Hildegarde Withers:
Final Riddles?

Stuart Palmer

Introduction by Steven Saylor

Hildegarde Withers: Final Riddles?

Stuart Palmer

Introduction by Steven Saylor

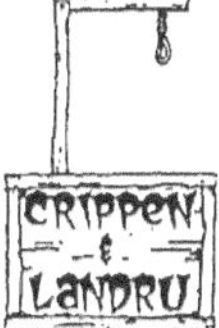

CRIPPEN & LANDRU PUBLISHERS
Cincinnati, Ohio
2021

Cover Design by Jacqueline Webber

FIRST EDITION

ISBN (limited clothbound edition): 978-1-936363-57-5
ISBN (trade softcover edition): 978-1-936363-56-8

Printed in the United States of America on recycled acid-free paper

Jeffrey A. Marks, Publisher
Douglas G. Greene, Senior editor

Crippen & Landru Publishers
P. O. Box 532057
Cincinnati, OH 45253 USA

Email: info@crippenlandru.com
Web: www.crippenlandru.com

Contents

Introduction
By Steven Saylor

Oh, Hildegarde Withers, how I've missed you!

We first met many years ago, in my darkened living room. You were on the TV screen and I was glued to the set, spellbound by the black and white splendors of *The Penguin Pool Murder*, filmed in 1932 and set in New York City. An actress named Edna May Oliver played you, and boy did she nail it! Later actresses would try their best, but none would ever come near Oliver's prim, vinegary portrayal of the quintessential spinster schoolmarm, a Depression-era amateur detective with a disapproving demeanor and the sleuthing skills of a Sherlock Holmes.

Assisting Miss Withers with her investigations (or was it the other way around?) was a crusty, cigar-chomping New York cop named Oscar Piper, personified in the movies by James Gleason, who, like Oliver, left an indelible mark on the role. Oscar and Hildegarde had the kind of salt-and-pepper, oil-and-vinegar chemistry that makes for a really great sleuthing team.

The Penguin Pool Murder, both the novel and the movie that quickly followed, launched the career of mystery writer Stuart Palmer, who would go on to a dozen novels about Hildegarde Withers and Oscar Piper, as well as Hollywood screenplays featuring the likes of Bulldog Drummond, the Lone Wolf, and the Falcon. Palmer became such a master of the mystery genre that he was mentioned in the same breath as Ellery Queen, Georges Simenon, Dashiell Hammett, Raymond Chandler, Erle Stanley Gardner, and John Dickson Carr. In 1954 his fellow authors elected him president of the Mystery Writers of America.

Palmer's stature in the genre was well deserved. His dialogue was tart, his settings atmospheric, his characters deftly drawn, and his plotting impeccable. Sometimes, as in the novels *Miss Withers Regrets* (1947) and *Nipped in the Bud* (1951), his virtuoso ability to confound and surprise the reader put him in a class with Agatha Christie.

Palmer was a master of the short story as well, and dozens of Hildegarde Withers stories appeared over the years. Two classic collections were published, *The Riddles of Hildegarde Withers* in 1947 and *The Monkey Murder and Other Hildegarde Withers Stories* in 1950. A few more Withers stories were gathered in *People vs. Withers and Malone*, a collaboration with Palmer's longtime writer pal Craig Rice that teamed up their two protagonists.

Diehard fans like yours truly knew there had to be more Hildegarde Withers short stories out there, and we were delighted when Crippen & Landru brought out *Hildegarde Withers: Uncollected Riddles* in 2002, featuring eleven stories along with a very useful bibliography (still available as an e-book).

But wait! There were yet *more* Withers stories not yet collected in a book. Now, at last, biographer and scholar Jeffrey Marks, something of a Sherlock himself, along with Doug Greene and Tony Medawar, have tracked them down, dusted them off, and presented them in these pages. Most are from the late 1950s and 1960s and were published in *Ellery Queen's Mystery Magazine*, but one is from way back—"The Riddle of the Black Spade" from 1934, which makes it one of Miss Withers' earliest adventures in crime-solving. And one story comes all the way from a different continent—"To Die in the Dark," which was published in 1944 in *Australian Women's Weekly*. Not to be missed is Miss Withers' encounter with Groucho Marx in the story that shares a title with his popular TV show of the 1950s, "You Bet Your Life."

Could there be yet more uncollected Withers stories? In 1952, Palmer claimed he had written about 50 Withers stories at that point, and if his math was correct, that still leaves over a dozen stories unaccounted for, perhaps buried and waiting to be discovered in miscellaneous American (or Australian?) newspapers of the 1930s and 1940s. Like Cher and certain other world-class acts, the short story career of Miss Hildegarde Withers may have more than one finale.

To round out this collection are a few items that broaden our appreciation of the author and his writing chops. Later in his career, Palmer introduced a sleuth who was about as far from Hildegarde Withers as can be imagined, a burly, gruff but good-natured, seen-it-all newspaperman-turned-PI named Howard Rook. One rare Rook short story appears here, "The Stripteaser and the Private Eye." Even the vocabulary in these stories is markedly different; it would be hard to imagine Miss Withers ever describing someone in such terms, though I suppose Oscar Piper might have done so—safely outside Miss Withers' earshot!

"How Lost Was My Father?" is something altogether different—and, for this reader, the biggest surprise in this collection. It's what nowadays might be called paranormal fiction. Not my cup of tea, I thought, raising an eyebrow and pulling a Hildegarde face—only to find myself unable to stop turning the pages. Frankly, this story gave me the willies. Curious, I looked up Stuart Palmer's listing at ifsdb.com, the Internet Speculative

Fiction Database. It turns out that Palmer, before the success of *The Penguin Pool Murder* set the course of his lucrative crime writing career, dabbled in the supernatural. From 1928 to 1931 he published almost two dozen short stories and purportedly true "essays" in a magazine called *Ghost Stories*, with titles like "A Sleeper Bewitched," "The Red Curse of the Mummy," "White Witch of Stonington," "An Unearthly Stowaway," "Phantom Dancer of Times Square," and even a five-part serial, "The Gargoyle's Throat." I had been vaguely aware that Palmer once wrote ghost stories, but I never sought them out. After reading "How Lost Was My Father?," I may do so. But I don't think I'll be reading them after dark.

Then there are Palmer's two forays into Sherlock Holmes pastiche, "The Adventure of the Marked Man" and "The Adventure of the Remarkable Worm." They are cleverly plotted and authentically capture the cadence and tone of Watson's voice. Palmer might have written more Sherlock tales, but it seems, from reading the essay that concludes this collection, "The I-O-U of Hildegarde Withers," that the Doyle estate put the kibosh on that idea. If only we had a whole book of Palmer's Sherlock stories! Alas, no amount of sleuthing in dusty library stacks or surfing the Internet will produce such a rich banquet, I fear. We must be happy with these two delicious morsels.

"The I-O-U of Hildegarde Withers" is truly a special treat—part memoir, part homage to Conan Doyle, part wistful meditation on the act of writing itself, and the curious connections a writer encounters over the course of a long and productive career. In this essay we hear the voice of Stuart Palmer—witty and wise, curious and clever, a boy who loved books who became a man who loved writing them. So vivid is that voice, you may even feel that Palmer's spirit is in the room with you, conjured up by the master's final, and best, ghost story.

The Riddle of the Black Spade

Uninvited and unannounced, a determined feminine figure marched into the sacrosanct precincts of the New York Homicide Bureau, with an afternoon paper under one arm.

Inspector Oscar Piper looked up from the little mountain of official memoranda which covered his scarred oak desk, and leaned back wearily in his chair. "Oh, it's you!" was his greeting.

But Miss Withers was undaunted. "Busy or not busy, Oscar Piper, you ought to be out on Long Island this afternoon instead of sitting here befouling the air with cigar smoke."

She opened the paper with a snap. A two-column head topped a box in the middle of page one, evidently the result of a last-minute change in make-up.

"'STATESMAN DIES IN FREAK ACCIDENT,'" she read. Then—"'David E. Farling, former state senator and present Manhattan attorney, was struck by a golf ball and instantly killed at about ten o'clock this morning. The accident happened at the small public course known as Meadowland, located near Forest Lawn in Queensborough.

"'Farling was discovered by fellow golfers lying face down near a large pool which forms one of the water hazards of the course. Beside him lay the golf ball which had struck his skull with a terrific impact, although the person who inadvertently drove it has not yet been identified'!"

"Yes, Hildegarde," the Inspector broke in testily. "I know all that."

"Well, do you know this?" she continued caustically. "The newspaper story goes on to remark that while there have been records of six or seven such accidents every year in the New York area, this is the first time that it resulted fatally!" She tossed the paper to him. "Now do you see what I'm talking about? Do you?"

"There has to be a first time for everything," Piper reminded her. "But if it makes you any happier, Hildegarde, you might as well know that I sent one of our best men out to help the Queensborough boys on the case. Dave Farling is too prominent a man to pass over easily, and there are too many people whose toes he has stepped on. But all the same—"

"All the same, you don't believe this could be murder?" Miss Withers sniffed. "There's something fishy about this business, Oscar. Just because it happened out in the bright October sunshine instead of in a locked room, and just because the weapon was a golf ball instead of a pistol, you leap to conclusions."

She drew a long breath. "Oscar, who was the person who found Farling's body?"

"Person? There was a whole raft of 'em. He was playing with Sam Firth, his partner, John T. Sullivan, 'the golden-tongued orator,' and his son, young Ronald Farling. They missed Farling when he didn't show up at the green, and after waiting for him a while to give him time to find a lost ball or get out of a sand trap, they started back to look for him. They got the Swiss who runs the place to help, and the whole party found Farling lying face down in the mud at the edge of the pool."

"Giving each other a perfect alibi, or something," put in Miss Withers. "Go on."

"That's all I know, so far," said the Inspector. "I'm only a cop, not a crystal-gazer."

Miss Withers stood up. "Well, what are we waiting for? Let's go out there."

"Donovan knows his business," opposed the Inspector. "And the precinct boys out in Queens aren't likely to welcome too much meddling. Besides, there's no use to try to make anything except a freak accident out of this case unless—"

His telephone shrilled, and he barked an answer. "Well, Donovan? What? Listen, is the body still there? Well, leave it. Hang onto the guy— wait for me at the course."

He put down the phone, and his voice was full of amazement. "Hildegarde, you're right. It's murder—and they've nabbed the dead man's son!"

She went through the door ahead of him, jamming her Queen Mary-ish hat a bit lower on her head. The thrill of the chase widened her nostrils, but as they sped through Manhattan's traffic in a long black squad car, heading toward Queensboro Bridge, she grasped the Inspector's arm and shook her head.

"I don't believe it," she announced. "I don't believe it was the son that did it."

"Such things have happened, and worse," Piper reminded her. "And don't think that Donovan doesn't know what he's doing. If he's made a pinch he's sure of his ground."

Miss Withers had a retort ready, but the sudden screaming of the siren drowned her out. They cut through red light after red light, raced over the bridge, and then on a long straightaway past mile upon mile of used-car lots, garages, hot-dog stands, grocery stores . . . far into the vastness of Queens, which enjoys the reputation of being the largest and most unlovely borough of New York.

The day had been warm for October, but now as the sun set behind the towers of Manhattan to the westward, a chill wind began to sweep down from the Sound. Miss Withers could not help shivering as the fast car swung off the boulevard and shot south over a narrow macadam road. There was a faded sign: MEADOWLAND GOLF CLUB—GREENS FEE 50¢.

On the right they could see a rolling green expanse of what had once been a succulent cow pasture. Now it bore signs of a sketchy landscaping and here and there a rain-streaked flag fluttered over a clipped green square of grass.

Far ahead of them they saw a small white building surrounded by autos, but at that moment their precipitous course was interrupted by a blue-clad figure which stepped out into the road ahead of them, waving its arms.

Brakes screamed. "The Sergeant says I was to tell you that if you cut across the fence right here you'll find him where the body is . . ."

"Okay," said Piper. He helped Miss Withers out of the car, which was simple, and over the barbed wire fence, which was fraught with difficulty and peril.

"Right straight toward the trees," their guide advised. They went onward over a little hill, and came down upon another fairway. Ahead of them, from the depths of a narrow ravine which cut across the open fairway in a wide diagonal, rose the tops of a cluster of elms. But there was no sign of human presence.

"Under the trees, Inspector," their guide insisted.

They came suddenly above the ravine, looking down upon a wide, leaf-choked pool near the elms. Smaller trees and bushes filled the canyon-like cut at the left, but ahead of them it lay open around the pool. Here were gathered an official little circle around a body which still lay face downward near the water's edge.

Photographers were taking their last shots in the fading light. Sergeant Donovan, red-faced and perspiring, came up the slope to greet his chief.

"Open and shut," he announced. "I washed it up pronto, Inspector. But you may as well have a look around." He noticed Miss Withers, and greeted her without enthusiasm. "Afternoon, ma'am."

"Open and shut," she repeated blankly. "Hmmmm."

They looked at the body—a sprawled, plumpish man of fifty dressed in plus fours and bright yellow sweater and stockings, and with a small circular indentation in the back of the skull. Then a tarpaulin was drawn over the grim exhibit.

"Right here was where they found the golf ball that did it," the Sergeant was saying. "About two feet from the corpse."

From his pocket he took a wadded handkerchief, in the center of which reposed a bright new golf ball, bearing on one side a tiny trademark consisting of a black spade—and on the other a dull reddish smear. "Exhibit A, Inspector!"

Piper nodded. "Seems to be clear enough. We may as well go on to the club house, eh, Hildegarde?"

Miss Withers had discovered a dead branch nearby, with which she was poking dubiously at the deep leaf-choked pool. Its murky waters were reflecting the last glow of the sunset.

"But we've found the body, Hildegarde!" he said jokingly. "Or do you think the murderer is lurking under water?"

She sniffed, and tossed aside the branch.

It was a good stiff walk back to the club house, a small building of rattletrap structure. In the rear was a three-room apartment sacred to the gnarled Swiss who leased the land and operated the course. In the front was an office furnished with a cash register, a counter displaying sun-hats, golf balls, patent tees, and the like, and a screened porch boasting half a dozen tables with chairs and a dispensing machine for soda pop.

It was on this porch that young Ronald Farling waited, with a plainclothes detective on either side and a burly captain in charge. That worthy hurried down to meet the Inspector on the lawn.

"Greetings," said Piper. "Miss Withers—Captain Mike Platt, Queens Division. Congratulations, Captain."

The Captain grinned. "Glad you agree that we've broken the case so early, sir. Just the same, I kept the young rat here so you could talk to him on the ground, so to speak. "

"Give us the picture, quick," ordered Piper.

"Well," said Platt slowly, "it's not a nice picture at all. Farling and his son Ronald, together with Mister Sullivan and Mister Firth all came out early this morning for a round of golf. They often come to this little course because it's never crowded and because it's ten miles closer to the city than the nearest full-size course.

"Or so they say. We got statements from Firth and Sullivan and let them go. It seems that on the seventh tee each one of the four drove his ball into trouble—except for young Farling, who's an expert. He drove right over the tops of those elm trees, almost to the green. Sullivan landed in the woods at the left, Firth saw his ball roll into the rough ground near the hill, and Dave Farling topped his a measly twenty feet or so.

"The others left him there and went on, for he was an unlucky golfer usually. From there to the green, where they knock the ball into the little hole. Inspector, each man was separate and busy with his own affairs. But though nobody saw him—excepting the murderer—Dave Farling must have knocked his second shot into the pool. And while he was down trying to find his ball, somebody knocked a ball into the back of his head, smashing his skull."

Miss Withers could see on the porch the drawn, handsome face of young Ronald Farling, between the two cops. "Somebody, you say, but—"

"But how do we know it was him?" Platt laughed. "Because he had a whale of a fight with his father yesterday in the office, over something his father wouldn't let him do. 'Not while I live!' said the old man. Firth, the partner, overheard it. And he told us. Moreover, the young lad is what they call a 'scratch' golfer. He likes to give exhibitions of driving a ball off a watch, or taking what they call a mashie and chipping balls twenty feet into a tin pail. He's probably one of the few men in these parts who could be perfectly sure of hitting just what he aimed at!"

The Captain was beaming. "Well, when Farling didn't show up at the green, the others figured he was looking for a lost ball. But then he didn't come and he kept a didn't coming as the saying goes, and finally the three of them started back. They saw old Chris Thorr on the other fairway raking away at the Autumn leaves, and called him to help. So the four of them came over the edge of the gully and saw Farling lying there, dead as a herring."

"And the boy admits the crime?" asked Miss Withers.

Platt shook his head. "Not him. He's a smooth one. But we'll make him talk before he sleeps or—"

"All right, Captain," said Piper quickly. "Medical examiner gone?"

Platt nodded. "Doc Farnsworth it was—and he didn't like the looks of things. It was him refused us a certificate of death by misadventure. Wouldn't give his final opinion until the autopsy. But Donovan and I figured we didn't need to wait for that before getting young Farling safe behind bars."

"Okay," said Piper. "Let's have a look at the lad."

They went up the steps and through a screen door. The young man was very pale, and seemed chilled through in his light blue sports shirt and dark flannels. He leaped to his feet impulsively.

"How long are you going to hold me here? I tell you, I had nothing to do with what happened. Do you think I'd kill my own father?"

"Father—by adoption, wasn't it?" Miss Withers put in softly. "Didn't I read something about it, some years back?"

Ronald Farling stopped short. His eyes clouded for a moment. Then—"Yes, by adoption. David Farling and his wife adopted me nine years ago, when I was twelve. It was just after my own father . . ."

"Yes? Go on!" Piper pressed forward.

The boy gulped. "Just after my real father was— was executed for murder! David Farling as his lawyer couldn't get him off, though it happened in a pitched battle between union men and company scabs. So he promised to take me, and bring me up as his own son. And he did."

The boy stopped short, realizing too late what he had said. His fists clenched, and then opened helplessly. "Like father like son, eh? I suppose that's what you're saying."

"You had a fight with your foster father in his office yesterday?"

Ronald nodded. "Well, an argument. But not—"

"What was it about?"

"He didn't want me to get married," confessed Ronald Farling simply. He drew a deep breath. "And if you want the name of the girl you can rot in hell before I'll tell you and drag her through this!"

He subsided sullenly into his chair. During the latter course of the questioning Miss Hildegarde Withers had been doing a little quiet snooping nearby. She reappeared with a leather golf bag full of sticks in one hand. The initials on the bag were "R. F."

"This is yours?" she asked the prisoner.

He nodded. Miss Withers opened the zipper pocket and brought out half a dozen golf balls. Three were old and battered. The other three were almost new, showing only a few nicks. Each bore a tiny red heart as a trademark.

"Could I see the one you have?" she asked the Sergeant. She took it gingerly. "Just as I thought. They don't match." On an impulse she showed Ronald Farling the ball with the smear of blood. "Recognize this ball, young man?"

He stared, and frowned. Then his eyes widened. "Why, that's my father's!"

The cops gathered instantly. "What?"

"It is! You see, when we started out this morning each member of the foursome bought three new balls Ask the girl inside at the counter—and of course we each got a different color and mark so we could tell them apart easily. Most makes of balls are designed in sets of four that way. Firth chose clubs, Sullivan diamonds, my father—I mean my foster father chose spades, so that left me hearts. They were kidding me about it."

"So David Farling was killed with one of his own golf balls!" said Miss Withers slowly. "Can we prove that by comparing this with other balls in his bag?"

But the dead man's bag was empty of balls.

"This isn't getting us anywheres," Captain Platt finally objected. "Okay for me to take young Farling away, Inspector?"

Piper looked at Miss Withers, rubbed his jaw, and nodded. "Keep him safe and sound," he said. "And don't yell at him all night," he added firmly.

The young man was half-led, half-dragged, to a waiting police runabout. Miss Withers had a last glimpse of his white, drawn, frightened face.

There was a brief interlude during which a gray ambulance lumbered out into the gathering darkness of the little golf course, its lights shining like two glaring tiger-eyes. At last David Farling was to be removed from the edge of the muddy pool. It was high time, thought Miss Withers.

The Inspector had left her to make a telephone call, and she wandered out through the littered yard in the rear. Here were old auto tires, sand boxes, broken greens, flags, and an ancient piano box—souvenirs of dead days. For the first time in her life she wished that she had taken up music and games and golf in her youth. A knowledge of what the Inspector called "pasture pool" would be a great help to her now. She had a feeling that an essential clue was eluding her—and the police. Perhaps it was a clue that would cry out like a trumpet to a more experienced devotee of golf.

She sank down on a convenient bench overlooking the fairway, and rested her chin in her hand. Far ahead she could see the lights of the morgue wagon swing across the sky and then beam back toward the club house, its silent passenger safely aboard.

"A ride that each of us must take—and some before our time," she was musing to herself.

At that moment a guttural torrent broke out almost in her ear. She turned suddenly, and realized that the speaker did not see her on the bench. He stood not far from the doorway of the living quarters, a gnarled, bitter figure leaning upon a long rake.

"*Ach, der Schwein.*"

Miss Withers had a vague knowledge of German and of French left over from her schooldays, and after a moment she realized that this endless torrent was a combination of both which must be Swiss. Yet most of the words were, luckily, unfamiliar to her. Here and there she caught one which made the back of her neck turn bright red.

She made ready. There was always something to be said for the power of a surprise attack. She jumped up like a jack-in-the-box.

"Who are you?" she demanded, raising her umbrella threateningly.

"Who am I? She asks me, who am I?" The harsh voice rose shrill and high. "Me, I'm poor Chris Thorr. Me, I'm the slave who must work week in and week out to make all smooth the grass where those *verdammte* pigs go joyriding with their unspeakable ambulance."

His voice was full of great sobs. Suddenly Miss Withers felt a certain sympathy for him, especially now that the ambulance came lurching back toward the club house, leaving dark furrows in the soft turf, wheels spinning erratically right and left.

She tried to make some properly sympathetic remark. But Chris Thorr turned back toward his lighted doorway, shoulders slumped despondently. "*Es ist nicht der Muhe Wert!*" was his parting shot.

Miss Withers turned to see the Inspector beside her. "I don't like that old buzzard," he observed. "What was that last crack?"

"Something about life being a bowl of cherries," Miss Withers translated freely. "I'm afraid Thorr is a pessimist."

"Maybe," said Piper, as they walked back toward the shack. "From what I hear he's got reasons. This place barely pays expenses, next Spring they're going to condemn most of it for the new Parkway, and his wife ran off with a traveling man or somebody last August."

"But didn't I see a girl in the office?" Miss Withers asked.

Piper nodded. "That's Molly Gargan, a neighborhood girl that he hires to take care of the office and sell tickets to the players. Which reminds me, I'd better tell the boys it's okay to let her go home. We've been holding everybody."

"Hold her a while longer," Miss Withers decided. "I want to see Molly."

Molly Gargan was something to see, beyond a doubt. Miss Hildegarde Withers was prone to attach more importance to feminine brains than to beauty, but the black-haired girl with the bright blue eyes and full sculptured body was positively breath-taking.

She sat at a stool behind the counter, staring out of the window at the darkness of the golf course. Oddly enough, her blue eyes were raining tears down an utterly calm and lovely face. She wore a modest pink dress that was obviously homemade, and as Miss Withers came through the doorway she noticed that Molly Gargan had torn that dress in five or six places along the collar. Now, as if no part of herself, her long fingers were busily tearing yet another place.

Miss Withers cleared her throat. "Whatever happened out on the course, it can't affect you, young woman, can it?"

Molly started, and then her lips tightened. "Of course not."

Miss Withers tried a rather mean trick. "The young man whom they arrested," she said casually, "insists that this morning, when the foursome started to play, they all purchased balls here."

Molly nodded her lovely dark head.

"And he claims that all four of them bought balls with a red diamond on them—is that true?"

"Why, no! They—" suddenly Molly stopped short. "Yes, that's right," she said evenly. "I remember now."

"Like fun you do," Miss Withers said under her breath. "Where do you live, Molly?"

Through the window Molly Gargan pointed to a white house perhaps a mile away, where the lights of the boulevard were glaring. "My father runs a filling station," she confessed.

"Very well, Molly," Miss Withers advised. "The police asked me to tell you that you may go home now."

"Thanks!" said Molly Gargan fervently. With one quick motion she pulled a sweater over her dress, slapped a tam-o'-shanter over her dark hair, and was out of the door.

Miss Withers watched the girl as she took a short cut across the darkened golf course in the direction of that dim white blotch in the distance which was home. Then she was aware that someone watched beside her.

It was Chris Thorr, shaking his head. "They are all alike," he observed gutturally. "Women!"

He crossed to the cash register, pressed the NO SALE key and scooped out the day's takings, a sorry morsel. Then he ostentatiously locked the showcase, as if Miss Withers would have been likely to go in for shoplifting golf balls and wooden tees.

"You can't blame her for hurrying away on a day like this," Miss Withers reminded him. "What if she did forget to close up? She's a very pretty girl."

Chris Thorr didn't seem interested in pretty girls. "Bah!" said he. "The prettier they are the less they know. I hope soon she gets married, and I hire a good sober girl homely as a mud fence, *ja!*"

He moved around, turning out electric lights. "You go home now— everybody go home, *ja?* I go to bed."

Everybody went home—except for one chilled and unhappy cop who was assigned, according to regulations, to cover the scene of the crime. Patrolman Walter Fogle spread out a newspaper on the damp grass under the elms, and prepared for a long and lonely vigil above the dark and leaf-choked pool.

The wind howled eerily in the tree-tops that night, and the pale October moon was hidden behind ragged wisps of cloud. Patrolman Fogle realized that it lacked but a night or two of being All-Hallow's Eve, and toward morning he dozed off into a nightmare of witches and goblins and howling, dancing wraiths.

He awoke with a jerk to see a spectral white figure moving near the edge of the pond. Fogle blinked, pinched himself, and blinked, again. But the figure remained.

"Hey!" he mouthed, through dry and trembling lips.

The white figure became a statue. "What the hell are you doing there?" demanded the patrolman. "Stop or I'll fire!"

The apparition dissolved in the direction of the clump of trees and brush further down the gully.

"Stop!" yelled Fogle. His gun came out, and he blazed away furiously.

But to no avail.

Next morning, shame-faced, he made his report. "Maybe it was a dead ghost and maybe it wasn't," he insisted to Captain Platt. "But I know for one thing that it could run like a rabbit. And it wasn't old Chris Thorr nosing around, because I went back to the club house and dragged him out of bed."

"Look at his shoes?" asked the captain. "Heavy dew, wasn't there?"

The cop nodded. "His shoes were dry, and he was sound asleep."

"Okay," said his chief. "Go home and grab some sleep. We may want you this afternoon."

At that moment Miss Withers and the Inspector were in deep conference. "It's funny about the medical examiner's report," Piper was saying. "The doc insists that Farling's skull was of normal thickness and that a golf ball would have to be traveling with the speed of a bullet to make such a wound."

"Oscar," suggested the schoolteacher, "isn't that an idea? I mean, couldn't you shoot a golf ball out of a gun?"

He shrugged. "Certainly not without leaving powder marks, even if you could get a gun barrel improvised out of a pipe or something. And as for that, Max Van Donnen just reported to me that while that golf ball bears traces of blood which check with Farling's, it has never been struck with a golf club! The waxy covering is intact, under the microscope! So there goes your gun theory."

Miss Withers nodded. "I suggested the gun because, you see, Oscar, I spent two hours this morning taking a golf lesson from a professional at the Lakewood Country Club. He's a better golfer than even young Farling, and he can drive a ball four hundred yards or lift one neatly into a tin pail twenty feet away. But not both at the same time, Oscar! By that I mean you can't combine speed with absolute accuracy in golf!"

"Which means that we're right back where we started," said Piper.

She shook her head. "We know that Ronald Farling didn't kill his foster father—at least not by driving a ball at him. Oscar, I think we're making this case too complicated. Did you get the report from the telephone company?"

He shook his head. "Takes them time to trace those calls," he pointed out. "But I don't see why you think we'd learn anything if we knew how many phone calls, if any, have been made from the club house to Farling's office on Broadway, and vice versa. You don't think—"

She nodded. "When there's a girl as startlingly beautiful as Molly Gargan in a case, you can take it for granted that she is somehow a part of the picture. Suppose the dead man had been playing regularly on that little course just to see the fair Molly, had become involved with her somehow, and then cast her adrift? And suppose the odd little Mr. Thorr secretly nursed a love for his pretty clerk, and wanted to avenge the slight?"

She stopped, and shook her head. "Thorr doesn't love the girl. On the contrary. And besides, Farling would not have brought his friends and son to play golf at the course after he was through with the girl." She sank into a chair. "I'm afraid we've drawn another blank."

Just then the telephone rang, and Piper listened eagerly. He made notes on a piece of paper. "Well!" he said. "In the past three months there have been fourteen phone calls from the golf course office to Farling's office—twenty-three from Farling's office to the course, and seven from the Farling home on Fifth Avenue to the course!"

"Which means that your case against young Farling is blown higher than a kite," Miss Withers reminded him. "Besides, he couldn't have been the midnight prowler who frightened Patrolman Fogle out of his alleged wits last night." She frowned. "Oscar, you ought to drain that pool!"

Piper laughed. "So you are looking for another body!"

"Another body—or another golf ball," she reminded him. "A golf ball with specks of powder burns on the cover, and a trademark which might be anything but a black spade."

"Draining that pool seems like something of an engineering problem," Piper objected. "Besides—"

"And I think you ought to turn Ronald Farling loose," she went on. "There may be more to discover from him if he's free than if he's in the lockup."

"The more we discover the worse off we are," Piper objected. "I naturally have had the other two members of that foursome investigated. Sullivan has been talking over the radio on behalf of the Citizens Committee, and naturally has been panning some of Farling's friends in politics. But the two men were personal pals. As for the partner, Sam Firth, he didn't gain anything from Farling's death, and he's probably lost a good share of his law business. Neither of them—"

"Business!" Miss Withers snapped. "We're missing the whole key to this affair. I wish I knew more about pretty Molly Gargan. I still believe that she's the catalytic agent—"

Piper shook his head. "Doesn't look like she'd throw a fit, to me."

"I said catalytic, not epileptic," Miss Withers snapped. "Don't you remember your chemistry? Well, with a girl as beautiful as she around, anything that happens involves her somehow. Oscar, I'm going to telephone her, and arrange for a quiet little talk—"

She asked for information, and then was connected with Gargan's Gas Station on Queens Boulevard. It was a worried Irish voice which answered her.

"Molly? This is her father speakin'. No, she's not here. She went out early this mornin', without giving me my breakfast. What? No, she didn't pack a suitcase. She was wearing a pink dress, I suppose."

Miss Withers put down the phone. "Oscar, doesn't pink look white at night?"

She gave him no time to answer. "Come on!" she insisted. "I think we're on the trail of something, and I don't like the scent."

"Now listen!" objected her old crony. "Good heavens, woman, I've got a Bureau to run. . . ."

"It'll run by itself," she came back. And the Inspector followed, for he knew her of old.

"We'll first have a talk with young Farling," she decided. "Tell the man to drive us to the Queens lockup."

But when they had reached that outlying station they found that the talk with young Ronald Farling would have to be postponed indefinitely.

"He's flew the coop!" was the way Captain Platt put it. "About half an hour ago Sam Firth, his father's partner, came out here with a writ of habeas corpus. They'd got wind of the medical examiner's report which cast doubt on the golf ball angle, so it was up to me to book the kid for murder or let him go. And we didn't have enough on him—"

"We can get him again if we need him," said Piper. "Well, Hildegarde?"

"We need him now," she said shortly. "Find out for me just what is the situation out at the golf course, will you? Anybody there?"

Captain Platt reported that Fogle was due to go back on duty at the course within the next few minutes, having had a short relief. "We always keep a cop around the scene of the crime for a couple of days," he informed her. "Otherwise the place is closed up."

Miss Withers then realized that Molly Gargan couldn't possibly be on duty. There would be no need to have her sitting on the stool behind that counter in the club-house, yet where was she?

"Oscar," she insisted, "will you take me over to the course? But for heaven's sake let's have no blaring of sirens this time."

They approached Meadowland very quietly indeed, and at Miss Withers' instigation the squad car was parked far down the macadam road.

Then, leaving the uniformed driver at the wheel, the Inspector followed Miss Withers over the wire fence and across the turf. "Good Lord, woman, are you still harping on that pool?"

She sniffed, and led the way. "I want a description from Patrolman Fogle of that ghost he saw," she admitted.

But Fogle was not on duty above the pool. Another uniformed man approached after a moment, crashing through the underbrush down the gully. He snapped to salute.

"Where's Fogle?" asked Piper sharply.

"Hasn't relieved me yet, sir. I guess last night was too much for him, because he was due at two o'clock and it's nearly half past."

"What were you doing off your post? Looking for him?"

The cop reddened. "No, sir. I—I thought I seen something moving down there."

Piper shook his head. "I guess all you men out here believe in fairies," he growled. "Was it a grinning skull or a snake with wings?"

"No, sir," said the patrolman seriously. "It was a young guy in golf clothes, and he could run like a deer."

"Yeah!" said Piper.

But Miss Withers, who had climbed back to the edge of the gully, was staring out over the course. "He still is," she remarked. "Running like a deer, I mean. And if he doesn't look out. . . ."

Piper and the cop joined her in time to get a clear, if distant, view of a young man who looked very much like Ronald Farling, as he vaulted a barbed wired fence into the road and was immediately clasped in the brawny arms of the uniformed man who drove Piper's car.

When the others came up he was arguing furiously with his captor. "Let him go!" ordered Piper.

Ronald Farling, looking a little wild and disheveled from his night in jail, faced them. "I suppose you want to know why I'm here?" he demanded.

Miss Withers shook her head. "You're looking for the same thing we are," she advised him. "Come with us, if you wish. In the words of the popular song, we're heading for the last roundup."

They crept toward the club house in silence, keeping always behind the rolling little hills, following gullies and the shadows of scattered trees. "Hildegarde, what are you up to?" Piper begged.

"I haven't the slightest idea!" she admitted. "But I'm going to learn something."

The wind still blew gustily from the north, driving dead leaves into their faces, and bringing the sound of loud voices from somewhere behind the club house. They crept steadily on, and finally reached the vantage point of a hedge.

From here they could get a good view of the club house, and of the littered yard in the rear where Chris Thorr stood, raking at the refuse. Beside him was Patrolman Fogle.

"Say!" broke out Piper. "There's something—"

But Miss Withers hushed him. "Listen!"

"Well, then—I bet you twenty dollars against five that you can't hit it in one out of three tries!"

Thorr's voice came clearly, and it bore an undercurrent of masked excitement.

Fogle scratched the back of his neck, and drew out his service gun. "You talk too loud, fella," he said. "I hate to do it, but I'm going to take your money."

They were standing perhaps twenty feet from the broken-down piano case which Miss Withers had noticed last night. Now she saw with a gasp of surprise that a homemade target of black and white circles had been tacked on the side of the box.

"Okay," Fogle said doggedly. "I've got three tries to put a slug in the center of that target, and if I do it you pay me twenty bucks." He raised his gun.

Miss Withers tried to scream, and found that no sound issued from her throat. She grabbed the Inspector. "Stop him!" she gasped.

"Illegal target practice within city limits of New York, illegal firing of service gun—" mumbled the Inspector. He stood up quickly. "Hey, there! What the hell do you think you're doing?"

The two in the yard whirled to face them. Miss Withers tottered on after the Inspector, who glared at the patrolman.

Fogle was in a spot, and he knew it. "I—sorry, sir. But he was razzing me about police markmanship, sir. On account of my firing last night at the ghost or whatever it was. Claimed I couldn't hit the piano box, much less the target. So we made a bet—"

Piper was grinning. "Oh, he thinks cops can't shoot, eh?"

Chris Thorr nodded. "Couldn't hit a barn if you were inside with the doors shut. Not like the police in Switzerland, let me tell you. Say—"

Piper rubbed his chin. "Fogle, how come you're stalling around here? Don't you go back on duty?"

"At two p.m., yes sir. But I just looked at the clock inside and it's only one-forty-five." He grinned. "So I thought I had time to show this guy . . ."

"Go ahead and show him," Piper ordered. "Just this once we'll forget regulations."

Miss Withers could hold herself is no longer. "Forget regulations and forget the common sense you were born with," she screamed. "But first let me get in that piano box."

She attacked it furiously with tooth and nail, but it was stouter than it seemed. Young Ronald Farling came forward to help her, while Thorr and the cops looked blankly on. Then at last a board was pried away, and another.

"Oh, God!" cried Ronald Farling. "Molly!"

It was Molly Gargan—her soft young body wound with cruel ropes, her red mouth gagged with a twisted rag. Tenderly they took her down from the hook which had held her there, with her heart beating just behind the bull's-eye of the target.

Only a half inch of soft pine lay between Molly Gargan and the leaden death which had hung poised above her.

It all happened in a split second. "Get that man!" screamed Miss Withers.

Gnarled, dried-up Chris Thorr had suddenly come alive. He flung Fogle head over heels, knocked the Inspector to his knees with the ever-present rake which he had snatched from behind him, and was running amok toward the two women.

His mouth was open and frothing, and a shrill endless scream of antic insanity filled the air.

Then Ronald Farling stepped in, dodged the swinging iron teeth of the rake, and brought his fist smartly into the madman's groin. Again—and then a right across to the chin that sent him backwards—

He did not rise. When things had calmed a bit, they found out why. He had fallen upon the tines of his own rusty rake, and three of the iron spikes had pierced his brain.

Farling and the girl leaned against the piano box, touching each other gently, wonderingly. They had no eyes or ears for anything else.

But the Inspector fairly gnawed at his cigar. "Hildegarde! It's a madhouse!"

"Not quite," she said. "Thorr wanted to get Molly put out of the way, and chose this means. Fogle was to have shot her as she stood bound and gagged in the piano box. Then later Thorr would have hidden the body out on the course somewhere—and with one or more bullets from Fogle's gun in the body, he would be the one to be suspected, particularly since he shot wildly at a phantom last night. "

"Yeah, but what phantom?"

"I imagine it was Thorr, in his nightshirt and barefoot," Miss Withers went on. "He didn't know that there'd be a guard at the pool, or at least wasn't sure. He had some unfinished business there—"

"So you say!" objected Piper. "But why would Thorr want to kill Molly here?"

"Ask her," said Miss Withers. "She knows."

Molly did know. It was because she had feared and suspected Thorr for some time, and therefore when her sweetheart was arrested for the murder of his foster father she had started scouting around.

"And you found what?" Miss Withers asked.

"I found that there were some brown stains on the end of Thorr's rake handle," said Molly Gargan. And suddenly the whole thing was clear to Miss Withers.

"That's why he tied you up when he found you examining his rake! It was the murder weapon—not the golf ball."

Piper shook his head. "You're still crazy. What possible motive would there be—"

"For Thorr to kill Farling? A very good one. Enter the pool once more, Oscar. You see, Farling must have been looking for his lost ball, and have poked at the water with that dead stick, just as I did. And Thorr, lurking nearby, saw him probing the pool and rushed up to hurl his rake like a javelin. The rake handle is just the diameter of a golf ball, Oscar. He thought of that when he had finished the deed, so he took the one remaining ball from his victim's bag, touched it to the wound, and dropped it nearby. He wanted it to appear like an accident, Oscar."

"But why, in the name of heaven, should Thorr object to having Farling poke around in that pool?"

"Your guess is as good as mine," said Miss Hildegarde Withers. "We won't know for sure until you drain the pool, as I've begged you to do, again and again. But I've got a pretty good idea that you'll find the sunken body of the wife who is supposed to have left Chris Thorr last August and run away with a traveling man."

"Well, who'd have suspected that?" exclaimed Piper.

"Who indeed—but I?" Miss Withers flashed back.

To Die in the Dark

"Now you look at murder," continued the Inspector discursively. "A certain type of house is apt to have a certain type of homicide happen in it. Take a run-down, respectable street of brownstones like this one. Ten to one any crime that happens along here will be cut to a pattern, sort of conventional, musty . . ."

"Yes sir," agreed the uniformed driver, peering at the house numbers. He brought the big limousine to a smooth stop at the curb and opened the door.

Inspector Piper went up the steps of the brownstone house with a dignified briskness, entering a door held open by a strapping patrolman who saluted and indicated the steep, narrow stair down the hall. "Third floor, sir."

The inspector wrinkled his nose at the musty smell of the old house, the reek of ancient cabbage, mothballs, and dust and tobacco, which were now mingled with a sharper, more acrid odor. Powder, eh? So this was a shooting. That made it simpler yet.

He was on the first landing when a door beyond suddenly opened and a plainclothes man came out, one hand firmly gripping the round elbow of a tall dark girl with magnificently large eyes. "Morning, inspector," the detective greeted him cheerily. "Remember me? I'm Castle."

"G'morning," said Piper, and would have gone on up the stair. But the dark girl suddenly jerked away from her guard and flung herself upon him. "Inspector! You've got to listen to me! Make them stop! Make them let me go! I don't know anything about this terrible thing, honestly I don't . . ."

The wide, terrified eyes blazed into Oscar Piper's, somehow both desperate and alluring. He turned and looked questioningly at the detective.

Castle said quickly: "She's the dead man's secretary. Miss Morna Dewey." He managed to accent the word "secretary" so that it became derisive, subtly humorous.

"You'll have your chance to talk later, Miss Dewey," said the inspector, and went on up the stair. But he could feel the dark eyes burning into the back of his neck as he went.

A stocky young man in glasses was standing on the third floor landing. Piper frowned, and remembered him. "Hello, sergeant."

"Lieutenant!" corrected the younger man. "Lt. Harold Branch, sir."

"Oh, yes I remember. You just got the boost. You in charge?"

Branch nodded. "It's my first case, and it's a corker. See for yourself. He's in there." He coughed. "We haven't touched a thing, except that, and Dr. Bloom looked at him."

Piper went in through the indicated door and found himself in a man's bedroom which had been decorated with Spartan simplicity. There were only the bare essentials of bed, bureau, chair, and rug. Beneath the two high windows fronting on the street had been set up a rough workbench, littered with melted wax, glue, scraps of leather and small, delicate tools which appeared to be the type used in book binding.

Beside the bench was sprawled the body of a thin young-old man in his fifties, clad in silk pyjamas and dressing-gown. The inspector looked closer and saw that a large caliber slug had made a neat entrance over the right cheekbone, and a remarkably messy exit in the rear of the skill.

He turned away. "Well, lieutenant, what of it?"

The younger man was watching him, eagerly. "Here's the details." He whipped out a notebook and began reading: "Name is Charles Portland, semi-retired rare book dealer. Lived in this house since he bought it eighteen years ago. Body discovered by the housekeeper, Mrs. Mattie Marple, when she brought up his breakfast tray at eight o'clock. Door locked, but she climbed up on a chair and peeped through the fanlight . . ."

At that moment a uniformed policeman came up to ask if the inspector would step into the library before he left. One of the suspects insisted on seeing him. Piper nodded vaguely, and then turned back to the lieutenant.

"Just what is so odd about this business that you have to bring me into it?" he demanded. "We're shorthanded down town, with half our best men in the Army. I don't see why you have to yell for help on your first case."

"But the door was locked!" Lt. Branch repeated. "And the only known key was found in the pocket of the victim's dressing-gown."

"All right, so it's suicide, and we can all go home," said the inspector, turning away. Then he stopped, at the look on Branch's face.

"Yes, inspector. But—but Dr. Bloom says he died instantly sometime between midnight and three a.m. He said—"

"Listen, young man. The medical examiner's report, and the ballistics report on the gun, will be on my desk in the morning, as a simple matter of routine . . ."

"Yes, sir. But there's one thing you won't have on your desk in the morning. There was no gun in the room."

"No gun?"

"Not a trace of it. We found a .45 shell case on the floor, and the slug flattened itself against the wall over there. But no gun."

A low whistle escaped from the inspector's lips. "Well, now! It could be . . ."

He was suddenly interrupted by the uniformed officer again, who said that if convenient Sgt. Castle would very much like to have the inspector come downstairs and speak to one of the suspects right away.

"Later!" snapped Piper, turning back to the lieutenant. "No way the gun could have got out of the room?"

"Those windows were locked tight," Branch said. "No gun got out of this room without somebody carried it in his little hot hand."

The inspector sighed, and nodded wearily. Another of those locked room things. "Who else was in the house last night?"

"Nobody." said Lt. Branch. "I mean, nobody but the murderer. The housekeeper goes home after dinner. We picked up a dame who claims to be the secretary, only if you ask me she's strictly gaol bait, when she came to work this morning. There's a nephew name of Sam Portland used to live here before he went in the Army, only after he got kicked out of the Service he had a fight with the old man and has been camping down in the village somewhere. We got an alarm out for him now."

"What more do you want, then?" Piper demanded.

"Wait, inspector. The nephew's a suspect all right, but we got a better one. A dame who's been cataloguing the library for a couple of days, name of Mrs. Fitzsimmons. Claims she's sent by the insurance company that's got a policy on the books, only there's something phony about her. She admits she's only worked for the company a few days, and the address she gave is a vacant lot on 135th Avenue."

"I think," decided the inspector quietly, "that I might enjoy a little talk with Mrs. Fitzsimmons."

It was, as things turned out, a bad guess. For as he entered the second floor library in which the three feminine suspects were being held, he suddenly stopped short. It appeared almost as if he intended to beat a hasty retreat, but it was too late.

Three women rose as one to greet him, but he had no eyes for the fat housekeeper with the straggly hair, nor for the lovely willowy brunette. He saw only the accusing face of an angular maiden schoolteacher wearing a hat which resembled a bon voyage basket.

"Oscar!" cried Miss Hildegarde Withers. "It's about time!"

The inspector recovered himself with Hibernian quickness. "If it isn't my old friend Mrs. Fitzsimmons!" he said. He turned to the perspiring sergeant. "I believe I'll question this suspect alone," he decided. "Bring her upstairs."

A moment later they were locked in a bedroom on the upper floor. "I don't see what's so funny!" the maiden schoolteacher was saying. "If your flat-footed nincompoops had the intelligence of a gnat—"

"And if you'd keep from pushing your nose into police business—" Piper took out a cigar, started to light up, and then scowled. "Wait a minute! This is one case you didn't learn about from the police radio. You were here before it happened!"

Miss Withers nodded. As self-appointed gadfly to the homicide division, she had many times felt it her bounden duty to interfere in the more interesting of the inspector's cases, usually in spite of him. But this time she held trumps, and she knew it. "Lower your voice, Oscar," she said. "And keep a more respectful attitude. I'm here professionally—and I was hired by Mr. McAllum, of Underwriters' Protective. That's a company supported by most of the old line life insurance companies to fight frauds . . ."

"I know, I know." Piper sat down on the bed, and put a match to a greenish-brown cigar. "Tell it your own way, but get to the point before tomorrow morning."

She sniffed. "Mr. McAllum had heard of my hobby. He said he was looking for a woman to do some detective work, but that a policewoman wouldn't do because they look like policewomen . . ."

"I know," sighed Piper. "Built like brick woodsheds, with low heels and boyish bobs."

"Exactly! You see, it all began when they got a report that Mr. Portland had taken out insurance policies totaling almost a quarter of a million dollars. That looked a little unusual . . ."

"I don't see why. Lots of people put their money into term insurance these days."

"It wasn't term, it was straight life. And no beneficiary except the estate. But what made the company worried was the discovery that Portland's total reported income amounted to just about the yearly premium on the policies!"

"I see," cut in the inspector. "They figured he intended to defraud the company by committing suicide."

"Not at all. Suicide would invalidate the policies. They figured that someone had talked Portland into insuring his life for an excessive amount, with the intent to murder him. And they wanted an investigator to get some concrete evidence which would give them an excuse to cancel the policies. They found out that Portland carried a small policy on his rare books, and got me into the house on the pretext of cataloguing the library."

"So what did you find?"

The schoolteacher hesitated. "Not much. I have an idea that Portland suspected something. Because he saw to it that I really catalogued the library. But I did have a chance to study the housekeeper. The Augusta Nack type if I ever saw one."

"The what?"

"Augusta Nack. The woman who cut up Guldensuppe some years before the turn of the century." Miss Withers had recently been making concentrated study of old murder cases in the files of the public library, and she liked to display her erudition. "But she didn't do it, even if she is a distant cousin of the dead man."

"Oh," breathed Piper. "She didn't do it. You're sure?"

"Of course. Because she didn't spill the breakfast tray when she found Portland was dead. If she'd been acting she'd have thrown the tray up in the air and there would have been spilled egg and toast and coffee all over the third floor landing. And you can see for yourself that she set the tray neatly on the hall table. Besides, the woman is lazy, and you can't tell me she would go to all the trouble of fixing up a nice breakfast tray when she knew nobody would eat it."

Piper nodded slowly. "What about the girl? Get a line on her?"

"Morna? There's something odd about that girl, Oscar. She hasn't had anything to do here for months—Portland's business is practically dead on account of the war. But he pays her a handsome salary to type a few letters and help him with his hobby of rebinding old books. Portland maybe was not too old to notice that she is about the most breathtakingly beautiful thing since Helen of Troy. But they were both very circumspect when I was around."

"What about the nephew?"

"Not mentioned, except by the housekeeper. She brought me my luncheon on a tray yesterday, and I pumped her a bit. In her opinion young Mr. Sam Portland is a misunderstood, abused lamb, and he never should have been kicked out of the Army."

"Well, well," said the inspector. "We'll see about that." Just then a knock at the door interrupted the conference. Piper opened it, and learned from Lt. Branch that Sam Portland had been picked up in a coffee shop on Sheridan Square, and that he was now downstairs in the front parlor, handcuffed to a couple of detectives.

"Now we are getting somewhere!" exploded the inspector, as he started for the stair. "You can tag along, Hildegarde, if you'll keep mum."

Young Portland turned out to be a well-fed, brawny youth in a worn tweed suit and a military haircut, wearing thick glasses and a truculent expression. He denied having seen his uncle for six weeks, denied having murdered him, denied everything.

"Then why weren't you at home in your apartment last night?"

"I was!" Portland insisted, "I got up early to go to the park."

"What for?"

"To look at the sun!" burst forth the young man angrily and would say no more.

"Of course you don't know that as your uncle's heir you inherit a quarter of a million dollars' insurance, do you?"

Portland kept his silence, but there was something more than surprise in his face at the news, something suddenly wary, thoughtful.

"You quarreled with your uncle—he was pretty sore because you got kicked out of the Army, huh?"

Portland shook his head. "It wasn't about that at all," he said, and then was silent again.

"Okay," Piper told the lieutenant. "Put him in with the others." He turned, and saw that Miss Hildegarde Withers was just entering the room. "Well," he greeted her. "I thought you were quieter than usual."

"I was having a look at the room upstairs," she said, "I knew I wasn't supposed to, but I thought—"

"That room was searched by trained officers!" Piper snapped.

"That's why I thought I ought to have a look," she said, frowning. She started out into the hall, where Sam Portland was being led away. "Yes, definitely the Ronald Molineux type," she decided. "Remember? He mailed poisoned headache powders to a gentleman he disliked. Very attractive to women he was, according to the newspaper accounts."

"All right, all right." Piper grew impatient. "So you got into the murder room. What did you find, if anything?"

"I'm not sure," she said. "Oscar, did you notice the workbench?"

"Of course I did, Portland amused himself by rebinding old books and stamping fancy gold doojiggers on the backs. There were tools scattered all over the place."

She nodded. "A sharp knife and a pair of thin pliers on the floor."

"Exactly. Portland must have been at work when the murderer came in. Oh, I get it. You mean that he must have known the killer, or he wouldn't have gone on working."

Miss Withers shook her head.

"Not quite that. Oscar, did you ever read of a case where a man, trying to make his suicide look like murder, tied a weighted rope to the gun and shot himself on a bridge, so the gun went to the bottom of a river?"

"Maybe. But no gun got out of those locked windows, nor through the fanlight. There isn't a fireplace in the room, so nothing went up the chimney on a rubber band. . . ."

"You're barking up the wrong tree if you think it's suicide. Because Portland couldn't have taken a step after he was shot. He didn't go out and dispose of the gun and then lock himself in the room and die." Piper laughed shortly. "Besides, there is one thing that proves it isn't suicide. The lights in the room were off and the shades drawn. You know as well as I do that nobody ever wants to die in the dark."

"It wasn't dark, Oscar. Didn't you notice the puddle of melted paraffin on the workbench? He had a candle."

"That was probably to heat the gold leaf that he applied to the book bindings. . . ."

She nodded. "But all the same, I don't believe that Charles Portland would have gone on working quietly at his hobby if the nephew he disliked walked into the room. And as for the secretary—"

"Ho, ho!" shouted the inspector. "He certainly would have put down his tools if she came walking in. As who wouldn't?"

"Crudely put, but accurate. According to Mrs. Marple the girl was setting her cap to marry her employer, only he had somewhat different ideas. That, of course, may be simply malicious gossip."

"All this is wasting time," Piper decided. "It's the nephew. He stood to gain plenty."

"No doubt. By the way, Oscar, did you notice his haircut? It made me wonder if—" She shook her head. "I should like to ask him one question."

"You won't get any answer," the inspector told her. But strangely enough, when they were downstairs in the library with the three detained suspects, Sam Portland answered without the slightest hesitation.

"What color was my discharge papers?" He smiled a twisted smile. "What color would it be? Blue, of course."

"I thought so," said Miss Withers pleasantly. She beckoned the inspector out into the hall again, the lieutenant following. "Oscar, did you notice?

When I questioned young Portland just now, the girl pretended not to be interested in the slightest. She kept her head turned away—but she forgot to breathe until he answered."

Lt. Branch pushed closer. "Oh, there's no connection between them," he said, "I have been watching, and since he came in the room she never looked at him nor he at her."

The schoolteacher was unimpressed. She said, "'The dog did nothing in the night time, and that was the curious incident.' A famous remark of Mr. Sherlock Holmes, Oscar. Any young man in his right mind would stare at that girl, whether he was suspected of a murder or not."

"Hildegarde, what in the world are you driving at? First you try to twist this thing into a suicide, and then you try to give that young couple a motive."

"I don't have to try," said Miss Hildegarde Withers softly. "They were given one without my help. Oscar, has any search been made of the girl's apartment? And of young Portland's?"

The inspector said he thought that one had or would be made, in the normal routine of the murder investigation, but he would find out.

"Do," urged the schoolteacher.

She was sitting in the front parlor, placidly cutting the pages of an uncut first of *Essays of Elia*, when the inspector burst in upon her. "I hate to admit it, Hildegarde," he cried, "but you hit the nail on the head! Not at the boy's apartment. Our men drew a complete blank there, except for a trunk full of uniforms, captain's insignia, and so forth. A guy that's kicked out of the Army isn't supposed to keep his uniforms, is he?" Miss Withers thought not. "Well, anyway," Piper continued jubilantly, "what do you think they found in Morna Dewey's second-best handbag?"

"A .45," said the schoolma'am.

Piper looked blank. "No, not that, but something just as good. It was a duplicate key to the room where Portland was killed! Just luck that they found it, because the key had been tucked down inside a rip in the lining."

The schoolteacher nodded. "But nothing in the boy's room. "Dear, dear. And I thought I had the entire thing solved. Wait a moment, Oscar, was this house searched?"

"For the gun, with a fine-tooth comb."

"All the same," she insisted, "I never consider a place searched until I have searched it myself." And she marched stoutly upstairs, finally stopping in a disused rear bedroom which appeared to have been Sam Portland's room during the happier days when this was his home.

The furniture proved empty and disappointing, and the closet produced only a set of wood shaft golf clubs, a pair of worn riding boots stuffed with heavy maple boot-trees, and a trout rod.

"No gun," said the inspector, "I could have told you. My boys know how to search."

"And some one knew how to hide," retorted Miss Withers, as she seized the brass ring of the boot-tree, jerked out the wedge, and then pulled out the curved shin piece and the smoothly shaped part which corresponded to the calf of the leg. The remaining part of the wooden tree was supposed to be a wooden foot . . .

The schoolteacher turned the boot upside down and a heavy .45 thudded to the carpet. "The gun, Oscar," she said. "It had to be there, because there was no place else for it to be."

Oscar Piper picked up the gun. "Government issue .45 Colt automatic, and I don't need a ballistics man to tell me it's been recently fired. There's an Army serial number, too, so let young Portland try to deny it's his." He dropped the weapon in his pocket, patted it.

"You're going to arrest them right away, then?"

"Huh? Certainly I am. Typical murder pattern. Loving couple decide to set themselves up with insurance money. It's perfectly obvious."

"Oscar, you must consider one factor," said the schoolteacher thoughtfully. "Beauty such as that girl possesses is a force, an unusual and dangerous force. It's enough to make me glad that I never possessed it myself.

"Morna Dewey has youth and bloom, but she also has a deeper, more fundamental thing—a synthesis of bone structure and glowing health, of hair and skin and eyes, which makes her walking dynamite."

"I know," Piper admitted. "She'll beat the chair. But that is not my funeral. I'm going to haul that precious pair down town and get a confession. Ought to have it all washed up before lunch time. By the way, I owe you something for your help in solving this case. Drop in the office round noon and I'll take you to Whyte's."

Miss Withers watched silently as the young couple were led away, noting that they still ignored each other with painful insistence. Her face was stony, but if any one had been noticing there was an odd softness in her pale blue eyes.

All the same, she turned up at Centre Street shortly after noon, to find the inspector at his desk. He was in the act of setting fire to a dead cigar stump by means of a desk lighter in the shape of a knight in armor. "Any minute now," he greeted her. "The girl is about ready to break. Got them both in separate rooms down the hall, with the boys working them over. Oh, nothing rough; just questions."

"Did the boy admit the gun was his?"

Piper nodded. "Says he bought it when he was expecting to go overseas with his division, but it was stolen some time after he came back to New York. And the girl denies ever seeing the key before, but she'll get tired of that."

"The bullet that killed Portland was fired from that gun?"

He shrugged. "The slug was too mashed up to see any rifling marks. But the empty shell was marked by the firing pin of the gun all right. No two are alike."

Miss Withers nodded noncommittally. "You sit here and I'll just step down the hall and see how it's progressing," Piper told her. "If our prisoners are still stubborn we'll have to work the old gag of telling each of them that the other has confessed. That always works. These things follow a definite pattern every time."

He stepped out of the room, carefully closing the door behind him. "You and your patterns!" exploded Miss Hildegarde Withers. Then she picked up the desk lighter and stared at it thoughtfully.

The inspector was on his way back down the hall when he heard the shot in his office. He plunged in through the hall door just as the white-faced desk lieutenant and two uniformed men came from the outer office. They all stopped short as they saw Miss Hildegarde Withers sitting placidly in the inspector's chair. In one hand she held the cigar lighter, still flaring, and in the other a small pair of pliers which now gripped the empty casing of a .45-caliber shell.

"I'm afraid I've shot a hole in your ceiling," said the schoolteacher calmly. "But I had to demonstrate to you that it's not the gun which kills, it's the bullet. You don't need a gun at all."

"Hildegarde, are you out of your mind?" Piper cried.

"On the contrary, I'm very much in it. Don't you see, Oscar? This is how Charles Portland killed himself, except that he held the cartridge pointed at his face instead of the ceiling. First, of course, he had taken out the ridiculously large insurance policy to set up a motive and settled the whole thing by planting evidence on the two people he hated most in the world."

"Oh, come, come. You were saying he had a yen for the girl."

"Hate and love are opposite sides of the same coin. If Portland couldn't have her, he wasn't going to see her marry his handsome young nephew. Spite work, Oscar, carried to its farthest, most vicious extreme."

"I don't see it. The bullet that killed Portland was fired from the gun we found hidden in his nephew's boot."

"Was it? Suppose Portland stole the service pistol which he knew could be easily traced to his nephew, took it out into the country somewhere and fired it until it missed fire, which I understand can happen with the best of ammunition? The shell would still bear the mark of the firing pin—and the dud would still go off if held in the heat of a candle flame."

The inspector swallowed, and then a slow smile crept across his face. "Hildegarde, I don't know what to say."

"Say it, with apologies to those young people," the schoolteacher advised him. "And double apologies to Portland. He got an honorable discharge for physical reasons, presumably eyesight. No man who was kicked out of the Army would keep his hair cut army fashion, nor retain his uniforms and insignia. He was hoping to regain his captaincy, Oscar. No doubt that is why he went out into the park to stare at the morning sun, which happens to be part of a special training for relaxing and stimulating eyesight. Many men who are trying to pass Army and Navy tests go in for it."

"I'd better do something about my own eyesight," said the inspector. "And something about my insight too." He turned. "All right, boys. Turn the suspects loose. And—and ask them if they would step in here on their way out."

Miss Withers smiled expectantly and waited. But nothing happened, Finally she crossed to the door and looked down the hall. "Mercy sakes, Oscar!" she cried. He joined her, to see that, while officers watched in an admiring circle, Sam Portland was embracing the lovely tall brunette.

Piper grinned. "Hildegarde, there's the happy ending, the clinch and the fadeout."

The schoolteacher looked again. "Oscar, you might tell your men to take the handcuffs off that boy!"

"O.K.," the inspector said. "But he's doing all right with them on."

Where Angels Fear To Tread

The honeymoon cottage, Miss Hildegarde Withers sensed immediately, was as deserted and melancholy as a last-year's bird's nest. "Dear me!" sighed the maiden schoolteacher uncertainly. A realtor's FOR SALE sign was not at all the warm welcome she had a right to expect from her favorite niece. What she had meant to be a surprise visit had reverse English on it, and her departing taxi had left her and her suitcase stranded in the desolate reaches of a half-built suburb in the drizzling rain.

By peering through the blinds she could see hanging above the cheerless fireplace the framed Picasso print of the *Woman in White* which had been her wedding present to the young couple only last June. The letterbox was stuffed with mail, but it was not the front of a house that told its story. Marching around to the rear, past the empty gaping garage, she lifted the cover of the garbage can to discover coffee grounds, cigarette butts, empty pint bottles, and the remains of a small table-model radio which appeared to have been sat on by an elephant.

Miss Withers was about to tackle the lock of the back door with a hairpin when she heard a loud "Hey!" and turned guiltily to see a slatternly young woman in slacks climbing over the picket fence from next door. "Say, didn't they tell you at the real estate office to ask at Rauthmeyer's for the key?"

"Why—it quite slipped my mind if they did," the schoolteacher temporized. The door clicked open, and she was ushered into a little kitchen stocked with modern gadgets, but in extreme disorder. The house itself smelled dank and sour. " But isn' t someone still living here? Are you quite sure the house is for sale?"

Mrs. Rauthmeyer nodded. "Furnished, too. The folks who lived here broke up a week ago. She's left, but he's still camping here off and on." Miss Withers obediently followed her guide on a conducted tour. There was dust lying thick on the bureau in the little back bedroom which Joanie had written would always be kept ready for Aunt Hilde, and the other chamber was a tangle of rumpled bedding and soiled masculine laundry. The closet was jammed with feminine garments. "Guess she just walked out in what she had on her back," the young woman suggested. "Probably she'll send for them when she gets settled."

"You have no idea where she can be reached?" Miss Withers asked, as casually as she could.

"Nope. We really didn't get to know the Sansoms very well, though they did come over to play bridge one Sunday. He works nights, you know. But even that bridge game broke up in a row when he took her out of a business double and they went down six."

"But surely a nice young couple wouldn't break up over a game of cards?"

"Easy to see you've never been married," Mrs. Rauthmeyer said wisely. "When a wife and husband fight, it's never really about what they seem to be fighting about. If you must know, I think that the main trouble was that radio program Joan was always listening to. Her husband hated it like poison—those war vets have jumpy nerves anyway, you know. Anyway, one night he up and smashed the radio to smithereens."

Miss Withers nodded. "Sinatra?"

"Huh? Oh, no, it was Dr. Somebody's Clinic on Family Relations, over one of those Mexican stations. Comes on at seven right when I'm getting supper, so I never listen." The door keys jangled. "Well, if you've seen everything . . . ?"

Standing in the midst of the bedraggled living room which had once been decorated and furnished with such loving care and such high hopes, Miss Withers took a last look around. She shook her head at the stained carpet, at the shelves where *David Copperfield* and *Swann's Way* had been elbowed aside by a dozen thick volumes on the psychology of marriage, and last of all her eyes turned to the wedding picture silver-framed on the table. There were Joanie and Neil coming out of the chapel, looking incredibly young and ecstatic.

"Yes," the schoolteacher said softly, "I've seen quite enough." But typically, as they were leaving, she had to rush back inside and retrieve her umbrella. "I guess I'd lose my head if it wasn't fastened on," she observed tritely, as she returned. But young Mrs. Rauthmeyer's smile was mechanical, and as Miss Withers went on down the street she felt eyes on the back of her neck. "Thinks I'm a nosey-Parker," she told herself. But she had to go all around the block and come back from the other side across the vacant lot, before she could retrieve her suitcase and scramble in with it through the window she had managed to leave unlocked during her search for the umbrella.

Twilight was falling, but she dared not turn on any lights. With the aid of a pocket-flash the schoolteacher set out to search the honeymoon cottage as it should be searched.

Half an hour later she knew the worst. Her suspicions had been amply confirmed. But this was far different, from her impersonal kibitzing on police homicide investigations in the past. This involved her own Joanie, whom she still thought of as a little girl. Why, somewhere in a trunk Miss Withers still had a sheaf of old letters, the first one printed in smeary red Crayola, and thanking Aunt Hilde for the "lovely dolly that wears diapaers."

She was so busy wool-gathering that she did not even hear anyone outside until the doors burst open and they were upon her.

Three thousand miles to the eastward a grizzled little leprechaun of a man, wearing only a towel and a big black cigar, picked up the telephone. "Inspector Oscar Piper? San Diego, California, is calling." A moment later he heard an all-too-familiar female voice saying, "Oscar? Is that you? Do you know what's happened?"

"What's happened is that I just had to get out of a hot tub and I'm dripping all over the floor! Hildegarde, if you want to play guessing games—"

"Wait, please don't hang up. I'm only allowed one phone call. Oscar, I got out here this afternoon to find that Joanie Sansom, my married niece, has disappeared without her clothes—"

"The girl ought to be easy to locate, if she's walking around in her skin."

"Stop trying to be funny! I mean without most of her wardrobe, and without even leaving a forwarding address. Oscar, there are signs that somebody tried to clean up bloodstains from the living room rug with hot water, and only a man would do that—women know enough to use cold. And there's no pistol in the house!"

"So what? Maybe there isn't a 75mm howitzer, either."

"But there is an *empty* holster for an Army automatic tucked away in a trunk under her husband's old uniforms, and a spare clip of .45-caliber cartridges. I just feel it in my bones that something's happened to Joanie. Nobody in the family really approved of her marrying that man because she'd only known him a few weeks and she admits she picked him up in the park. . . ."

"Well," said the Inspector dryly, "I seem to remember that you picked me up in the Aquarium some years ago. Relax, Hildegarde. The girl's probably in Reno."

"Without her best dresses? If she was getting a divorce she'd certainly want to look her best at a time like that. Besides, the neighbors overheard them having a terrible fight one night about a week ago, and Joanie hasn't been seen since."

"It's out of my territory. Why don't you call in the local police?"

"*Call* them?" Miss Withers snorted. "Oscar, I guess I forgot to tell you that I'm in the San Diego police station, charged with illegal entry and grand larceny and I-don't-know-what-else." Her voice sharpened. "Are you laughing at me?"

"Just choked on my cigar," Piper hastily assured her.

"Oh. Well, anyway, while I was searching the house the snoopy woman next door noticed my flash-light through the window and called the police. I had my own suitcase with me, of course, and they took that as proof that I'd just finished looting the place. So here I am—they say my bail will be two thousand dollars."

The Inspector choked again. "Okay, Hildegarde. Put whoever's in charge on the line and I'll see if I can talk you out. But let this be a lesson to you. . . ."

The toll-call ran through eleven dollars and ninety cents with tax while a suspicious Latin-American detective-lieutenant listened, and even when he had hung up there was little warmth in the brown shoe-button eyes. "Guess we'll have to turn you loose," he said reluctantly. "That New York inspector says you're just a meddlesome old battleaxe of an amateur detective, but that you've no criminal record."

She tossed her head, rather like a startled horse. "Well, I must say!"

"And besides," Detective-lieutenant Villalobos went on, "while you were phoning we opened the suitcase. The stuff inside must be yours all right—there's nothing that a young bride like Mrs. Sansom would wear even to a dog-fight."

"Never mind that. Now that you've satisfied yourself as to my *bona fides*, what are you going to do about my niece?"

"We're reporting her to Missing Persons."

"Not good enough. Don't you see, you must arrest her husband at once! She wrote me that he is junior chemist for an oil company here in town."

Villalobos gestured with both hands. "We can't arrest anybody on your suspicions."

"Not even if I'm willing to sign a complaint?" Her fountain pen appeared.

"Okay," said the detective, when the deed was done. "It's you that's climbing out on a limb, not me." Picking up her suitcase, he escorted her firmly outside and hailed a taxi. "Now, ma'am, you just run along and let us do our job."

"But you'll really send out a broadcast on Neil Sansom, and stake out a couple of your men in the cottage to grab him if he comes home?"

"Sure, sure. Goodbye, Miss Withers."

"But Sansom works—" she started to say, and then bit her lip. The taxi was moving away, and after all the man might be right. In a way she was out on a limb. Moreover a tiny red light was flashing off and on in the back of her mind, a warning that she had forgotten something she should have remembered. But what?

"Take me to the—the Signal Hill Oil Company plant," she told the driver, on a wild impulse. As they crawled through the down town traffic, he switched on the radio and filled the taxi with hillbilly music. The schoolteacher suddenly remembered something, and looked at her watch, which showed a little past seven. "Can you get Mexico?"

"Sure can, lady. The Tia Juana stations, anyway." After some fishing around through bits of a sister-act singing "La Paloma" in Spanish and a re-running of the day's races at Hollywood Park in Brooklynese, Miss Withers at last heard a throbbing, feminine voice saying, ". . . work, work, work from morning to night cleaning and cooking and washing and then when he comes home, he just eats and goes to sleep, or else goes out bowling—he says. I'm just fed up, I am. Sometimes I get to crying and can't stop." There was a short pause, and then a man's voice: "That's her side of it, Doctor. But what about me? I work hard at the office all day and when I get home she hasn't even got her hair brushed, and around the house she's always nagging because we haven't got a new station wagon like our neighbors. . . ."

"But it's in English?" Miss Withers wondered. "I thought—"

The driver turned to grin lopsidedly. "Sure—they only broadcast from across the border to keep out of the jurisdiction of the Federal Communications Commission. Some of 'em sell snake oil. But this Dr. Doan is pretty good—my old lady swears by him."

". . . and it is obvious here," a deep, oddly heart-warming baritone was saying, "that the marriage of our good friends Mr. and Mrs. Blank is gravely endangered by a growing anxiety-neurosis and sense of emotional frustration on the part of both husband and wife. It is not easy to sublimate the emotions of courtship into the workaday relationship of everyday married life. . . ." The hypnotic voice went on and on, and as she jounced around in the back seat Miss Withers' prominent nose began to wrinkle.

"Only thus," the mellow tones continued, "can you both make the necessary adjustments and find domestic security and peace. Here is a copy of my new book, *Pitfalls of Love and Marriage*, with my compliments." There was a brief musical phrase, and then: "And to you of our radio audience—are you one of those who are puzzled and confused by the problems and conflicts of modern living? Do you need counsel? Then sit down and write me a letter—just Dr. Doan, Radio station XBYO, Box 131, San Diego. My help is free, as a public service. However, if you want an immediate answer on the air or in writing, just enclose a five-dollar bill to insure a number-one priority. And now for the mail-bag as time will permit. . . ."

There was a great deal more of the same, blasting forth the intimate secrets of a dozen or so unhappy human beings, with every problem glibly analyzed and solved in a few smooth sentences stuck full of the catchwords of psychiatry like a cookie full of raisins. When they arrived at her destination and the schoolteacher got out, it was with a deep sense of relief, for not even the smoking plant of an oil refinery smelled as bad as that radio program.

She approached a low white building surrounded by vast looming spheres and cylinders of shining metal, interlaced with a spider-webbing of pipes, and here and there erupting belches of flame into the sky. Miss Withers wasn't at all sure of what she was going to say to Neil Sansom when she found him. You couldn't just up and ask a young man if he'd murdered your niece—or could you?

As it developed, she needn't have worried. For Sansom wasn't at work today, not had he shown up yesterday either. She received this news from a pudgy young man in soiled linen who said that his name was Hank and that he worked out of the same test-tubes with Neil Sansom. "When I heard that there was a lady out here looking for him, I thought maybe it was his wife," he confessed. "The poor guy's been almost off his rocker for the past few days. We were afraid he might do something desperate."

"So was I," the schoolteacher admitted. "Or that he already has. But you *must* have some idea of where I could locate him?"

"Well, "suggested Hank helpfully, "there are only 194 bars in the San Diego area. You could start with those." More dispirited than ever, Miss Withers thanked him and returned to her waiting taxi.

"Back to town, lady?"

There seemed nothing else to do. "The trouble with me," she told herself, "is that I'm acting like a mother-hen instead of a bloodhound. If I only had half my wits about me I'd—but of course! *The wedding picture!*"

"Beg pardon, lady?"

She realized that she had spoken the last words aloud. "Turn around," said Miss Withers firmly. "I've decided to go down to Tia Juana."

"But that's a long haul, and I been driving this hack all day!"

"I'm already too far out on a limb," she told him, "to turn back now. Take me across the border." She leaned back in the seat, nodding almost happily. This is what she should have thought of in the first place.

The man muttered something to himself, but made an abrupt U-turn. A moment later he switched the radio on again, bringing back the mellifluous tones of Dr. Doan: "And in conclusion I say to the young woman who signs herself Miss Puzzled that since her fiancé has shown fixed infantile behavior patterns and evidently is in the grip of a mother-fixation with schizoid tendencies, she should forget him and—"

"And *frammis* the *stanportis*," Miss Withers put in tartly. "Driver, do you mind turning off that double-talk?" They rode on in silence, in the wrong direction.

A few miles northward along the coast from San Diego sleeps the village of La Jolla, famous for Torrey pines, abalone shells, and for having the most mispronounced name in recent history. In one of the most secluded of its neo-Moorish beach homes, shielded from the street and the curious gaze of the tourist by a line of pepper-trees, Dr. Charles Augustus Doan sat in his comfortably furnished study and listened to the sweet sound of his own voice.

Dr. Doan stroked his neat little Van Dyke complacently, making a mental note as the XBYO station identification came on in staccato Spanish that the program just ending was his 2,940th. Then he loosened the cord that held the heavy wine-colored dressing gown around his ponderous body, and turned again to his hobby. Other men of standing might collect first editions or Flemish paintings, but the doctor fancied five-dollar bills. With the dexterity of long practice he removed these from the heap of letters which represented yesterday's mail. Through wide French doors he could look out as he worked upon the rain-washed, moonlit garden filled with cacti and rare succulents, to the garage at one side which held his two late-model sedans, and a little farther to the low vine-covered retaining wall and the shimmering Pacific beyond. Somewhere nearby a mocking-bird was singing.

Not bad. Not bad at all for a man who only twelve years ago had been trying to eke out a hand-to-mouth existence as Professor Charles, mental-ist and lecturer on sex (Miracle of the Unborn, 12 count 'em 12 genuine human embryos in bottles, carnival bookings available for next season, address care of *Billboard*).

Though he had a competent staff, this was one operation which Dr. Doan always liked to perform in person. Into his pocket went the money, and into a wire tray beside him went the letters, to be dramatized on the air, answered briefly at the end of the program, or directly by mail. Letters without any enclosure went into the waste-basket unread, but luckily these were few and far between.

After a while there came a discreet tap at the door, and without remov-ing the big Corona from his mobile mouth, Doan said, "Come in, Patty."

The secretary was a pale, wispy woman on the rocky side of thirty-five, addicted to shapeless knitted dresses and open-toed shoes. As was her almost unvarying custom, Patty Givens gave a dry little nervous cough before she spoke. "Excuse me, Doctor—"

"All set? Everybody here?" Doan started to rise. "Might as well get it over."

"Er—no, Doctor. Dora and the writers are in the living room, but Julio hasn't had time to get back from the studio. It's something else. A young man insists on seeing you. He's sort of wild-looking—perhaps I ought to call the police?"

"Police? Of course not,"

"Doan cut in hastily. "Would I be doing my duty if I turned away a poor soul who is in need of counsel? Just explain to him that I don't keep office hours for consultation, but that I'll try to see him later—"

"You'll blamed well see me right now!" came a high, excited voice from the hall, and a young man entered the room as if blown by a high wind. His clothes were hung on his thin body scarecrow style, and there was dried blood above his eye.

The doctor looked at him in cold, offended dignity. "My dear sir, you can't come bursting in—" he began, and then noticed that the uninvited guest was brandishing a large and nasty-looking automatic pistol. "Please sit down and put that thing away," he said quickly and firmly. Then his voice softened. "Something tells me that you are in serious trouble. You don't have to make threats to receive any help that it is in my power to give. Tell me about it, lad. Just what is your problem?"

"*You* are!" blurted Neil Sansom.

From the doorway Patty cleared her throat. "Doctor, hadn't I better call—?"

"Of course not," Doan told her sharply. "But you might get our visitor a stimulant."

"Save your liquor, I don't want it. I came here about my wife!"

"Ah, yes." The doctor sighed. Even at his age, which was pushing sixty, there were a good many phone numbers in his little black book. Some no doubt had husbands. This was likely to be awkward, unless the fellow identified himself."

"Perhaps, Miss Givens, you had better step outside and leave us in privacy," he suggested.

Once the study door was closed, even with her ear pressed close against a panel, Patty could only hear the rumble of their voices. She sighed, and then went back to the kitchen and—first making sure that the Mexican cook had left for the day—helped herself to a glass of cooking sherry, chasing it with a peppermint. "For my nerves," she told herself. Not that she lacked confidence in Dr. Doan's ability to handle any conceivable situation. . . .

When the buzzer sounded, summoning her, she raced back into the study and stopped short. There was the doctor standing alone beside his desk, smiling as he ground out a cigar butt in the tray. "That awful young man—" she cried. "I didn't see—"

Dr. Doan nodded toward the garden door. "I gave him what help I could, but he is still in a nervously disturbed state and I thought it just as well that nobody meet him in the hall."

"Doctor, you're wonderful!" Patty gazed on him with dog-like devotion. Then she saw that Doan was holding the pistol.

"Yes," he continued, "I suggested that your young friend take a good stiff walk along the shore and cool off. And I convinced him that in his condition it would be wiser to leave the weapon with me." Doan dropped it into his desk drawer. "By the way, aren't we ready yet?"

"Oh, yes, Doctor! They're all in the living room waiting. I don't think they suspect a *thing*." Patty stepped quickly aside to hold the door, and Dr. Doan started down the hall. To a fresh Corona he held a gold cigarette lighter bearing a caduceus made of tiny emeralds, and on the obverse *To Dr. Charles with gratitude from Lana*, which had been his birthday present to himself a year ago.

In the vast, underlighted living room, filled with arches and niches and wrought-iron, were gathered the four people to whom Dr. Doan liked to refer as his fellow-workers. Dora Dinwiddie, Lady of the Hundred Voices, was a veteran of vaudeville who never let anyone forget that in the early days of radio she had been featured on Ed Wynn's show. Dora played all the feminine parts for this program, from teen-age daughter to doddering crone, though in person she was a handsome forty, hung with bracelets and bangles.

Nearby, sprawled on the big divan were the Carnehan brothers, graduates of the Hollywood quickie studios, a pair of paunchy, graying adolescents in sweat-shirts and slacks. Ray and Sam, known respectively as the Drinking One and the Chasing One, wrote and arranged the program, read some masculine parts, and ghosted Dr. Doan's books.

At the moment they were sharing their *Racing Form* with Julio Barnes, a thin, waspish man with the manner and the flying hair of a concert maestro. He handled music and sound effects, cut the recordings, and each evening drove down across the international boundary and supervised the actual broadcasting of the program from the little studio at XBYO.

It was a tribute to Dr. Doan that they all rose—even Dora—when he entered the room. Patty Givens assumed the role of hostess, and bustled around refilling their glasses and gleefully recounting how the doctor had overpowered and disarmed the wild-eyed intruder by sheer mental force. But Doan cut her short.

"My friends and fellow-workers in the cause of human welfare," he began in his honeyed baritone, "tonight I have a very important announcement to make, as you perhaps have guessed. Contracts were signed today between myself and a relative of a very big *politico* across the border, which will make us equal partners in *El Negro y Blanco*, the Black and White network, Mexico's first television chain. Originating here in Tia Juana but sent by wire to be rebroadcast from Mexicali, Nuevo Laredo, and Matamoros will be the new video program—*Judge Doan's Court of Human Problems!*"

There was a little stir among the listeners, the beginning of surprised congratulations, but Dr. Doan raised his hand. "As you know, we have waxed enough platters to carry the old show until the first of the year, when it will go off the air. You have all worked with me hard and faithfully, and therefore I have a sort of bonus, an advance Christmas present, for each." Doan produced a sheaf of envelopes from his pocket, much as he might have taken a rabbit from a silk hat, and handed them to the hovering Patty to distribute.

Dora Dinwiddie opened hers first. "A check for two months' pay!" she cried delightedly, and then read on, in a voice that suddenly went harsh: "In final settlement of all claims and obligations." Her bracelets fluttered and jingled. "But—"

"Oh, yes," said Dr. Doan. "You see, television is quite different from ordinary radio. For instance you, Dora, have a hundred voices. But you have only one face. The new show will require a completely new cast of characters for each broadcast, except for myself of course. Also a completely different sort of preparation and script, and a technical staff trained in the video field. It is with deep and heartfelt regret that I say goodbye to you, and I wish you success as you go on to other fields of service." The doctor's smile warmly embraced them all, and then he bowed and swept out of the room.

The four of them stood there, flat-footed. It was Julio Barnes who first found his voice. "That—that *cabrón!*" he whispered, and spat on the rug.

Ray Carnehan for once in his life put down a highball half-finished. "Why, I owe my bookie more than the amount of this check! We'll get a lawyer and sue—"

Sam interrupted. "You know what we'll get in the Mex courts. Besides, our contracts are with the program that's being killed. Line forms here for unemployment insurance." He was thinking of the golden, laughing girls of the Hollywood Sunset Strip and how far twenty dollars a week would go with them.

"We've made Doan a million dollars and now he kisses us off with two months' pay that he'd owe us anyway!" Dora Dinwiddie cried, for once in her own true voice with the Iowa twang to it. "Slaving away for ten years on less than Guild scale for that flea-bitten chiropractor. . . ."

"*Judge* Doan now," Julio Barnes put in. "It's a wonder he didn't go the whole way, and ordain himself Father Doan!" He snorted. "The Confessional on the Air!"

Patty Givens cleared her throat from the doorway. "You shouldn't say such things about a brilliant man who's devoted his life—" But the four of them stamped out of the house, making rude remarks about what Dr. Doan could do with his life, and the front door slammed behind them. Patty peered out of the front window, in an odd state of fluttery happiness, as they held a further indignation meeting on the sidewalk under the pepper-trees, and then she let go a sigh of relief as they separated and drifted away, In her opinion they were crude, vulgar people and unworthy to have shared in the doctor's great work. She was happy to see the last of them.

She almost said as much to Dr. Doan as a little later he lay stretched out on the big red-leather couch in the study and—cribbing occasionally from his library on popular psychology—dictated answers to the day's mail. It was in moments like this that Patty Givens was coziest, just the two of them alone in the big rambling house. She felt even more intensely than usual the glow of the sherry inside her, the tingling sweetness of the peppermint in her mouth, and the warmth of the tiny electric heater on her ankles.

It would have been altogether perfect if the doctor would only let her close the doors into the garden and draw the shades. Sometimes the looming shapes of the giant cacti made her nervous. In the moonlight one Joshua tree in particular resembled a lurking man, with an arm upraised in warning. . . .

Patty was still busy with the doctor in the study when the doorbell rang. A pause, then it rang again, and finally someone hammered as with a nightstick. "Just a *minute!*" the secretary muttered, and then hurried down the hall and flung open the front door. "You're here, thank heavens—" she started to say, and then her jaw dropped. For instead of the blue uniforms she was expecting, there was only a tall bony woman with a long face which vaguely resembled Man o' War, topped by a hat straight out of *Godey's Lady's Book.*

The apparition held an umbrella poised, ready to knock again. "I wish to see the doctor at once," announced Miss Hildegarde Withers.

Patty coughed. "Oh—but well, you see the doctor doesn't practice. I'm his secretary—you could write him a letter if you wish his counsel. . . ."

"I don't," said the schoolteacher. "But I've been tracking Dr. Doan all over Tia Juana and back, and I'm not leaving until I see him. I—" Suddenly she stopped, her eyes curious and almost sympathetic. "What are you afraid of? I won't bite."

"Oh—why, I expected it to be the police at the door," Patty admitted.

"Why? What's wrong?"

"Nothing, really. But you see, I thought I saw somebody in the garden. I've imagined it lots of times before when I've had to stay and take dictation late at night, but tonight there really *was* something there. And the doctor finally said I could call the police if it would make me feel easier. I just know it was that same awful young man who was here earlier, waving a gun."

"Oh, dear!" sighed Miss Withers. "A young man with a gun . . . but I suppose that a man like the doctor has many enemies . . . ?"

Her remark was abruptly punctuated by the sound of a shot, incredibly loud and clear, from somewhere back in the house. "Oh, God!" shrieked Patty Givens. She whirled and ran.

Though left at the starting gate, Miss Withers made up ground on the straightaway and they were neck and neck at the study door. Flinging it open, she was met by the acrid stench of cordite. There had evidently been a fierce though brief struggle, for the desk drawer was gaping, papers and letters were scattered like autumn leaves, and the electric heater had been kicked over.

The big, bearded man in dressing gown and slippers lay crumpled on the floor between desk and couch, eyes staring at nothing. In a second Miss Withers satisfied herself that Dr. Doan was forever finished with human problems, including his own. Yet there was no wound, no bullet-hole that she could see.

Patty Givens, who had snatched up a vase and rushed out into the garden like a tigress defending her cub, now came slowly back. "I heard the murderer—running away," she said, half-choking.

Miss Withers came to the door and listened, but there was by this time nothing to hear except the swishing of the surf on the beach, and the distant singing of the mocking bird. Out of the corner of her eye she could see that the secretary was doing a nervous little dance-step, an absurd hop which increased until her whole body was shaking. "Oh-oh-oh," moaned Patty. "I'm going to—"

"You are not either," said the schoolteacher, and slapped her. Then the woman subsided into great shuddering sobs, clinging to her like a scared child. It was at that opportune moment that the police finally arrived. Just her luck, Miss Withers thought, that when for once in her life she had been on the scene of a murder ahead of the authorities, she had to be entangled with a hysterical woman.

The officers took one look at the body and then one of them raced for the phone, the other shepherding the two women into the living room where he stood guard over them. Nor did he seem disposed to pay heed when Miss Withers tried to give him a few well-intentioned hints about the handling of the case. "Lady," he told her, "I only work the prowl-car beat."

Outside, autos arrived hastily, and there was the banging of doors, heavy steps in the hall, and the tantalizing masculine voices that she could almost hear. The schoolteacher tired of sitting on the sidelines and listening to Patty Givens coughing and sniffing, and of the scent of peppermints. "This has gone far enough," she finally burst forth. "I demand to see the person in charge. After all, I've been working on this case longer than anyone else, even if I did guess wrong about the victim."

"Shut up—please ," said the patrolman. "Your turn'll come."

When it came, Miss Withers was rather sorry she had insisted, for it was none other than her old acquaintance Lieutenant Villalobos who came into the room, wearing an old trench-coat and a worried scowl. The shoe-button eyes flashed in recognition. "Oh, *no!*" he said, wincing. "Not twice in one day."

"Lieutenant, I didn't expect to see you in charge way out here."

"La Jolla happens to be part of the city of San Diego," he told her. "I was never sorrier." Wearily he took out a black notebook. "Now ma'am, how do you explain."

"I came here, after bribing the people in Tia Juana to give me Dr. Doan's home address, because I happen to know that my niece Joanie Sansom *always* listens to Doan's radio program. I thought that maybe she isn't dead after all, because if he'd killed her, Neil wouldn't keep their wedding picture around to look at. I hoped to persuade Dr. Doan to include in his next broadcast an appeal to her to come home or let us know where she is."

"And it was just a coincidence that you happened to be on the spot when he got killed. Is that your story?"

"But I wasn't! I was standing in the doorway, trying to get his secretary to let me see him, when the shot was fired. And for that matter I don't know if the man was murdered or not. I didn't see any wound anywhere."

Villalobos smiled grimly. "You should have lifted his toupee, then."

It was Patty Givens who gasped. "His *what?* But the doctor didn't—"

"Oh, sure. They make 'em nowadays so nobody can tell. Anyway, Doan was shot in the center of his bald spot at close range, the bullet angling down into his body. We figure the hair-piece must have got knocked off in the struggle, but the murderer took time out to replace it, neatly covering the wound. The gun itself—"

"An Army .45 automatic," whispered Miss Withers.

"I was about to say that the gun is missing, though we found an ejected .45 shell under the bookcase." The dark eyes narrowed. "You seem to know a lot about this."

"Put it down as a lucky guess," the schoolteacher said, somewhat feebly.

But she was saved for the moment by Patty Givens, who could keep silence no longer. She blurted out the breathless story of what had happened that evening, of the awful young man forcing his way in with the gun and how Doan had taken it away from him, of the session here in the living room when the doctor fired his staff, and of how later she had seen someone or something moving in the garden.

Villalobos listened patiently, making notes only of the names and addresses of the four members of the staff who had been paid off. He tore out the sheet and handed it to a uniformed man. "Pick them up," he said.

"But Lieutenant," objected Miss Withers, "don't you think it unlikely that people would commit murder just over losing a job?"

He gritted his teeth. "I've seen murder committed over eighty-five cents. Killers aren't reasonable."

But it was really Patty who answered the question. "You don't know them," she insisted. "They'd all been with the doctor so long they thought they owned their jobs. Dora Dinwiddie has a young husband and she knows he'll walk out on her if she stops making big money. Julio Barnes was in prison once for trying to strangle a man in an argument over the proper way to adjust a microphone. And the Carnehans—they both live up to every dime they make, and Ray can't do without liquor any more than Sam can do without little blond extra girls."

"Surely there are lots of other jobs," the schoolteacher objected.

Patty shook her head stubbornly. "Nobody goes back to one of the big networks again after ten years with a shoestring station down here. This is the end of the line."

"Okay!" growled the lieutenant. "I'm asking the questions. What you're saying is that one of the four people who got their final pay check tonight thought it over and then sneaked back through the garden to get even with Doan. Is that it?" He tugged thoughtfully at his lower lip. "Now who besides yourself knew that the gun was lying there handy?"

"Why—" the secretary flushed. "Maybe I *did* mention about how magnificently the doctor quieted and disarmed that young man, when we were all in here."

"So the Dinwiddie woman, both Carnehans, and Barnes knew the gun was somewhere in the study?"

Patty nodded, and started to speak, but Miss Withers interrupted. "There was somebody else who knew—the person from whom the gun was taken."

Villalobos' bow was exaggerated. "Could be. Also could be that that person's name is Neil Sansom. Anxious to swear out another warrant?"

"Certainly not! Because whoever did murder Dr. Doan, I'm positive that it wasn't my unfortunate nephew-in-law. If he had been going to commit homicide he'd have done it on the spur of the moment when he first arrived. I'm also positive—"

"If there's anything you're *not* positive about, let me know!" the lieutenant told her. He turned Patty Givens over to a subordinate with orders to have her sign a written statement. "That'll be all for tonight," he told Miss Withers, taking her by the elbow and steering her down the hall.

"But, Lieutenant, I want to make a written statement too! And shouldn't we have another look around Dr. Doan's study? I was thinking of the papers on the floor, and the ashtrays, and his checkbook. . . ."

"I said that would be all!" Villalobos repeated, in a queer, strained voice. But as they reached the front door, it was flung open and in came two bulky detectives, with Neil Sansom handcuffed between them. He looked sulky, scared, and guilty as Cain—but still in the pale, handsome face Miss Withers could see the boy of the wedding picture.

"Found him walking along the beach," was the report. "Says it was a nice night and he was just taking the air. But guess what we found in his pocket, Loot? A nice big .45 automatic that he happened to find a few minutes ago right below this house, left high and dry by the tide."

Neil only muttered, "Why shouldn't I have picked it up? It's mine."

"You poor boy," cried Miss Withers quickly, "don't say one thing more until I get you a lawyer. I'm Joanie's aunt from New York, and I'm afraid I've helped get you in a lot of trouble. Just tell me one thing—where is she?"

Neil Sansom seemed to be too tired to be surprised, even at this. "I haven't seen Joan since she knocked me cold with an ashtray and walked out of the house. I don't know where she is and I don't care anymore."

Then his captors jerked him along, and Miss Withers found herself being escorted out the front door in what was almost the equivalent of the bum's rush. "That fellow in New York warned me over the phone that you'd get in my hair," Lieutenant Villalobos muttered through clenched teeth. "Goodbye, *please.*"

However, the schoolteacher had to give him credit for one thing. The man was courteous enough to have a police car take her back to San Diego. It was not until they passed the ferry terminal and pulled up outside the familiar big brick building with the barred windows that she realized the lieutenant's hospitality included putting her up for the night.

After a sleepless night in a detention cell and a breakfast of mush and jail coffee Miss Hildegarde Withers did not think that anything could make her more miserable than she was already. But she had not counted on being hauled out to the house in La Jolla again shortly before noon, and coming face to face with her missing niece in the front hall.

The girl clung to her tearfully. "I was in Las Vegas," Joanie cried. "But I hopped a plane as soon as I heard it on the radio."

"But, child, why didn't you let anybody know?"

"I was afraid if I wrote anybody or sent for my stuff, Neil would find out where I was and come after me. I wanted to give him a real good scare, but I really wasn't going through with a divorce. Only you see, when we quarreled he tried to spank me!"

"The beast!"

"No, he isn't! It was all my fault, every bit of it. And now they're going to hang him for murdering that awful doctor—"

"No, they're not, child." Miss Withers tried to keep her voice confident.

"But yes they are!" Lieutenant Villalobos came briskly toward them, a look of smug satisfaction on his newly-shaven countenance. "Just a few things to straighten out on the time-table, which is why I've got everybody rounded up here. Will you follow me into the living room, please? You too, Mrs. Sansom— you're the motive." Then he dropped back to take Miss Withers' arm. "Sorry we had to hold you last night, but you know how it is. By the way, I'll have to admit that was a good steer you gave me about Doan's checkbook."

"Was it?" She blinked. "And the ashtrays?"

"Nothing in them but cigar butts."

"Oh," said the schoolteacher, her mind racing like a fly-wheel. But there was no time. The lieutenant ushered them into the living room, already rather crowded with uniformed men and material witnesses. Dora Dinwiddie sat on the edge of a hard chair, playing with her bracelets. The Carnehan brothers, both stiff and sober now, shared the piano bench, and Julio Barnes and Patty Givens slumped in easy chairs. On the divan, manacled to a stony-faced policeman, was the guest of honor. Neil looked up at Joanie as they came in, let out a breath, and then turned back to stare at his shoe-tips again.

"I'll make this short and sweet," began the lieutenant. "It's important that we have the times established. At eight-thirty last evening Miss Patty Givens came into the doctor's study and told him that there was a young man insisting on seeing him. She has identified the prisoner as being that man, and he doesn't deny it. At that time Miss Dinwiddie and both Carnehans were waiting in this room, and Mr. Barnes was on his way here, right?"

They all nodded. "Okay. At eight fifty-five Dr. Doan rang for Patty Givens and showed her a gun he'd taken away from Sansom. . . ."

The brisk, confident voice went on and on. Miss Withers racked her brains, but no inspiration came. She felt that she was drifting in a boat without oars or rudder, caught in a swiftening current and with the roar of a cataract ahead.

"Okay. At approximately nine o'clock Dr. Doan came into this room and made a little speech, after which he distributed pay checks to four of his employees. Around nine-fifteen they left—" He referred to his notebook again.

"And I for one went straight home," said Dora Dinwiddie. "My husband will back me up!"

Sam Carnehan spoke up. "If it's alibis you want, I spent the rest of the evening with Mimi, the day cashier at the Casa. She's not supposed to date guests, so I imagine she'll deny it."

His brother Ray confessed to having spent the previous night in a round of bar-hopping, starting at the Beach and Tennis Club and ending up on Skid Row in downtown San Diego. Julio Barnes said he'd gone home, played his violin for a while, and then taken his spaniel out for a long walk. All alibis, of a sort, but nothing Miss Withers could get her teeth into. It had to be one of them.

Villalobos continued summing-up. "So after you four had left, Patty Givens and the deceased started cleaning up the dictation in the study. At this time Sansom was taking a walk along the beach and trying to cool off. Finally he wandered back from the beach and came up into the garden and Patty Givens saw him out there, and called the police. That was at ten fifty-eight. At a minute or so after eleven Miss Withers arrived and rang the doorbell, so Patty had to leave Doan alone in the study to answer the front door—"

"I wouldn't have," Patty cried. "Only I thought it was the police answering my call!"

The lieutenant nodded. "I'm not suggesting that her arrival at that moment was a put-up job, but it did give Sansom the chance he was waiting for. Seeing that the doctor was alone, he slipped in from the garden and grabbed the gun out of the desk, or maybe he even asked Doan to return it to him. Anyway, once it was in his hand—"

"But what about the checkbook?" Miss Withers cut in desperately.

"Oh, yes." Villalobos nodded. "There were four stubs in it dated today, filled out properly for the four final pay checks. And there was a fifth check torn out, stub and all—that was the check he wrote to Neil Sansom, trying to buy his life!"

Across the room Neil started to rise, but felt the jerk of the handcuffs and sank back again. "Probably," continued Lieutenant Villalobos, "the shot was fired while Doan was bent over to write the check, thus accounting for the location of the wound. Sansom destroyed the check when he got outside, but then he lost his nerve. He remembered that Patty Givens could identify him—so he wandered up and down the beach, probably trying to get up courage enough to use the gun on himself."

Joanie leaned down and whispered in Miss Withers' ear. "He's innocent, I know he is! Neil wouldn't do anything like that in a million years. He couldn't!"

But the schoolteacher only sat there, still held in her nightmare. There was nothing, nothing at all she could offer in its place. It was that, or else she had to take her pick of the four—Dora, the Carnehans, or Barnes—and they all had the sort of alibis innocent people usually have.

Through Miss Withers' mind flashed the events of last evening, like film being hastily rewound on the reel. Neil's arrest, the lieutenant's questions, the wait with Patty in the living room, the scene in the room with the body, the sound of the shot—

"I'm afraid, Lieutenant," she said a few moments later, "that my niece is going to faint. Perhaps I might get her a glass of water?" Without waiting for an answer she whisked out of the room, plunging past the uniformed man in the doorway so swiftly and erratically that she almost threw him off balance. In less than five minutes, however, she was back with the glass of water. But now there was a look in her eye which—had this been one of Oscar Piper's cases—would have made that wise little Irishman order full speed astern.

Lieutenant Villalobos, however, still had the bit in his teeth. "Now listen," he was saying to Neil, "you can save yourself and everybody a lot of grief by making a full confession. You killed Dr. Doan because you knew he had advised your wife to leave you, and no doubt a jury will take that into consideration. But it's an open-and-shut case—"

"Please don't shut it just yet," interrupted Miss Withers airily. "By the way, Lieutenant, I just noticed in the bathroom that you're having the plumbing opened up. An excellent idea. I was sure that the missing check and stub had been burned or disposed of right here in this house."

Someone in the room sighed, very softly. "What the—?" began Villalobos.

"And remember, I tried last night to tell you that I thought it odd the killer replaced Doan's toupee neatly over the wound. That would seem to imply a squeamish person, who had to stay in the room with the body for a while and couldn't stand the sight of blood. Did I mention to you too about how Patty Givens here went rushing out into the garden after the murderer, she said? Up to then she'd been timid as a mouse. And how did she know that Doan was murdered then? She barely looked at him and there was no visible wound."

"Oh-oh-oh!" screamed Patty furiously. "You horrible woman, to say such things! Why, I worshipped the ground he walked on!"

"No doubt you did," Miss Withers conceded. "Until he told you that you were fired too. What could be more natural than after getting rid of the rest of his staff he'd get rid of his secretary? They say there's nothing more aggravating than an office-wife, especially one that coughs and sniffs and eats peppermints constantly. . . ."

"And that jiggling little dance-step that Patty was doing in the study last night," the schoolteacher continued. "I thought at the time that she was only shaking with hysteria, but *it was really the open-toed shoes!*"

"That's enough of this nonsense," Villalobos cut in. "You're trying to pin this thing on the doctor's secretary, but you're way off base. Haven't you forgotten that in your own statement you said you were talking to Patty Givens when Doan was shot?"

"Yes, Lieutenant—*but Doan was already dead when I rang the doorbell!* Patty Givens had killed him and thrown the pistol into the ocean—but not far enough—before she phoned the police. She thought I was the law, so she made a quick last minute adjustment in the study and hurried to answer the door, thinking that she was about to give herself a perfect alibi. Because nobody can tell within five or ten minutes the exact time a body expires."

Miss Withers stopped for breath. Something had gone terribly wrong, for it should have happened—

Then a bullet ricocheted screaming down the hallway, and the sound of a shot boomed through the house.

For an instant everyone in the living room was paralyzed, and then the cool Bostonian accents continued. "What you just heard was a pistol cartridge that I snatched from the belt of that officer in the doorway and stuck into the filament of the electric heater," she announced. "When the heater got red hot, the thing went off. Of course I should have faced the heater toward the open door, so the bullet would go harmlessly out to sea as it did for Patty last night." Miss Withers peered toward the secretary. "But it had to appear that there was only one shot fired, didn't it? You wanted to get rid of the *second* empty shell, but of course you didn't think it would be that hot. You worked it into the open toe of your shoe, and that's why you were dancing." Patty Givens suddenly stood up.

"There's no need to say any more," she told them dully. "Since you're tearing up the plumbing you'll find the scraps of the check anyway." Once started, she kept on talking endlessly, on and on. But long before she finally ran down, Miss Withers and the Sansoms were far away. It was a fine bright day, with little clouds like tufts of cotton-wool.

"But you're coming home with us for your visit, after all?" Joanie was begging, Neil's arm around her and her head on his shoulder.

Miss Withers thought not. "You young idiots deserve a chance to get together and pick up the broken pieces without anyone else butting in," she told them. "Perhaps I'll come later on. Right now, I think I'll make a long distance call to a certain hard-headed little inspector in New York and give him a piece of my mind. 'Meddlesome old battleaxe' indeed!"

The Jinx Man

Roscoe Brock had always been Fortune's fair-haired boy, and then his luck ran out. If coming events cast their shadows before, then his life was just one shadow after another, all with the same grim outline.

He went for a canter one Sunday morning—and came galloping back with a bullet-hole through his hat. Then there was the birthday bottle of cognac that seemed spoiled, and had to be thrown away. It was retrieved by the colored scrubwoman, who showed up weeks later to get her pay, looking as if she had been in the Valley of the Shadow, as indeed she had. Again, caught by a sudden shower, Brock descended into the subway for shelter and was somehow crowded off the platform to land in front of a train, which stopped only inches from where he sprawled.

Three narrow escapes. It was the kind of luck which couldn't hold out forever. The next thing to happen to him was Miss Hildegarde Withers, which must have seemed a little like adding insult to injury.

The spinster schoolma'am was sitting in the comparative coolness of a little garden restaurant in the village, and over the coffee had been giving a brief review of a book she'd read. "And victims are born or shaped by society just as criminals are. Oscar Piper, are you listening to me?"

The Inspector came out of his meditations with a start. He had been trying to decide what it was that his dinner companion reminded him of in the odd hat she was wearing tonight. Perhaps one of those funny angular Dutch houses, with a stork's nest on top. "Yes, Hildegarde. Very interesting, but—"

Her sniff was audible. "Dr. von Hentig's book is *more* than that, it presents a totally new approach to criminology. He suggests that many victims of crime practically ask for it; they stand in the path of the deed and tempt the criminal."

"Horsefeathers!"

"But insurance experts say some people are accident-prone. Haven't you run into others who seem murder-prone?" As he started to shake his head she added: "Oscar, would the name *Roscoe Brock* refresh your memory any?"

Piper jerked as if stung. "You been listening at keyholes or something?"

"No, but I have my sources of information. By the way, is it true that Brock's reason for taking out a $100,000 life insurance policy is that he's resigned himself to the fact that he must keep his appointment in Samarra, and soon?"

"Judas Priest in a Mixmaster!" yelped the Inspector. "It's the weather! This time of year, with the dog-days and the humidity, is the silly season for sure." He mopped his face. "Look, Hildegarde, this Brock thing— well, the other afternoon a Mrs. Millicent Jones comes barging into my office. One of those meek, prettyish women who look as if they wouldn't say 'Boo!' to a goose but who always stick like a cocklebur until they get their way. She introduces herself as confidential-secretary to this fellow Brock—"

"I know. Once called 'the Boy Wizard of Wall Street'; has made and lost several millions; twice married to and divorced from the same woman, an arty dancer named Nadia something who's wasting her sweetness on the desert air of Hollywood. Don't look so surprised, there's nothing much for a retired schoolma'am to do *but* read the newspapers. Anyway go on, I'm all ears."

"Ears? You mean *nose*. Well, anyway, this Jones woman insists that her boss is headed for a hearse. She wants us to drop everything and keep him from what she calls 'Foul Play,' though she can't suggest any suspect or any possible motive."

"The lady then is more worried than the potential victim?"

"Less fatalistic, anyway. Seems she's worked for Brock for years, ever since he started on a shoestring, and she isn't going to see him cut down."

"And I suppose, Oscar, that with your usual tact you told her that if and when Mr. Brock actually *got* himself murdered you'd investigate, but now run along?"

The Inspector had the grace to look sheepish. "Well, the bureau is too busy with homicides that have happened to be able to spare men for preventive detection. And those accidents—or near-accidents—could happen to anybody."

"Murder can happen to anybody," snapped Miss Withers. "And does, to some resident of our fair land, on an average of every 45 minutes. Nor am I convinced that those were accidents, though I'm going to find out. You see, one of my former pupils at P. S. 38 has grown up to be an executive at Guardian Assurance, and he tells me that they're worried about Brock's new policy. They've heard rumors, and they want to know if the man actually does have a shorter expectancy than he should have at his age. I've been called in as a sort of unofficial consultant to help them decide if the policy should be cancelled. So you see, even if the police are calmly going to sit on their thumbs and let Brock die, I'm not!"

"Curfew shall not ring tonight, eh?" The Inspector was amused. "Okay, Hildegarde. But I'll bet you a new hat you're wrong. Real murderers don't fool around with fake accidents that misfire—they come right to the point and it's usually the point of a knife or pistol. So sleuth all you want, just as long as you keep out of mischief—and out of my hair."

"What hair?" murmured Miss Withers, eyeing him critically.

But she was into mischief at the crack of dawn next morning. Before 7 o'clock the schoolteacher was prowling along Central Park South outside the apartment house in which Roscoe Brock kept a modest ten-room duplex. She even looked up hopefully at the fifth floor, but all the eyes of the building were lidded against the sun with closed venetian blinds. Then a woman came suddenly striding out of the apartment house entrance like a young queen, to step into a taxi. She bore herself as if a long scarlet evening gown, four diamond bracelets, and a sable stole were required uniform for this early hour. She also wore tears, one on each cheek.

It was not until hours later, when Miss Withers was deep in the bound volumes of old newspapers in the public library, that there was anything to connect this fine-feathered but unhappy lady with Roscoe Brock. Then, in the columns of an eight months' old Sunday supplement she saw that same proud face, under a headline: LOVE-TWICE STRANGLED BY TICKER TAPE. The story, seemingly written in a perfumed solution of benzedrine instead of ink, recounted how "exotic Nadia Nordica" was off to Palm Springs to divorce the Boy Wizard of Wall Street for the second time. The artist had depicted her lightly clad in wispy scarves and skipping nymph-like into the forest, pursued by an apathetic Pan who had paused to read the financial section.

"Dear, dear!" murmured Miss Withers. Some women obviously didn't know when they were well off. She hesitated, and then decided on a frontal attack. After a phone call and a ride downtown in the subway, she came at last to a tower above the famous street that starts in a graveyard and ends in the river. The names of the Roscoe Brock enterprises lettered on the door outnumbered the employees loitering within. But Mrs. Millicent Jones was waiting for her. "You're Miss Withers? I must say I thought somehow that you'd be—different."

"I am. Sometimes, Mrs. Jones, it's an advantage in my line of work *not* to look like a policewoman," the schoolteacher declared brazenly.

"Just call me Jonesy, everybody does." The secretary dressed and bore herself in a manner that insisted she was younger and prettier than was actually the case, but she oozed competence. "R. B. isn't down today—naturally he's still a little shaken from his experience in the subway. Men are such babies, aren't they?"

Miss Withers murmured that her experience with men and babies too had been limited. But she was being led along by Jonesy. "Come this way. We'll use R. B.'s office, it's private and cozy." Jonesy unlocked a door with her own key.

About as cozy as Grant's Tomb, the schoolteacher thought—all dark wood and heavy leather, with too many gadgets. She declined a cigarette, and waited while Jonesy plunked herself down behind a big mahogany desk and lighted her own, blowing smoke through wide, eager nostrils. "All right, let's get going. You see, I handle all R. B.'s personal problems."

"The immediate problem, I believe, is how to keep him alive?"

"Yes. What we want is a murder investigation, only before-the-fact." Jonesy went on to answer a number of pertinent questions about the accidents. The shot on the bridle path had come when R. B. was spending a weekend with the Stevenses. Bob Stevens had been his business partner years ago. The breakup had been as amicable as those things ever can be, and the two men had remained friends, though hardly intimates. At first the shot had been blamed on some careless hunter.

"But May is hardly the season for Nimrods," Miss Withers observed.

"Exactly. And it couldn't have been some small boy with a .22, because the hole in R. B.'s hat—it was a beautiful Borsalino—was big enough to have been made by a 30-30." Jones went on to discuss the birthday cognac, which had been delivered by messenger, she supposed, among other gifts. Even though the card had been lost, everyone had taken it for granted that the bottle was a gift from some old friend, because it was Brock's favorite brand. It had immediately been opened for an office party, along with a cake with LIFE BEGINS AT 40 in pink candies from "the girls" and a box of cigars from the men. Jonesy herself had given him a pair of Glen Argyles knitted by her own hands. Anyway, a toast had been proposed in Lily-cups but someone had discovered that there was something wrong with the cognac. Perhaps it had turned to grape-dust and vinegar, as old brandy will. It had been recorked and dropped into the wastebasket. And of course by the time they heard about the scrubwoman and learned the seriousness of the matter, the original wrappings had long since vanished in the trash. "But wasn't it lucky," Jonesy cried, "that R. B. only took one tiny sip of the awful stuff?"

"Lucky for everyone except the scrubwoman," Miss Withers pointed out dryly.

"Yes, poor Verzine. That was her name, Verzine Colman. The building super said that when she came to get her pay she looked grayish-green, like a zombie. R. B. had me send her a check for a hundred, though we weren't obligated. She had no business scavenging in the waste-baskets, though of course they all do."

The conference was interrupted endlessly by the telephone. Jonesy made and broke appointments for her employer, squabbled with his shirt-makers and tailor, and reminded the tobacconist that again he had sent the wrong cigars. "R. B. is just a little boy at heart," Jonesy explained. "He knows he shouldn't smoke those big heavy Coronas, but you have to watch him every minute!"

"I can imagine," said the school-teacher. She finally managed to get back on the subject of the incident in the subway, which proved to be the most baffling of all. The attack could hardly have been premeditated. Nobody could have known that Brock would take off early that afternoon and go shopping near Times Square, seeking cactus and tropical plants for his terrarium . . .

"His *what?*" demanded Miss Withers blankly.

"Terrarium. Above the bar in his living room. It's like an aquarium only instead of water you put in sand cactus and maybe a lizard or a toad. The idea is to make your guests thirsty."

"My, how the other half lives!" The schoolteacher shook her head. Anyway, Jonesy went on to explain that a sudden thundershower had caught R. B. unawares, without a taxi in sight. Having had a lifetime fear of thunder and lightning he ducked into the 47th Street subway—and had been innocently reading his newspaper in the midst of the rush hour crowd when he found himself shoved off the platform.

"But surely there were plenty of witnesses this time?"

"Too many. In a jam like that nobody notices anything, not even the trainmen and guards. It all happened so quick, and R. B. was engrossed with his paper. The one who pushed him must have just melted away in the crowd. So taking the three incidents together, they prove—"

"Among other things, that the would-be murderer is more persistent than dexterous. By the way, just what sort of business do you people carry on here?"

"A little of everything," Jonesy admitted. "Apart from playing the market, we buy up bankruptcies, promote inventions, and deal in subcontracts.

But that's all over now. There's only a skeleton staff, to wind things up. We're retiring. R. B. always said he'd retire when he got to be forty and just enjoy life."

"That usually means fast women and slow horses, does it not?"

"You don't know R. B. No chorus girls for him. He had enough of that sort of thing when he was married to *that woman*. Why, he even backed concerts and recitals and two musical shows, trying to buy her way in, but each time he got his fingers burned. Not that she didn't have some talent, but—" Jonesy smiled smugly. "Anyway, R.B.'s ready to settle down. He has a place up at Loon Lake in Maine, where there's trout and salmon fishing."

"He'd like to settle down, if someone doesn't settle him first. And yet there is no one with a motive to want him dead. What about his former partner?"

"Oh, Mr. Stevens was sore as a boil at one time. You see, R. B. bought him out when it looked as if the firm was going under, and then next year we hit the jackpot. But that's' all forgotten. Besides, Mr. Stevens was here at the birthday party, and took a drink of the cognac. He wouldn't have done that if—"

"I see. Well, there's always *cui bono*. Who benefits by Brock's will?"

Jonesy shook her head. "There isn't one. And the only relative I know anything about is a distant cousin who's a medical missionary out in Korea."

"Beyond suspicion, surely. As well as out of rifle, poison, and subway range." Miss Withers suddenly stood up. "You've been most helpful. And now if you'll phone Mr. Brock and tell him that I'm on my way up to see him . . .?"

The woman looked childishly disappointed. "But I thought we'd have lunch and I'd outline what ought to be done for R. B.'s protection, and then I'd take you up—"

"Thank you, but I'm afraid I must play a lone hand, and have a free one." Overruling all protests Miss Withers departed, feeling more than a little confused.

Back uptown again, she was kept waiting for some time outside the door of apartment 5A. Finally, after she had identified herself by shouting through the closed door, it was opened by a man in dressing gown and wrinkled silk pajamas who could only be Roscoe Brock in person. "Sorry to keep you waiting," he said. "But I was resting. Didn't get much sleep last night, as you can well imagine." Miss Withers, thinking of Nadia and the wispy scarves, let her imagination run riot.

Her host was explaining that he had let his servants go, as a precaution. "The worst thing about the awful fix I'm in is that I can't trust anybody!" Miss Withers followed him into the living room. A slight, tense man, this Boy Wizard of yesterday. He had a round, youthful face marked by a pert nose, and a muscular but knobby body. For all his fitness he was afraid— she sensed that beneath the surface flippancy. "So you're the hotshot murder expert the insurance company has sent to end all my troubles?"

"I also work with the police at times," she advised him, and sat herself primly down on a hard chair. The room was striking and colorful, but hardly relaxing. In spite of herself the schoolteacher kept staring at the collection of primitives, and the carved wooden gods from Africa and Polynesia which decorated the place. Polymorphous, nightmarish deities, full of ancient guile.

"Don't mind the parlor pantheon," Brock told her. "When I took this place last winter, after the separation, I let Jonesy plan it with the interior decorators and I guess they went overboard on jungle sculpture. But they say you can get used to anything. Now and then I have a feeling that some of them are waiting for me to offer up a goat without horns." He indicated a particularly ugly little mahogany godlet who squatted on the piano. "That's Dumballa, from Haiti. Doesn't he look as if he'd relish a bloody sacrifice?"

Miss Withers sniffed, and started to say something about graven images, but the doorbell interrupted. Brock came back bearing a little armful of letters, papers, and packages. "Only the morning mail, late as usual. One moment . . ."

"Expecting something important? Perhaps a threat, or a demand for money?"

Brock flicked a glance at her, and nodded. "Perhaps. Because there must be some pattern behind this persecution. I keep hoping they'll come out into the open." He was tossing letter after letter aside half-read. Miss Withers decided that he was not as youthful as he had seemed at first. Perhaps he was one of the men who, like Lindbergh or the Duke of Windsor or Mickey Rooney, go straight from boyishness into old age without ever passing through maturity at all. A green apple withering, a wrinkled youth.

"Hello, what's this?" Brock said suddenly. In his hand he held a small cardboard carton punched with holes, the top nearly covered with cancelled stamps. "This must be the lizard I ordered for my terrarium! Sent down to a novelty house in Texas for it—what most people call a horned-toad. I thought it would give some of my hard-drinking guests a jolt to look up and see one of these little beasts blinking at them through the glass." He rose and started toward the other end of the room, ripping off wrappings and lifting the cover. Then he gave a cry, and flung the box from him with a round Elizabethan oath. He leaped lightly into a chair. "Look out, for God's sake!" he screamed, pointing.

"I *am* looking out!" Miss Withers found herself perched on the grand piano with her feet tucked underneath her skirt. The first thought that popped into her head was that somebody had sent Brock a Gila monster by mistake. But those creatures were only mildly poisonous, and nothing to make all this fuss about.

Then she saw it. A gaudy worm, no more than ten or twelve inches long, flowed sluggishly across the carpet toward her. It looked like something created in a nightmare and decorated by a child playing with kindergarten colors—blunt at head and tail, ringed with black and red and yellow, a creature garish and incredible and altogether evil. The ophidian eyes were alert, unblinking.

"*Coral snake!*" Brock croaked hoarsely. "Deadlier than ten cobras!"

"Habitat Central America, Mexico, and the Gulf States," Miss Withers chimed in automatically. She reached out for the wooden deity beside her, prayed a silent prayer to Dumballa, and then dropped the heavy statuette squarely on the wriggling reptile.

It was all over. The schoolteacher slid limply off the piano, walked over to the nearest divan, and passed out cold. When she regained consciousness she found Roscoe Brock inexpertly trying to pour whisky down her throat. "Take that awful stuff away," she cried, strangling. "It's worse than the snake."

He was staring at her with a new and grudging respect. "I guess I underestimated you. But what would anybody think, with you wearing that low-comedy getup?"

"Never mind the pretty speeches. My hats are my own business." Miss Withers stood up, wavering a little. The snake was real—it still lay there in a smashed puddle of bloody pulp. A near thing. Perhaps Brock had underestimated her, but she had certainly overestimated herself. She looked questioningly at him. "Where—?"

"The bathroom? Right down the hall, on the left," he said quickly.

"I'm not going to be sick, I'm going to telephone!" Miss Withers snapped.

And soon the apartment resounded to the heavy tread of men in uniform. There was much dusting of fingerprint powder, and glaring of flashbulbs. The hat with the bullet-holes was produced and photographed. The smashed snake was photographed. Even Dumballa, leering obscenely, had his picture taken.

But Inspector Oscar Piper liked to get his hands on something tangible, something that might eventually be Exhibit A in a courtroom. His original skepticism forgotten, he pounced happily on the cardboard box, the wrappings, and the typed address label. Without taking the dead panatela from his mouth, he assigned one man to start tracing the box and paper, another to the post-office angle, and a third to work on all typewriters accessible to anyone connected with the case. "The snake I'll work on myself," Piper decided. "I suppose it came from some zoo."

At one end of the room Roscoe Brock had at last found willing ears to listen to his tale of woe, and fingers to take it down in official notebooks. He obligingly stuck the Borsalino on top of his head, while a ballistics expert decided that if the bullet had been an inch lower it would have been *finis* right there. Brock drew a map of the bridle path near the Stevens home, and located the attack in the subway. It had been near the north end of the platform, halfway between the gum machine and the newsvendor's stand, directly opposite a theatrical poster advertising the latest musical hit.

"Brock's very cooperative, for a millionaire," the Inspector observed softly.

"And why not?" Miss Withers sniffed. "Right now he's a *murderee* first and a millionaire second. But Oscar—four attacks, and still no sign of a motive!"

"Thousands of people with motives," admitted Roscoe Brock later. "I've been thinking it over. Nobody can fight his way to the top in business without stepping on toes here and there. My conscience is as clear as the next man's, but I must have wrecked competitors, fired employees who never got another job, and been lucky where better men have failed. There must be countless people who hate my guts. One of them must have brooded over his imagined wrongs until he cracked mentally."

"Homicidal maniacs?" The Inspector couldn't swallow that.

"Well, who but a maniac would try to kill me by mailing me a poisonous snake?"

He had a point there. "If you look at it in the proper perspective," the schoolteacher put in "no *sane* person commits murder. Too much risk involved."

"Just what I said!" Brock cried. Out of all those thousands—"

Piper said he'd settle for just one suspect, closer to home. "How about this ex-wife of yours?"

For the first time in days Roscoe Brock laughed aloud. "Nadia? No!"

"Of course, in a way you did block her ambitions," Miss Withers suggested softly, watching his face.

"What do you mean? I poured hundreds of thousands into Nadia's career. I gave her recitals at Carnegie, I hired the best coaches and teachers for her, and even a symphony pianist to play her accompaniments. I backed shows, I got other dancers fired so she could have the main spot. Everything that money could do—"

"Exactly," said Miss Withers. "You smothered her. And then when she wanted you to choose between her and your business, you let her go. Hell hath no fury . . ."

He shook his head. "Not Nadia. Besides, we're still friends, in a casual way."

The schoolteacher wondered how casual one could get by 7 a.m. But Piper waved his hand impatiently. "Okay, Mr. Brock. What about your former partner?"

"Bob Stevens? Oh, he was bitter for a while, because he had an idea I'd made things look worse than they were during that bad year, so I could buy him out cheap. Once in a while I still catch a funny glint in his eye when I complain about high income taxes. He's the moody, introspective type, though he's been grateful enough for the bite of business I toss him now and then. But he's out as a suspect."

"I know," said Miss Withers wearily. "He took a sip of the poisoned cognac."

Piper frowned. "Well, your employees then? How about the Jones woman?"

"But Jonesy's my right hand! She's a regular Rock of Gibraltar. For fifteen years her job has meant everything to her. Oh, she did have a husband, but he drifted away and is supposed to have drunk himself to death. She lives for her work—she's been more like a partner than an employee."

"Now you're retiring, and what has *she* got?" demanded Miss Withers. "Perhaps she was more like a partner than a secretary, but she only got a secretary's pay."

Brock looked blank. "I hadn't thought of that. But still—I tell you that Jonesy is incapable of anything like this. She was the one who went to the police. Besides, did you notice the stamps on that package the snake was in?"

"The man is a bit of a detective himself," said Miss Withers a little later, when she was alone with the Inspector.

"Maybe so. But he only seemed inclined to knock down the suspects as we set 'em up. And what was that about the stamps?"

"He meant that Mrs. Jones was not the type to put on a dollar's worth of postage when thirty cents would do. A point well taken."

Piper shrugged. "Well, what can I do with a guy like that? Except maybe hold him in protective custody."

"You couldn't keep him locked up forever, and when he came out it would start all over again. Oscar, one thing does occur to me. Homicidal maniac or not, the person we're seeking is close enough to Brock to know his favorite bridle path, his pet brand of cognac, his fear of electrical storms, and even his terrarium."

"Inside job, eh? Maybe we better go down and have another talk with that Jones woman. She might be just clever enough to ask protection for her intended victim."

But for once Miss Withers had no desire to get into the act. "You go ahead, Oscar. I think I'll try to locate Brock's former wife, and ask her why, after she spent the night in his apartment, she left at 7 A.M. in tears."

Leaving the Inspector flatfooted, the schoolteacher started off by her lone, sniffing at a cold scent. Her luck was in. At a taxi stand on Central Park South she found the driver who had picked up a lady in evening dress early that morning and taken her to the Hotel Griffon, one of the small theatrical hostelries on West 47th St. But the desk clerk was unwilling to commit himself to anything, even that it was a hot day. Miss Nordica might or might not be registered. Maybe she'd checked out.

"Well! I'm from her husband's office, and I was only trying to do her a favor. The police will be here any minute to ask her a lot of embarrassing questions."

"One moment," said the clerk, starting to back away into an inner office.

"And you may tell her," called Miss Withers, "that I'll stay here in the lobby till she does decide to see me. She'll have to come down some time."

It was a short wait. "You can go up to 11B after all," the man reported back. Something in his voice implied that whatever happened it served her right.

At her knock a woman's pleasant voice said, "Come in!" and Miss Withers came in to receive a chilly squirt of soda-water full in the face. For a long moment the two women stood staring at each other, equally paralyzed. Nadia broke first, dropping the siphon and clutching her face dramatically. "Oh, no!" The flood of apologies was almost as breathtaking as the fizz-water had been. "But I thought—they said you were from Roscoe's office, and when you were so insistent about seeing me I was positive that you must be that Jones woman!"

Miss Withers stood dripping, in injured dignity. The dancer was less queenly today, wearing a tight halter and slacks. But still beautiful, the schoolteacher conceded, with the detachment of one who never in her palmiest days had any pretentions. She permitted herself to be mopped at with a towel. "Is this the way you usually greet your husband's secretary when she comes calling?"

"I'd like to make it buck-shot! That office-wife! Office-mother, rather. The way she's got her hooks into that man! But I am sorry you got wet."

"One of the hazards of the trade," Miss Withers told her. "I see that I'm interrupting your unpacking." There was an open suitcase on the day-bed.

"Packing, you mean." The dancer stood against the wall, taut as a bow-string. "I never should have come back anyway. But what's this about the police?"

Miss Withers explained somewhat sketchily why she was involved in the case. "You see, something almost happened to Mr. Brock again. This time it was a snake."

"But how horrible!" Nadia sank into a chair. "Then I was wrong! When Roscoe wrote me about the other accidents, I thought he was lying. I thought he was making it all up, to get me to come rushing back to him."

"And yet you did come rushing back?"

"But of course! If he cared that much—"

"I see. Love is a wonderful thing, and sometimes I'm sorry that I have had so little first-hand experience. At any rate, he cared enough to have you spend the night in his apartment, didn't he? May I ask why you were leaving at seven this morning, dressed to the teeth?"

The red lips opened, thinned, and shut like a trap.

"I'm sorry, but I'm investigating a murder even if it hasn't happened yet. You are quite aware, of course, that spending the night under the same roof with your husband during the interlocutory period of one year invalidates your California decree? It makes you his wife again—and his widow and heir, if anything happens to him." The schoolteacher, having loosed her petard, stood up to go.

But Nadia blocked the door. "What if I were to tell you that I got in late last night, and when I couldn't reach Roscoe by phone I went to a party at the home of some friends—a very late party? I thought he might be there, you see. What if I said that when the party broke up—at dawn— I felt sentimental and worried, and rushed over to Roscoe's apartment, and he wouldn't even let me in?"

"Offhand, my dear young woman, I'd say you were telling a big fat lie."

"But you couldn't be sure, could you?"

Miss Withers, somewhat nettled, said that there were ways of checking such things. "What friends gave the party? The police will be asking. Only by that time I suppose you'll have arranged with somebody to back up your story." She moved to the door.

Nadia smiled an odd smile. "Don't climb on your broomstick and take off quite yet, please." She turned, raising her voice. "Bob! Come here!"

The bathroom door opened and a man came blithely in. He was the man of distinction, from the tanned face beneath gray temples to the highball in his hand. "This is Miss—I'm sorry I can't seem to remember your name, I know it was part of a horse. Withers, that's it. Miss Withers, Robert Stevens."

"Delighted," said Roscoe Brock's ex-partner. He even looked delighted.

"Bob and I were having a talk, about Roscoe and everything," the dancer explained. "He wanted to leave, but I thought if it really was Jonesy bursting in on me I'd better have a witness." She turned. "Bob, was I at your place last night—all night?"

Without hesitation he said "But of course. Lovely party. Our latch-string is always out, pot-luck, and all that sort of thing." He laughed easily, and Nadia chimed in.

"Well!" said Miss Withers. "It isn't funny." She paused in the doorway. "Roscoe Brock is in grave danger. Right now anything may be happening to him."

"Fine!" cried Nadia. "I hope it's something with boiling oil in it!"

The schoolteacher made a quick exit, clutching her hat and the shreds of her dignity. Somehow she felt just a little confused. Deep in the bottom of her mind a little red light was flashing off and on, warning her that there was something she had failed to notice, something like a stone left unturned. But there was so much to do, there were so many places she had to go! If she could only be like the man in that story, and leap on a horse and gallop off in all directions . . .

She did her level best to do just that. It was not until almost six that evening that she came rushing into the Inspector's office, to find her old friend and sparring-partner not in one of his better moods. "Well, Oscar, why the long face? Don't tell me the machinery has bogged down? Didn't the fingerprints match, and couldn't the paper be traced?"

"How right you are," he told her heavily.

"The address label was probably typed on some demonstration machine on a shop counter when the clerk was busy elsewhere? And the wrapper was second-hand and had been taken, stamps and all, from the remains of some old package in a trash can?"

"How'd you know that?" Piper demanded, a little startled.

"A good guess. I did notice that the postmark was Grand Central, a week old. Which would imply that the snake never went through the mails at all."

"Probably," sighed the Inspector. "The killer could have just left it at the desk in Brock's apartment house. Worse than that, I found that there isn't a coral snake within a thousand miles of here, not even in a zoo. Animal dealers don't supply them." Just then a uniformed man came in with a paper sack, a container of coffee, and change for a dollar. "You should have warned me if you expected to be squired to a spaghetti joint tonight," Piper told Miss Withers apologetically. "I'm eating in, because I have work to do—"

"Heavens, I forgot lunch! Even-steven on the pastrami sandwiches."

A little later, over her share of the coffee, Miss Withers said, "Did you call on Jonesy?"

"Yes—a dry run. She says she hates snakes and she never fired a gun in her life and she finally tried to slap my face and went into hysterics because she said I was insinuating that she was responsible for the attacks on Brock, her one ewe lamb. Loyalty is a wonderful thing, if not carried too far."

Miss Withers nodded. "Oscar, almost from the beginning one thing has been clear about this case. The person behind these attacks on Roscoe Brock is not only someone close to him, someone who knows his every move, but who—"

"But who hates his guts. Elementary, Miss Watson."

"That's the catch, Oscar. Whoever it is has a sort of psychological block that makes him shoot an inch too high, use an easily detected poison in the cognac, push his victim in front of a train that was already slowing down for a stop. Doesn't it seem almost as if the killer has a sort of sneaking fondness for his victim, and is pulling punches in spite of himself—or herself ?"

"With Sherlock Holmes it was the needle," said the Inspector. "With you it's worse. You've been at those big books again."

"No, Oscar. I've had a most active afternoon. I was squirted with soda-water by Brock's ex-wife, who sincerely hopes he'll be boiled in oil. I've been laughed at by Bob Stevens, who used to be Brock's partner but got shuffled off, and who has a big expensive house on Long Island but wears a threadbare Brooks Brothers suit."

Piper listened, nodding. "Nadia needs some looking into. She's suspect Number One, according to Jonesy. The secretary pointed out that if Nadia flew here yesterday she could have done it before, and pulled those stunts . . ."

"The wife and secretary waste no love on one another, do they? But of the two I prefer Nadia."

"Well, Jonesy hates to see her boss get back in Nadia's clutches. She really hit the ceiling when I let it slip accidentally on purpose about where the dancer spent the night. But as I told her, the ex–Mrs. Brock has no motive."

"None that I could figure out—until last night. If anything happened to him now she might make a case for her being the legal widow. Only I think she really loves him."

"She loves him—but she wants him boiled in oil?"

"Exactly. Her pride is hurt. She came rushing back for a reconciliation and something went wrong. A woman scorned—" Miss Withers frowned.

"By the way, Oscar, have you detectives trailing the principals in this affair?"

"As a matter of fact, I have. Except for Nadia—I didn't know where she was. But I'll attend to that right now." And he did, with a phone call. "Go on, Hildegarde. What other mischief did you get into today?"

"I made a trip up to 125th Street to pay a call on Verzine, the scrubwoman. It seems that the poison in the cognac she drank burned out her stomach lining, and the poor thing is living on crackers and milk, unable to work. My next stop was the American Museum of Natural History, where I spent some time looking at the habitat groups. Then I put in an hour on the 47th Street subway platform, just watching the trains go by, and I found time to stroll in Central Park and watch the equestrians. I was even whistled at by two sailors who were riding horseback."

"I thought," said the Inspector through a mouthful of sandwich, "that you had to have 20/20 vision to get in the Navy?"

Miss Withers gave him a look. "Well, they were riding side-saddle, and I'll concede that they might just possibly have been celebrating."

"Never mind, Hildegarde," he told her kindly. "I'll whistle at you any old time if you'll only get this Brock case settled."

"Oh, but it is," said the schoolteacher slowly. "At least there won't be any more attempts on Brock's life."

"What? How can you be so sure of that?"

"I just am. Besides, I talked to him on the phone and he's going to get out of town, first thing in the morning. He has a fishing lodge up in Maine . . ."

Piper suddenly stood up. "Have you lost your wits? A killer can strike up there just as well as—"

"Relax, Oscar."

"What do you mean 'relax'? Am I supposed to mark the case Closed just on your say-so, just because you've had a hunch or something—" At that moment the phone rang. "Inspector Piper speaking . . . okay then. Report back to your precinct." He turned, looking happier. "Anyway, we can scratch out one suspect. Brock's ex-wife checked out of the Hotel Griffon half an hour ago, headed for the airport."

"But—but that means she's going back to Hollywood! I don't like it—"

"Well, I like it fine. The more people in the Brock case who leave my jurisdiction the better!"

"But Oscar, I'm worried."

"What's the matter, did you read the tea leaves wrong or something?"

"I still wish you'd put the Jones woman in custody, just for tonight."

"But why? She can't pull any fast ones, with Officer Purdy on her tail."

"Couldn't you have him bring her in for questioning or something, and then hold her here, for her own protection?"

The Inspector gave her a sharp look. "I suppose I could, next time he gets a chance to phone in. But why should I?"

"Because—well, I just realized how ugly this thing can be. Perhaps—"

"Perhaps you've been barking up the wrong tree again, huh?"

"Thank you very much for the sandwich!" Miss Withers snapped, and departed slamming the office door. She hurried back uptown, and rang the bell of Roscoe Brock's apartment. This time it opened immediately.

"Oh, it's you," he said, his round boyish face falling a little. That meant he expected someone else. Jonesy—no, not she. That meant he didn't know Nadia had left town. "Come in," Brock invited, pointing at the pile of fishing rods and tackle in the hall. "You see I'm taking your advice. It'll be wonderful up in Maine this time of year. Those land-locked salmon—"

"I," said Miss Withers, "am a fisher of men."

"But it still seems somehow like running away."

"My grandmother always said that he who fights and runs away will live to fight another day. You're planning to leave early?"

"The sooner the better. I've a lot of packing to do, and Jonesy is on her way up here with some important papers from the office. She's also going to pick up my car at the garage and bring it over—I thought maybe I'd better stay locked in here until I take off, just in case . . ."

"Very prudent," murmured the schoolteacher. A complete set of little red lights were now flashing their warnings in the back of her mind, but she didn't quite know what to do about them. Then she saw that Brock had his checkbook out.

"By the way, I suppose I owe you something for your help in all this?"

"Nothing at all," said the schoolteacher. "Under the circumstances. But if you do feel any obligation I wish you'd send the check to that unfortunate scrubwoman. She's really in quite desperate straits, you know."

"The woman asked for it, didn't she? Taking things from wastebaskets . . ."

The doorbell rang, and Brock excused himself. He came back in a minute or so, tucking something into his pocket and smiling, Miss Withers thought, like the cat that ate the canary. "Telegram," he explained. "Just business. Now what were we talking about?"

"Verzine, the scrubwoman who drank the poisoned cognac."

"Oh, of course! I'll have Jonesy send her something tomorrow."

"Your secretary isn't going up to Loon Lake with you, then?"

He snorted. "Lord, no—not now. I mean, I see enough of her at the office. I did take her on a trip once last spring—it was to Bermuda—and she was in a perpetual tizzy because she thought I was being overcharged. For everything."

"I—I see." Still somewhat uneasy, Miss Withers took her departure. Back at her own apartment she aired her gangling apricot poodle and then in desperation set about washing her hair, always a last resort at moments like this. Before it was half-dried she was on the telephone. Her last call was to the Inspector, who turned out to be still at his office. "Oscar, I just called to see if you did what I asked about putting Mrs. Jones in protective custody?"

"The answer is no."

"Oh, dear. Because I called the Hotel Griffon, and just before Nadia checked out she had a call—from a woman. It's obvious that Jonesy has been doing her best to prevent the reconciliation in the Brock family."

"Relax, Hildegarde," said the Inspector. "You're behind the times. But the reason we didn't pick up Mrs. Jones—well, it was one of those things. Purdy lost her. He's a good cop, but she went into the ladies' room at the Astor and must have come out another door. It could have been on purpose or just an accident."

"Oh, dear!"

"That's not all. We checked the airport, and Nadia Nordica didn't take a plane for Los Angeles. She left at seven this evening via Eastern Airlines for Bangor."

"Bangor, Maine? Of course! That's what the telegram was about. Then perhaps everything is going to be all right, after all!"

The Inspector started to say something about Hildegarde and her happy endings, but Miss Withers cut in with—"I'd be considerably happier if I knew where Mrs. Jones was right now. I suppose you tried her apartment?"

"Don't try to teach your grandmother to suck eggs. Of course. No dice."

"Did you try Mr. Brock's apartment?"

"We called there too. She'd been there, to deliver some important office papers that he wanted to take with him, but she'd left."

"How about the office down on Wall Street?"

Piper snorted. "Are you nuts? Why would she be there, at this hour?"

"Oscar, you don't understand. It's the only real home she has. Please—"

"Now don't give me that. I'm a patient man, but—you're not trying to hint that Jonesy was the one who took a pot-shot at Brock, sent him the queer cognac, pushed him off the subway platform, and mailed him the snake? Because—"

"Oh, no! Contrariwise. This is a queer case, Oscar. Skim milk masquerades as cream and things are seldom what they seem. But murder is a two-edged sword, not to be fooled with. And if you act out the shadow often enough, it well may become the substance. I have a premonition . . ."

"You and your crystal ball! Hildegarde, go to bed and sleep it off." The Inspector hung up forcefully. Enough was enough. It was time to call it a day. But still, when he came out onto the street, he told the taxi-driver to take him downtown, instead of northward to his home.

It was the sort of a case where it was worthwhile to eliminate all the blind alleys. . . . Then he found that there were lights still on in the offices of Roscoe Brock Enterprises, though the rest of the building was in darkness. He hammered on the door. "Open up—it's the Law!"

But nobody opened. By and by he went back downstairs and got the night watchman with his keys, and later still he put through a call to Miss Hildegarde Withers, who had taken his advice and was deep in slumber.

"You and your premonitions!" he said savagely. "We found Mrs. Millicent Jones sprawled over her boss's desk, more dead than alive. The ambulance men say it's some metallic poison, and she has about one chance in five."

"Oh!" said Miss Withers ineffectually. "Oh, dear! Then there must have been something planted there—perhaps the poison was in the water bottle on his desk, where she'd help herself . . ."

"I knew if we fooled around with this mess long enough there'd be a murder," said the Inspector grimly. "Save it. I'm picking you up in ten minutes, and then we're going to get to the bottom of this."

The schoolteacher was ready and waiting on the steps when the big black Headquarters car came up the street. The Inspector opened the door, with a grim invitation. "Get in, and talk fast," he said. "This isn't funny."

"I thought the answer was obvious enough, even for you," she said.

"You mean to say that Brock got wise to the fact that his love-sick secretary had been trying to kill him, and got back at her by planting poison in the office hoping she'd take it accidentally? Horsefeathers!"

"Horsefeathers indeed," said Miss Withers. "Oscar, if only—" But the howling of the siren drowned out her voice. They cut down to Central Park South, and pulled up outside the apartment house with a jerk that jarred her back teeth. The Inspector was out of the car before it stopped rolling, but the bird was flown. The startled man at the desk said that Mr. Brock had left for his place in Maine fifteen minutes ago. In his yellow Lagonda.

"Oh, sure!" snarled Piper, biting through his cigar. "Any place but! He'll ditch the car, too—"

"No, Oscar." Miss Withers was tugging at his sleeve. "Brock is really going to Loon Lake—because Nadia is waiting for him there."

"Judas Priest in a whirlwind! Will you—"

"I thought that by this time you must have realized that Brock faked all those attacks on his life. Didn't you suspect that at all?"

"Of course I did!" he roared. "But he couldn't push himself off the subway platform!"

"I can explain even that—"

"Explain it in the car," he told her roughly, and pushed her back inside. Then he paused to detail one of his men to send out a general alarm for Roscoe Brock. "We'll go after him. If he's headed for Maine he'll take the Parkways as far as New Haven, and maybe—" They roared away again.

Between screams of the official siren Miss Withers said, "He could jump off the subway platform in front of a train—if he knew that ten-car expresses always stop at a certain point. Brock was too familiar with that subway platform for a man who claimed to have only been there once. He must have spent hours . . ."

They careered around a corner, missing a streetcar by a whisker, and snapped through an intersection like a scene in an old Mack Sennett comedy. "Of course," the schoolteacher went on, "Brock wasn't wearing his hat when he shot the hole through it. People who ride horseback jam their hats low down or else they'll jostle off. The cognac and the snake were easier still—it wasn't even a real coral snake, though he tried to make me think so. Up at the Museum they have mounted snakes—coral snakes and also the harmless cane-brake adders that look just like them only the colors are reversed . . ."

The Headquarters car swerved onto Riverside Drive, and then on and through a toll-gate without hesitating. "Keep talking," demanded the Inspector. "Make it good. Why would a man go through all that monkey-business . . ."

"It's obvious, Oscar. Because he wanted desperately to win back his ex-wife. He'd tried everything else, and failed. But Nadia is the dramatic type, and he thought she might respond to drama. If she heard about his narrow escapes she'd come back to him—as, in fact, she did. Only she saw through him, and that cut his pride to the quick. By that time Roscoe Brock was carried away with his play-acting. She simply had to acknowledge that he'd been in great peril. The night they spent together was spent quarreling, and he decided to fake one more attack, this time with a witness in the person of an insurance investigator—meaning me. He was determined, like so many liars, to make his lie stick. Of course he must have had that harmless snake packed and ready for days. . . ."

The detective who sat beside the driver was in radio-telephone communication with the suburban centers through which they were racing. White Plains, he said, had just reported that a yellow car, foreign-make, had gone past the Sawmill River turnoff headed northeast.

"That's him!" cried the Inspector, and for once Miss Withers refrained from correcting his grammar.

"They want to know should they call ahead to set up a road-block?" asked the detective.

"No," decided Piper. "We'll catch up. I want to handle this thing personally." He turned toward the schoolteacher, a little easier. "All right, I'll buy it so far," he conceded. "But why should Brock want to poison his secretary?"

"I—I don't know," she admitted honestly. "Especially now. At one time I thought—well, he obviously must have been comforting himself with Mrs. Jones after his wife left him. That was almost inevitable, for a man like Brock. But suppose Jonesy took it seriously, and kept on taking it that way even after he wanted the interlude closed? When she talked to me she twice mentioned what a little boy he was, and that's always a bad sign. She knitted socks for his birthday, and she fussed about the cigars he smoked. You yourself said that the woman stuck like a cockleburr when she wanted something. I was thinking that Brock might have come to the conclusion that Jonesy had to be removed from the picture if he hoped to get Nadia back, but . . ."

The Inspector's hand was tight on her arm. "There goes the son of a—"

"Oscar!" But sure enough, their lights stabbed at a low-slung yellow car far up ahead.

"Kick it!" ordered the Inspector.

They were doing 80 already, but the driver kicked it up to 90.

"Hit the howler!"

The siren screamed, but the gap between them and the yellow Lagonda remained the same. Then suddenly the voice of the police dispatcher back in White Plains came booming through the air. "Calling New York HQ Car Three. Inspector Piper, your office reports Millicent Jones just died Bellevue Hospital from poisoning thought to be *mercuric fiumerin*. There's more coming in . . ."

"Never mind the rest," ordered Piper "It's murder now! Keep the siren on."

The yellow Lagonda was actually drawing a little away from them, in spite of the fact that this section of the Parkway was full of wide curves. Miss Withers clutched the Inspector with a deathlike grip, praying as she had never prayed before. But her eyes could not tear themselves from that tiny red tail-light ahead.

Suddenly it went up into the air, and vanished. Then their headlights caught a blinding vision of the great yellow car turning end over end, rocketing across the highway to smash against the guard-rail—like a garden snail flung against a stone. Somehow their driver managed to fishtail the big Headquarters limousine to a standstill, brakes screaming.

But it was all over. There was nothing for them to do except set up red flares to warn off other traffic, and to call in for the meat wagon and the wrecker. Miss Hildegarde Withers had no part in all this. She sat alone in the back seat of the limousine.

A startled scream escaped her lips as the radio suddenly boomed out again. "This is White Plains. Still standing by, New York HQ Car Three? Here's the rest of message. Before she died Millicent Jones confessed taking poison out of remorse for having murdered her employer, Roscoe Brock. That is all."

"Oscar!" cried the schoolteacher.

The Inspector finally heard her, and came back. His voice was bitter.

"A blowout," he explained.

Breathlessly she told him about the radio message. "But it doesn't make sense! How could Jonesy murder Mr. Brock when she was already dead?"

"Neat," the Inspector said. "Very, very neat. The three remaining tires on that fancy imported heap are all inflated to over a hundred instead of the normal thirty-two pounds. He was a cinch to crack up on one of those curves at high speed. She fixed him good."

Miss Withers subsided into a silence that lasted until they were heading back toward the city. "I think I see it all now, Oscar. When you came down to get Mrs. Jones and put her in protective custody—because of my hunch that she was in danger—she thought you were arresting her for murder. So she took poison."

"Go on. It's your case."

"If Jonesy couldn't have him, nobody could. Of course! That has to be it. She got the idea from Brock's own fake accidents. That's the trouble with playing with murder—it's apt to come true. Naturally she thought that she was going up to Maine with her boss. And then when he got the telegram telling him that his ex-wife was flying up to meet him there for another honeymoon, he told Jonesy to go back to her typewriter."

"Sure," said the Inspector.

"And now Brock's money will go to that distant cousin who's a medical missionary out in Korea, and also you owe me a new hat!"

"Which will look just as funny as the old ones," the Inspector reminded her. "And hold your horses before you get carried away with the idea of a happy ending. If Brock's ex-wife really spent the night with him and invalidated her interlocutory decree, then she's the widow, and she gets—"

"She gets her just deserts, which is nothing. Don't forget, Oscar, I have her own word for it. He wouldn't let her in."

Hildegarde and the Spanish Cavalier

There were times, and this was one of them, when Inspector Oscar Piper wished he had taken up some line of work other than man-hunting. Such was his deep depression, as he sat that morning at his littered desk in the offices of the New York homicide division at Centre Street, that he barely winced when he heard a familiar voice greeting him from his doorway.

"Oscar," cried Miss Hildegarde Withers. "Do you know what day tomorrow is?"

"Thursday," he grunted. "All day."

"*And* the twelfth of March!" The wind and rain outside had left the maiden schoolteacher's hat looking like nothing other than a fallen *soufflé*. She plumped herself down in a chair and waited, with obvious expectancy.

The Inspector frowned in mock concentration. "Let me see. Can't be your birthday—you stopped having those years ago. Wait! Is it the anniversary of the day we *didn't* get married?"

"It is not—I jilted you in the autumn. Stop pretending to be so dense. I can see very well whose file it is that you have spread out on your desk, so you are already aware of who is being graduated from Sing Sing tomorrow."

"Juan del Puerto!" exploded Oscar Piper. "And just why are you so interested in the Spanish Cavalier? I admit he's good-looking, if you like the dark, oily type . . ."

She sniffed. "I happen to have a natural antipathy to Lotharios who prey on defenseless, middle-aged women. And so should you—the way he made monkeys out of the police! You were all so positive that he killed the lady doctor he had married, and somehow disposed of the body on the honeymoon cruise to Tampico. Imagine going to all the trouble of having him extradited, and then finding that you couldn't pin anything on him but a bigamy charge—and a weak one at that!"

"Oh, yes?" Piper's fist hit the desk so hard that the cigar butts in his ashtray sailed up into the air and looped the loop. "Well, when the gendarmes finally ran him down in Mexico City he was shacked up in a hotel with this other wife—Consuelo or something—and she was wearing part of Maggie Gustavson's trousseau and all her jewelry. We even proved that he had bought half a dozen cartons of safety-razor blades just before sailing day—"

"So if he didn't murder her, who did? The customary police attitude. If Maggie wasn't killed, and her body cut up with razor blades and thrown out of the porthole piece by piece, then why didn't she come forward and say so? Why did she never make any effort to communicate with her sisters in Newark, or to recover the money she had turned over to del Puerto just before the wedding bells chimed? The newspapers still hint that it was the Perfect Murder—and now, after only five years in prison, the man goes scot-free!" Miss Withers shook her head. "Something has got to be done, Oscar."

All this, to the Inspector, was like turning a knife in an open wound. "All right, Miss Smartypants," he snapped. "What can we do that we *haven't* done? I took pains to see that del Puerto didn't get parole or any time off for good behavior; he served every day of it. I tried to block his recovering Maggie's life savings, which he was wearing in a money-belt when arrested, only he's now got Matt Sherwood for his lawyer, and all they have to do—once he's out—is to apply for a court order, which is just a formality. Nobody can prove that it wasn't a free gift to him before the marriage, like he swears. Maybe she did—women of a certain age, particularly pent-up, inhibited women who have never had time for love, usually fall hard when they fall, and do foolish things that they regret later."

"I never did a foolish thing in my life," the schoolteacher retorted. "At least, not one I have regretted. Except perhaps not marrying you twenty-years ago."

He grinned. "Thanks, Hildegarde. Anyway, I've lost plenty nights' sleep trying to figure out some way to get that guy, but all I could think of was to tip off the immigration authorities to give him the bum's rush out of the country the minute they can—"

"Oscar!" she cried. "You must untip them, and at once! Remember the Uncle Remus story about Br'er Rabbit, who was caught by Br'er Fox and who screamed, 'Do anything you like, but *don't* throw me into the briarpatch!'—when that was exactly what he wanted most of all? Don't you see, we mustn't let del Puerto get away!"

"What's the use? Judas Priest in an electric fan, if we couldn't make a case against him then, how can we now with the trail as cold as last Christmas's goose?"

"You could—" Miss Withers started, then stopped. "It is a problem, isn't it? But if we could set a trap for the man somehow, surprise him into giving himself away, let him get stuck with his own story? He claimed that Maggie had a fight with him at the dock and walked off in a huff, leaving all her clothes and baggage behind. And hasn't he always insisted that she's alive somewhere, and hasn't he kept issuing statements to the press begging her to come forward? He's a consistent liar, Oscar. By now he thinks he has nothing to worry about. No doubt he has kept his spirits up through the years in prison by planning what he will do with the money when he gets his hands on it. Suppose—suppose that just as the court is about to order it handed over to him, Maggie herself appears out of nowhere to contest it!"

The Inspector closed his eyes and sighed. "She can't," he said, as if speaking to a child. "She can't—for the simple reason she's dead."

"But isn't that just what Juan del Puerto will blurt out when we spring the surprise on him? Isn't there a good chance he'll incriminate himself?"

"I don't see—"

"You will. It doesn't have to be the *real* Maggie, does it?"

Oscar Piper was way ahead of her. He held up his hand. "No, you don't!" he told her firmly. "Not even if he did know her only two weeks, and not even if all this did happen almost seven years ago. People don't change that much. Here, look at her picture. Maggie was a good-looking babe in her late thirties, a big-bosomed Scandinavian type. You couldn't possibly fool anybody."

There was a wicked glint in her eyes. "No, Oscar? With a blond wig here and some judicious padding there?" She gestured.

"*Never!*" pronounced the Inspector. "Never in a million years! Look, thousands of pictures of Maggie Gustavson have been printed in newspapers and magazines, and we've sent out world-wide telephotos. You'd only make a laughing-stock of yourself." He sighed. "Not that I wouldn't do anything—and I mean *anything*—to crack the case. The whole thing hurts like a splinter in the seat of my pants. But that's the way it is. At 9 o'clock tomorrow morning the big gates up at Ossining swing open, and out he comes. His shyster lawyer will probably drive up to meet him, and they'll rush back to town and start proceedings to get hold of the money."

Miss Withers nodded, rubbing her lower lip. "By the way, Oscar, just what was the exact amount?"

"Thirty thousand was what she drew from the bank the day before they were married, and thirty thousand was the amount found in his money-belt. He hadn't had time to touch it yet. A nice round figure for a lady to turn over in advance to her murderer. I imagine there'll be some court fees out of it, and the lawyer will want his share, but there'll be enough left so del Puerto can cut a wide swathe back in Mexico."

"I see. He laughs best who laughs last." Miss Withers stood up. "I must be running along. Please ask the immigration people to hold off for a few days, while I try to think of something. By the way, how long will it take for the court to turn over the money to him?"

"Sherwood has probably already applied for a hearing. It should come up in a day or two. Only take a few minutes—it's just a formality."

The maiden schoolteacher murmured something under her breath which the Inspector did not catch, and then with a vague wave of her hand she turned and hurried out of the office. It was still storming when she reached the street, but she had walked half a block in the rain before she came back to earth and remembered to unfurl her umbrella.

The rest of her morning was spent in the 23rd Street branch of the Public Library where she ferreted through mountains of old, bound newspapers, now and then making brief entries in the little black leather book she always carried in her capacious handbag. She lunched frugally at a drugstore fountain, and then headed for the subway and Newark. The Inspector telephoned her at 5 that evening, and again after dinner, but there was no answer.

The old girl was out sleuthing again, he told himself with a wry grin. It would be the coldest trail she had ever struck; she'd have to get up early in the morning to crack this one.

As a matter of fact, Miss Hildegarde Withers rose on that Thursday the twelfth of March well before the sun, which did not begin to brighten the dingy train windows until they came out above the Hudson north of Yonkers. By half-past 8 she was staked out in a hired taxicab under the gray walls of Sing Sing Prison in Ossining, New York, peering at the gates through a pair of 3-power opera glasses unused since her last attendance at *The Pirates of Penzance.*

Early as it was, a reception committee was already formed, consisting of half a dozen newspaper reporters and photographers who lounged on the curb, smoking or beating their arms against their chests for comfort against the raw wind off the river. So del Puerto was still news, Miss Withers noted grimly.

Shortly before 9 a little crowd of curious townspeople began to gather—a boy on a bicycle, a night watchman with his dinner pail, several dumpy women with babies or shopping bags. There were even a few private cars and a taxi. "Everything but a brass band for the scoundrel," the schoolteacher observed to herself.

At exactly 9 the gate opened and a swart, stocky man came out, wearing a fedora pulled low over his eyes and a trench-coat that seemed too tight for him. He stopped short—whether to take a breath of the raw fresh air or in surprise at the popping of flashbulbs, she couldn't be sure. After a moment he hurried forward into the middle of the street, shoving aside the circle of reporters with their chorus of questions.

Then seemingly out of nowhere came a long black sedan, cruising so as to time its arrival perfectly, and slowed almost to a stop beside him. Del Puerto leaped inside as the door was opened, the motor roared, and it was all over. One of the spectators, a fat woman in an apron, stepped out into the street to stare after the speeding car.

"You want I should follow him?" demanded Miss Withers' driver, who had been somewhat intrigued with it all. He seemed disappointed when she told him to take her back to the Ossining station. There was no use trying to follow lawyer Sherwood's limousine.

When they turned around at the corner Miss Withers noticed that the taxi was also turning. There was someone in the back seat—a girl with a bright scarf tied around her hair. She was holding a handkerchief to her face as if she were crying.

The train from Albany was late, and when Miss Withers finally got aboard she found all the coaches crowded. When the train lurched ahead she was still staggering forward, clutching the back of one occupied seat after another. Then, in the very last car of all, she caught a glimpse of a bright scarf above glossy black curls—the girl in the taxi—and alone in the seat!

"Nothing ventured, nothing gained," said the schoolteacher to herself, and bustled forward with a new light in her eye. She plumped herself down beside the girl, who was leaning wearily back, her sloe-eyes almost closed, smoking a long brown cigarette. There was some commotion as Miss Withers arranged herself, her coat, her handbag, and her umbrella. "Mercy, it's crowded today, isn't it?"

The girl smiled and nodded politely, then blew another smoke ring.

"That's right, go right on and smoke, I don't mind. My, what unusual cigarettes you use—aren't they the kind sold in Spanish America?"

"Yesss," the girl said, smiling, but only with her lips. Her eyes were wary now. She started to rise, but Miss Withers put out her hand.

"Please don't go," she said firmly. "I'd like to talk to you, *Señora* del Puerto."

The dark eyes flashed wide open. "No *hablo* Eengleesh—" she began.

"I think you *habla* enough to understand that I want to be your friend," the schoolteacher went on. "What's the matter, child? Are you hurt perhaps because your Juan did not greet you when he came out of prison?"

The girl drew herself back into the corner of the seat, almost crouching. "You are reporter?" she whispered. "Or are you police, maybe?"

"Neither—just a citizen. You are in trouble?"

The eyes flashed. "I take care of myself. Please leave me 'lone, leave us both 'lone. I only come here to get my man, to ask him to come back—"

"Back to Mexico or back to you? Both, I presume. By the way, why were you hiding outside the gates in a taxicab so that he couldn't see you even if he wanted to?"

"Because—because I must see Juan alone, not when the reporters and that lawyer, that Meester Sherwood, are around. I do not like that Sherwood, he give Juan bad advice. He tell him to plead guilty so—so—"

"So the police would drop the murder charge that they couldn't prove anyway?"

"Of course they couldn't prove! But bigamy—poof! We are not legally marry with the *Justicia* and the padre; we are only what you call common-laws. So where is bigamy?"

Miss Withers decided to prod a little. "You mean to tell me that you want to take a suspected murderer back into your loving arms?"

Consuelo laughed. "You think I am his woman for two years and do not know him outside-in? Juan, he cheat a little because he love easy money, but he love his neck too much to commit any murder." The sloe-eyes softened with memories. "Why, he take baths every day with perfume soap, some days twice. He wear silk underwear and always, always he is shaving. He take care of himself like a prima donna, that man. He only marry that old cow because she want him very much and she has much money. When she got mad and run away, he come back to me."

"Yes, but—" The schoolteacher seemed to be getting nowhere. "I have some important contacts," she suggested tentatively. "If you'll tell me just why you want to see Juan alone, perhaps I can fix it."

"It is because he is mad with me. He believe the police when they say they find me in our apartment wearing that woman's clothes and jewelry, and he had told me never to open that suitcase. But I swear I do not open it—never! The Mexico City police, they only try to make a better case, so they say what is not true. I must tell him that—and tell him to forget her money. I have money now. That will make him forgive me, *por Dios.*"

Miss Withers nodded. "I quite understand, my dear. There are many things that cannot be said before an audience, many things indeed . . ." Her voice trailed away, and a little shiver went up her spine. She might have gone on to say that one of the things not to be mentioned in public was the weight of what might be a small-caliber pistol in a lady's handbag, a soft woven handbag which she had just touched with shamelessly exploring fingers. She edged a little away from Consuelo, who leaned back against the seat, staring at nothing. The lovely Latin face slowly froze into a mask, resembling some ancient Mayan carving, alien, stoic, aloof—and cruel. She seemed asleep.

After a while the schoolteacher rose quietly, gathered her belongings, and went back to the vestibule, as if in a hurry to get off. The train was already pulling into 125th Street, but before the departing passengers elbowed her aside she saw through the glass door that Consuelo was rising and going forward to the room marked WOMEN, handbag in hand.

"It's just possible," Miss Withers said to herself, "that she knows I know, and that she's getting rid of the gun. And also possible that it was only a compact I felt, and that she is simply going to touch up her face before arrival."

The schoolteacher was first off the train at Grand Central, hurrying along the platform and up the ramp to secure an eagle-eyed vantage point behind the Information Desk. She was resolved to shadow Consuelo— the Mexican beauty was a new factor in the situation—and a fascinating one.

Miss Withers waited and waited, and Consuelo didn't appear. After half an hour Miss Withers gave up—who could know, in that labyrinth of labyrinths of Grand Central Station, what twist and turn the girl had taken? "I must have put her on her guard, somehow," Miss Withers said absent-mindedly to the man at the Information Desk, and went away.

Her next stop was Centre Street. She had known the Inspector, that gray little leprechaun of a man, better than she had ever known any member of the opposite sex; but never in all their association had she seen him as let down as he was that noon when she came into his office. It was no time for her to play the gadfly—he had evidently been gadded quite enough.

Oscar Piper looked up from the tangled pile of newspapers and gestured. "You seen these?"

"I hardly need to," she admitted. "They've dug up the del Puerto case?"

"Exhumed is the word. Dammit, I've spent thirty-five years as a cop, and nothing to show for it but a couple of months' pay in the bank and a stake in the retirement fund. I've personally helped send over a hundred murderers to the Chair, and stayed up all night drinking black coffee and hating myself the eve of their executions. I've been beaten up by thugs, I've had gangster lead pried out of my carcass twice, I've worked twenty-four hours a day for days on end when a big case came up, and all the thanks I now get for it is a tabloid's editorial beginning: *Police Sit on Their Hands as del Puerto Goes Free!*"

"Consider the source," she said.

"Here's another—*Man Third Degree Couldn't Break Goes Free Today—Gustavson Disappearance Still Unsolved!*" The Inspector snorted. "I wish to heaven I could have that guy in the back room with only me and a rubber hose. But believe me, we never laid a finger on him—not even a pinkie—and he wouldn't even agree to the lie-detector."

"But Oscar, nobody can be right all the time."

He wasn't even listening. "The case was so simple—like ABC! It was Maggie Gustavson's own fault that she trusted a no-good she'd picked up in the park and only known two weeks—but as I said, there's no telling what a woman of her type will do."

"Or any woman," put in Miss Withers.

"But we owe it to her to see that the rat is sent where he belongs, which is the Hot Seat. And yet we had to back down and settle for giving him five easy years in the pen."

The schoolteacher had her own opinion about how easy any years in the penitentiary would be, but she kept it to herself. "Oscar, if I remember correctly you've often said that the way to solve a murder is to look for the one thing wrong in the picture—the unnatural factor."

"That's right. In this case, it was del Puerto stocking up on all those razor blades. For a thin dime you can buy a handle that makes a regular scalpel out of a razor blade—nice and handy for dissection."

She shuddered. "Perhaps. But Oscar, I was thinking of the—of the *exactly* thirty thousand dollars."

"*Yeah.* And tomorrow at 11 o'clock in Judge Black's branch of the Municipal Court comes up the application of Señor Juan del Puerto for the swag. Murder pays off."

"Everyone gets paid off eventually, in some coin or other," Miss Withers said softly. He hadn't quite got her point, but that could wait.

"Never mind, Oscar, tomorrow is another day." The Inspector told her that she could take the Pollyanna stuff and go away and let him enjoy his headaches in peace and quiet.

She went, closing the door behind her very firmly. "But if you think, Oscar Piper, that you've got headaches today, just wait until tomorrow," she whispered in the hallway.

Tomorrow's headache broke ahead of time, shouted to the skies by newsboys waving copies of the early editions of the morning papers, at theater time that same evening. Clutching a paper still damp from the presses, the Inspector dialed Miss Withers' number. Through his mind went the many strong words and phrases he intended to use—but they were to stay pent up within him, for there was no answer. He tried again and again, until he was sick of trying. He even reported the phone out of order, but it got him nowhere. Miss Withers was not at home.

"Out riding her broomstick, probably," he said with unusual bitterness.

He was hammering on her door with the dawn, but still no answer.

A bottle of milk, a half pint of cream, and the morning paper lay on the mat—headlines still screaming at him: CLAIM MAGGIE GUSTAVSON ALIVE—TO BE IN COURT TODAY! He kicked viciously, strewing newsprint all over the hall, and then stalked out of the apartment house. For once Hildegarde had gone too far with her shenanigans.

It was, as he well knew, no time to be going down to his office. The Commissioner would be calling, the press would be on his neck for a statement. Finally he ducked into a telephone booth, dialed SPring 73100, and asked for Lieutenant Swarthout in the detective division. "Send out a broadcast to pick up Hildegarde Withers!" he ordered. "She'll probably be wearing a blond fright-wig and falsies. Pick her up and hold her—for her own protection."

A blank "Why?" came from the other end.

"Oh, the old girl has gone completely off her trolley. She has a wild idea of surprising Juan del Puerto into a confession by appearing in court. Now the big surprise has somehow leaked out ahead of time. Del Puerto will be wise that it's just a gag—not that he wouldn't know it anyway, since he knows where the poor woman's bones are rotting. But Hildegarde is going to get herself in seventeen kinds of trouble for impersonation, contempt of court, and God knows what else. Get going and find her!"

The lieutenant got going, and the word went out over the radio and the teletype. But that was all. As the hands of his watch neared 11 the Inspector gave it up as a bad job. For a few moments he debated whether or not to go near the courtroom and the fiasco that he knew must follow, but in the end he succumbed. Somebody ought to be there to pick up the pieces.

It seemed that everybody was there. The big courtroom was filled to overflowing when he arrived. Near the doors a slatternly scrubwoman was mopping the same place over and over again, straining her ears to catch what was going on inside. There were a lot of standees, although at the moment His Honor was only wearily passing sentence on a smallish gentleman in a sharp tweed suit who was pleading guilty to bookmaking on the corner of 47th Street and Broadway, evidently not for the first time. There was a brief pause while the bookie expressed his preference for paying fifty dollars over ten days at Welfare Island, and paid off with a smooth treasury note. Half a dozen spectators, evidently partisans, got up to go—and the Inspector slid into a chair quite near the rail. At least, he had a seat. After all, it might teach the old girl a much-needed lesson not to butt into other people's business.

"Would you mind moving over, please?" came a crisp, familiar voice, and Miss Withers crowded in beside him, beaming. "How nice of you to come, Oscar!"

He stared at her blankly. The maiden schoolteacher was dressed as usual in sober serge, with her own hair and bosom.

"But—but—but—" he began.

"Stop making noises like an outboard motor. Oscar, you didn't think that I would actually try to masquerade, did you? But I did do a little investigating, and I found that the late Maggie Gustavson has three sisters, all blondes, still living in Newark. There is bound to be a certain family resemblance, you know. We studied her old photographs and picked the sister who looked most like her—it was Hulda, three years younger, but all the more likely to resemble the Maggie he'd remember. With a little changing of hair-do and make up, and with the addition of some of Maggie's old clothes that she'd kept at home, I think we've produced quite a passable Maggie. Worked most of the night on it, too—we just got in from Jersey."

He shook his head doggedly. "But you can't actually hope—"

"Why not? Of course the newspaper stories may give del Puerto a chance to prepare himself—but it will hit him all the harder when instead of the obvious fake he's expecting he sees the living breathing image of Maggie popping up here in court and snatching the money out of his hands just when he was so sure of getting it. I wouldn't be surprised at anything that happens!"

"Neither would I, but it'll be nothing good," the Inspector said glumly.

"Oh, I don't know. Look, Oscar. Over there, across the room—the pretty girl with the dark curly hair. That's Consuelo, from Mexico City."

"The first wife of his?"

"She told me the relationship was somewhat more informal." Miss Withers went on to whisper the story of her train trip down from Ossining, but halfway through she was interrupted by the calling of the plea of Juan del Puerto versus the City of New York. On the other side of the railing a tall, handsome man suddenly appeared, ruffled his graying curly hair with manicured nails, and said that his client was ready.

"Sherwood doesn't look worried," Piper whispered.

"Neither does Juan," Miss Withers said. "But keep your shirt on, Oscar." The plaintiff entered and sat down beside his counsel, buffing his fingernails against his palm, impeccably dressed in a new blue lounge suit with peaked lapels and a pinched waist. He did not seem to have sensed the commotion in the courtroom when his name was mentioned, nor to listen to the brief plea of his attorney as Sherwood set forth claim to the money which had been taken from his client at the time of arrest.

"Just a minute," His Honor said. "I understand that this money has been the subject of another claim—"

"Which was dropped, I believe, with the consent of the District Attorney's office, Your Honor."

The Judge hesitated. He was a sincere-looking old man, and he obviously disliked his duty. There was a deep silence in the court. "I hear no objections," Judge Black continued. "I therefore—"

A slim young man, with an eager fox-face, suddenly arose from the attorneys' bench. "If it please the Court—"

"Yes, Mr. Nicolet? I understood that the District Attorney's office had no further interest in the matter, and had withdrawn all claims?"

"We had, Your Honor. But something has just come up. I wish to ask for a continuance in the interest of justice. There is an obvious necessity for establishing the legal ownership of this money, which was originally the property of Dr. Margaret Gustavson, and was allegedly transferred by her to the plaintiff shortly before their wedding on December fifth, 1945, a marriage since declared bigamous and therefore invalid . . ."

"Your Honor!" Sherwood stood up again. "We do not maintain the legality of the marriage. That is quite immaterial."

"So ruled," said Judge Black almost reluctantly.

"My client deposes and states that the money was a free gift, and nothing else."

"Quite right. A gift is a gift. The only person who can lawfully question that gift is Dr. Gustavson herself, and since I understand that—in spite of some wild prophecies in local newspapers—she is unable to appear, I see no valid reason—"

"If it please Your Honor," Nicolet interrupted, "I wish to call Dr. Margaret Gustavson to the stand!"

There was a moment of dead silence, followed by a muffled clamor from the crowd. Then a blond woman, buxom yet still attractive, suddenly rose to her feet in the back of the room and started down the center aisle. For a moment the sharp rapping of the Judge's gavel was lost in the hubbub. "This court will be cleared if there is any more disturbance!" Judge Black was purple with anger. But Miss Withers wasn't watching him—she had eyes only for Juan del Puerto, whose face was turned blankly, incredulously, toward the woman who was coming forward so resolutely. . . .

Did he look like a man who had gambled everything for thirty thousand dollars, and now realized that he had lost? The Inspector strained his ears to hear del Puerto mutter something along the lines of "But she can't be here—she can't, because she's *dead!*"

Across the room there was an outbreak of hysterical sobbing, and Consuelo suddenly stood up, biting at her handkerchief and muttering in Spanish, either thanking or imploring her Dios. She almost ran out of the room.

The blond woman had come slowly all the way down the aisle, and now was passing through the gate in the railing, which Nicolet politely held open for her. "A good man," Miss Withers whispered. "He owed me a favor. I do hope he doesn't get into any trouble over this."

"I hope you don't!" Oscar Piper whispered back.

The surprise witness paused as she came into the enclosure, and then she turned slowly and looked straight at Juan del Puerto, her blue eyes stony-cold.

He was standing up now, oblivious to the fact that his hands were shaking like leaves in the wind. His face had somehow lost its swart rotundity and was suddenly stark and drawn, the features working as if moved with hidden springs. The heavy, passionate lips trembled, and there were real tears in his eyes. "Maggie!" he cried, chokingly. "Maggie, it is you! You did come back!" He started forward suddenly, as if to embrace her, and only the quick warning hand of his lawyer held him back.

The humming as of a hundred hives of bees arose from the crowd, and again Judge Black banged fiercely with his gavel. Bailiffs and court attendants were shouting for quiet, with Nicolet and Sherwood both talking at once. The elder lawyer finally got the floor.

"My client wishes to withdraw his claim—"

"Yes," del Puerto cried. "It's her money—let her have it!"

The gavel crashed. "The Court declares a fifteen-minute recess, during which time I must request that the attorneys in this case confer—"

Del Puerto was beyond all that. "Your Honor, don't you understand? I am not under suspicion of murder anymore! I am not a marked man, a thing of shame! She's alive, she's come back!" He was effervescent, jubilant.

"Oscar, I assure you that I had no idea—" whispered Miss Withers. "But does he sound like a guilty man? Nobody could be that good an actor!"

The Inspector wasn't listening. He was watching the blond woman, Hulda Gustavson, who stood in the center of the stage in a deep freeze, an actress who had forgotten her lines and couldn't improvise. . .

And then there was the sharp *cr-r-r-rack* of a pistol shot sounding above the confused din of the courtroom, like a venetian blind suddenly loosed. Nobody knew just where it came from, but the uniformed officer at the door prudently threw himself on the floor. Juan del Puerto threw up his hands and gaped foolishly, then slid into a heap against the counsels' table. Miss Withers heard a woman screaming, and then realized that it was herself.

The Inspector was gone, fighting his way up the aisle through the pandemonium. She sprinted after him, like a football carrier following his interference, and they burst out into the corridor together. It was empty.

There was nobody in sight except the old scrubwoman standing open-mouthed, with a pail in one hand and a mop in the other. "Somebody just shot a man through an opening in that door," Piper yelled at her. "You saw it—who was it?" She shook her head vacantly, and then at the Inspector's increasing volley of questions she only retreated into a sort of paralysis of terror, saying only "Yes" and "No" to anything, and obviously not knowing or caring what she said. Finally Miss Hildegarde Withers pushed the Inspector aside.

"Nobody is going to hurt you," the schoolteacher said gently. "Just tell me—who opened that door a crack and shot through it? And which way did that person go?"

The woman pointed a shaking finger toward the nearby stairs. Piper set off at a run, but was back again soon enough, shaking his head in disgust. Neither the elevator man nor the guards in the lower hall had seen anyone running or had noticed any other suspicious circumstance. People were passing in and out all the time. The Inspector had drawn a complete blank.

By this time the corridor was filling up with people, curiosity-seekers and courtroom attachés—among them the uniformed man who should have been standing outside but who had slipped in because he wanted to hear better. The Inspector worked off part of his steam on that unhappy patrolman, implying that there was no punishment in the book which fitted this particular crime but that he, Oscar Piper, would improvise one. . .

"'Something with boiling oil in it, I think,'" quoted Miss Withers softly. But during the interval she had calmed down the scrubwoman, had learned that she was Mrs. Mamie Schultz of 433 Tenth Avenue. The old lady's story, told in broken phrases, was that she had been scrubbing over there in the corner, had looked around at the sound of the shot, and had seen somebody running away—she thought that maybe it was a woman. There was only time for a glimpse before whoever it was turned the corner and went down the stairs.

"Now," said the Inspector, "we're getting somewhere. Was it a smallish, dark girl, Spanish-type, very pretty?"

"Maybe . . ." said the scrubwoman, hesitantly.

"Or," put in Miss Hildegarde Withers, "was it a woman of about fortyfour, the blond, buxom type?"

The bedraggled woman gaped stupidly, and then pointed toward Piper. "It vass like he say, she vass liddle and dark."

"So!" said the Inspector triumphantly.

"So nothing!" Miss Withers came back. "Perfect nonsense. On your cue, she's describing Consuelo who left minutes before the shot was fired." The schoolteacher turned full face on the frightened woman. "Wasn't there another—a buxom blonde type?" But the bewildered old crone only shook her head.

"I think I don't see no other woman," she insisted stubbornly.

That was that. The Inspector turned his attention toward the routine direction of the rapidly growing corps of uniformed men—there was to be a search of the courtroom and of everybody in it. "Not that it will get us anywhere," he predicted.

He was right—it didn't. One after another, the people in the courtroom were given a cursory search and then released; no guns were found.

In the Judge's chambers, Miss Withers came closer to the Inspector, and whispered, "Oscar, I'm truly sorry if I upset the apple cart and changed del Puerto from a suspect into a victim. But really, this simplifies things. There was only one person who had a motive to shoot him."

"Yeah?" he said, with heavy sarcasm. "Who's your guess now?"

"The real Maggie Gustavson, of course! The woman he had tricked into marrying him and giving him her savings. Not all her savings, naturally—because nobody ever saves such a nice round even amount. Savings come out to odd dollars and cents—I suggest that Maggie had a good bit more, a sort of nest-egg. Every woman likes to have a little money of her own, that she doesn't have to account to anybody for—"

They stood back as ambulance attendants carried Juan del Puerto away, his face a deathly gray in color, almost the same shade as the dingy blanket which had been wrapped around his pudgy body.

"Maggie wasn't murdered," Miss Withers continued. "She cracked up—in a state of amnesia or close to it, when she found that her new husband was already married. She hid out, enjoying the hue and cry as del Puerto was dragged ignominiously back to be charged with her murder. She must have been disappointed when he pled guilty to the minor charge, but she still would have taken a deep pleasure in his suffering."

The Inspector was unimpressed. "You're making this up out of whole cloth. It's all rubbish. She'd certainly have contacted her family."

Hildegarde gave him a look. "Not Maggie. She'd risen far above them, and she knew how they yearned for her money. Look what lengths Hulda was willing to go to, just to make a valiant last try for it! But when Maggie read in the newspapers about Juan getting out of prison, when she heard the astounding news that someone posing as herself had appeared out of nowhere to contest his getting the money, wild horses couldn't have kept her away from this hearing."

Piper frowned. "I don't get it. You mean to say that you were intentionally putting del Puerto on the spot?"

"Not exactly. But I suspected that somehow she'd manage to be here. I'm afraid I underestimated how much she hated him. Hell hath no fury, Oscar . . ."

"But the Mexican wife had as good a motive, no?"

"Hardly. He had come back to her once, and she knew he would again. Besides, she stuck up for him—it was she who cleared him on the razor blade business. She told me about his fetish for being immaculately neat, and I have discovered that there is a prohibitively high tariff in Mexico on American razor blades."

"Maybe." The Inspector shook his head stubbornly. "But I wouldn't believe your Consuelo under oath."

"Well," said Miss Hildegarde Withers firmly, "I wouldn't believe the police under oath when they say that they found that slip of a girl wearing Maggie Gustavson's trousseau at the time they arrested her in Mexico City. Nobody lucky to have a firm trim little figure like Consuelo's would ever think of putting on clothes that would fit her like a tent. It just doesn't make sense!"

"You're up to something," said Inspector Oscar Piper. "I only wish I knew what."

The line of people waiting to be searched was dwindling now, and it was all too evident that the murder weapon was not to be found.

"I have an idea," said Miss Withers.

"You and your ideas." Piper shrugged. "Might as well let the boys finish up and get out of here."

"But Oscar—look at it this way. Nobody can criticize you now for not being able to pin Maggie's murder on del Puerto, because it never actually took place. This is really a feather in your cap."

Oscar Piper turned and glared at her. "One more feather like this and I can fly right out of the Department. At times like this, I feel like turning in my badge."

For once, Hildegarde Withers had nothing whatever to say. She tagged along behind him, biting her fingernails. They marched out in silence, out into the main corridor again. Wincing at the sight of the waiting battery of the press and the photographers, the Inspector suddenly turned and headed toward the back stairs. He was going down, almost at a run, when he felt Miss Withers' hand on his arm, whirling him around.

"Oscar, wait!"

He stared at her blankly. "Wait for what?"

"Oscar, look there—at the scrubwoman." Miss Withers pointed to where Mrs. Schultz was trudging dispiritedly along, dragging her mop and pail. "Oscar, she could have been lying! And of course nobody thought of searching her."

He was patient. "Of course she was searched—she insisted on it. I guess she enjoyed her little hour in the limelight. So—"

"So wait until I ask her one more question, anyway." Miss Withers hurried back toward the old woman, who had set down her mop and pail and was now backing away apprehensively.

"I tell you all I know—everything!" the woman cried.

"But you didn't tell us why the halls are scrubbed in the daytime—instead of at night, as they usually are." The schoolteacher pressed closer. "Mrs. Schultz, I have just one more question—"

Miss Withers stumbled clumsily against the pail, so that it overturned and flooded the hall with a soapy Niagara. The Inspector leaped, trying to save his shoes. Then he saw Miss Withers triumphantly pointing—to a big cake of soap and some dirty rags sliding across the floor. One of the rags was wrapped around a small automatic pistol.

"Mrs. Schultz," went on the schoolteacher, "isn't it time we got down to cases? You are Dr. Margaret Gustavson, aren't you?"

The woman straightened suddenly, her eyes widening, her shoulders squared.

"I'm glad I did it!" she cried out, almost as if the Inspector's hand was not firmly on her elbow. "I've been waiting for this chance a long, long time—ever since that day at the dock when I saw Juan's passport and a snapshot of that other woman. That's where he kept her picture—hidden in his passport. He lied to me—he lied, he lied!"

She began to laugh—shrill hysterical laughter that went on and on.

Hildegarde Withers turned away. She remembered what she had said to the Inspector: "I underestimated how much she hated him. Hell hath no fury like a woman scorned . . ."

You Bet Your Life

Walter McWalters looked upon the imminent end of Walter McWalters with considerable calm. His voice over the phone showed just the proper blend of hurt surprise and immediate cooperation. He would be glad to come down to the District Attorney's office for the "little talk" they requested so urgently; since he was tied up today would ten o'clock tomorrow morning be all right? He hung up the instrument without the slightest trembling of his well-manicured hand. Half an hour later the prominent clubman and mining investment counselor was out of the big house in exclusive Brentwood which late wife Claire had bought just after their marriage four years ago, taking with him only such necessities as his clothes, shaving gear, and a brief case containing $200,000, mostly in hundreds. McWalters had always liked the feel of hundred dollar bills.

He was out of the house—and out of this world. He disappeared with less splash but more finality than a stone dropping into the water starts ripples. . .

Six months later a certain whimsical, eccentric spinster made her debut on television. Just before zero hour Miss Hildegarde Withers felt more than a little nervous, because she was not at all sure of her lines. There was more at stake here than any jackpot prize, and she felt that she should have been better prepared for her ordeal than just the short briefing in the little backstage dressing-room and the powder the makeup man had dabbed on her weather beaten face.

The clock ticked away, and then loud and clear came the honeyed voice of the announcer, a Mr. George Fenneman. "And now, Groucho, I have another interesting couple for you to meet—a Mr. Wilton Mulvey and a Miss Hildegarde Withers." A youthful, collar-ad face appeared around the backdrop, and a hand beckoned. "Come in, folks, and meet—*Groucho Marx!*"

Miss Withers and her nondescript little partner were jostled gently from behind; they took a few steps forward and then they were *on*. She was vaguely aware of the studio audience, the lights, the cameras, the orchestra—but once on stage she had eyes only for the dapper, graying man in the spectacles, the neat tan suit and bright blue bow tie, who perched behind a high desk where a bowl of asters concealed his microphone. In the flesh, Groucho looked like his filmed self only perhaps more so;

his famous mustache was undeniably real, too. She had always wondered about that; Miss Withers had had a secret fondness for the zany Marx Brothers ever since *Animal Crackers* days.

"Welcome, welcome to *You Bet Your Life*," cried Groucho cheerily. "Say the Secret Word and you'll receive an extra hundred dollars." He relighted his cigar. "Miss Withers, do you mind if I call you Hildegarde?" There were more of the usual pleasantries, with the famed comedian going into his usual routine of trying to play matchmaker for the two of them after Mr. Mulvey admitted that he was a bachelor. It also developed that Mulvey spent his life engraving things on the heads of pins, which gave Groucho an opening for some jocose remarks. Then he turned on Miss Withers, with a pixy-ish cock of his head. "Hildegarde, may I ask where you're from?"

"You may, Mr. Marx. I taught public school in New York City for many years. Now I live in a little white cottage in Santa Monica, by the sea. I've retired."

"How often," sighed Groucho, "I've wished all schoolteachers would retire, back in my early days. But I'll have you know that it isn't true they had to burn down the schoolhouse to get me out of the third grade. It was the *fifth!* But Hildegarde, is that all you do, just retire?"

"Of course not. My avocation is criminology."

"Face cream or dairy cream?"

*"Crimi*nology, Mr. Marx."

"Oh," Groucho said. " I don't hear well, my glasses must need adjusting. So you're a criminologist. Does that mean you read murder mysteries and try to guess who-done-it before the author tells you in the last chapter?"

"Certainly not! I'm interested in real crimes, particularly in the offbeat sort. It occurred to me long ago that the police have a tendency to follow beaten paths, which works out well enough only when the criminal runs true to form. But—"

"So you're a sleuth, Miss Withers?" Groucho interrupted, picking an aster from the bowl and delicately sniffing at the stem end. "Have you ever actually solved a real crime?"

She shrugged modestly. "Quite a few, as it happens. Do you remember the Rowan murders in New York City, and the Ina Kell affair that wound up out here in Tia Juana, and the capture of Eddie the Actor in Chicago? Those were some of my successes."

"A schoolteacher sleuth, doing the work of the police! And I suppose they're very grateful to you for your help?"

"On the contrary, Mr. Marx. Even though I've always been willing to stay in the background and let them get the credit. But—the official mind, you know!"

"Are you working on anything interesting right now, Hildegarde?" Groucho asked.

The schoolteacher steeled herself, then lunged. "Yes. I've become very interested in the McWalters case, right here in town."

Groucho managed a mammoth surprise-take. "McWalters! Isn't he the socialite who's supposed to have walked off some months ago with a suitcase full of somebody else's money—the one who did a disappearing act more famous than anything since Judge Crater's? Isn't he the man the police are looking for all over the United States, to say nothing of Canada and Mexico?" In an aside, he added, "But who am I say nothing of Canada and Mexico, good neighbors that they are?" He paused. "And Hildegarde, do you really think you have a chance to solve the McWalters mystery, when the biggest police manhunt in recent history has failed to turn up hide or hair of the man?"

In a hotel room in Las Vegas, Jack Finn, licensed private investigator, came out of the bathroom with a highball in his hand and noticed that Sugar had the TV set on. Something caught his eye. "Migawd!" he cried. "Is this Thursday? Where went Wednesday? Look, baby, get packed—and fast! We got to get back to L. A.!" But the big, pasty-faced man himself stayed beside the set, while the ice cubes melted in his drink. . .

Over the air waves Miss Withers was saying, "I don't think, Mr. Marx. I *know*. I have the McWalters case solved."

Groucho's eyebrows went up even higher than before. "What?"

"Yes. By a combination of common sense, feminine intuition, a clinical study of what is known of the man's habits and behavior, plus one lucky break, I know *everything*, including his approximate whereabouts. They all make one mistake, you know."

"And are going to tell our vast unseen audience—most of whom are probably out at the refrigerator getting a can of beer at the moment—all about your discovery?"

"I'm afraid not, Mr. Marx. It's top secret."

"Oh, I see. You're just telling the police, then?"

"No, Mr. Marx," Miss Withers replied. "I most certainly am *not* telling the police. They have been too rude to me. I'm writing it all up in an article. Of course, when it's published the police can no doubt arrest McWalters in a matter of minutes. But I mustn't say too much—"

In a little bierstube in New York's Yorkville, Inspector Oscar Piper sat frozen on his stool, his face upturned to the TV set hung above the bar. "Lady, you've said it already!" gasped the grizzled little skipper of Homicide West. Hildegarde, he feared, had lost her marbles. And he was fond of the preposterous old biddy, too. They had been friendly enemies since their first meeting above a corpse and frightened penguin in the old Aquarium, more years ago than he cared to think. His lager slowly went flat, untasted before him.

On the TV screen Groucho Marx was saying, "So you're a writer, too?" For once in his life, Groucho was playing straight man, but he gave her a conspiratorial wink.

The schoolteacher nodded brightly. "I expect to finish my little exposé article this week, and I'm quite confident that it will be snatched up by the editor of one of the largest Sunday supplements. He used to go to school with me, so I have an *in.*"

"Well, Hildegarde, I'll watch the Sunday newspapers, and I only hope that the missing Mr. McWalters reads them too, so he can learn about his mistakes. Good luck. And it's been a lot of fun talking to you two, but now it's time to play *You Bet Your Life.*"

Miss Withers' phone buzzed like an infuriated rattlesnake just after midnight, while she was in the midst of giving her hair in its requisite hundred strokes with the brush. Naturally she was on Cloud Nine at hearing the familiar voice of her old friend and sparring partner; also, and just as naturally, she hardly gave him a chance to put a word in edgewise.

"How thoughtful of you, Oscar, to call me! Didn't the show go well? Wasn't it a shame about my idiot partner doing us out of the grand prize? What did you think—?"

"Shut up and listen! Hildegarde, do you know what you've got yourself into with this insane yak-yak over the air?"

"Certainly! One of my more brilliant inspirations."

"Didn't it occur to you that McWalters might be tuned in?"

"We hoped so. Naturally, Oscar, it was a put-up job, my being a guest on the show and all. But one of the first things I learned about McWalters was that he never missed watching a quiz program and that his favorite was *You Bet Your Life*—so I thought that might be the way to trap him. And with the help of Mr. Marx and Mr. Fenneman and the writers, I baited a hook."

Oscar Piper was almost choking. "Baited with your own gizzard! You bet your *own* life . . ."

"Don't be silly, Oscar. If the man saw the broadcast of the show, or listened to the radio version, he's sure to think that I know his secret and that I'm going to publish it to the world. So naturally he'll have to come out of hiding, try to break into my house, and get a look at my manuscript . . ."

"You think McWalters is just a con-man?"

"But he *is*, Oscar! He skipped with $200,000 and there is a big reward out for him that I can well use, though I may have to split some of it. But that isn't my main interest. It's to nab one of these men who prey on defenseless women!"

"Hildegarde," the inspector said, as to a small child. "McWalters is not *just* a con-man and a thief. The grand jury out there indicted him for that, but there are other indictments pending. He's wanted in several states on suspicion of *murder*!"

"Oscar!"

"So when he comes calling on you it won't be just to sneak a look at your imaginary manuscript. It will be to silence you for keeps!" She gasped, and he continued mercilessly. "The guy's last wife *disappeared* nearly a year ago, didn't you know that?"

"But I thought she was supposed to be in a sanitarium."

"That was just one of McWalters' phony explanations to account for her absence. She's dead, all right—and so are several other ladies who got in Mr. McWalters' way. I hope you've got police protection?"

"N-n-no, Oscar. The police said if I bothered them any more about this case they'd have me locked up for observation."

"Not a bad idea. But don't tell me you're home, *alone?*"

"I have Talleyrand—and a toy pistol that nobody could tell from the real thing."

"Oh, *no!* A silly French poodle who loves everybody in the world, and a squirt gun! Hildegarde, you're absolutely out of your mind, and if I may say so it's not much of a trip at that."

Her sniff was audible three thousand miles away. "I might add that a Mr. Finn, a private detective, is having me guarded . . ."

That did it. Oscar Piper was about to let go with one of his better blasts, but the brittle voice of the long-distance operator cut in on him. "But damn it, miss, where am I going to get two dollars in change at this hour of the morning? Operator, do you know who I am?" But she ruthlessly cut him off.

Miss Withers sighed philosophically and went back to her hairbrush, but she had lost count. Oscar's warning had not really made her nervous—but she did find herself putting sunburn oil instead of wrinkle cream on her face just before she turned out the lights. Once in bed, sleep seemed miles away.

Visions flashed through her mind, bits of the incomplete picture puzzle she had been forming for weeks. She knew a little more about Walter McWalters than the police did, but not really enough. The man seemed to have had no past—except for what the Inspector had hinted about previous wives. His life had apparently begun when he drove up to the best hotel at Lake Tahoe in a foreign car, cut a wide swath with the ladies who were vacationing there, and finally carried off her feet the prettiest, plumpest, and richest of the widows—one Claire Visscher. Everyone had said it was a truly romantic marriage, though she was in her thirties and he was on the shady side of fifty.

They had bought—presumably with her money—a $60,000 home in Brentwood and lived in it for some years, uneventfully. McWalters had joined the Jonathan Club; they had been members of half a dozen exclusive country clubs and beach clubs and bridge clubs. There had been no friction in the household, according to Mrs. Lemmon, the housekeeper—who seemed, like most members of her sex, to have a soft spot in her heart for McWalters. He had been away a good deal of the time, investigating mining properties upstate and in Nevada; Claire had missed him very much and had been lonely. She played a lot of solitaire and kept a bottle of brandy in her closet behind her hats. McWalters neither smoked nor drank, was always immaculately dressed, kept himself in tip-top shape by golf and swimming, and liked to go only to the fanciest resort hotels and the finest restaurants. They had many acquaintances, but no close friends.

The housekeeper had said, "The McWalterses seemed to a very devoted couple and she was always kissing him and fixing his tie. I heard him raise his voice to her only once—when she slipped off her diet. Once morning when I came to work she was gone, with some of her clothes. He told me she'd gone away to take a cure for alcoholism and sleeping pills, and not to talk about it to anyone."

Mrs. Lemmon thought that McWalters touched up his sideburns and mustache with a dark tint, and that maybe he even wore a toupee. She had seen a denture brush in his bathroom cabinet. He was of average height and weight—about five-ten and 155 pounds—wore glasses only for reading, was fond of bridge and poker, but would always interrupt the game to watch TV quiz shows.

In fact, he seemed to have been the average well-to-do man—the Man on the Street, or at least the Man on the Boulevard. But when the District Attorney's office listened to the appeals of his wife's distant but hopeful relatives and called him in to ask the whereabouts of Claire and why he had told so many conflicting stories to account for her absence, he finished looting her bank accounts and took off in their second-best car, his gray '53 Ford sedan, down The Street of No Return.

So much for the man supposed to be a multiple murderer of *women*. And Miss Withers realized with a shiver—if he was already wanted for several killings he wouldn't have any reason to hesitate at one more.

The minutes crept by, with the little house silent as a tomb except for Talley's soft snores at the foot of the bed. Everything was too still; there was not even the usual rumble of the Pacific surges against the breakwater, or even the sound of a distant auto horn or siren.

And just then she knew there was something in Oscar Piper's dire predictions—because somebody was moving softly, but not quite softly enough, through the dead eucalyptus leaves that littered the side yard. Miss Withers tried to stop breathing, for now the intruder must be just outside her thin-screened windows. No, he was going stealthily on again, toward the rear of the cottage.

She slipped out of bed, pausing only to take the flashlight and squirt gun from under her pillow. She tiptoed back into the kitchen and saw to her horror that the knob of the back door was slowly turning. Next would be a skeleton key, or celluloid strip. . .

At that moment the poodle came yawning up beside her. "Talley, *bark* or *growl* or something!" she whispered fiercely, but he only looked puzzled. Miss Withers took a deep breath. *"Gr-r-raugh!"* she snarled, in what she hoped was a reasonably accurate facsimile. Then in her own voice: "What is it, Wolf ? *Down,* boy!" She spoke louder, "Who's there?"

A man's voice mumbled something that might have been "It's all right."

In a flash of sudden relief she guessed the answer. "Oh, you're from Mr. Finn's Agency?"

"Yes, Miss Withers. Just checking." The voice was discreetly hushed, but it was deep and masculine and very comforting. In another moment she would have asked him in for a cup of coffee, but now she heard the man going down the steps and away.

Weak with relief, Miss Withers went back to bed and was almost immediately asleep. What you don't know won't hurt you, they say—and they never said falser. Jack Finn had only one operative in his hole-in-the-wall agency, and that one was the blond girl known as Sugar, now dozing by his side as he drove across the wide Mojave Desert at ninety miles an hour. He pulled up when they reached the town of Barstow, then nudged the girl awake and led her into the rear booth of an all-night café. "Java time, kid," he told her. "But drink it fast. We've got to get back to L. A. pronto, even if you have to drive, God forbid."

"You really think it will pop that soon, Jackie?" She spiked their coffee generously.

He shrugged. "The cops think McWalters is in Mexico, the D.A.'s office thinks he's in Canada. His car's been seen in half a dozen places, but as that schoolteacher dame says, it could be just a red herring. He could have laid a lot of false trails and then doubled back. And if he *did* see that broadcast—"

"You think he'll try to knock her off ?"

"Likely. She did a good job on that TV pitch—almost had me believing it myself. He just might fall for it."

"You've always said that the easiest person to con is a con-man. But you don't care whether he knocks her off or not, do you?"

"Damn little," admitted Mr. Finn. "And I'm not out for a piddling piece of the reward, either. I hate that guy's guts—hiring me to look for his missing wife just to make it look good later! And after I'd wasted a month looking for a dame he'd dumped in the ocean or somewhere, paying me off with a check on an account he knew was impounded. All I want is to get to that monkey a few minutes before the cops do."

"Why the revenge stuff?"

Finn smiled. "Not that at all, Sugar. I want to make a deal, that's all. He tells me where his dough is, so I can get it and let him have half for his defense and maybe a little bribing of witnesses. He'll fall for it—all there's against him, unless they find his wife's body which they won't, is forgery of her name and misappropriation of funds. With dough he can beat that rap."

"Only my Jackie will cross him, huh? You'll lose your license."

"Who needs a license, in South America? Let's roll."

The morrow came, as morrows always seem to do. It was far from a bright day, in more ways than one. A thick, pea-soup fog drifted in from the Pacific; it was what the fly-boys call "bird-walking weather," as Miss Withers firmly explained to Talley as she turned him out into the little fenced backyard. From then until after dark, the schoolteacher tasted the dubious delights of being an overnight celebrity; her doorbell and her phone never stopped ringing. By eight o'clock in the evening she was at her wits' end and on her fourth pot of coffee, with the phone off the hook and the doorbell disconnected and almost all the lights turned off. She felt more absolutely alone than she ever had in her life.

She froze when suddenly there came a hammering on her front door. It was repeated, louder. "Open up, it's the law!"

"You don't fool me with that one! Go away!" she cried.

Somebody laughed. Hardly daring to believe her ears, she slipped off the chain—and then Oscar Piper came in, to find himself embraced and soundly kissed.

"Oscar!" she cried, hastily putting aside the water pistol. "You've come to my rescue!"

"Well—it was just that we want this McWalters pretty bad back in New York. And I had some vacation time coming . . ."

"You look peaked. Have you eaten? Why didn't you phone me from the airport? How long can you stay? What—?"

He sat down wearily. "Relax, Hildegarde! Yes, I ate on the plane. Yes, I did try to phone, but your line was busy. I can stay—" he looked around. "Hey, something's different. Yeah, where's the pooch?"

"Poisoned, Oscar. Early this morning somebody threw some biscuits loaded with weed killer into the yard. I found him and gave him some mustard water, and the vet says he has a chance. But—"

"But somebody wanted him out of the way—to get to you."

She nodded slowly. Talley, as they both knew, was a poor excuse for a watchdog, but no stranger would know that—especially after her synthetic growls of last night. And she herself had given the intruder his cue by leaping to the conclusion that he was from the detective agency, and blurting it out! She told him about that.

The Inspector accepted a cup of coffee. "So that proves McWalters saw the broadcast and is right here in the area!"

"I've thought that all along. But I also believe the man was right here in this house today!"

He almost dropped his cup. "You mean while you were out?"

"I wasn't out. I didn't have a chance to go out, or even to make my bed and clean the dishes. But let me tell it my way."

It had begun early, with the vet's coming to take Talley away in the pet-ambulance. Everything had come thick and fast after that. . . phone calls from cranks and curiosity-seekers, but most of them hadn't bothered to phone, they had just come barging in.

"You should have charged admission," the Inspector said.

"Be quiet!" There had been the freelance photographer who wanted to take pictures of her, but she had sent him packing. Before he had stepped off the porch there had been a Mr. Karff who claimed to be a TV talent agent and wanted to try to get her on *The $64,000 Question.* A Mr. Beale had wanted to collaborate with her on a book, *Murderers I Have Known;* there had even been a swami, turban and all, who offered for a fee to go into a trance and tell her the real whereabouts of McWalters; there had been umpteen reporters, and even a representative of a *Confidential*-type magazine who wanted to bid for her article. . .

"You mean your imaginary article?" Oscar Piper cut in.

"It isn't *entirely* imaginary, Oscar," The schoolteacher indicated a card table set up near the window, complete with typewriter and assorted papers. "I left the bait right out in plain sight, as even you can see. But my callers were coming so thick and fast—" She shook her head. "I couldn't keep my eye on all of them. But during the day one of the carbon copies of my manuscript disappeared!"

"Wow!" gasped the Inspector. "Then—"

"Then somebody lifted fifteen pages of gibberish, because the thing made sense only on page one. My real article is here." And she touched her forehead.

He nodded. "Who else was here?"

"Dozens, but all the rest had credentials, or else were too young or too old or of the wrong sex."

"Yeah, how about that? Couldn't McWalters have come dressed like a woman?"

"No man could fool me in women's clothes—not if he spoke," said Hildegarde firmly.

"But which one fits McWalters' description?"

"They *all* do! Remember, he has a phobia against being photographed, and there's only the police artist's re-creation sketch. Remember, too, he's such an *average* man, except for superficial. If he took out his upper plate, removed his wig, shaved his mustache, stooped or started wearing elevator shoes, quit tinting his hair, got fatter by not exercising or not dieting, changed his entire manner of dress and his habits and way of life, McWalters could be an entirely different person!"

"Criminals aren't that smart," Piper objected reasonably.

"Not the ones you *catch,* you mean! But you'll admit that police usually locate missing persons by working on the old theory that a man in flight will in spite of himself revert to his original tastes and habits—if he's a gambler, look for him at the racetrack or in Las Vegas, and so on. But suppose a man were clever enough to make himself into just the *opposite* of his former self, what then?"

"Impossible. He couldn't keep up the disguise."

"That's what the man from the District Attorney's office said when he was here today. He accused me of withholding evidence, but I soon made him see I haven't any evidence—yet."

"They're surely going to give you police protection now?"

"No, Oscar. They're still positive McWalters is out of the country. Besides, I've been trusting to Mr. Finn, the private detective. He was out of town on business until today, but he's very much in on it now. In fact, he's in that old abandoned building across the street right now, keeping an eye on me with a pair of binoculars. He set that up an hour ago . . ."

"Phooey on private detectives. Anyway, to sum it up, it looks like McWalters tried to sneak in on you last night and was scared off, either by your watchdog imitation or by news that there might be agency men around. He came right back this morning to get rid of your dog, then returned later in some disguise to steal your so-called manuscript—"

"More likely in the hopes of doing me in then and there, only there were so many people going and coming that he didn't dare."

"Looks that way. Anyway, he must be pretty close. But you forgot to tell me about the D.A.'s man, and Finn. Who else was here?"

Miss Withers was always nettled when he used the official tone on her. "Why—there was the postman. He delivered my mail in person just to get my autograph. And one of those old bleary men who collect old newspapers for the Welfare League, but they come this time every month. And the vet, of course, to get Talley. I guess that's all. You listening?"

He stood up. "Thinking. You say Finn is on the job right now?"

"Certainly. Behind that second floor window shade . . ."

"Then why didn't he show when he saw me barge in?" Piper snorted. "Answer me that!" But she couldn't. "Then he's either double-crossing you or he's drunk or asleep! I'm going over there!" He was out of the door in a second, with Miss Withers close on his heels.

By the light of the Inspector's pocket-flash they entered the building across the street—a building the wreckers had already started to demolish.

Up the creaking stairs and along the hall to the front apartment they went. The door was closed; the schoolteacher was about to knock when Oscar Piper caught her wrist. Then he turned the knob quickly, and plunged in.

The room was bare as a bone—except for a folding chair set up by the window, a thermos flask half full of coffee, an empty whiskey bottle on the floor, and a pair of binoculars on the window sill. It was Miss Withers who noticed the thermos cup that had rolled into a corner—and that the few drops of coffee in it were still warm!

"He could have just stepped out for a minute," she whispered.

The Inspector was studying the scuff-marks in the dust. "And he could have been dragged out," he said, pointing. "This ties it! I bet you the body is in this building—and probably the killer too!"

"McWalters? But how could he have known—?"

"Ten to one he was already using this building to spy on you himself, and heard Finn come in. It's logical."

"You could be right," she said, shivering.

"I'm going to search this dump from top to bottom. But it's no place for you. Rush over and pack some duds and get in your car and scram to the nearest hotel, fast!"

"But Oscar—!"

"Get going," he whispered fiercely. "You're in the way!"

She went. She rushed across the street and into the cottage, finding that in her haste to leave the cottage before, she had left the door ajar. Everything looked undisturbed, but still she snatched up the toy pistol— the model of a Colt .38 that would fool anybody, the sales clerk had said— and methodically searched every inch of the place. Nobody was there. It took her no more than five minutes to fling some necessities in an over- night bag, and then she was out of the back door and running toward the garage.

Me, running away! she thought bitterly. And the dear Inspector alone in a dark ruin of a building with probably a corpse and a killer for company. But what must be, must be. She flung open the doors to the alley, swooped behind the wheel of her ancient coupe, and jabbed at the rusty starter.

And then, just as the motor began to cough and snort, it happened— right out of the world of nightmare. A man stepped quickly out of the shadows and slipped into the seat beside her. In the gloom she could only see that he was a medium-sized man, slightly overweight, wearing thick glasses. He also wore the cap and uniform of the Welfare League pickup detail, the trash scavengers who were always coming around for her old rags and newspapers—the hopeful, sobered-up, washed and shaved vagrants who had seen the light and were trying to reform.

"I knew it!" she thought.

"Don't bother to scream," the man said quickly, in a voice that was over-pleasant, almost syrupy. But she knew it was the same voice she had heard outside her kitchen door last night, the same voice she had failed to recognize in the whine this morning, when he had come to ask for her discarded rubbish.

She felt something sharp against her side. "Just drive, please," said the man who had once been known as Walter McWalters. "And keep driving."

Something sharp entered her side an eighth of an inch, just as she was about to say "I will not!" So she put the car into gear, and started to drive. There was nothing else to do. But while she drove, being Miss Withers, she talked. She hoped that her voice was calm and normal—they said you had to humor them. "I've been looking forward to meeting you," she said. "So you were hiding out down on Skid Row right under the noses of the police! Very clever, Mr. McWalter."

The man beside her flicked a smile, and put one arm almost lovingly across the back of the seat behind her shoulders, close to her throat. They were out on the street now. "Just keep driving," he told her.

There were a few cars passing, and a number of pedestrians. If she could twist the wheel and cause a collision. . .

"Don't try it," McWalters advised.

She must try to get him talking. "I suppose you keep your money handy in a baggage locker at Union Station, where it's safe as long as you put in a quarter every day, and where you can dig into it for spending money?"

"Bus station," he corrected. It was the first information he had volunteered, and she felt a faint flicker of hope. She was also looking and praying for the sight of a police car, but now they were going south through lonely streets in the manufacturing and lumberyard area.

"If I'm being taken for the proverbial ride, you might at least satisfy my curiosity," she pointed out reasonably. He did not answer, so she plunged blindly on. "I'd really like to know how you disposed of your wife's body so completely. It's unique in the annals of crime, you know."

"Is it now?" he said easily.

"You took all those trips up into the uranium country, I understand. I've driven through some of that, and I noticed that when anybody takes a claim they mark one corner with a pyramid of stones, a sort of cairn several feet high. You see them all over the desert. Seems to me that would be an ideal place to hide a body. Like Poe's 'Purloined Letter,' right out in plain sight."

"Talk away, my dear lady," he said, unruffled. But she had felt his body tense at the word "desert" and tense again at the word "cairn." So she was sure now. At least it would be a moral victory, a triumph of her intuition—even if posthumously.

"Turn left here, please," McWalters told her, still in that intimate, oozy voice. They turned, and with the turn went her last chance to sideswipe another car.

They had entered a new subdivision with vast curving, unpaved streets lined with little gimcrack houses still in construction. It was—at least, at night—as desolate a spot as anyone could find. On and on they plowed, through red mud and little pools of water.

"Stop here," McWalters said finally. She braked the car to a shuddering halt. "Last stop," he said. He reached past her and flipped the door latch. "Out," he told her, pushing gently.

"I—I won't!"

"None of that." The thing in his hand pressed hard against her. "I just want to borrow your car for my getaway . . ."

Oh, sure! And he didn't want it all blood-stained. Suddenly she jammed her bony elbow hard into his stomach and flung herself out of the car, only to take a few steps and then bog down to her ankles in hopeless mud. She whirled to face him, as he slowly came closer, with the ice pick in his hand held low and menacing. "He actually enjoys this sort of thing!" she thought frantically. He took another step, and in spite of herself she screamed for the first and last time—a scream that echoed futilely and unheard through the raw lone streets and the gap-windowed houses. The pale moonlight showed no place for her to go, no hold for her to crawl into. And McWalters came closer, closer. . .

"*Please!*" she gasped, and her hand went fluttering to her bosom. Then in a flash her hand reappeared, with the water pistol aimed straight in his face. "You stand back and put up your hands!" she screamed. "Or I'll shoot!"

McWalters hesitated for a moment, a wide grin on his face. He seemed to be savoring the moment. "Miss Withers, you kill me!" he said. "I noticed that silly squirt gun of yours a little while ago, when I looked through your house. But I thought this would be more useful." He waved the ice pick—her own ice pick—in her face.

He reached for her, arms held out almost lovingly. Even a cornered kitten will bare its claws and spit in the face of an enemy. Miss Hildegarde

Withers shut her eyes and pulled the trigger. And seconds later it was all over. . .

Meanwhile, Inspector Oscar Piper had been having rather a bad time of it too, back in the condemned apartment house with the corpse of Jack Finn, skull crushed in, which he had finally located stuffed into a broom closet. His trouble however was not with the corpse, but with the Santa Monica police, who took a dim view of his discovering dead bodies in their territory, New York inspector or not.

Visiting police officers are required to check in with the local authorities unless their visit to a municipality is purely social. Nor was the local sergeant, whose usual duties only included such crises as noisy beach parties, drunks, and petty theft, especially fond of being told how to conduct a murder investigation.

"I wouldn't handle that bottle if I were you, Sarge," Oscar Piper had said.

"I think it rather fits the hole in the dead man's skull. Ever heard of fingerprints?" The Inspector was a very tense and worried man, or he might have been more tactful. As it was, they kept him in their little headquarters, making out and signing statements, for the next four hours. Finally they let him go, with grudging apologies, and he made a beeline for the nearest phone and started calling hotels. No Hildegarde, and nobody answering her somewhat unusual description. He tried her home with no avail. As a last resort he tried the downtown Los Angeles station.

"We were just going to send out an all-points on you," the dispatcher said. "Get down here fast, Inspector." And he told him why.

"Judas Priest in a revolving door!" murmured Oscar Piper.

"Naturally I used full-strength ammonia in that squirt gun you were so funny about," Miss Withers told him tartly much, much later. "You see, I read somewhere that postmen sometimes used that trick on unfriendly dogs."

They were having a huge and expensive lunch at Perino's, on Wilshire Boulevard. He swallowed a bite of filet, and shook his head. "You're really one for the books," he confessed.

"Maybe I'll even write it up someday," she said. "With you, of course, as comic relief."

"Well, at least it's over." He sighed. "They say McWalters will be the first blind man to go to the death chamber at San Quentin, and even if they don't find his wife's body he's booked for the Finn job. And I hear there's no question about your getting the reward."

"My chief reward, Oscar, is the news that Talley will be all right and can come home tomorrow," she said firmly.

"Then what?"

"Well, Groucho Marx sent word that they'd all like me to do a followup performance on *You Bet Your Life* as soon as possible. But I think I'm more the spectator type. I was just wondering, Oscar, if when I get the reward money Talleyrand and I might not take a little trip back to New York. Somehow, after all this, I feel the need for the peace and quiet of Times Square."

The Inspector grinned. "Well, remember the Sullivan Law—and leave your pistol home."

Who is Sylvia?

"Don't say it!" cried Miss Withers from the doorway. "I will concede that my new hat looks like something designed by a trained chimpanzee using finger-paints, and that I burst into your sanctum sanctorum unannounced, but your outer office was empty and you *did* send for me! You have a *problem*, Oscar, right?"

"My worst immediate problem," whined the long-suffering Inspector past his inevitable cigar, "is a sudden ringing of the ears. But sit down, Hildegarde."

She was already sitting, on the edge of a hard chair. "You want any help on a new murder case—I hope?"

This all happened, it might be explained, back in the halcyon days when Miss Withers was still teaching school in Manhattan and devoting a good deal of her spare time to acting as self-appointed gadfly to the police department, especially Homicide.

Oscar Piper shook his head. "It isn't murder—at least, not yet."

"But it involves a recent appointment with a charming feminine visitor. You got a haircut, and you are wearing what looks suspiciously like a new tie. And there is the faint aroma of expensive perfume in the office, and a lipstick-stained cigarette in your ashtray. What did your fair visitor want that you wouldn't give her?"

"Now, how in the world—?"

"Elementary, my dear Oscar. I think I passed her in the hall, looking madder than a wet hen. A smallish woman in black, with pearls under a mink-trimmed Alaska fur-seal jacket, fighting the Battle of the Forties, heart-shaped face, determined chin?"

"That's Mrs. Lola Mills. A wealthy socialite, has her own antiques and *décor* shop up on Madison. Sent down to me by the Commissioner himself. Wanted to have her new daughter-in-law arrested and deported so that the wedding can be quietly annulled."

"That's *all* she wanted?"

"Yeah. I gave her the polite brush-off by sending her down to look through the mug files. You see, Mrs. Mills is convinced that her precious son Donald has gotten himself married to Miss Lizzie Borden—"

"Oscar, have you been *drinking*?"

"No, but it's a dandy idea. I was going to say—to Miss Lizzie Borden, or a reasonably accurate facsimile thereof. Anyway, an adventuress, Mrs. Mills says, traveling under an assumed name because she is wanted by the police somewhere, who married a rich playboy for his money and is probably planning to poison him at any moment. Not a case for the department."

"Naturally not. You're never interested in murders until *after* they happen. But I happen to be a firm believer in preventive detection. What grounds has this Mrs. Mills for her suspicions, or is she just being a mother-in-law? Tell me more, I'm all ears."

The Inspector carefully relighted his cigar. "I don't know if the woman has any real basis for worry or not. But her son came into a pile of dough from his late father, and took off on a round-the-world yacht cruise with some friends. The cruise broke up in the Mediterranean and Donny went on catch-as-catch-can, probably seeing the world through the bottom of a highball glass. On the last leg of the trip, between Hawaii and the mainland, he met a girl—and married her as soon as they hit Frisco.

"So he brings his bride back to mother's big duplex apartment on East Seventy-third, where I gather that three's a crowd. The girl is an oddball, according to Mrs. Mills. Secretive about her past, seems to have no family or background, didn't want any wedding announcements sent out, and refuses to have her picture taken."

"Many woman don't think they're photogenic," Miss Withers said. "Even I—but no matter. There must be more than *that*."

"There is. The girl claims to be an American citizen, but at times of distress she lapses into a British or Australian accent. What else? Oh yes. Likes to cook, and dabbles in rare herbs. And about the only personal possession she has that predates the marriage is a sort of dispatch case, a big leather bag that she keeps locked in a closet and guards with her life."

"Oscar, I'm very much afraid that Mrs. Mills was once frightened by that old Broadway play, *Night Must Fall*, where the menace carried around a leather hatbox with his latest victim's head in it. Surely the situation could be cleared up with few simple questions—?"

"I gather from Lola Mills that things are too strained for that. She's afraid that if she pries any more, her son will blow up and take off and she'll never see him again. He's on the defensive, completely infatuated with the girl."

"So he's in love with his own wife! Oscar, I'd like to give this Mrs. Lola Mills a piece of my mind."

"Believe it or not, I may ask you to do just that little thing. But first tell me one thing. Did you phone Missing Persons about a week ago in regard to a girl named—let me see—Sally Burris? And if so, why?"

"Because she seems to have disappeared into thin air. You see, I had a letter from a Max Bailey, now a real estate man in Hawaii. He used to be a pupil of mine—I keep in touch with a number of them. I remember Maxie as a little urchin who usually needed a handkerchief, but he seems to have grown up and fallen in love. He and this Sally Burris had an understanding, he wrote me. But the girl was stage-struck, and she left Honolulu and headed for this city, where she had reservations at the Equity Club, a residence hall for young actresses and dramatic students."

"I know the place. The Martha Washington with make-up kits."

"But Sally never showed up there, not even to ask for her fifty dollar deposit back or to pick up her mail. Max's letters have gone unanswered. Only the next-of-kin can report a person as officially missing—but the girl is an orphan. Max is worried, and so am I now. Oscar, has something dreadful happened?"

The Inspector looked very pleased with himself. "Well, she's not on a slab in the Morgue—if that's what you mean. Stop trying to be the Little White Mother of all the Russias, will you? I'm afraid you have some bad news for your former pupil, that's all. Hildegarde, it seems that for once instead of getting into my chair, you've taken me off the hook."

"And just how, pray tell?"

"It wasn't until after Mrs. Mills had flounced out of here that I remembered something—the similarity of names between your Sally Burris and her son's new wife, Sylvia Burris. Sally being the diminutive of Sylvia, naturally."

Miss Withers's eyes widened,."Why, Oscar! How neat!"

"Yeah. Nothing has happened to Max's girlfriend except that she's jilted him and married somebody else. And Lola Mills has got herself in a stew about nothing. All the same, she'll take some persuading, the mood she's in. Did this Max Bailey give you some description of his Sally?"

"He said she is delectable and curvaceous, and I quote, 'with eyes like stars!'"

Oscar Piper snorted. "That's a description?"

"Weren't you ever young, Oscar, back around the turn of the century?"

"And look who's talking!"

"Max also enclosed a snapshot." Miss Withers produced it.

"Just another pretty girl at the beach," said the Inspector. "A bandanna around her hair, dark sunglasses. The picture's not quite in focus, but definitely a dish. I might even say——"

"Stop drooling! I also saw Sally's application form at the Equity Club, in which she says that she's twenty-four, five-seven, a hundred and twenty-five pounds, white, American, and a graduate of Honolulu High. Acting experience includes road shows, repertory, and stock. References were a theatrical agent named Moske and the aforesaid Mr. Bailey."

"Good. With that information we ought to be able to set Mrs. Mills's mind at rest. Maybe she won't be happy about her son's marrying an actress, but it's better than a fugitive from justice. Wait a minute, I'll see if the woman is still downstairs looking at pictures." He pressed a button on his squawk-box, spoke briefly, and then turned back, shaking his head. "She seems to have got tired of barking up that tree, and walked out."

Miss Withers was stalking uneasily up and down the office. "She probably decided to take matters into her own hands. Oscar, I smell trouble—the woman sounds desperate——"

"Oh, come now. Your imagination is working overtime again."

"And one of the things Mrs. Mills hasn't stopped at is petty theft, if I'm not mistaken!" The schoolteacher pointed. "Oscar, when the woman was here earlier this afternoon did you happen to leave her alone in the office for a moment, and at that time was your prize trophy in its usual place of honor there on the shelf?"

The Inspector jumped up, staring at a very empty little plush-lined case. "My silver-mounted Grussbacher Positive that I won at the Pistol Team tournament in Boston eighteen years ago! Why that no-good, light-fingered——" He grabbed for the phone, crimson with fury.

"Wait!" Miss Withers commanded. "*Please* let me handle this, Oscar. Remember, the woman has influence with the Commissioner. And you don't want it known that a visitor stole a lethal weapon right out from under your nose." She snatched up her umbrella and handbag, and headed for the door. "I'll rush up there and straighten things out before she gets into trouble with your pistol."

"*Women!*" snorted Inspector Piper, his eyes traveling ceiling-ward.

The languid young man behind the apartment house desk asked who was calling, and she said "Miss Withers, from Inspector Piper's office at Headquarters!"—which in one sense was true. Up on the 30th floor a massively carved oak door was opened by a young woman wearing a gingham apron and a wary expression, who said, "Yes?"

"Will you please tell your mistress—" then Miss Withers bit her tongue. This was not the maid; her apron was too functional, her bearing too unmaid-like. "Excuse me, I was looking for Mrs. Mills."

"*I'm* Mrs. Mills." The girl wore no lipstick, no make-up except possibly eye-shadow. A large diamond solitaire and diamond wedding ring were in evidence. "I fancy you want my husband's mother, Mrs. Lola Mills. She hasn't come home yet."

"Thank heaven for that!" murmured Miss Withers. She found herself being ushered into a drawing room only slightly smaller than a tennis court, decorated with a lavish simplicity. There were some weird, avant-garde paintings, and a number of leering African witch-doctor masks. But the schoolteacher had eyes only for the girl. "You must be Sally?"

"I—I've been called that, but I'm Mrs. Donald Mills—Sylvia Mills." The voice was cool, aloof. "Will you excuse me? I have something on the stove." The young woman swept out, rather like a duchess in spite of the apron. Miss Withers chose the least unfriendly-looking chair, completely at a loss. For the life of her she could not decide if this was the girl in Maxie Bailey's snapshot, or not!

She seemed taller than five feet seven, slimmer than a hundred and twenty-five pounds, older than twenty-four. Miss Withers took another hasty look at the picture, wishing it were in better focus. It *could* have been she, if that was black hair under the bandanna, and if those were blue eyes under the sunglasses. Still. . .

In a matter of minutes Sylvia was back, bearing a silver tray. "Would you like a cup of tea, maybe with a spot of rum in it? Or a cocktail? Or perhaps you're not supposed to drink on duty."

"Er—why, no thank you. Tea would be just fine."

The young woman poured, with a studied graciousness. But for all her poise, Miss Withers sensed that Sylvia was tight as an E-string.

A frontal approach seemed best. "You're a long way from home, aren't you, my dear?" Hildegarde asked chattily.

Sylvia put on a wistful Katharine Cornell expression. "Home? I never really had one."

"I was only referring to the charming trace of accent. Isn't it Australian?" This was purely a shot in the dark; Sylvia's speech was without ethnological overtones, almost carefully so.

"Oh? Why, yes, I have traveled down-under. But I didn't know any of it had rubbed off. The Aussies myke an 'abit of dropping their haitches, as the saying goes." Sylvia smiled faintly.

"And you like to cook? How unusual for a young girl nowadays!"

"Oh, sometimes I like to mess around a bit in the kitchen with rare herbs and spices. Perhaps because for so many years I never had anything but an electric hotplate. My mother-in-law thinks it's odd of me, but then she thinks everything about me is odd." The dark-shadowed eyes narrowed a little. "I suppose that's why she sent for somebody from the police to ask me personal questions. Oh, don't bother to deny it. She even tried to have me tailed by private detectives!"

Miss Withers hastily took in sail. "I am neither a policewoman nor a private investigator," she announced. "You don't have to fence with me, my dear. I was asked to look you up and see if you were all right—by a young man in Hawaii, a former pupil of mine. Of course you remember Max?"

The blue eyes flickered, but there was only the faintest hesitation. "Max Bailey? Poor dear, I'm afraid I have been too busy to send him a card. But he was never anything to me, I assure you. Oops—excuse me again." Sylvia made another quick exit to the kitchen, eventually returning to say, "Just didn't want my *Boeuf Alouette* to burn. Now, about Mr. Bailey. I think he has his nerve, asking you to spy on me!"

"I'll be glad to tell him so, and report that you are happily married. You are happy, aren't you? In spite of this situation with your mother-in-law?"

"What makes you think there is a situation? What did she tell you?"

"I've never met Mrs. Mills. But she talked to the Inspector, who happens to be one of my oldest friends. I promised him I'd look into it. As far as I can see, your mother-in-law is just a little upset because you seem so—well, so secretive. For some reason she seems to think that you're not what you say you are—"

"Well, that's just too bad! I'm Sylvia Burris, born at sea twenty-five years ago on the American passenger-cargo ship *Victoria Reina*, graduated from Honolulu High seven years ago last June, girls' basketball team, French club, second lead in class play. My parents died in the bombing of Singapore, and I was brought up by various relatives, also now dead." She was rattling it off as if by rote.

"Have you ever used any other name?"

Sylvia's laugh was quick. "Various stage names, which is quite natural around the theater. I was Sally Sims on a U.S.O. tour. My life has been full of ups and downs, and there are some things—"

"Things you can't or won't talk about?"

"Well, my husband knows all he needs to know, and he's satisfied! I didn't marry his damn mother, too. I guess you mean well, Miss Whatever-your-name-is, but I'm sick and tired of being pried at and questioned. Now that's all—I really must get back to the kitchen." The girl started out, then paused in the doorway for an exit line: "Tell Lola Mills I just want to be left alone."

Miss Withers frowned, sipping her tea. It was hard to imagine Mata Hari in an apron—yet there was something strange about the girl. She seemed to be hiding inside some sort of shell. . . .

Just at that moment came the click of a key, and there entered a very handsome gray Cheviot topcoat and ultra-smart bowler hat. At least that was the way Miss Withers would have described it, for the man inside the garments was a trifle on the vague side. "What a tremendous personality he *needs*!" she quoted to herself. But Donald Mills slipped out of his coat, hanging it and the hat meticulously in the hall closet, and then turned to cry, "Sylvia? Sylvia doll?"

And Sylvia came running, arms outstretched. Their embrace would have been cut out of the film by most movie censors. Then the young man announced breathlessly, "Darling, I got the reservations! Just think, by this time tomorrow—"

But Sylvia nudged him. "Donny, this lady is from the police." And Donny paled visibly.

"Nothing very serious," Miss Withers spoke up quickly. "Just something about your mother's antique shop. Shoplifting, we think." She gave Sylvia a meaningful look.

"Oh," said Donny, immediately uninterested. Suddenly he turned to Sylvia, who was silently waiting. "Doll, what say you get changed and we shake the dust of this dump off our feet and go out somewhere gay for dinner?"

"But—but I was making *Boeuf Alouette* to surprise you!"

Donny lowered his voice, but not quite low enough. "Come on, we can't take another evening *en famille*, you know that! Mother will have the vapors when I tell her we're leaving."

"Of course, dear. I'll put the stuff in the fridge and slip into a posh frock in 'arf-a-mo!" She rushed off to the kitchen, rattled pots and pans for a moment, then came back to parade up the stairs with her husband.

"My mother should be back soon," said the young man over his shoulder, quite without warmth. "Make yourself at home."

As soon as the young couple was out of sight. Miss Withers made herself at home by casing the hall closet; she had noticed a suspicious bulge in the pocket of Donald Mills's topcoat. Yes, the bulge was a snub-nosed Savage .32 automatic. There was also an envelope from a travel agency, with two first-class airline tickets to Guatemala City via Mexico.

She put everything back where she had found it, returned to her chair, and picked up a book. She was just in time, for Donny Mills suddenly ran down the stairs, a scowl on his vaguely handsome face.

"I know why you're here," he said sharply. "Shoplifting my eye! As if anybody could walk off with one of my mother's Governor Winthrop desks." He snorted. "Mother hired you to come here and smear Sylvia!"

"Young man, I am only trying—"

"My mother would stop at nothing, literally nothing, to break up my marriage! She's a monomaniac! She's an incubus!"

"I'm not too well versed in demonology, but don't you mean succubus?"

He wasn't listening. "I've had enough! That's why we're getting out, for good. Because if we don't, something terrible is going to happen!"

"Then you feel that your wife is actually in danger?"

"We all are!" Donny crossed to the little bar and tossed off a jigger of brandy. "So you can tell my dear mother for me—" He broke off as Sylvia appeared at the head of the staircase. Her dark hair was coiffed, and she was molded into a long, high-fashion black evening gown which did things for her, as did the mutation-mink coat. Yet Miss Withers could only think of Vampira on television, or the woman in the wonderful Charles Addams drawings.

And then Sylvia caught one of her spike heels on the stair, and started to tumble. Donny, a trifle slow in his reflexes, just barely managed to catch her in his arms.

It was over in a moment. And it all seemed a little unreal to Miss Withers, who rose as they prepared to leave, "Perhaps I should be running along. . . ?"

Donny Mills shook his head, "No, you may as well wait. You can break the news to my mother that we're leaving." And the door slammed behind them.

"Well, really!" said the schoolteacher to herself. Then she went over to the phone and dialed SPring 7-3100. Luckily the Inspector was still at his office. He sounded worried. "Well, Hildegarde?"

"Not so well. I'm at the Mills apartment, but Lola has not come home. I met the young couple, but since I have no badge or official status—"

"I'm glad you realize that. But is the girl Sally Burris from Honolulu, or isn't she?"

"I can't ask questions and demand answers, as you policemen can. There's something about the girl that doesn't ring quite true. She's putting on an act of some kind. Her speech is guarded, though she did lapse once or twice into what I imagine to be Australian slang. Sylvia *could* be Sally— she did recognize the name Max Bailey. But Oscar, I can't for the life of me decide if she is really the girl in the snapshot or not."

"When you're undecided about anything, that's news!"

"Thank you. Oscar, I wish you'd check and see if Donald Mills has a pistol permit—because if not, he's violating the Sullivan Act."

"This is all I need!" yelped Oscar Piper. "Lola Mills has a gun and she thinks Sylvia is going to try to kill Donny, and Donny has a gun and he thinks his mother is going to try to kill Sylvia, and—"

"Nobody is going to kill anybody!" interrupted the schoolteacher sharply. "I shall see to that. I'll confront Mrs. Mills when she arrives and straighten this whole thing out in no time at all, even if I have to commit a technical misdemeanor. Don't worry, Oscar."

" 'Don't worry, Oscar' my foot! You're sitting on the lid of a volcano, and I'm to wait and cool my heels until the whole thing blows up in the newspapers tomorrow! Remember, I'm up before the retirement board in a month or so!"

"Take a couple of aspirins, my dear," said Miss Withers, and hung up. Then she sat herself down to wait with all the patience of a cat at a mousehole.

Lola Mills did not arrive home until well after eight-thirty, and when the intense, birdlike little woman did put in an appearance the odor of cognac was mingled with her perfume. Nor did the enameled perfection of her still beautiful face crack into any surprise at the presence of an uninvited visitor. But of course the man at the desk downstairs must have tipped her off.

"The Inspector sent you? How thoughtful of the dear man!"

"It's about the pistol," said Miss Withers bluntly.

"What pistol?"

The schoolteacher sternly said exactly what pistol, and Lola Mills said loftily that the whole idea was quite preposterous and that she would be glad to lay bare the contents of her handbag or submit to search. "So you simply checked the gun at the desk downstairs when you heard somebody from the police was here! No matter—but do you mind telling me how you were planning to use it?"

Lola Mills smiled coldly. "Conceding nothing—but mightn't such a weapon just possibly be useful to *force* the truth out of somebody?"

"I've met your daughter-in-law, and I doubt if she'd scare easily. The Inspector has told me all about your problem—"

"Oh, I do hope that you're not one of those private eyes! I've tried them, and they got nowhere. Except to find out that there once actually was a Burris girl who went to high school in Honolulu. Only the description doesn't fit my son's wife at all!" When shown the snapshot, Lola Mills laughed in derision. "The woman my son married is thirty if she's a day—she's no sweet high school graduate!"

Miss Withers doubted if her own high school graduation picture would be identifiable today, but this situation was beyond further argument. "I'm going to nip this in the bud, Mrs. Mills. Obviously there is only one way to set your mind at rest. Where's this mysterious leather bag that Sylvia's supposed to keep hidden?"

"Upstairs, in her closet. But—you wouldn't *dare!*" Lola Mills was suddenly cold sober.

"Your son and his wife are out for the evening. Now is the time. And I'll venture to bet that the bag contains only keepsakes of her childhood, or perhaps old family photographs and dance programs or something equally harmless. And I want your promise that if I'm right you'll stop trying to play the serpent in this Eden of theirs."

"But you don't understand!" cried Mrs. Mills as she led the way up the stair. "Nothing in the world would make me happier than to have Donny safely, happily married. But he was tired of the nice girls in his own set before he was twenty. He got mixed up with an awful girl in the Village who wrote bad poetry to be read aloud to the music of a threeman orchestra, and then there was that Mexican lady bullfighter, and I had to buy off that dancer from Cairo . . . But *this?*"

They came into a large bedroom, designed as a man's room but now showing a considerable overlay of feminine frippery. There were books—expensive, beautifully bound, esoteric: Mirabeau, Verlaine, Huysmans. There was a massive hi-fi set, its records running largely to "progressive" jazz and atonal, Oriental stuff. But both books and records were now almost snowed under with copies of *Playbill* and *Theater Arts.*

Lola Mills was trying to find a key that would fit the closet. "Try your own," suggested Miss Withers. And it worked, after some jiggling. Then, from behind a mountain of brand-new feminine apparel, from the darkest recesses of the cubicle, the two women lugged out a worn, very heavy leather case and placed it on the bed.

"You'll notice that she's scraped most of the labels off, but you can still see most of the word 'Melbourne,' " Mrs. Mills pointed out accusingly.

"The girl admits having traveled in Australia." Miss Withers squinted at the lock, then attacked it cautiously, using a bent bobby-pin. "Mustn't leave any scratches," she pointed out. "Now if I can only—*there!*"

The case suddenly flew upon, its contents spread out before them. "Just as I said!" announced the schoolteacher with heartfelt relief. "Nothing but a lot of old scrapbooks and newspapers."

But then they looked a little more closely. . . .

"It's happened!" was Miss Withers's greeting to the Inspector as he arrived at Centre Street next morning.

"Not a murder? *Who? Where?*"

"A man named Paul Hykes, in a suburb of Sydney, Australia, almost five years ago. I'd have phoned and got you up in the middle of the night to come down here, only I knew that probably you couldn't get Australia on the phone at that hour, so—"

"I don't want to get Australia on the phone at any hour!" The veteran policeman sat himself heavily down behind his desk. "Don't come at me so fast with all this before I've even had coffee! Hildegarde, what have you got into?"

"Believe it or not, Lola Mills seems to have been perfectly justified in her suspicions. Poor woman. I had to call her doctor for a sedative, and then—"

"And you left her in that condition, *with my gun?*"

"Oh, never mind your old gun. Oscar, we burgled the lock of Sylvia's mysterious bag. From now on just call me Pandora!" And then she went on to tell him everything in detail.

"You mean to tell me that girl's bag was crammed with press clippings from Australian newspapers about some old murder case?"

"Yes. *And* the pistol, of course. A Korean war souvenir, of Chinese make. But the clippings were all about the murder by slow poison of a wealthy, retired sheep-man named Hykes, and the subsequent trial of his cook-housekeeper for the killing. Her name was Mullen—Sylvia Mullen."

"*Sylvia?*"

" 'Who is Sylvia, what is she. . . ?' as the poet sang. I don't suppose you know anything about the case, but I saw enough in the scrapbooks to see that it must have been something of a *cause célèbre* down on the other side of the world. The Mullen girl, only twenty at the time, expected to inherit in her employer's will. There seems to have been a good deal of public sympathy for her, as there often is when the accused is young and attractive."

"She was acquitted?"

"I didn't get to read that far. Lola Mills was practically in hysterics, and I was afraid that Sylvia and Donny would come home and catch us in the act. As it was, I had to spend the night with the poor woman, and the young couple didn't come home at all. Or at least not until after I'd made Lola some coffee this morning and deposited her at her antique shop."

Oscar Piper was very grave. "And to think that I gave Mrs. Mills the brush-off. I don't suppose there's the slightest doubt that the girl is the Australian poisoner? Any press photos?"

"Just one." She handed him a newsclip of an enlarged snapshot, not improved by newspaper processing, showing a girl in shirt and dungarees, and wearing large earrings. He scowled at it.

"Not much better than the one from Hawaii," admitted Miss Withers. "But there *is* a resemblance, allowing for the years, some dieting, and a smarter hairdo. Maybe if your lab would blow the pictures up big—"

He nodded. "You're right. I've got to call Sydney. If Sylvia Mullen was found guilty and executed, or if she's in prison somewhere, then okay. But if she got off, changed her last name, and sneaked out of the country—"

"And assumed the identity of a young actress named Sally Burris—we musn't forget that angle."

"Yes. This may be murder on murder, with one more to go. Poisoners almost always repeat, if they get off the first time. Okay, here goes."

He picked up the phone, but it developed that all the radio-telephone circuits in the Pacific were fouled up by sunspots, and there would be at least a considerable delay.

"Then cable!" commanded the schoolteacher. "Remember, Sylvia and Donny have plane tickets for seven o'clock tonight. And if she once gets him out of the country—"

So the official query went out, addressed to a Chief Inspector of the New South Wales C.I.D.

"And while we're waiting, you could check on passports," Miss Withers prodded hopefully. The Inspector objected that the girl wouldn't need a passport traveling from Hawaii to the United States. "But Oscar, she would on arriving in *Guatemala*."

There was no record of a passport issued to a Sylvia Burris. But a passport had been issued four days ago to a Sylvia Mills.

"With that, they can go anywhere!" Oscar Piper snapped. "Sylvia will have Donald Mills to herself down in one of the banana republics, where they never heard of a medical examiner, an autopsy, or even extradition!"

And the minutes ticked by—with deadline getting closer and closer.

Then, just as they were about to send out for their third jug of coffee, came Australia's answer. Sylvia Mullen had stood trial before the Assizes, and the jury had disagreed. Indictment finally nolle prossed by the DPP. Failure to convict due to disagreement by forensic chemists about the poison, thought to be derived from a weed the natives called "pituri." In accordance with the laws of the Commonwealth, all pictures and fingerprints of the accused had been destroyed on her release. Present whereabouts unknown.

"I knew it in my bones!" said Miss Withers.

"Of which you have a complete set!" muttered the Inspector, quite ungallantly.

"This is no time for flattery, Oscar. You could send out a broadcast to have Sylvia arrested and held—"

"On what charge? We've no proof, even if we're morally sure that she murdered this Hykes, did away with Sally Burris, and now has her sights set for Donald Mills!"

"Oh, dear. And they did seem such a loving couple."

"Sylvia loves Donald Mills like a snake loves a bird," retorted Oscar Piper. "Did his mother tell you that night right after the ceremony Sylvia got him to write a new will, and that he also made her his sole beneficiary?"

But the schoolteacher was studying the faded old newspaper photograph of the Australian Sylvia. "Imagine a girl having the bad taste to wear earrings with dungarees," she mused. "All the same, Oscar, I do wish you'd have somebody make an enlargement of this picture—the head, and especially the ear."

"Come off it! Even an amateur like you should know that Lombroso's theories about criminals having a special type of ear-lobe were exploded years ago!"

"I'm quite aware of that. I wasn't born yesterday."

"Nor day before yesterday, either! Oh, I get it. About the earring. But there's no reason to suppose the girl is wearing that same ornament after all these years, or even has it in her jewel case. You're grasping at straws—" Just then the phone rang, and he grabbed it eagerly. "It's Lola Mills," he said out of the side of his mouth—as if the shrill feminine accents did not echo halfway across the office. It was a very one-sided conversation, which he ended only by promising to call back. "More trouble," he sighed. "Mrs. Mills says she went back to the apartment at lunchtime and found that Donny and Sylvia had been there and gone, bag and baggage."

"*The* bag, too?"

"Yes. Not even a tender good-bye note from her son. The woman's desperate. I guess I ought to have her locked up, for her own protection."

"Thank heaven she doesn't know when and where they're leaving."

"She does. I guess she called all the airlines."

"Then I imagine," said the schoolteacher thoughtfully, "that Mama will make a point of being out at the airport to say good-bye—and not with bon voyage flowers."

Oscar Piper threw a perfectly good cigar into the wastebasket. "There's too many loose guns knocking around in this case! I've half a mind to have everybody picked up and charged with Sullivan Law violation."

"Which publicity should make the Commissioner very happy, to say nothing of your having to admit that one of the guns was stolen right out from under your nose."

"Yeah, that damn gun. I'm going to call Lola Mills and order her to bring it in . . ." But nobody answered at the Mills apartment. Nor was Lola Mills at her antique shop, though a clerk said he would be *delighted* to take a message. . . .

The Inspector started to give him one, being pushed beyond his strength.

"Oscar, you should have your mouth washed out with soap," said the schoolteacher as she headed out of the office. "I'll see you at the airport, if not before."

"Last call! All passengers for Pan-American Airlines Flight Twelve, Mexico City and Guatemala City, now loading at Gate Three," came the booming, impersonal voice of the public address system, echoing hollowly through the dingy stone vaults of the air terminal at Idlewild—so-called because it is neither idle nor wild.

Inspector Oscar Piper waited helplessly beside a pillar, chewing one cigar after another into bits. He had arrived late because of a traffic foulup on the Parkway. No sign of Hildegarde anywhere, no sign of Lola Mills. And no sign of the young couple, either—at least, of a couple who fitted the schoolteacher's somewhat sketchy descriptions: a young man in a bowler hat and Cheviot topcoat with a girl who looked a little like Vampira. Yet they could be anybody—almost all the passengers now boarding the vast, super-science-fiction jet that was poised outside in the dismal drift of rain seemed to be couples, half covered by umbrellas. . . .

And the clock ticked inexorably away.

Finally Oscar Piper went outside and pressed his way to the wire barrier, checking on his aides. He had six plainclothes detectives, two of them women, planted at strategic intervals. And a lot of good that would do him.

Mechanics were giving a last minute touchup to the plane, the last of the baggage was being stowed in its cavernous belly, and the cargo hatch was slammed tight. And then, out of the blue, he heard his name called out over the loudspeaker. "Will Inspector Piper please report to the Security Office on the mezzanine? Will Inspector Piper . . ." He raced inside and up the stairs.

Meanwhile Donald Mills and his adored Sylvia, who had come aboard separately, each wearing a raincoat, with the girl in slacks and a mannish hat, settled themselves back comfortably in two forward seats and caught the first relaxing breath of freedom. "I told you Mother wouldn't pull anything," Donny whispered. "Didn't I?"

"It wasn't your mother I was so worried about," the girl whispered back. "It's that Withers woman, Donny, she has eyes just like a wombat back home, a *digger's* eyes." She broke off at the pained look on her husband's face. "Oh, there I go again! I'm sorry, dear."

"For God's sweet sake, will you remember you're Sylvia Burris Mills, and that you were born on an American ship at sea and went to school in Hawaii?" he said intensely. "Never mind the past—it's over and done with! Darling, you *must* remember—"

He broke off as a shadow loomed overhead. "Mr. and Mrs. Mills?" The speaker wore an airlines uniform. "I wonder if you'd mind stepping off for a moment? Some mistake about your seats . . ." They froze. Yes, they would mind very much, but it was an order, not a request.

Up in the Security Office a troubled airlines official was shaking his head. "Inspector, I can't hold that flight any longer. Not unless you show me a warrant."

"We can show you more than that, young man," snapped Miss Hildegarde Withers, who now swept into the room like a ship under full sail—with Lola Mills in tow. "You wait right there in the chair," the schoolteacher told her.

"And say nothing!"

Lola Mills nodded and sat down, surprisingly meek.

Miss Withers faced the airlines man. "If you give orders to send that plane off, I'll plant myself right in front of the nose and defy you to run over me!"

"She would, too," said the Inspector dryly, and the official mopped his forehead. Just at that moment Donald Mills and Sylvia were ushered into the room, the young man avoiding his mother's glance.

"I demand to know what this is all about!" Donny blustered. "What possible charges--?"

"Oh, be quiet!" the schoolteacher snapped. She caught the Inspector's arm and whispered to him fiercely. "Oscar, you'll have to trust me! Have I ever given you a—a bum steer?"

"Yes," he answered truthfully.

"But my average! Oscar, this is terribly important, and much bigger things than the letter of the law are involved. I think I have it solved. Just have the three of them sent into the inner office to us, one at a time. . . ."

He hesitated—and was lost. Through his mind flashed memories of the dozens of times the intrepid, meddlesome old thresher had in the past swept aside the chaff and come to the wheat. . . . And Oscar Piper nodded against his better judgment. He gave the orders, and then followed her into the other office, a bare little cubicle with only a desk, a filing cabinet, and two chairs. Nobody wanted to sit down, anyway.

"Lola Mills first," said Miss Withers.

"Yeah. But how did you get hold of her?"

"Lay in wait for her at her apartment. I knew she'd want to change into something modish for what she had in mind, so she'd have to go home before coming. Show her these enlargements, Oscar—and explain what they mean." She produced blowups of Sylvia Mullen's undisputed snapshot reproduced in the old Australian newspaper, and of the other. "Notice the ears, Oscar!"

And then, at long last, he saw what she was driving at. "Judas Priest in a handbasket!" And his manner was very grave as Mrs. Mills came into the room. "Here is the evidence, ma'am," he said gently. "Notice the ears?"

Lola Mills saw, and nodded slowly. Her eyes began to fill with mascara-stained tears, and she went silently out.

Donald Mills was next, his face dark with sullen fury, his eyes fearful. He had had about enough, he said.

"There is very little more," the schoolteacher told him. "It is out of my hands now, and a matter for the police. The Inspector just wants to ask you one question. Oscar?"

"Mr. Mills," asked Piper quietly, "have you ever seen the contents of your wife's dispatch case?"

There was a silence. Then "Yes!" cried Donny Mills. "You mean those old clippings? Well, why shouldn't my wife be interested in a big murder trial that took place when she was visiting in Australia? The similarity of first names, and of appearance and all that—why, my wife's always been interested in the theater, so she collected background material. . . ." His voice trailed away as if he didn't expect anybody really to believe him.

"But do you actually know—" began the Inspector.

"I said *one* question, Oscar!" Miss Withers cut in. The Inspector felt the grip of her fingers on his arm.

Donny Mills, more bewildered than ever, turned and went out.

"But Hildegarde, we're supposed to be clearing up this mystery, and you won't let me—"

"Get Sylvia herself in here," said the schoolteacher. "Oscar, you've got to leave this to me, or it still can blow up in our faces. Go out and keep an eye on Lola Mills—I don't want her talking to her son—at least, not yet. Though he probably won't believe her, anyway."

"I hope you know that you're doing, because I don't!" said Oscar Piper.

But he left, and in a moment Sylvia walked in, like Joan of Arc marching to the stake. The girl stood stiff as a ramrod, and her lips were pressed tight together.

"Well, what are you waiting for, applause?" Miss Withers smiled enigmatically. "Fancy yourself as an actress, do you? Well, I *know!*"

Sylvia's eyes were like two burnt holes in a blanket. "What are you going to do about it, then?"

"I haven't made up my mind. It's not as if the Australian police wanted Sylvia Mullen for anything. She was released, and she disappeared. Of course, if the other Sylvia—the one from Hawaii—were to turn up some day—?"

"She won't!" said Sylvia. "But—but how did you know?"

"It just occurred to me to have two pictures enlarged—the one of Sylvia Mullen and the one of Sally Burris. The shape of the human ear is one feature that never changes. And you haven't the right ears to be the Australian Sylvia."

The girl hesitated. "Did—did you give me away to Donny?"

Miss Withers shook her head.

"Oh, thank you!" cried the girl, the ice finally breaking. "I do love him! It started as a joke, aboard ship. And then I began to see that Donny was fascinated with the idea of being in love with a dangerous, glamorous poison-murderess! That's really all the hold I have on him, don't you see? He thinks that I'm Sylvia Mullen playing Sylvia Burris—*only he's got it the wrong way around!*"

"Hardly a firm foundation for a marriage, is it?"

"But I'm making him happy! I'm playing a lifetime role, for an audience of one! And I ought to be good at it—I really did sit in the courtroom at the trial to get the Mullen girl down pat, and I did play the lead in *Black Widow,* the play based on her life that got laughed off the boards in one week in Melbourne. But now I'm going over great!"

"Far be it from me," said Miss Withers wistfully, "to come between a woman and her natural prey. I never quite snagged a man, myself. So be off with you!"

The girl gave her an impulsive hug and ran out of the room. And a few minutes later the two best friends and favorite sparring partners stood arm in arm at the barrier and watched the big jet soar up into the night.

"Imagine their life together," said Oscar Piper dryly. "Every time Donny Mills fancies she's angry at him, he'll taste his soup the way porcupines make love."

"And how's that, Oscar?"

"*Very* carefully!"

"Some men like to live dangerously," the schoolteacher told him. "And speaking of danger, that mother of his has gone home. I hope she's gone for keeps, because I don't like good-looking rich widows hanging around you. And if you're worried about your trophy, I gave her a chance to save her face—she slipped it into my handbag when we were coming over in the taxi. Here it is, good as new."

But in taking the gun from her capacious carry-all, her finger quite by accident caught the trigger. There was a flash of flame, a fearful blast, and the screaming whine of a bullet losing itself in the sky. Before a crowd could gather, the Inspector seized the gun and ran hell-bent for the exit. But Miss Hildegarde Withers beat him by a nose.

The Return of Hildegarde Withers

Miss Hildegarde Withers knew that something was afoot as soon as she came into the Inspector's outer office and saw that his door was closed. It was a chill wet December morning, and unwilling to go back into the drizzle or to interrupt one of her friend's official "conversations" with some unlucky suspect, the spinster school-ma'am sat down and proceeded to cool her sensible heels.

She pricked up her somewhat prominent ears as the sound of excited feminine voices came faintly through, and then the door opened and Inspector Oscar Piper ushered out of his office three attractively dressed young ladies who were strange visitors indeed for this center of the grimmest police activity. They were very young, alike as three peas in a pod except that the girl in the seal jacket was a little younger and prettier and more distraught than her companions, one in civet and one in squirrel.

"Last door at the end of the hall," the Inspector said to his departing guests, and then held the door for Miss Withers.

"Well, Oscar," Hildegarde observed tartly, eyeing a little mound of red-smeared cigarette ends in the midst of his cigar butts, "your clientele seems to be changing its tone."

The Inspector grinned sheepishly. "They got in here by accident. Some sort of a hysterical story about their dancing teacher disappearing up in Carnegie Hall last night. Seems this woman, name of Carla Monterey, popped off into thin air, leaving her clothes on a chair. She even left a hot shower running in the bath—to steam a velvet dress, so the kids say. I sent them up to the Bureau of Missing Persons."

"And just what good will that do?"

"Not much. The Sergeant will fill out a blue slip for the file."

"But Oscar—" There was a glint in Miss Withers' eye.

"Nothing in it for Homicide. We got rules, you know."

"*Have*, not got! Fiddlesticks! Rules are made to be broken. What's the rest of their story?"

A little nettled, Oscar Piper went on: "Just that they are all students in the school of this Monterey woman. Sometimes she books herself and her advanced pupils for professional engagements. Last night they were having a late rehearsal, which ended in some sort of row between the Monterey woman and her manager, an Argentine calling himself Emile

Valentine. Valentine, yet! Anyway, this gaucho character and the girls went out for supper, and when some of them came back to pick up a handbag that had been forgotten, the dancing dame was gone. Studio's on the twelfth floor, and the elevator man said he hadn't taken her down. This morning she didn't answer her phone, so the girls really got worried and came down here. I figure it's just another case of artistic tantrums. Ten to one the woman will show up before the day is out."

"So she walked out and left a dress to steam," said Miss Withers thoughtfully. "You might have gone up there and looked around."

"I'm up to my ears. But if you're so all-fired interested—"

"I believe I will!" decided Miss Withers, rising suddenly. "School closed yesterday for the holidays, and I've had my Christmas shopping done since Labor Day—"

"Naturally!" said the Inspector, but she was already starting out of the door, umbrella grasped in a firm hand, looking like some ungainly bird of prey.

She was lucky enough to catch the three disconsolate maidens on the stairs. "The man says that a person isn't missing until after forty-eight hours!" the girl in civet complained to Miss Withers, after that lady had introduced herself as practically a member of the Force. "He says it's up to the immediate family to make a report, and that she'll probably show up all by herself."

"I can well imagine what *they* think," the schoolteacher said. "The official mind! Well, let's do a little sleuthing ourselves. And while we're in the taxi, let me hear all about it. Start at the beginning, go on until you come to the end, and then stop."

"Said the Queen to Alice," spoke up the girl in sealskin, and the older woman beamed at her for recognizing the quotation. This one turned out to be Lucille Jeffers, and the others were Sally and Babs Dell. The name Lucille Jeffers meant little to Miss Withers, who did not follow the adventures of this year's debutantes in the society pages.

Lucille Jeffers, speaking a mixture of finishing school and slang, obligingly began at the beginning as the four rode northward from Centre Street. "We were all working our tails off at the studio last night, Sally and Babs and I and some others, rehearsing. The *señorita* had been teaching us the swellest Andalusian peasant dance—she had promised us a long while ago that if we caught on to it she'd let us do it with her as part of her professional act at hotels here during the holidays. But—"

"Everything was going *beautifully*," cut in squirrel-clad Sally, who spoke in breathless italics. "Until Mr. Valentine came *bursting* in about eleven—"

"With a telegram offering the *señorita* a chance to bring her group and make a New Year's Eve appearance at the Corals Hotel in Miami Beach," finished her sister Babs, a high soprano.

"I understand that started an argument?" Miss Withers pressed.

"Well, sort of," continued Lucille Jeffers. "Because without even asking her, he'd gone ahead and telegraphed an acceptance. Of course, all us girls are crazy to dance professionally. But most of us know darn well that our families won't let us go that far from home, and some of the others wouldn't give up their New Year's dates here in town."

"All but you, darling," cut in Babs Dell.

"All but me, because my mother's in Europe and my aunt doesn't care. Besides, I'm crazy to take that trip! Anyway, the *señorita* was furious with the girls because most of us wouldn't go, and furious with Valentine for getting carried away with the offer and wiring an okay. He wanted her to go alone, then, and just do the solos, or perhaps work just me into the act, but she wouldn't listen.

"And Valentine argued with her while we were changing back into our clothes, and we could hear them yelling at each other. So he left her there in her bathroom where she had the water running, and took us all out to eat."

"Carla usually has supper with us when we dance late," explained Lucille. "But last night she wouldn't come. So Valentine said good night to her and we all said good night and she just slammed the door."

"She didn't really slam the door. I think she just threw a shoe or something—" put in Sally.

"But after you ate, you did go back there?"

"Yes, because I'd left my purse," Lucille Jeffers explained. "Emile went with me, because Carnegie is dark and scary that late. The studio door was locked, the lights were all on, and the water was still running in the shower where the dress was being steamed. But she was gone."

"You're sure she wasn't hiding somewhere in the studio?"

"Where could she hide? Emile and I went all through the place together, even looking into the closets. She hadn't taken the elevator, and she knows none of the other permanent tenants in the building, and I don't believe she'd walk down ten flights of stairs."

"What about windows?" demanded Miss Withers.

"They open out above the street, with no fire escapes. There's one from the bathroom onto an air shaft, but it's tiny." Lucille shook her head. "Her practice clothes were right there on the floor, and I think all her street dresses were in the closets, although I can't be sure because the place is so full of costumes. Anyway, it was well after midnight, so we turned off the water in the bathroom and put out the lights and Emile took me home. This morning we girls got together, and we decided maybe something dreadful had happened—"

"*Babs and I* were the ones who thought so!" corrected Sally.

"Well, I thought so too," insisted Lucille. "Only if Carla had wanted to go away for a little while, I couldn't help thinking how mad she'd be if we turned in a false alarm!"

"I feel it in my bones," said the schoolteacher, "that this is *not* a false alarm."

"You mean—you mean *suicide?*" Sally gasped.

The taxi drew up before the entrance to the studios of Carnegie Hall, one door east of the venerable portico beneath which three generations of music lovers had stood in line for symphony tickets. There was even a line there now, but the three girls and the inquisitive schoolteacher pushed past and made their way into the little raised foyer.

Here an ancient and solitary colored man dozed inside an ancient and solitary elevator. They entered, and it rose beneath them, haltingly and painfully, past one floor, then another. . . . Miss Withers was somewhat surprised to notice that the sixth and eighth floors came on the same level, with the seventh above them!

"Buildin's powerful old," explained the venerable operator as he noted her surprise. "Levels sorta scrambled here, and easy to get yo'self lost in." The steel cage faltered to a stop, and Miss Withers followed the girls out on what she hoped was really the twelfth floor. Then she stopped to ask a question. "No, ma'am, ain't seen Miss Carla this mornin', not hide nor hair."

They set off down a narrow hall, turned right, then left, then right again, went down three steps and came up seven, and arrived finally at a gateway and grille beyond which was a thick oak door bearing the sign: *Carla Monterey—Home of the Danse Espagnole.* Lucille fumbled for a moment in the maze of Moorish wrought iron, and withdrew a key. "She showed us where she keeps it," the girl explained as she unlocked the door.

Miss Withers found herself in a gaily tiled hallway, hung with shawls, ancient armor, and professional photographs. At one side was a mammoth Spanish writing desk, its drawers all awry. The air was thick and stuffy, as if all the windows had been closed for a long time. The girls called out, "Carla? Carla, you here?" But there was no answer.

Walking on tiptoe, the four females passed through the foyer and came into the wide expanse of the main practice hall, a long high room with a parquet floor, unfurnished except for practice barres along the wall and a battered Victrola. At the right, doors opened into a smaller practice room and dressing rooms for the students. Directly across was a curtained doorway leading to the dancer's private apartment.

They came next to a living room, bright with scarves and shawls and Spanish art. It was also a bedroom, for against one wall was the bulk of an old-fashioned Murphy bed, the doors of two closets overflowing with costumes, shoes, and the like, as well as a small bathroom and a kitchenette bright with blue oilcloth. It was all hushed and silent as a tomb.

This was where the missing dancer had last been seen. Now only pictures of her remained—a great many pictures, some of them in the styles of yesteryear. From each wall Carla Monterey stared down, eyeing the intruders with the imperious scowling smile of the Spanish danseuse.

Miss Withers ignored the pictures and went at once to the bathroom, to study the velvet dress. It was of fine, plum-colored velvet but was sadly ripped at the seams. The window onto the air shaft, she discovered, was barely large enough to get her head through but she peered out of it and down, seeing nothing of importance.

Nowhere were there any indications of bloodshed or violence, although even at that moment the schoolteacher would have given odds that Carla Monterey was dead. Yet if the students and this Mr. Valentine had all left together, with Carla alive and in the midst of having a tantrum. . .

The girls, back in the studio, were chattering excitedly. There was no sign anywhere of the clothes that had been scattered around on the floor and on the chairs last night!

"Then she *has* come back!" cried Sally happily.

"Yes, of course she has!" Lucille agreed, in a voice totally without conviction.

Miss Withers was prowling about, apparently aimlessly. It seemed strange to her that there was not a single picture of a man anywhere in the place. "Was there no love interest?" she demanded. *"Cherchez l'homme,* you know."

"Not Miss Monterey!" said Babs loyally.

Lucille Jeffers started to say "No," but Sally interrupted. "Not since Emile!" she said firmly.

"*Since* Emile? But wasn't—isn't Mr. Valentine still around?"

"I guess they *used* to be lovers," Lucille said, with weary sophistication. "But they broke up months ago, and decided to be just friends. He stayed on as her manager, which isn't odd if you know show business."

Miss Withers looked thoughtful for a moment, then led the way back toward the entrance. In spite of her hunch, this case seemed to be falling to pieces. If only she could get her teeth into something!

The hall door suddenly opened, and a young and dapper gentleman stepped into the foyer, a key in his hand. He was well, almost exquisitely dressed, in a Chesterfield, pearl-gray Homburg, and spats. No, they were suede-topped shoes—but in Miss Withers's book that was just as bad.

"Oh, excuse me!" he said, his handsome face blank. "I didn't—"

"Oh, Emile!" cried Lucille. "Mr. Valentine—this is Miss Withers, *of the police*. She's going to help us find Carla."

"Of the police?" echoed the Argentinian. Then he smiled, showing beautiful teeth. It was a warm smile, and Miss Withers found herself changing her first impression of him. This was no gigolo, in spite of the long sideburns. He walked swiftly toward them, with hand outstretched.

But he was not trying to shake hands. "If you are of the police, madam," he said in a voice almost completely free of accent, "then it is right that you should see this." He extended an envelope. "I found this last night here in Carla's desk," he explained, "when Miss Jeffers and I were looking around. I opened it, naturally—though at the time I didn't feel like showing it to anybody." He gave Lucille Jeffers a pleading look.

To the police was written in a scrawling, childish hand across the envelope. *If anything happens to me, arrest Emile Valentine*, was the message inside. It was unsigned.

"That's Carla's writing, all right!" said Babs, looking over the schoolteacher's shoulder.

Miss Withers drew a deep breath. "Well, Mr. Valentine?"

He bowed with resignation. "I confess I toyed with the idea of destroying this. But do not credit me too highly for turning it in. Knowing Carla, I would guess that she left others around. She—she is a very peculiar woman." He sighed.

Miss Withers put the letter in her handbag. She found herself far beyond her depth, and the three confused, frightened girls gave her no moral support. "I suppose you must arrest me?" the man asked her, almost cheerfully.

The schoolteacher shook her head. "I'm not exactly a policewoman," she confessed. "And I don't see any real evidence that a crime has been committed. Perhaps it is just that somebody wanted to make it look that way!" She tapped her teeth with the handle of her umbrella. "It seems to me that we ought to be looking for Miss Monterey, here in the building."

"Why don't we ask at all the neighboring studios?" suggested Lucille Jeffers eagerly.

"And we shall," the schoolteacher pronounced. "I'll go to the right and you go to the left. Perhaps Babs and Sally will do the same on the floor above. See if Miss Monterey is there, or if they heard or noticed anything unusual last night."

"Could I perhaps help?" Mr. Valentine said hopefully. "I could take the floor below. After all, I have more reason than any of you to find Carla now!" And Miss Withers agreed with him.

The ringing of doorbells began in earnest. During the next fifteen minutes the schoolteacher managed to interrupt one class in adult tap dancing, four singing lessons, one luncheon party, and got an elderly male violin teacher out of bed and out of temper. And everywhere she drew a blank. There was only one studio left, a studio entered from another hall but presumably abutting on the missing dancer's quarters. Here lived two maidens of seventy-odd, surrounded by potted plants and Siamese cats. It took Miss Withers almost no time at all to win the confidence of the kittens, and then of her hostesses.

She could hear, from where she sat on a sofa, a cacophony of piano lessons, voice culture, and stringed instruments through the thin walls, which gave her some hope. "Of course you ladies heard the commotion next door last night?" she fished.

"Why, we always go to bed about nine—"

"But you know how difficult it is to sleep as one gets older—"

Miss Withers sniffed, but let that go by. "What *did* you hear?"

"There was nothing unusual, except that about eleven—"

"Dear, it was nearer twelve!"

"Between eleven and twelve we heard the girls leave the dance place next door. . . ." The old lady shook her head. "The Monterey studio, and if you ask me that woman is no better than she should be, with men calling at all hours, and—"

"There hasn't been a man there, at least not late at night, these last few weeks," corrected the other. "And if you ask me, it wasn't so quiet last night even after the girls and the man left. I could hear the Monterey woman playing castanets."

"It wasn't castanets, it was those Cuban gourds filled with shot—mariachis, I think they call them . . . or do I mean maracas?"

"You're both positive it was something, though?" The little old ladies were positive. The sounds hadn't lasted long, and then later someone had gone through the studio calling "Carla"—a girl and a man, they thought.

"We don't usually hear anything from in there," they agreed. "Just voices, and never clear enough so we can make out the words, really."

"Too bad, isn't it?" said Miss Withers, and left in deep thought. For a moment the mystery had seemed to be clearing, and now she was faced with a fog even denser than before.

She returned to the dance studio, although there was something uncanny and unwholesome about it, something that made her feel like walking softly and speaking in a whisper. Perhaps that is why she opened the door silently when she entered.

Then she froze. Across the main hall the drapes of the studio doorway were open, the tall dressing-mirror outlining a distant but distinct picture. There was lovely Lucille Jeffers. As Miss Withers watched, the girl's coat slipped from her shoulders, revealing her slender body wrapped in a man's arms—the arms of Emile Valentine. Their lips met in an interminable kiss—a kiss obviously not meant to be seen by anybody else in the world—and Miss Withers backed hastily out into the hall and leaned against the grille.

So that was the secret she had sensed in the depths of Miss Lucille Jeffers's dark eyes!

The schoolteacher's meditations were shortly thereafter interrupted by Sally and Babs Dell, who announced clearly and loudly that they had discovered a violinist upstairs who had heard someone beating on a drum last night, around midnight. But that was the total of their findings.

With the two girls, Miss Withers went back into the studio, making sure to make plenty of noise. They found Lucille smoking a cigarette and curled up in a chair, while Valentine walked nervously up and down. Both announced that their searches had drawn a blank, which did not surprise the schoolma'am to any great degree. She looked at her watch, and found that the afternoon had slipped away. The Dell girls hinted that they were expected home, and that they had dates. They were obviously fed up with playing sleuth.

"Run along," Miss Withers told them. She reached for her bag and umbrella. Strangely enough, while she had purposely left them with the umbrella handle at right angles to the monogram on her bag, it now lay parallel! It was an old trick, one she had successfully used with her pupils, and she felt suddenly elated. She must be getting close, or someone would not have been interested in her bag!

She rode down in the elevator with the others, and in the lower hall stopped to scribble her phone number on a number of cards. "If any of you hears anything, please call me," she instructed them. "I have a strong notion that this evening will bring some word of Carla."

Lucille Jeffers gasped. "Then you don't think she's dead?"

"Yes and no," said the schoolteacher, and summoned a taxi. Once alone in the cab, she opened her handbag, but as she had guessed, the envelope marked *To the Police* was gone.

Across the table in their favorite spaghetti joint Miss Withers was consulting with her old friend and sparring partner, the Inspector. Painstakingly, point by point, she gave him the developments in the case. "Of course, I haven't the *slightest* proof of foul play."

"You're always leaping to half-baked conclusions," said Oscar Piper. "I suppose you think this sheik Valentine lured her somewhere and bumped her off? But how? She was alive when they all left, and besides, where's the body?"

"Don't put words in my mouth, Oscar!"

He jammed his cigar into the ashtray. "They'd be superfluous. Wait! Suppose the Monterey dame took a runout powder down the stairs and left the note to throw suspicion on her former boy friend, hoping to get back at him? She could be hiding out—"

"But why? And you forget the sounds that came from the studio just after the others left her last night," the schoolteacher told him. "You forget the rips in the velvet dress, and the letter which Valentine produced and which someone snitched."

"Oh, that! I have a duplicate," the Inspector sprung on her. He showed her a long legal envelope, with a smaller one inside. "It came this afternoon. The law firm that sent it refused to talk. Same message as yours, only the Monterey woman signed this one."

She nodded. "Mr. Valentine was right, then."

"Perhaps you'd better let Homicide handle this, after all."

"Over my dead body!" Miss Withers had come to a decision. She wrote busily on the back of a menu for a moment, and handed it over.

Piper whistled. "Spanish dancer disappears," she had written. "Leaves poison pen letters attempting to implicate manager, but letters proved false by police investigation. Nation-wide search for Carla Monterey is on . . . You want me to try to plant this in the newspapers?"

"My reasons should be obvious, even to your limited intelligence."

"Flattery will get you nowhere. There's barely time to get this into the morning rags, but I'll try. It's your funeral." And neither of the two oddly assorted partners guessed how close to truth that was to be. . . .

Miss Withers went home, and waited for something to happen. Remembering the old story about the girl who had to take three baths on Saturday night before the phone would ring, she even tried that desperate experiment. Then she washed her hair, and gave it exactly one hundred strokes.

The early editions of the tabloid morning papers, she knew, came on the streets about 8:30 p.m., the *Herald-Trib* and *Times* somewhat later. The hands of the clock moved past ten, past ten-thirty, past eleven. . .

The phone rang. And there was the suave voice of Mr. Valentine. "Madam, you are a genius," he announced. "You were right! I just received a message from Carla!"

"'O my prophetic soul!'" quoted the schoolteacher. "Where are you now, young man?"

He barely hesitated. "I—I'm at Miss Jeffers's. I simply had to tell her the good news and show her the telegram. It was filed at Miami Beach, Florida, and it reads: SORRY CAUSED WORRY WILL EXPLAIN EVERYTHING WHEN I SEE YOU AM GOING AHEAD WITH ENGAGEMENT HERE PLEASE FOLLOW AT ONCE WITH COSTUMES AND LUCILLE IF SHE CAN COME and it's signed carlissima, which used to be her pet name, so I know it is genuine."

"Well, are you going to follow her instructions?"

"Why not? I'm still her manager. And I expect almost anything of an artiste like Carla."

"Naturally," Miss Withers said. "All's well that ends well. May I speak to Lucille Jeffers, please?"

"Hello!" came Lucille's vibrant young contralto. "Isn't it wonderful? It all must have been just a silly joke!"

"Silly, but hardly a joke. Well, I hope you enjoy your trip to Florida."

"Why—how did you know I was going to go?"

"I didn't, until just now," said Miss Withers sagely. "Good-bye."

She hustled into her coat, and ten minutes later was climbing the steps of Carnegie Hall again. A different Negro was on elevator duty, and he took her up to the twelfth floor. It was late, very late, but Miss Withers had no mercy at all. She pounded on the door of the two little old ladies until they and their cats all came to the door to see if the building was on fire or something.

"I just wanted to ask you," the schoolteacher demanded, "did you ever hear a Spanish dancer playing castanets on the stage? Or see anybody playing mariachis or marimbas or whatever they call those things you shake?"

Both of them shook their heads. "I thought so!" Miss Withers said softly, and leaving them convinced of her utter madness, she went resolutely back down the hall, pausing only a moment at the Carla Monterey studio to make sure that the place was dark, the door locked, and the key gone. But she had enough, at least to sleep on.

When she woke bright and early next morning she knew that, except for one important detail, the puzzle had been completed by her subconscious while she slept. She knew what she must do, but first there remained the necessity of toast and orange juice and coffee. As calmly as if she faced nothing worse than her usual classroom of students, Hildegarde Withers prepared and ate a leisurely meal.

Then she strode southward through the crisp December morning toward Fifty-seventh Street and the ancient, grimy magnificence of Carnegie Hall. She rode up to the twelfth floor, walked down the hall to the dance studio, and knocked confidently on the door. Inside there sounded a cheerful male voice: "Just a second!"—and then the door opened and she looked into the surprised and disappointed face of Emile Valentine.

"Oh, it's *you!*" he said.

"And you were expecting someone else? Miss Jeffers, I presume?"

He nodded, mopping his sweaty face. "She promised to come down early and help me pack the costumes." He nodded toward the two great wardrobe trunks in the studio ahead of them. "I had the elevator man bring them up from the basement," he continued, "and the packing is about finished. But a man is never any good at this sort of thing."

"I certainly wouldn't trust any man I know to touch my clothes," Hildegarde admitted. "Perhaps I can help?" One trunk was closed, and the other stood gaping amid a litter of scarves, castanets, high-heeled slippers and brilliantly colored silks and satins.

"You're very kind, but I'm just about done," said Valentine. "Excuse my appearance, but it is a big job to pack forty costumes."

"What? Good heavens, how long is this Florida engagement to last?"

Valentine stared at her, as if he would very much like to ask why she had come, and why she was interested in other people's business. Then: "It's for New Year's Eve, and the dates before and after," he said slowly. "But the *señorita* is temperamental. She never decides until almost curtain time what fits her mood, so she usually takes her entire wardrobe along. Only this time, adding insult to injury, she leaves me to pack it."

He turned to stuff a wad of chiffon into a trunk drawer. Then, as Miss Withers prepared to ask the question that was foremost in her thoughts, he turned, his face a mask of puzzlement. "Tell me, as one who knows of detective matters, is there any way of making sure this telegram is not a hoax?"

Miss Withers found the wind blown from her sails. Slowly she took the message he offered her. It was a genuine Western Union form, she could see that. Strips of yellow paper from an automatic typewriter were pasted across the page. According to the data at the top, the message had been filed in Miami Beach at 10:15 last evening. It was just as it had been read to her over the phone. She scowled at it thoughtfully.

"I'd feel foolish if I carted the costumes all the way down there and found that Carla had skipped again," he said. "I tried to phone the hotel, but she isn't registered."

"The telegram certainly looks genuine," Miss Withers told him. "But young man, tell me something. Carla Monterey was prodigal with money, extravagant like most artists, was she not?"

He shook his head. "She was not! Carla appreciated the value of a dollar—anybody who knew her will tell you that."

"I see," said the schoolteacher. She roamed idly about the place as he continued packing. She fumbled with the telephone, straightened a picture, looked at herself in the tall mirror, and then sat down on a piano stool, sensing that the young man would very much like her to go but dared not suggest it.

He finished the second trunk, and slammed it shut. Then he looked impatiently at his watch.

"The girl seems to be late," suggested Miss Withers.

He nodded. Then he came over to the piano. "You're not really satisfied that the case is settled, are you?" he challenged. "What's on your mind? Is there anything I can do before the expressmen come for the trunks—they're due here at ten."

Miss Withers consulted her watch, and then told a bare-faced lie. "Why, it's almost ten-thirty now!"

Valentine looked again at his watch, shook it, then listened to it. He turned toward the electric clock on the wall of the practice hall. Its hands pointed to twenty after ten; Miss Withers had seen to that detail.

"Got to phone!" cried Mr. Valentine. He hurried to the instrument, dialed furiously, and then emitted a string of soft Latin oaths. "The thing's dead!" he announced. "And we've got to make that noon train. I must call the express office, and that—that girl. Would you mind waiting here and watching things until I get back? If Lucille comes—"

"I wouldn't mind at all." Miss Withers gave him time to get to the elevator, and then began a survey of the place. To her surprise, the closets really *were* empty! The man actually had packed all forty costumes—which spoiled her hypothesis. She poked at the trunks, but they were both tightly locked.

Then heavy knocks came on the door, and the expressmen came in trundling heavy truck rollers. They seized the trunks before the agitated schoolteacher could make up her mind. "Okay, lady," said one. He shoved two tickets into her hand, and they departed, their rumbling slowly diminishing down the hall.

Things were going too fast for Miss Withers, and in the wrong directions. She made a circuit of the place again, noticing that the kitchenette door was open. The place looked cheerless, but perhaps that was because the bright oilcloth had been stripped from walls and dining alcove, leaving only rough bare boards. She came back into the foyer, with an eye on the phone. Suddenly the door opened.

Miss Withers whirled defensively, and looked into the youthful, worried face of Lucille Jeffers, dressed for traveling and carrying a suitcase in her hand. "What are you doing here?" the girl demanded. "What's happened? He *hasn't* left without me!"

"I think he just went to phone." Miss Withers was trembling with excitement, but she drew the girl in and closed the door. Then she ran across to the telephone, sliding her fingers along the cord to the point where a common pin had been inserted to short the connection (one of the little details she had attended to earlier) and removed it with a jerk. She lifted the receiver and was rewarded with a buzz. Hastily she dialed SPring 7-3100, while Lucille Jeffers waited with frightened eyes.

"Inspector Piper's office, and hurry!" she begged. Then—"Oscar! I'm in the studio at Carnegie Hall when I should be minding my own business. The fat is in the fire. Understand?" And she hung up, because Lucille was tugging at her sleeve.

"What's *happened?* What have you done to poor Emile?"

"That is beside the point. My dear, I've got to speak to you—"

"Speak nothing!" the girl exclaimed. "Haven't you eyes to see with? Don't you realize that this is all a frame-up, a plot to incriminate Emile? She *hated* him, I tell you. She didn't want him and she didn't want anybody else to have him. If she's dead, she killed herself to make him suffer, and if she isn't dead, then she's in hiding and hoping he'll be arrested!"

"If that is true," said Miss Withers gently, "there's a way to prove it. Suppose we open those trunks in the other room?"

"The trunks? They should have gone already! But if you think there's anything in them that will incriminate Emile, I'll show you! I'll open them myself, with a hammer!"

Miss Withers said, "Then never mind the trunks. Your offer relieved my mind, though." Somehow she had known that a girl who still liked *Alice in Wonderland* couldn't be mixed up in murder. "We haven't a moment to lose, child. You've got to get out of here."

"Not without *him!*"

"But you must! Do you care for him so terribly?"

Lucille Jeffers' young body was stiff as a ramrod. "Of course I love him! In three weeks I won't need my parent's consent, and we're going to be married!"

"Child, you don't know what you're saying." Miss Withers was saddened, but she did not soften. "You mustn't run away to Florida or anywhere with this man," she said.

"I won't believe a word you say against Emile!"

"But if you go, that will only play into the hands of whoever plotted this diabolical thing," she pointed out. "If you travel across a state line with Mr. Valentine, even in separate Pullmans, he can be arrested for violation of the Mann Act, and thus be doubly framed!"

The girl fell for it, hook, line and sinker. "Would anybody actually *do* a thing like that?"

"You'd be surprised at what some people are capable of doing. Trust me, Lucille, and let's get out of here!" Taking the bewildered girl by the arm, Miss Withers hurried her out of the studio and down the hall. Her carefully laid plans were all going to pieces. But to get out of this place was the first step.

Her thumb pressed the elevator button, and she held it there until the machine started up. Somewhere on a lower floor it halted, and she thought she heard a man's voice. "Can't you hurry?" she called down. For a moment nothing happened, and then the cables started going by again. At last the door clanged open, and Miss Withers pushed the girl through, then followed as the man in the uniform cap slammed the door shut.

"Down!" gasped the schoolteacher, and as the car started to drop she saw the face of the man at the controls, and gave a little cry.

"Emile!" cried Lucille Jeffers. "Darling, what in the world—?" She tried to embrace him, but he flung her out of his way.

"Trick me, would you?" Valentine screamed at Miss Withers. "Well, I tricked you right back by getting rid of the old fool who runs this elevator. Now you're going for a ride—"

Suddenly there were shouts echoing up the shaft, and the sound of running footsteps on the stairs. "Oscar!" screamed Miss Withers. But Valentine stopped the elevator so suddenly that both women were thrown to the floor; then it shot upward again. The girl had succeeded in fainting in a heap in the corner; Miss Withers would like very much to have followed suit but somehow could not.

The running footsteps mounted steadily below them, almost keeping pace with the antiquated elevator, which the frenzied man fought desperately, as if he wanted to take it through the roof. There was a command from below, and then a shot was fired, perhaps as a signal to those in the lobby. But Emile crouched down.

"*Gendarme!*" he shrieked. "Hold your fire or I cut the women into bits and fling them down to you. Do you hear, coppers?"

The feet pounded steadily upward. And now Valentine had a knife in his hand. The car was nearly at the top of the shaft. Suddenly the man reversed it, and sent it hurtling down. Miss Withers had a glimpse of blue uniforms, of red angry faces shooting upward.

"I speak only with your leader," the man screamed, halting the car between two floors. "I bargain—my life for the two women. Is it yes?"

At the moment he was very much in command, though heaven knows he had no place to go. "Trapped in a trunk with a skunk!" Miss Withers whispered to herself, quoting the old singsong verse. But she could not take her eyes off the knife, which Valentine was brandishing wildly with his right hand while he ran the elevator with his left.

Then she heard a calm voice—perhaps the sweetest words she had ever heard in her life. It came strangely through the top grille of the cage, from somewhere up above—where a man peered down the shaft from an open door.

"Stoop a little lower, Hildegarde!" said Inspector Oscar Piper. In his hand—the first time she had ever seen him with firearms—was a police positive. As she flung herself down on the floor beside the limp figure of Lucille Jeffers, the gun spat—once.

Valentine collapsed slowly—and the weight of his body forced down the controls. The car shot down suddenly. It increased speed, plummeting.

Miss Withers rose to her feet, pried Valentine off the lever, and as the daylight of the lobby came rising up beneath them, she cleared the mechanism and stopped the car dead-still.

She opened the door, still several feet above the landing, and then fainted dead away into the arms of her would-be rescuers.

"*Must* you drown me?" The schoolteacher received part of a glass of water in her open mouth, and prudently shut it again. The Inspector was leaning over her, looking concerned. Then she tried to rise, for she saw that she had been carried all the way back up to the dance studio.

"Take it easy," said Oscar Piper. "It's all over, whatever it was. But when you feel well enough, I wish you'd tell me what this is all about. You've been out for twenty minutes. I've sent a colored elevator man to Bellevue to have stitches taken in his scalp, I've sent a little girl over to Park Avenue with a broken heart, and a dead gaucho to the morgue. Suppose you fill me in on just what happened?"

Hildegarde sat up straight in her chair. "Of course it was Valentine who did away with the Monterey woman," she began. "But I wasn't sure of it until this morning. Everything that happened only seemed to make it more confusing." She quickly outlined the high spots. "I didn't know until Lucille Jeffers was willing to open the trunks that she was innocent of any complicity. That completed my task."

"Okay, so I know what happened—but I don't know *why!*" said the Inspector. "Why did Valentine kill the dancer?"

"Because she loved him and wouldn't let him go. And he saw a chance to marry a pretty, rich deb. So he got rid of Carla. He did it in the studio, while the girls were dressing. Do you remember the girls said that after he came out of the room and called good night to Carla, she slammed the door?"

"Yeah, so she was alive then—"

"Oscar, there are portieres between the hall and the studio," she pointed out. "You can't slam a drapery. Anyway, Carla was dying then. While the handsome Argentinian took the girls out to supper, the woman who had loved him was strangling to death, *upside down!*"

"Hildegarde, you feeling all right?"

"They had a row, and he decided to kill her. Things played right into his hands. He tied and gagged Carla, and then turned on the shower to cover any noise she might make. The velvet dress was to explain the shower—but it was ripped so badly that I knew nobody would have bothered to steam the wrinkles out of it. It was a lucky break for him that Lucille Jeffers forgot her handbag, because that gave him an excuse to come back and make sure that everything was under control. But he couldn't let Lucille know, or even suspect. He wanted her to think that the disappearance was a phony, a frame-up devised by Carla to injure him."

"And he thought he'd *clear* himself by producing the letter?"

"Yes. Carla had probably been threatened by him before, and showed him the letters. He knew there'd be others, so he beat us to it. Then the two little old ladies telling of the noise they'd heard. Each one picked a different cause for it—castanets, or maracas, and someone upstairs thought he'd heard the beating of a drum! But I'll come to that point later.

"It was Lucille Jeffers who took that letter from my handbag, thinking to protect him. That convinced me that she loved him, but was not entirely in his confidence. So I set a trap, or rather I had you set one for me. I mean the announcement in the papers that the police took no stock in the poison pen letters. That gave Valentine confidence and a new idea. In his attempt to make the case seem like a hoax, it occurred to him that if he received a wire from Carla in Florida, the investigation would probably be dropped. The suggestion was that she had seen the New York papers, realized that her plot had failed, and decided to call it off."

"But you can't get New York papers in Florida as soon as they're off the press."

"Exactly, Oscar! I knew the wire was a fake, if only because it so conveniently offered Mr. Valentine an excuse to get out of town and take the girl with him. Heaven only knows what he expected to tell Lucille when they got to Florida."

"But you yourself saw the wire, filed in Miami Beach!"

"Remember, Valentine had received an earlier telegram, offering the dance engagement. He simply went out and sent himself a message signed Carla, and then soaked off the typed matter and pasted the fake date and message on the genuine base!" She paused for breath. "Of course he was mad as a hatter—I think most murderers are. But he was clever. He almost convinced me that Carla, who was careful about money, was in the habit of paying excess fare on trunks containing forty dance costumes—for a three-night performance!"

"But the costumes *are* gone!" objected the Inspector. "Why should he send them anyway?"

"Get me some fishhooks and line, and I'll find them for you," the schoolteacher said.

"Huh? Oh, there's a regular grappling iron in the car downstairs," Piper told her. "But it's not heavy enough to lift a dead body up an air shaft."

"But there's *nobody* down the air shaft!" she told him. "Just the forty costumes, or most of them anyway, if I'm not mistaken."

"Then—then where *is* the body of Carla Monterey?"

She handed him the two red baggage checks. "You can pick up the trunks at the station," she said. "You'll find Carla in one of them, wrapped up in blue oilcloth."

The Inspector ran for the phone, returning almost instantly. "I've started the boys," he said. "And I've also found out the real motive of this murder. They discovered at the morgue that Valentine is really a bigamist and wife murderer named Ramez, wanted in all the Americas. Suppose the Monterey woman threatened to tell the Jeffers girl of his past?"

"Brilliant, Oscar. Now that you have it all figured out, I think I'll trot along home—"

"No, you don't! Where did he hide the body until he was ready to put it into the trunk?"

"Elementary," said Miss Withers. "Step this way, Oscar." The school-teacher led the way back into the studio living room. "Why, of course—he left her right where she died. In this thing!"

She tugged at the Murphy bed, and finally it swung down to the floor. The Inspector gasped. "Good Lord! You mean he hid the body *in* the bed?"

"Still alive—alive and kicking, I would say. Head down in a tangle of bedclothes. Strangling brings muscular spasms, and that accounts for the noises, the 'slammed door' that the girls thought they heard, and the 'casta-nets' and 'drum playing' and all the rest of it. They heard Carla Monterey's *last* dance—her feet rattling against the door in a true Danse Macabre!"

"Let's get *out* of here!" said Inspector Oscar Piper.

Hildegarde Withers is Back

A muffled din sounded in the anteroom, and then the door banged open and an unexpected guest backed her way into the Inspector's office, fending off the uniformed guardian of the gates with handbag and umbrella. "Oscar! *Do* something!" she cried.

"Hildegarde Withers, as I live and breathe!" gasped the grizzled skipper of Homicide, managing to get out of his swivel chair and restore some semblance of order. "Don't mind the sergeant, he's a new man and didn't know you from Adam—I mean, Eve. If you'd let me know you were coming to town I'd have had the welcome mat out. But I thought you were safely retired, and busy with your African daisies out in California."

"African *violets*, Oscar." The schoolteacher was preening her feathers like a ruffled Buff Orpington. "And if you dare to add insult to injury by making one of your characteristic snide remarks about my new hat—"

"That's a *hat?* I thought it was a fallen *soufflé!*"

"This is hardly the time for persiflage. Not when I've just flown all the way across the country to come to your aid on the Barth case."

"By broomstick? Well, dear lady, we've been getting along pretty well here at Centre Street without any amateur help since you quit being selfappointed gadfly to the Police Department—" Here Inspector Oscar Piper broke into a slow double-take. "The *what* case? "

"Barth, Cecily Barth. You do recall the name?"

"It may ring a bell somewhere, but just now—"

"Oscar, I sometimes think that you are being intentionally dense! Cecily Barth happens to have been one of Hollywood's most famous stars in her day. You yourself must have been just about the right age to have had a schoolboy crush on her, back when she was the Love Goddess of the Silver Screen, unquote."

"I used to be a Tom Mix fan, myself," he said almost apologetically.

"But even you must have seen some of the recent newspaper publicity about how the great independent television producer Mr. Boris Abbas is producing the life story of Cecily Barth as a special on filmed TV, bringing a famous Hollywood writer here to do the script in collaboration with Cecily herself, testing dozens of young sexpot actresses to play the leading role, and so on and so forth?"

The Inspector carefully relighted his cigar. "Oh, *that* one! I've got the flimsies here somewhere. Yeah, right here. You call it the Barth case, but it was some scenario writer name of Gary Twill who did the Dutch Act out of his hotel window late yesterday afternoon. According to all reports, it was a simple case of suicide."

"Suicide is never simple! Oscar, most criminologists agree that falls from high windows, like drownings from canoes, are automatically suspect. Perfect murders, perhaps. I am quite aware of the fact that you police don't believe there is any such thing as the perfect murder, but remember, if it were perfect, you wouldn't know of it! And Gary Twill's death was no suicide, I'll wager a pretty penny. I feel it in my bones."

"Of which you have a complete set," Oscar Piper put in unkindly but accurately, softening the wisecrack with a Hibernian-type grin. "Look, Hildegarde, old girl, I'm personally delighted to have you back in town and tonight will joyfully buy you a spaghetti dinner at any place you name. I think I know just how bad you're itching to make like the old firehorse at the sound of the siren, but believe me, this case just *ain't* it!"

"*Isn't* it," she corrected automatically.

"Okay, *isn't*. This Hollywood writer, the guy named Twill, had been out of work a while and he got this plush assignment to come to New York and do a TV script, with free hotel room and everything—and then it all went blooey. He had a thing going with the boss's playgirl-type secretary and he had a contract and he lost them both at the same time, the girl *and* the job. So he did the Dutch Act, like I said. What more do you want, chimes?"

"A suicide note or an eyewitness would help. Oscar, there is more here than meets the eye. I have known some screenwriters in my time—Los Angeles is crawling with them. They don't take their lives when they lose a girl, or a job either; they feel sure that another one, girl or job, will be along in a minute. Meanwhile, like Miniver Cheevy, they keep on drinking."

"Miniver *who?*"

"A character in an almost forgotten poem by an almost forgotten poet named Edwin Arlington Robinson. No matter. I became interested in this case because of a certain letter which was shown to me over a week ago by a neighbor of mine out in Santa Monica, a Mrs. Marcia Connell, whose three children are usually trampling down my flowerbeds. She happens to be the niece and presumably the only blood relation of the once glamorous Cecily Barth.

"I've caught glimpses of the old lady arriving on Christmas and birthdays, in an ancient Cadillac with equally ancient chauffeur, to deliver presents to her grandniece and grandnephews. Lady Bountiful—but she *never* has helped when Marcia needed a new washer and dryer or the children's teeth needed straightening. And I've seen Cecily mentioned in the newspapers; she's a fanatic anti-vivisectionist, makes speeches for the SPCA and Humane Society drives, and once—before arthritis totally crippled her below the belt and confined her to a wheel chair—she even tried to lead a protest march against the Chicago stockyards because of what she considered cruelty in slaughtering methods. Quite a personality, Oscar. Would you care to read the letter she wrote to her niece, a week or more ago?"

"Yes, but not very much," said Oscar Piper. Nevertheless he meekly accepted the note, neatly typed on Hotel Harlow Towers stationery, and read:

Darling,

Rain rain rain here in New York, and I wish I was home in my own house in Coldwater Canyon where I belong. I hope Jack is still working at Douglas and bringing home his paycheck intact. And darling Loramae and Timmy and Ricky! I hope to be back home for Christmas, but if I am still tied up here I have just oodles of goodies I've collected in these wonderful toy stores like Schwartz's, all wrapped and ready.

The script goes well, except that Gary Twill, the writer—who is right handy in the room next to my suite—is sometimes a bit stubborn and wants documentation for things that happened instead of trusting my memory, which as you know is perfect. I usually get my way, however. He does the structure and first draft of the scenes and then we hash them over and finally I type up the finished version and correct the dialogue and so forth. We are now on the final scenes.

I confess I'll be glad when it's over. The weather has been so nasty that I don't have Felicio, the most obliging Puerto Rican bell-boy, push my wheel chair out on any more shopping trips. I don't feel so safe in this big town, either. Somebody doesn't want this film released—I've had some threatening phone calls and so has Mr. Abbas and Gary Twill.

And I tell you, dear, I can almost smell Death around this hotel—close to me and coming closer. When I tell my fortune with the cards, I get the Queen of Spades or some other dismal symbol almost every time—and you know what that means!

I rescued a lost forlorn black kitten in an alleyway and sneaked it into the hotel—you know black cats are lucky! I named him Asmodeus, and I intend to bring him back with me and present him to our darlings.

If I ever come back! Marcia! I have a terrible presentiment that Death hovers over this old hotel—I mean it! Just as soon as the TV script is finished and approved by Mr. Abbas—a very strange man but you know producers, almost always the enemies of talent—and as soon as the picture is completely cast and costumes picked, I am getting out of here. Maybe I'll come back when they actually start shooting and maybe I won't. This Lilith Lawrence who is to play me looks the part all right—she is beautiful enough—but she underacts terribly. I hate to say it about anybody but I fear she's a Method actress!

Must close now—room service will be bringing up my dinner and I have to lock Asmodeus in the closet as the little black devil will dash out through any open door and then I have to chase him, in my wheel chair, yet—unless Felicio or Gary Twill is around to help.

Don't worry about what I said—at my age Death is only a heart-beat away anyhow. And I know how to protect myself. I have a very authentic-looking pistol that shoots ammonia, plus some other pre-cautions, like a chain on the door.

Kiss the dear kiddies for me.

Your affectionate
Auntie Cecily

The Inspector handed back the letter and shrugged. "Sounds like some kind of a nut," he observed. "And I thought black cats were supposed to be unlucky."

"I am not interested in primitive superstitions, Oscar. During the Dark Ages in Europe—and even in England during the witchcraft hunts—hundreds of thousands of cats were tortured and killed because they were thought to be witches' familiars, and rats and mice overran the land. How any cats survived I'll never know, but I prefer dogs myself, particularly big Standard Poodles like my dear old Talley, who is languishing in a boarding kennel at the moment."

The Inspector looked at his watch pointedly.

"Very well, Oscar we'll get down to cases. Perhaps Cecily is a bit of a psychic, or has some ESP precognition power. Coming events do cast their shadows before: Abraham Lincoln foresaw his own death in a dream, and the day before President Kennedy was assassinated a clairvoyant ran all over Washington trying to get to somebody and warn him not to go to Dallas."

"Coincidence," said Oscar Piper.

"Perhaps. But suppose somebody actually *doesn't* want Cecily's life story to come out—somebody who knew her 'way back when and has since, shall we say, reformed and hoped that the wild oats would stay buried?"

"Come off it! The old dame is strictly a has-been! Who cares about scandals that happened more than forty years ago? It's ancient history. And how would knocking off the writer—or Cecily either—prevent Mr. Abbas from making the picture anyway?"

"I don't know—yet! But I have all the newspaper clippings here in my handbag. There is something rotten, and I don't mean in Denmark. I'm not just working on a hunch, or on my so-called feminine intuition either. Oscar, how deeply have you looked into this Gary Twill death?"

"Things have changed in the Police Department, Hildegarde. I'm strictly administrative now, and other men on precinct level do the leg-work. I'm supposed to be an Inspector."

"Well, then—*inspect!*"

"Hildy, why are you getting the wind up and making all these waves?"

"I'll tell you exactly why. I only got into town this morning—I tried to phone you from the airport and got a fast brushoff from that uniformed ape in your outer office. He told me you were in conference!" She sniffed. "You were not to be disturbed!"

"That's right, I was down having a look at the morning lineup."

"I got another brushoff at the Hotel Harlow Towers, where Cecily Barth is incommunicado and Mr. Abbas is too tied up to see anybody, and so on. But I had noticed that Gary Twill, the man you say committed suicide, was reported by hotel employees to have gone out on a brief errand shortly before he died. He returned with a paper bag which he took up to his room. Right?"

"According to these reports, right. But it all fits. He thought he needed some Dutch courage—"

"I do wish, Oscar, you would stop insulting the people of Holland. And why should Gary Twill go out in the rain? Why buy liquor himself when he could have called room service and had drinks sent up from the bar and charged to Mr. Abbas? Or at least sent a bellboy out on his errand?

It just doesn't fit! So having nothing better to do, I provided myself with a newspaper photograph of Twill—who, I must say, was a distinctivelooking man well over six feet, with prematurely white hair, and I went out cruising the neighborhood shops to see if I could discover the *real* purpose of his last errand." She paused dramatically.

"And so what?"

"So *this!* He not only bought a bottle of champagne at a package store on Sixth Avenue, but he also stopped in at a travel agency on Fifth and purchased a first-class airplane ticket to Los Angeles on the eleven p.m. flight! Now, don't tell me that a man who intends to die the hard way would go out and spend almost two hundred dollars on a plane ticket that he didn't intend to use!"

The Inspector frowned. "Then something must have happened to push him over the edge—"

"Exactly! Something—or someone."

"I mean, to make him change his mind." But Oscar Piper was not quite as sure as he had been a few moments before.

"These are deep waters, Oscar. And getting deeper. If we could only look back in Time, and see Yesterday . . ."

It was late morning on a rainy Wednesday. Or a rainy morning on a late Wednesday. Gary Twill wasn't quite sure and didn't care which. He opened his bloodshot eyes somewhat gingerly, to survey the ceiling of his hotel room, wishing fervently that he were far, far away from this dingy pad, far from the darling if slightly demented old bat of a Cecily—he sometimes thought of her as "Nightmare Alice"—in the next suite, far from Boris Abbas in his office up in the penthouse furnished in silver-and-black upholstery, and most particularly far from Janey Roberts, Valkyrie-cum-vixen.

Far from Manhattan. The big city, to a native Californian, always seemed dirty, raw, and cold—when it wasn't dirty, hot, and humid. Twill had worked almost all night on the final sequence of *The Thousand and One Loves of Cecily Barth*—a title he loathed, but maybe he could talk Abbas into changing it later. He had turned the final ten pages over to Cecily for her to read and approve and type up the final version with two carbons; it kept her feeling that she was a part of it all to bang it out on her portable electric typewriter, and she could do nice clean copy. She was to take it up to Abbas, or at least leave it with Janey for the great man to read later. Anyway, the damn thing was done, finis, complete.

What a wild assignment! What a wild collaboration, with this crazy old relic who fancied herself as a writer because she'd taken some correspondence course in screen-writing and had turned out a dozen or so dramas that never even got to first base with movie or TV story editors! But today not even a former Oscar winner could pick and choose his assignments; there was 80% unemployment in the Writers Guild West.

The big man sat up in his tangled blankets and sighed, ruffling his almost white but still very curly locks. Then he fumbled for the phone and called down to room service for breakfast—not that his stomach was really awake yet.

After a while the ubiquitous Felicio rolled in a cart bearing a pot of coffee, orange juice, some cold toast and obviously colder eggs. Felicio also wore his hopeful Puerto Rican smile, beneath the nose which had been flattened during some earlier attempts to become the terror of the welterweights—but you had to give the guy credit for trying.

Sometimes he was very trying, like now. For he had another manuscript with him; Twill could see it sticking out of a pocket. The Great American short story again. "Oh, God!" moaned the man in the bed. "Not today!"

"But you have feenish the job. You will go back soon to Hollywood. You take my manuscript and show it to Mr. Goldwyn like you promise?"

"Yes, yes. Just leave it on the bureau."

Gary Twill might just as well have said "wastebasket"—and the hypersensitive Felicio sensed it immediately. He withdrew into his Latin sheath, with injured dignity. "I guess it was all just kidding, no?" There was a sentence or two in mumbled Spanish, too fast for Gary Twill to catch—except for one or two words, and those not customarily found in Spanish-English tourist dictionaries. The door closed behind Felicio, and none too gently.

Twill sighed and shrugged. These would-be authors! He really should not have jollied Felicio along—now he'd probably made another enemy in this God-forsaken place. Twill drank the orange juice and a few sips of the cold coffee, then went back to a troubled sleep, from which he was rudely awakened around 2:00 p.m. by the sound of a key in the door and the entrance of a somewhat oversize but very blond and very curvaceous young woman whose secret Mona Lisa smile boded no particular good.

She had been here many times before, under happier circumstances. It was obvious that at this moment she was not on loving dalliance bent, to put it mildly. "You could have knocked, Janey dear," he said, as he drew a sheet over the bare and exposed portions of his muscular figure.

"I could have knocked with a hammer on your thick skull, buster," said Jane. "With joy and gusto. But as it happens I just dropped by to return your room key, and to be the first to bring you some good news. Good from my point of view at least. Not from yours."

"Don't be unkind when I have a king-size hangover. What happened? Didn't Cecily approve the script? She's already okayed all but the last ten pages."

"Oh, she typed up the last scene real neat, and she said she approved the whole thing. She'd do anything for you, Lover Boy, like most women. But when His Nibs read your hunk of tripe—"

"Rewrite required?" asked Gary Twill, moaning.

"Rewrite my sainted painted toenails! Mr. Abbas read it and then he blew up and he said—and I quote—that it is the most misbegotten, unshootable, useless one hundred and eighty pages of junk that he has ever seen, even in a lifetime involved with writers who can't write, and that it turns out to be sophomoric fantasy instead of the objective semidocumentary biography he hired you to do, and that if he could he'd hold up your check and that he fervently wished someone would restrain him from coming down here and strangling you with his bare hands for wasting over four grand of his hard-earned money and then delivering a package of pure garbage!"

Jane was enjoying this, Gary Twill suddenly discovered. She was trying to get a bit of her own back, as our British cousins say. But he was now fairly wide-awake. "Come now; what was so wrong with the damn script?"

"You ought to know! You fictionalized the whole thing!"

"Suddenly I feel confused—I didn't think it was fiction. But dear sweet love, knock it off! So what if Abbas puts another writer on the final, shooting version of the script? Forgive and forget; come back to Hollywood with me and live it up a little! We fit together so good—you make me happy!"

"Slap-happy," said Jane. "Mister Twill, I wouldn't go to Hollywood with you if by any chance I wanted to go to Hollywood and you were the accredited, uniformed driver of a brand-new Greyhound bus! I don't mess around with a guy who's already had three wives!"

"Two, and both legally divorced. I only pay token alimony." He sighed, the handsome if slightly raddled face looking hurt. "You shouldn't insist on taking it so seriously. I should have told you in the beginning, I know. But please, baby—I got a headache. I worked all night. Everybody hates me. Cecily thinks I didn't do her amours full justice, now you say Abbas isn't satisfied with the script, and Felicio hates me because I don't flip over his short stories cribbed from O. Henry—"

"And don't forget Lilith Lawrence, buster!"

"Lilith? Hell, she got the part, didn't she? She's set to play Cecily, thanks to me."

"And you soft-talked her into testing for the role on the Beautyrest, which got her into trouble with her agent who happens also to be her boy friend, a guy even bigger than you are and considerably stronger if not meaner, by the name of Hymie Rose. Keep out of dark alleys, darling, while you're still in Manhattan."

"You *do* give a damn, then, Janey, darling!" Gary Twill said hopefully.

"Not for you, for Hymie. He might just possibly get caught, though it would be justifiable homicide in my book, you—you rat-fink!" Jane went out, slamming the door behind her.

Twill winced and then slid out of bed, stark naked. He paused to take a medicinal gulp from the almost-empty bottle of whiskey on the bureau and then—when the warm glow had hit his insides to a satisfactory degree—set about showering, shaving, and putting on some clothes. He'd phone Abbas pretty soon and find out how much Janey, in her vicious, holier-than-thou mood, had exaggerated the foul-up with the script. Probably she had exaggerated quite a lot, because while it wasn't going to be nominated for an Emmy it was still a damn good piece of work, considering what there had been to work with. Cecily's life story almost outstripped *Fanny Hill* and *Forever Amber* combined.

When Gary Twill was half dressed he stopped short, sniffing. There was a strange smell in the air. It wasn't Janey's too liberal sprinkling of "My Sin," or the breakfast eggs, or Cecily's damn cat that had its litter box in the otherwise unused connecting bathroom; it was something else—something Gary couldn't identify.

"New York just smells, I guess," he said to himself. "Too many people too close together." Being an essentially factual and objective man, he did not once consider the odor to be the smell of death, nor did he—for all his sensitivity—hear the beating of dark, invisible wings overhead.

"Here goes," he said aloud, and finished the bottle. Then he mentally girded his loins, put on his armor, and went down the hall and up the elevator to the penthouse. Abbas had both his offices and his living quarters here, plus a tiny and somewhat bedraggled patio and garden outside, forty stories above the street.

Miss Bixby, the built-in receptionist, was a dour old doll, a sort of birdlike old biddy from whom he had never even been able to win a smile. Not at least until this afternoon, when she told Gary Twill that the great man was much too busy to see him, and that his severance check would be mailed to his agent. Gary Twill ruefully chalked up another sworn enemy, but he headed for the inner door.

It was locked. "He's got Miss Lawrence and her agent in there now," proffered Miss Bixby. "And I don't think waiting around will do you any good, frankly. Jane distinctly said that I was to tell you not to wait."

But Gary Twill waited anyway, reading an old magazine from the coffee table without actually seeing it. After a while the inner door opened and Lilith Lawrence—the spitting image of Cecily Barth at twenty-five, even to the dark sleek hair and the billowy hips—emerged, closely followed by her agent. Hymie was a robust, sharply dressed man with close-shaved but darkish-blue chin and cheeks, who looked straight through Gary Twill and headed for the exit. Lilith Lawrence (born Mae Klotz) hesitated for a moment, giving the writer her sweetest smile.

"So sorry, Gary darling," she trilled. "But that's the way the ball bounces, isn't it? I only—" Hymie Rose grasped her by the elbow and propelled her hastily out of the place.

"So now can I see Abbas?" Twill demanded of the woman at the desk.

She shrugged and picked up the phone. After a moment she put it down and said, "Mr. Abbas says to tell you that he's very busy and that your room rent is paid up only through today and that if you keep hanging around and bothering him I am to call Mr. Durkin, who as you know is the house detective, and have you forcibly eee-jected!"

"I get the message," said Gary Twill. "Have a good time at the next coven." He departed, with whatever dignity was left to him. Which was not too much.

As he rode down in the elevator he decided to travel westward under the alias of George Spelvin or something; no use letting everybody in the trade who read *Daily Variety* and its "NY to LA and LA to NY" column know that screenwriter Gary Twill had flopped in the big city and was returning ahead of time with his tail between his legs. . . .

In Inspector Piper's office Miss Hildegarde Withers was holding forth. "But don't you see, Oscar, this man Twill was out of his element here in New York. He was surrounded by people he didn't understand and who didn't understand him. This independent producer, Mr. Abbas, is reputed throughout show business to be a man of violent temper. According to the newspaper accounts, in his earlier days he was a professional wrestler in Hungary and a protégé of Sandor Szabo, whoever that was—"

"Just one of the greatest mat men in history," said Piper, brightening.

"You see? If he became enraged at his writer—?"

"Hildegarde, you're tilting at windstorms."

"It's *windmills,* if you insist on quoting from books you've never read! Abbas is a possibility, anyway. He had the physical ability to throw anybody through a window or over a parapet. And then there is this Jane Roberts person, the blonde Amazon type. With whom Gary Twill was for a time intimate, to put it politely. A woman scorned, Oscar—you know how dangerous they are."

"Dream on, dream on. In this day and age women don't kill for that, not good-looking ones anyway."

The spinster schoolteacher was consulting her sheaf of newspaper clippings. "Then what about Lilith Lawrence, the girl chosen to play the part of the young Cecily in the TV film? Here's a night-club photo of her and Gary Twill, holding hands at some place called El Morocco and looking very fatuously at one another. A girl as physically equipped as Lilith must have plenty of boy friends, some of whom might have resented a Hollywood writer getting into the act, as the phrase goes. An obvious jealousy motive. And there is also the unpleasant Mr. Durkin, the house detective, who was very nasty to me this morning when I tried to see Cecily. According to the newspaper stories he had had several altercations with Twill over noise and high jinks in the hotel room. He's a suspect to be reckoned with."

"He's also an ex-cop," Piper said. "I remember vaguely that there was some beef connected with his leaving the force. That I will look into, if you insist. But don't let me stop you—go on with your brainwashing."

"I think you mean brainstorming, but no matter. You're a real Mr. Malaprop, Oscar. There is also this bellboy named Felicio Bonaventura, who keeps cropping up in the affair and who seems to have told each reporter a different story. Anyway, not one of these people has an airtight alibi for the time of the murder—if it was, as I believe, an actual murder."

"But do they *need* alibis? And while you're making up your list, better put down dear old Cecily Barth too. I don't see any motive for her—but you never know. And the wheel chair can be only a prop and she can really walk as good as anybody else—"

"As *well,* Oscar! And I think you have been watching too many old movies on the Late Late Show. Even if it weren't for her crippling arthritis, even if she could get out of the wheel chair and walk, how on earth could she—a frail woman weighing less than a hundred pounds—throw a big man out of a window?"

"It's your frammis," said Oscar Piper. "Personally, I think it was the butler. Only I guess there really isn't any butler in our cast of characters, is there?"

"You're not being very funny. And you haven't explained the bottle of champagne or the airline ticket. I think the ticket alone proves that my worst suspicions are justified."

"Do you ever have any *best* suspicions?" He grinned, and chose a fresh cigar. "Hildegarde, I'm very fond of you, but sometimes you're nuttier than a fruit cake."

"In case you don't know it, there are some new recipes for fruit cake. Remember, Oscar, that Cecily Barth did step on a lot of toes in her heyday, and no doubt she made a lot of enemies. In her time as a movie queen she was, according to legend, no better than she should be, leading men on and then throwing them aside—"

"Like a worn-out glove?"

"—and wrecking many a marriage and many a career. Her life story, if presented on television, might just possibly ruin certain people who have since grown mature and respectable. Suppose for a moment that she, and not Gary Twill at all, was the intended victim? Remember Cecily's letter to her niece? Suppose Gary Twill had been trying to protect her, and somehow got too close to the truth?"

"My supposer isn't quite that active nowadays, Hildegarde. But let's look at this thing seriously for a moment. It just *has* to be suicide. Twill was a big, powerful, athletic-type man and nobody could have thrown or pushed him out of a hotel window, not without a hell of a lot of commotion anyway."

"Unless he was knocked unconscious first, perhaps?"

"You're *reaching*, Hildegarde. No, I have a hunch he took the easy way out."

"Suicide is 'easy'?" she snapped. "That could only be suggested by someone who has never experienced it. Oh, you know what I mean! And my dear Oscar, time was when if I came into your office with a bee in my bonnet, you'd have come instantly alive, grabbed your hat and a handful of those dreadful stogies, and we'd have taken off on the chase."

"Time *was*," admitted the Inspector soberly. "I'm strictly desk level now; I don't actually go out on cases and try to do the work of the precinct men. And remember, neither of us is as young as we used to be."

"Speak for yourself, Oscar!" And Miss Withers gathered herself and her belongings together and made an abrupt exit, slamming the door so hard that, out in the anteroom, the sergeant swallowed his gum.

Thirty seconds later the sergeant had another shock, as he saw the skipper erupt from the inner office, hat and topcoat and cigars in hand. "Closed for the day," Inspector Oscar Piper barked in passing. "Hold the fort. I got to take off and try to keep my best friend from becoming her own worst enemy." He hurried out into the main hallway—where he found Miss Hildegarde Withers leaning against the bulletin board with a patient yet cryptic smile on her somewhat equine visage.

"So here we go again," she said. "Better late than never."

A little later the two oddly assorted sleuths climbed out of a taxi at the Hotel Harlow Towers, that once plush and now slightly rundown hostelry on Central Park South. They stood on the sidewalk, a chill autumnal wind whipping about their ankles, at presumably the same spot where Gary Twill had come plummeting down out of nowhere to splash his brains out on the cement. Just before 6:00 p.m. would have been a very busy hour at this location, as they both knew.

"It was only by the grace of God that the fool didn't take some innocent passerby with him on his trip to the Hereafter," observed Oscar Piper. "As it was—according to the reports—three people were knocked down, and one woman had to be hospitalized."

"Another argument against suicide," pointed out the retired schoolteacher. "Unless Gary Twill had no compassion."

Unfortunately there had been no actual eyewitnesses. If Twill had stood for a few moments in the window, or had hesitated on the narrow ledge outside while he screwed up his courage, nobody had seen him. It had all happened during one of Manhattan's sudden, blustering rainstorms. With no buildings across the street, nothing there except the reaches of a practically deserted Central Park, no one had been in position to catch an accidental glimpse of the beginning of the high dive—if indeed it had been a voluntary dive. Naturally, all the people in the street below were either shielded by umbrellas or by folded newspapers held over their heads; no eyes had been turned up against the slashing, icy rain.

"The first cruise car got here just two minutes after six," Oscar Piper was patiently explaining. "The officers took statements from several persons, including one newsboy—"

"Who very probably might be that little man in the kiosk over there," Miss Withers interrupted impatiently. "I wonder!"

For once she wondered correctly. Mr. Herman Gittel, age fifty-six, professional newsvendor, proved reasonably amenable to conversation after Miss Withers had purchased one copy of each of his evening newspapers, noting with sadness that the *Herald Tribune* was gone.

"Sure, I seen it," said Mr. Gittel. "And I heard him yelling all the way down. He sounded real weird, like he was nuts or something. Stuff musta blown out of his pockets, because the air was like a snowstorm with bits of paper."

"I really wish I knew exactly what bits of paper," remarked the schoolteacher wistfully. "But I suppose the street cleaners have done their work." She surveyed the gutter, poking into a storm drain with her umbrella.

"I kept me one sheet as sort of a souvenir," offered Mr. Gittel. And from his well-worn leather jacket he produced a wrinkled, rain-stained piece of manuscript paper—which proved to be Page 172 of what seemed to be a teleplay script. Miss Withers and the Inspector read:

SCENE 88—EXT COLDWATER CANYON HOUSE—MED CLOSE SHOT—DAY Cecily and Norman, she in daring and revealing swimsuit, he in smart yachting costume of the time. They are seated on a stone bench with profusion of flowers in B.G. He is concealing displeasure. Cecily is, however, mistress of the situation.

CECILY (*moving closer*)
Don't be difficult, Normie-pie. Isn't it enough to be my lover—do you have to be my leading man too? It really isn't your type of role anyway, Mr. Lasky says. And when *The Hunchback of Notre Dame* is released, you can write your own ticket at Essanay or anywhere.

NORMAN
It isn't just that, beautiful. You're a lovely cheat. We were supposed to have a date to go down to Ensenada and gamble a little over the weekend—you broke it because you had to stay home and read the script of *Passion's Pawn* or something, and then you were seen dancing at the Miramar with somebody whose name I intentionally don't remember.

CECILY

Don't be difficult, darling. You have your career and I have mine. Let's leave it that way.

The rest was indecipherable. Which, Miss Withers thought, might be all for the best. "Oscar," she said on impulse, "will you buy this for me?"

Somewhat reluctantly, the Inspector invested two dollars for the tattered souvenir.

"So the guy took his rejected manuscript with him," he said. "You getting morbid or something, collecting mementoes yet?"

"One never knows," the schoolteacher pronounced mysteriously.

"Anyway," Oscar Piper pointed out impatiently, "whatever personal stuff blew out of his pockets on the way down, his billfold was there and he was immediately identified."

"Did the airline ticket show up?"

"Not according to the report. Somebody probably found it and cashed it in. But he had a California driver's license, membership cards in the Writers Guild West, Greater Los Angeles Press Club, Ace Hudkins Health Club and Gym, Civil Liberties Union, the NAACP and CORE, and the usual jumble of credit cards. There was also over $300 in currency, and his room key tagged Hotel Harlow Towers 2466. Our men went right in and upstairs and reported that 2466, a single, was something of a shambles. Bed unmade, a litter of coffee cups and empty liquor bottles, and manuscript pages scattered all over the floor. The room was sealed off, but if you insist on taking a gander at it—"

Miss Withers had been vainly trying to count up to the windows of the 24th floor, but had only managed to get a crick in her neck. "If you count the lobby and presumably the mezzanine, and skip the thirteenth floor which no hotel ever has, then—" She sighed, and gave it up.

"It was the twenty-fourth all right," put in the cooperative Mr. Gittel. "I seen the open windows."

"*Saw*," corrected the schoolteacher absently. "But are you sure?"

"The hotel is forty stories, and I counted down to where I saw the open windows—"

"Windows? *Plural?*"

"Well, the one on the left was wide-open, curtains flying, and the second over to the right was just a little open. Before the cops got here it was closed."

"Very interesting," said the schoolteacher.

Inspector Oscar Piper found it less so. "Well," he grumbled, "there doesn't seem to be any question about the guy going out the window of his own room. I suppose you're hell-bent to go up to the pad and have a look for clues; but Hildegarde, I warn you, those were trained investigators who handled this case, working on modern scientific lines."

"And using computers, no doubt!" she said scornfully.

"Computers don't guess, like you do! Well, do we go upstairs?"

Miss Withers was deep in thought. "I suppose so. But I am more interested in *people* than in the scene of the crime. I want to see Cecily Barth and make sure that the poor crippled old woman isn't the victim of another 'accidental' suicide or something, and I want to meet the various people who had reasons, large or small, for disliking Gary Twill."

"Okay," said the Inspector resignedly. "Let's go."

They entered the ornate but somewhat musty lobby of the old hotel, almost but not quite a relic of the Gaslight Era, and immediately learned from a supercilious desk clerk that Miss Barth wasn't seeing anybody or taking any phone calls, and furthermore—

"Who's your house dick?" demanded Oscar Piper.

"Why—our security officer is Mr. Durkin, but—"

"Get him here, fast." For once the schoolteacher had to admit the usefulness of a shiny gold badge (denoting over thirty years with the Department) which the Inspector flashed briefly. Because wheels turned, and Mr. Durkin (who had given her a sort of bum's rush earlier in the day) made an instant appearance from the restaurant-bar, where he must have been enjoying a very late lunch or a very early dinner for he was sucking his teeth and chewing chlorophyll mints.

"Was there something, Inspector?"

"There was and is."

The stubby, choleric house detective lost no time getting into the record that he was very shocked that a thing like this should have occurred at a quiet, respectable hotel like the Harlow Towers but what can you do? A suicide is a suicide, and the least said about it, the better. And after all, this Twill twerp wasn't the sort of guest who would have been made welcome at the hotel, only he was working for Mr. Abbas, a long-time resident of the penthouse and anything Mr. Abbas asks for—

"Okay. Abbas took a room here for his imported Hollywood writer, and a suite next door for Cecily Barth—is that right?" The Inspector was getting more than a little impatient, perhaps because he had had a light lunch and was thinking of dinner. "Anybody else?"

"Just Miss Lawrence, the star. She's in 2634. There's a reservation for the director when they pick one, and for the casting director and costumer. Mr. Abbas likes to have all his staff right on hand. Only his secretary, Jane Roberts, lives home—I think in Brooklyn Heights. And Miss Bixby, the receptionist, who doesn't really count. I'll be glad to take you upstairs—"

"You better be," said the Inspector. "You know, Mr. Durkin, I seem to remember something. You were a sergeant, working out in Queens or Staten Island or somewhere. There was a mishmash, and you were allowed to resign rather than stand charges. So you went out to California and didn't make out and then you came back to Manhattan and got this job."

They were going up in a rocky old elevator. "Can you cool it, Inspector?" Durkin was sweating. "I need this job, and what's past is past. You know how it is, Inspector."

"Maybe," said Oscar Piper. "We'll see how it plays. Where's the room the guy jumped out the window of?"

Durkin led the way down a long hall and then to the right, past a door which he pointed out as Miss Barth's. Then they came to Gary Twill's door.

"It's been sealed," said the house detective.

"Then I'll just unseal it," said Oscar Piper.

They went into the room, Miss Withers entering with some trepidation for the place was—from her point of view—in a mess. The bed looked as if some insomniac hippopotamus had been in it, the desk and surrounding territory were littered with pages of crumpled manuscript, the bureau bore an empty whiskey bottle, and clothes were strewn everywhere.

"Yet he seems to have died," the schoolteacher pointed out, "rather nattily dressed in tweed jacket and slacks, including a necktie. Suicides usually don't care how they look. I think I have 'cased the joint,' as you would say. Let us go."

"Okay, okay," said the weary Inspector as he resealed the door. "So now you're satisfied?"

"Not at all! There were no signs of a fight or struggle, no broken furniture or other indications of combat. Yet still—"

"So it was suicide!"

"With the airline ticket?" The schoolteacher shook her head. Then she turned suddenly on the house detective. "Mr. Durkin, just why did you intimate that Gary Twill wasn't the type of guest welcomed at the sacrosanct Harlow Towers?"

Durkin said uneasily, "Well, he was a sort of Bohemian type—loud stereo music at all hours, hipped on the liberal bit and fraternizing with the help and giving 'em ideas. He had Felicio all steamed up about becoming a writer. And he had all sorts of people visiting his room. We can't have that sort of thing."

"Dear me, no! We must live in the last century, mustn't we?" Her glance was scathing.

"Okay, okay!" put in the Inspector. "Let's go see the movie queen."

"Miss Barth isn't going to let us in," predicted Durkin. "Since this happened she's been locked in tight, and she won't hardly even let the maids in to do her rooms."

"No room service? How does she eat?" asked Piper sensibly.

"Didn't you know? Miss Barth is a vegetarian, and lives mostly on wheat germ and crackers and stuff like that, all out of cans and boxes." They were now standing outside the door of the suite, and Durkin knocked. He knocked again, and then called out in a wheedling tone, "It's just Durkin, Miss Barth. Can we see you for a minute?"

There was not the slightest sound from within. Inspector Oscar Piper who was not the most patient man in the world, saw a bell and leaned on it. "Open up, lady—this is the police!"

"Go away!" came a querulous voice from within. "You're not fooling me with that old one!"

Oscar Piper sighed, and nodded at the house dick—who reluctantly produced his master key. It worked, at first. The door swung open and then held, caught by a heavy chain.

Miss Withers felt that this had been mismanaged enough, and spoke up. "Cecily, will you please listen?" she said in her best classroom voice of authority. "Mr. Durkin and Inspector Piper of the New York Police Department are with me, but I started the whole thing. You may not know me but my name is Hildegarde Withers and I happen to live next door to Marcia, out in Santa Monica, and she showed me your letter—"

"Prove it!" The voice was still hostile.

"Well, Marcia is on a new diet and has lost three pounds. John is working the swing shift at Douglas. Loramae had summer flu but got over it and she and her brothers are now trampling my flowerbeds again. Is that enough?"

"All right, I guess," came the disembodied voice. The door closed, a chain rattled free, and then they were permitted inside—all but Mr. Durkin, who found his way blocked by the Inspector's right arm.

"Look, I got my job to do," complained Durkin. "I got to tell her we got rules about not installing chains and keeping pets and—"

"Blow," said Oscar Piper, with the disdain of an honest cop for one who had cheated. Mr. Durkin blew.

And Miss Withers and the Inspector were entering a big, dimly lighted drawing room that smelled of perfume and cat and cigarette smoke. The schoolteacher had eyes only for the woman in the lightweight wheel chair who faced them, sitting on it grandly as if it were some sort of throne. She wore a flowered housecoat as if it were ermine and velvet, and her chin was high and defiant.

What was left of Cecily Barth, presumably in her seventies, was mostly spirit and spunk, though there were traces of ruined beauty under the heavy makeup and in her deep dark eyes. And her hair was still as raven-black and as sleekly arranged as it had been back in the halcyon days when this woman had rivaled Theda Bara and Nita Naldi and Clara Kimball Young. . . .

"It was so good of you to come," Cecily was saying, holding out her hand. "You must forgive my seeming rudeness at the door. But my nerves are in a dither. However, any friend of dear Marcia's—"

Her words were for Miss Withers, but her attention was turned to Oscar Piper; he was a man. For a few seconds she was a faint echo of the Screen Vamp, the Sex Goddess of the Silver Screen, unquote. Quite evidently she expected the Inspector to kiss her hand, but he only held it for a second and then sheepishly dropped it.

Meanwhile Miss Withers was gathering impressions, as was her habit. This elderly, crippled old woman was in fear of her life; the schoolteacher could almost feel the fear, could almost smell it above Cecily's perfume.

"You must excuse the way the place looks," Cecily was saying, waving her hand vaguely. Indeed, the room was a jumble of untidiness. The tables, chairs, and even the mantelpiece suggested Christmas Eve in the family of a dozen or more small children: everything was piled high with toys, plus rolls of fancy wrappings, balls of varicolored string, and boxes of bright Santa Claus stickers. There was a stack of packages, wrapped and ready for mailing, in one corner.

"Christmas—in September?" said the Inspector, unbelieving.

"I'm afraid I went simply mad in your New York toy stores," admitted Cecily as she made ineffectual efforts to find them a place to sit. "I had such fun shopping before—before I got too scared to go out anymore, even with dear Felicio pushing my wheel chair. But now, I really don't trust anybody!"

The Inspector was seated uneasily on the edge of a sofa and had taken out a fresh cigar, while Miss Withers prowled the room, the packages, the typewriter table. There were many scrapbooks, many old newsclips and photos of an earlier era. But what she was interested in was *now*.

"About this suicide next door—" the Inspector began.

"If indeed it *was* suicide," said Cecily Barth meaningfully.

"You didn't hear any sounds of a struggle, any raised voices?"

"No," admitted Cecily. "But there is an unused bathroom between, where I keep my cat's litter-box. Mr. Twill and I were working very closely together on the script, and we never locked the connecting doors. That would have made a fine scandal once upon a time, wouldn't it? But I'm afraid I wasn't here to notice anything yesterday afternoon; my cat had got out and down the hall and I was looking for him, as I often have to do when I can't get anybody to do it for me."

"Let's get down to cases," the Inspector went on firmly. "When did you last see Gary Twill?"

"Well, he brought in the last sequence of the script early in the morning, around eight o'clock. He'd worked on it all night, poor dear boy. Like most writers, he hated to make carbons and he always made a lot of typographic errors, so I had to type the final version of everything."

Cecily nodded toward the corner of the room, where there they saw a bridge table, a portable electric typewriter similar to the one used by Gary Twill, and several piles of white and yellow paper.

"It wasn't actually as intimate and deep a collaboration as I had hoped it would be, but I'm still going to try for co-screenplay credit. The lovely TV residuals, you know! That's the payment to writers for re-runs, and it can go on for years." She beamed at them. "A sensational life story like mine will be released and re-released over and over again."

"You were satisfied with the script, then?" asked Miss Withers.

"More than satisfied! Gary had caught the spirit of the really great days of Hollywood. Such a dear brilliant man! I can't believe he took his own life."

"Who could have done it, then?" demanded Oscar Piper.

"Really, my dear man!" Cecily made a dramatic gesture. "How on earth should I know? I'm a stranger in town."

"'I a stranger and afraid, in a world I never made,'" said Miss Withers softly. Cecily was obviously winding the Inspector around her little finger, with a practiced charm that dated back two generations. The schoolteacher was less easily impressed. "You're quite sure you heard nothing in the next room yesterday afternoon, and that you were out chasing your kitten at the time Gary Twill died?"

"Quite sure."

"And you received Twill's version of the last sequence of the script about eight yesterday morning, and retyped it with carbons and then took it up to Mr. Abbas, say around ten or ten-thirty?"

"Exactly. Only I gave it to Jane, his confidential secretary. I can manage these automatic elevators very well, if I take my time. I told Jane that I was delighted with the script and that I would sign formal approval anytime—I have that right in my contract."

"And did you hear anything from Mr. Abbas yesterday?" the school-teacher pressed.

"Nothing directly. I phoned Jane Roberts sometime after lunch to learn what the great man's verdict was, and she said he was still studying the script but that storm warnings were out. That didn't worry me; he's the sort of producer who never likes anything on paper in the first reading."

She broke off when there was a sudden interruption from the bedroom. What erupted was at first sight a rather furious battle between two small black kittens. The fracas moved into the drawing room—and then it turned out to be a mimic battle between one black kitten and one very naturalistic toy kitten, with the former naturally getting the upper hand—or upper paw. Then just as suddenly it was all over; the live kitten turned its back on the stuffed kitten-on-a-string, stalked over to Cecily, and leaped lightly into her lap.

"Asmodeus baby!" said Cecily Barth. She turned to her visitors. "I almost named him Lucifer—only then his nickname would have been 'Loose,' and I couldn't have that, could I?"

"We'll wait and see the film," said Miss Withers ironically, conscious that they weren't getting anywhere. "Miss Barth, I moved heaven and earth to get the Inspector to come up here with me and look into this affair, and all because of Marcia. But I don't think you're being altogether frank with us. We happen to know that you saw Gary Twill die. So you weren't chasing your kitten—you were looking out of your open window. A newsvendor in the street below looked up and saw two open windows—and then yours was swiftly closed. Right?"

If the sally was supposed to put Cecily into one of her dithers, it failed completely. "I wasn't going to admit that," the aged screen star said. "I just wanted to keep out of it. Yes, I had recovered Asmodeus, and I was sitting here and I heard the commotion. I did rush to the window and it was raining so hard I had to raise it to see anything—and I wish I hadn't." She faced them defiantly, like an angry child caught with a hand in the cookie jar. But Miss Withers was thinking. This ridiculous old woman knew something which she was not prepared to disclose. It might be important, it might be minor. But it was something.

"What I am really interested in," said the schoolteacher, "is the bottle of champagne. The one Gary Twill went out to buy shortly before his death. But he didn't drink it as a sort of stirrup cup into Eternity, because the empty bottle wasn't found among the other empties. Can you help us there, Miss Barth?"

Cecily hesitated for a very long second, and then she smiled. "I thought that some things could be kept private," she said, as she put the black kitten gently down out of her lap. "All right, since you press me, I'll tell you." She wheeled herself over to the hall closet and almost immediately reappeared with an unopened, gold-topped bottle of champagne in her hand. It was, Miss Withers noticed, of 1938 vintage—whether a good year or a bad year she didn't know. But that did not matter.

"A going-away present," Cecily explained. "Just like Gary."

"But no note with it?" pressed Miss Withers. "I know writers."

Cecily hesitated. "I don't know just when Gary left the bottle: it was in the connecting bathroom, just inside the door on my side. And since you make such a point of it—yes, there *was* a note."

Wheeling herself with a certain calculated dexterity, Cecily went over to the typewriter table and came back with a sheet of manuscript paper, which the Inspector and Miss Withers read as one.

Cecily dear, the hell with everything. I am taking it on the lam (as we used to say in the old Cagney pictures) and getting outa here. Don't say it hasn't been fun, because it hasn't. Drink this in good health, and think of me as not one who is dead but just gone far away. (Quote from Elizabeth Barrett Browning, I think). Anyway, I have had it. Your affectionate collaborator, Gary.

It was the Inspector who spoke first. "Well, Hildegarde? You said you would be happier with an eyewitness or a suicide note. You now have the latter. Okay? Let's go somewhere and have dinner."

"Let's not," said Miss Withers, who was in a state of confusion but who had a little red light flashing on and off in the back of her brain. She faced Cecily. "You have, you know, been withholding evidence and in essence you have been resisting police officers in the performance of their duty and otherwise impeding justice. I am quite sure that Inspector Piper can find some grounds for having you held as a material witness in Women's Jail for a few days—"

"It might be a most interesting experience," said Cecily Barth. "But if he did something foolish like that to me—while Jane Roberts, who is the one person who actually might have had real animosity to Gary, goes free—well, Inspectors have become sergeants overnight. Or even sent to a beat over in Canarsie?"

The dear old lady had claws, it appeared. Longer than those of Asmodeus (named after a minor demon), who now was purring contentedly in a chair. A live prop for an ageless actress who was determined always to be on stage . . . Cats, Miss Withers had observed, always had means of taking care of themselves.

"I think—" began Miss Withers. And then the telephone rang.

"I'm not supposed to have any phone calls," Cecily pouted. But she wheeled herself over to the instrument. "Yes?" Her voice changed into a dulcet tone. "Yes, Mr. Abbas?"

The voice at the other end was loud and emphatic; it could be heard across the room. "Cecily, mine darlink, ve got problem. Somebody making stink about that fool Twill. Some old dame who minds other people's business. So ve haf a conference here in de office at eight dis evening, right? All of us! So ve agree on our stories. Hokay?"

"I think I can arrange to be there," said Cecily. She hung up and turned back to her guests. "You perhaps heard," she said. "Mr. Abbas is disturbed at this reopening of the case. So he is calling a conference—"

"We know," said Miss Withers. "Things get more complicated all the time. And my best advice to you is—"

Just then the doorbell rang. Cecily wheeled herself over, put on the chain, then opened. Both Miss Withers and the Inspector caught a glimpse of a frightened girlish face through the crack.

"It's me—Lilith!" came the voice. "Miss Barth, I have to tell you something, but the switchboard girl won't ring you."

"Those were my personal instructions, dear. I—I'm not feeling well and I'm not seeing anybody or talking to—"

"But you don't understand!" the voice from the hall persisted, "We're all in trouble and the picture is in trouble. This whole thing is going to hell in a handbasket. Somebody is trying to reopen the mess and make out like Gary didn't kill himself! There's some old biddy rampaging around—she has some sort of *in* with the fuzz—and she's here only to try to make trouble. And any more bad publicity might frighten away Mr. Abbas' backers. So if anybody asks you, don't tell them about Gary and me—it was only a night or two anyway and all in the course of show business. Really, it doesn't count!"

"Yes, dearie," said Cecily calmly. "My lips are sealed."

"And another thing," said the voice through the crack in the door. "His Nibs wants us all up in the penthouse at eight tonight, for a sort of council of war. It's an ultimatum. We have to get our stories all straight or this picture isn't ever going to get made!"

"Roger—out and over," said Cecily. She closed the door and turned back to her uninvited guests. "You see what I mean?" she demanded a bit plaintively. "I just don't know how to cope with it all."

"You don't have to cope with it all by yourself, not now," said the schoolteacher. "But these are deep waters, and I feel there is more here than meets the eye, unquote." She gave the Inspector a signal, and they made their departure—with Asmodeus the black kitten making a determined but vain effort to go out with them.

"Well, Hildegarde?" said Oscar Piper as they approached the elevator. "Did you see anything I didn't see? I figure that was a genuine twenty-four-carat suicide note, and—"

"And a genuine, twenty-four-carat plane ticket, don't forget. Oscar, I'm afraid I can't take you up on that dinner invitation, I have other things to do. But I suggest that we both crash Mr. Abbas' party at eight."

"Well—if you say so. In for a nickel, in for a dime. Fine old dramatic tradition—to have all the suspects gathered together in one place, while the great Hawkshaw unravels the mystery. Only, in this case, I don't see any possible motive for murder."

"So then it might be an *impossible* motive," Hildegarde retorted. "I am not trying to be cryptic, Oscar. But a little red light is flashing on and off in the back of my head, a warning that perhaps I have missed something. And besides, I have an errand to do—some shopping, as it were."

"Not another hat—when I was just getting used to this one!"

"No, not a hat. Something more in the line of a toy, but a rather unusual toy." She nodded. "And now, if you will be kind enough to hail me a taxi, I'll be off. We'll meet here again in the lobby at eight o'clock, right?"

"Right or wrong, we'll meet," said the Inspector wearily.

The penthouse apartment-cum-office where the self-admittedly great Mr. Abbas lived and had his being was originally a magnificent (if now a somewhat rundown) center of operations. The drawing-room office, in which he was now having a supposedly secret conference with his employees, protégés, and disciples, was large enough for a tennis court or at least a badminton court; it had been furnished in 1932 Moderne—plenty of glass and everything in black and silver, with sharp angles.

The paintings were early imitations of Picasso, the books were sumptuously leather-bound copies of Mr. Abbas' scripts, the lighting was soft and slightly off-green. Miss Bixby loved it; Jane Roberts wished she had kept her date to go bowling; Lilith Lawrence thought belatedly that she should have taken up some other line of work. Hymie Rose sat beside his client and was chewing on an enormous but un-lighted cigar. "He should get me out of here and find me some nightclub bookings," Lilith was thinking.

But a TV picture was a TV picture, with audiences in the millions. One mustn't forget that. And it meant so much to dear old Cecily. . .

Abbas was speaking, as from the mountaintop. He was directing his diatribe at them all, but looking at Cecily in her wheel chair.

"Ve got troubles," said Mr. Abbas. "Troubles vith script and troubles vith publicity. Everybody here, including me myself, has goofed. But ve don't got to go on goofing. Don't any of you talk to no more reporters, understand? So vat is it if a fool bellboy suggests that maybe I trun—I trew—Gary Twill over the parapet? The script vas bad, but not dat bad. He musta kill himself, de no-goodnik."

Just then there was a shrill alarm from the doorbell, which Miss Bixby hastily arose to answer. And in came Felicio, smiling apologetically. "Sorry. Mr. Abbas—but he have badge and what am I to do?"

So Inspector Oscar Piper, followed closely by Miss Hildegarde Withers, joined the party, though very much uninvited. "As you were!" commanded the Inspector. "At ease! This isn't a pinch, yet." Again he flashed the persuasive gold badge.

But the situation was obviously strained, and Miss Withers was, so to speak, up in arms. "We are gathered together," she began, "all of those who knew Gary Twill here in Manhattan, to try to find out how and why he died—"

"Everybody but Mr. Durkin," put in Cecily Barth softly. "A very nasty man."

"Thank you," said the schoolteacher. "Which gives me an idea." She winked to the Inspector, who frowned and then caught on. He stepped catlike to the door and threw it open, disclosing the house detective crouching outside.

"Come in and join the party," said Miss Withers. "I had a hunch you wouldn't want to miss this."

"I was only keeping tabs—" began Durkin defensively. Then he came sheepishly in.

"I shall continue," the schoolteacher said firmly. "But this is not a simple matter."

"Understatement of de year," put in Boris Abbas. "I resent—"

"Go ahead and resent," said Oscar Piper. "But shut up when the lady is talking."

"We have the case," continued Miss Withers as if in a classroom, "of an athletic, two-hundred-pound man, in full possession of his faculties, who went to his death out of a hotel window. I discount the theory advanced by Felicio in one press interview that Gary Twill was hurled over the parapet by Mr. Abbas—"

"I do not really mean it—I am a writer of fiction!" cut in the bellboy hastily. "I let the imaginations run wild."

"Because that would have required premeditation and an accomplice down on the twenty-fourth floor to open Twill's window. So I eliminated Mr. Abbas."

The producer bowed.

"But may I see the script which you found so disappointing?" she went on. Abbas nodded to Jane, who got it from the files. As she continued, Miss Withers riffled through the neatly typed pages. "I also had to eliminate Mr. Hymie Rose, who though he possibly had motive, could hardly have thrown Gary Twill out of the window without creating a battlefield in the room."

"But if poor dear Gary had been sandbagged and was therefore unconscious?" suggested Cecily helpfully.

"He wasn't unconscious—he screamed all the way down. And pages of a manuscript went flying with him. I have one page of that manuscript which was rescued from the gutter and is still legible, and I note that it doesn't match the corresponding page just handed to me. On page 172, in the version Gary Twill took with him to his death, Cecily is playing a love scene in a garden with another Hollywood star of the time, one Norman Kerry—"

"Dat vas in the original outline," cut in Abbas.

"And in the final version just given to me the scene is played with the Prince of Wales, no less! And later Cecily romances with Jack Dempsey and Charles Lindbergh and heaven knows who else!"

"Vich is vat makes me so infurious!" yelled Abbas. "How to get releases from such big names?"

"Let me explain," Cecily cooed. "I simply took a few liberties as I typed the final version and livened it up a bit. Who remembers dear Norman today? Now Edward, later King of England—"

"His intimates, I understand, always have called him by his real name, which is David," said the schoolteacher pedantically.

"I met him once at a party," Cecily said defensively. She looked like a child who had just been told there is no Santa Claus.

"To continue," said Miss Withers. "I once liked Mr. Durkin for the killer. He had left the police force under a cloud, and lived for a while in Los Angeles until the heat was off and he could come back and get this sinecure of a job as hotel security officer. If Twill had known him out west and learned of the old scandal, and if Mr. Durkin had been afraid that Twill would talk and cost him this job—"

"You're dreaming, Hildegarde," said the Inspector.

"I know. I was clutching at straws. But again we face the problem of why the window was open on a stormy, rainy day, and why there were no signs of a struggle. I had to come to the conclusion that this was not a strong-arm job, to use the vernacular. Even though Jane Roberts here has—obviously strong arms—"

"*And* the only real motive!" Cecily put in gleefully. "You should have heard them quarreling!"

"You bitch!" said sweet Jane, with feeling.

"I must confess that at one time I even considered Miss Barth herself as a suspect," continued Miss Withers.

"I wouldn't want to be ignored!" the old lady said happily. "This is the most exciting thing that's happened to me in years!" She was obviously enjoying every moment of it.

"But it's only in old B-movies that a supposed cripple suddenly arises from a wheel chair and performs deeds of mayhem and murder."

"I really am crippled," Cecily said sadly. "Look at my legs, once the most famous in Hollywood!" She lifted her skirt and displayed pitifully atrophied legs, like pipestems. "So if strong men couldn't have pushed poor dear Gary out of a window, how could poor little me?"

"Exactly. How could you?"

"So that seems to leave only me," spoke up the fair Lilith with some spirit. "But how on earth—"

"You could possibly have called his attention to something down in the street, and then—"

"But *why*? He played fair with me, I got the job. And since we are getting down to cases, I didn't just romance him for the job, I really went for him!" And Lilith gave Hymie Rose a defiant stare.

There was a silence. Then the Inspector coughed and murmured, "Well, Hildegarde? Having eliminated everybody, we come back to suicide."

"Not quite, Oscar. Not with that plane ticket." She turned back to Cecily Barth. "Cecily, you took liberties with Twill's script. Didn't you know he'd scream with rage and insist that Mr. Abbas read the correct version—if he was still around? And that your machinations would all go for nothing?"

Cecily was suddenly quiet.

"It may seem to some of you that this is an insufficient motive for taking a man's life. But the human ego is a strange thing—especially the Hollywood ego. Cecily, you convinced yourself that with Gary Twill out of the way you could talk Mr. Abbas here into using the more sensational version of your life story. True or false?"

The people in the big room were hardly breathing; you could have heard a soap bubble explode.

"Utter nonsense," said Cecily finally, in a small voice. "Granting for a moment what you say about the script, how could I, a ninety-pound cripple, throw a big strong man out of a window?" She finished on a high squeak of triumph.

"To make a long story longer," said Miss Withers almost sadly, "I suggest to you, as they say in British trials, that you worked out a clever and devilish scheme—playing on Gary Twill's good-hearted willingness to help you search for your kitten who was always getting out. You bought a life-like stuffed black kitten, which could easily have been mistaken for the real thing in a rainstorm, and with a cane or some other implement shoved it out on the ledge that runs beneath your room, the bathroom, and Twill's room. Then you rushed to him and asked him to try to reach out of his window and rescue it."

"Pure fantasy!" said Cecily. "I suppose I was right behind him in my wheel chair and gave him a superhuman shove? What jury would believe that?"

"I'm not quite through," Miss Withers said quietly. "I remembered that for years you've been an ardent worker for the Humane Society and the SPCA and kindred organizations, and that once you tried to lead a protest march against the Chicago stockyards. You had seen how they force cattle into the chutes. So you got an inspiration and you bought this."

From her capacious handbag the school ma'am produced an Xmaswrapped parcel, and slowly and dramatically unwrapped it. The article inside looked something like a large flashlight, with no bulb.

"What on earth is that?" demanded Oscar Piper.

"It's known as a Shock Rod. At the stockyards it's called a cattle goad. Oscar, I don't suppose you would let me demonstrate, with you as the subject? I guarantee that if this instrument is applied to your anatomy you will automatically and involuntarily jump farther than you have ever jumped before."

"No, thanks," said Oscar Piper grimly.

Miss Withers pressed the button, and the Shock Rod buzzed like an angry rattlesnake. "Cecily, now we know why Gary Twill went out the window. And how can you explain why we found this nasty thing among the Christmas toys wrapped up for your grandnieces and grand nephews?"

"You didn't! You couldn't! I mailed it—" Then the ex-movie star realized what she had said.

Miss Withers and the Inspector had their spaghetti dinner after all, if a bit late. Over the zabaglione he suddenly frowned. "One thing bothers me. Oh, it's not the old woman; she won't stand trial—"

"Psychiatric care?" asked the schoolteacher.

"Some private place, with bars. For the rest of her days. No, I'm wondering how you got into her suite and found the gadget."

"But I didn't! I hunted all over town until I found a place where you can buy them, and I got some Christmas gift paper like Cecily's and wrapped it, figuring it would shock her into a confession. Shock treatment can work both ways, Oscar."

He grinned, and lifted his glass of Chianti. "To you, Hildegarde. Long may you wave!"

Hildegarde Plays it Calm

Alas, there was no welcoming committee at the gates of the sprawling Los Angeles International Airport. Inspector Oscar Piper, feeling forlorn and also conspicuous in his too-Eastern dark suit, was forced to the conclusion that he had been stood up. He was just in the act of retrieving his suitcase from the dizzily revolving carousel in the baggage room when he was set upon from behind by a breathless female of uncertain years but of determined disposition.

"Oscar, you're late—" began Miss Hildegarde Withers.

"Well, I had to stay up there with the plane, didn't I? Your smog and fog socked us in for a while." The two old friends and sometime sparring partners stood back and surveyed one another, as people often do after a lapse of years.

"You're looking a little peaked, Oscar. If you ask me, it's high time you took this overdue vacation."

"And you've changed, Hildegarde. You're different, somehow."

"Well, for one thing, I happen to be wearing a scarf instead of a hat, so for once you can't make any of your invidious wisecracks. And I was going to say—your plane was late and I'm glad, because I'm late too. I almost didn't get to meet you at all because just as I was about to leave I had a most surprising phone call. I'll tell you about it as I drive you to your hotel. My car's right outside."

"Illegally parked, I see," said the Inspector as they came out onto the concourse.

"I was in a tearing hurry. Besides, if I'd received a parking ticket I'm sure you could have had it fixed for me."

"You flatter me. A New York cop hasn't much drag in L.A." She whirled her ancient Chevrolet coupe past a threatening truck, bluffing out two other drivers who hooted their horns at her in frustrated fury, and then she nosed into a lane marked San Diego Freeway.

"But I don't happen to want to go to San Diego!" Oscar Piper protested.

"Relax! The San Diego Freeway goes to Bakersfield, only we'll turn off at Santa Monica where I live. The Santa Monica Freeway goes to Los Angeles, and the Hollywood Freeway goes to Van Nuys. It's all very simple."

"I'll bet! What's this about the mysterious phone call?"

"You won't be able to guess who it was, not in a million years!"

"Look, I only have a week's vacation. So come to the point, if any."

"Very well. The call was from Eileen Travis. That name should ring a bell. Don't you remember the case up in Las Vegas umpteen years ago? You weren't directly involved in it, except for having to vouch for me over long-distance when the police were being difficult."

"Wait a minute!" His leprechaun-ish face brightened. "Wasn't that the one where the suspect's fingerprints didn't match those on the murder weapon, and you pulled one out of the hat and suggested that the Chief of Police make her take off her shoes?"

"That's right—the famous toe-print case. It was *that* Eileen Travis who called me, out of the blue!"

"You mean she beat the murder rap, after all?" Oscar Piper threw his cigar butt out of the car window in deep disgust. "Another case of an allmale jury refusing to convict a pretty dame?"

"Wrong, Oscar. Eileen was found guilty on two counts of Homicide One, and she sat in Death Row at Nevada State Penitentiary for months on end. Then there was a commutation of sentence and she served ten years or so but now she is out and trying to make a new life for herself."

"Or looking for a new victim, maybe."

"Oscar, you think too much like a policeman. This woman has paid her debt to society, and we ought to give her the benefit of the doubt. I've often wondered what happens to the people I've helped to catch and convict during my meddling in affairs that really shouldn't have concerned me. This is the first time I have ever had a chance at firsthand to see what they're like when and if they get back into the world. Perhaps Eileen is a different person now. She may just want to thank me, for changing the course of her life."

"Sure, I'll just bet."

"Anyway, she called to ask if she could drop by this evening. I could hardly say no. So you and I will have to postpone our trip to Disneyland until tomorrow."

"Okay with me, my stomach is full of butterflies anyway. I'd just as soon spend the rest of the evening reading a good book, curled up in my hotel room."

"What good book—*Fanny Hill?* And speaking of hotels, here we are."

The schoolteacher pulled up in front of the old Miramar, which now faced a wide expanse of wine-dark sea and a remarkable sunset full of

Technicolor clouds. The Inspector dragged out his suitcase, and then hesitated.

"I really wouldn't turn my back on that dame, if I were you," he said earnestly. "I know how the criminal mind works. She may have been brooding all those years in stir, nursing a grudge against you."

"I don't think so. Heavens, there was nothing personal in what I did! She just outsmarted herself."

"Then probably now she wants to play on your sympathies and borrow some money, or have you give her a character reference. Anyway, I bet you she wants *something* out of you!"

"You're on, Oscar. For a whole dollar. I'll phone and give you a full report when she leaves, if it isn't too late."

"Phone me anyway. And well—I hope I'm wrong!"

Miss Withers drove the six blocks back to her modest cottage, thinking that the dear Inspector must be getting mellow with the years. This was the first time she remembered his ever hoping he was wrong, about anything!

At precisely eight o'clock the doorbell rang. "We must give the lady an A for promptness, anyway," said the schoolteacher to Talley, her big Standard Poodle. He was getting rheumatic in his autumn years, but he still lumbered up from his couch to answer the door and give his warm greeting to any human being. Talley, as somebody had said years ago, was a dog who would gladly have held the dark-lantern for Jack the Ripper.

"Come in, come in," said Miss Withers. The handsome, well-dressed woman looked a little apprehensive. "Talley doesn't bite, he just wants to sit in your lap, Miss Travis. Or is it Mrs.?"

"It was just a number until a couple of months ago." The tone was bitter.

"Let me say that I'm very glad things have turned out so well for you," offered the hostess tactfully. "You must have been a very model prisoner indeed. Or would you rather not talk about it?"

Eileen shrugged, and accepted a cup of coffee and a cookie. "As a matter of fact, I don't just want to talk about it, I want to do something about it. Penal reform, I mean. I'm not down here just for fun. I'm having conferences with some movie people at the Westwood-Hilton about the possibility of doing my life story on film—*The Doll in the Death House*, or something like that. I want the movie money, when and if, to go to CALM. That's Citizens for the Abolishment of Legal Murder, you know."

"Yes, I do know. And a worthy cause it is."

"But you—you're practically a policewoman. And isn't the fuzz—I mean the police—always in favor of the death penalty?"

"Most of them, because they're under the impression it's a deterrent. I think it fails in that, and besides, it's inequitable. Few people with enough money to hire a good lawyer ever get the death penalty, and in the entire history of this country I believe that only fourteen women have been legally executed. But you didn't get in touch with me to argue that point, did you?"

"It said in the article I read about you that you usually work, or used to work, hand in glove with the New York police—"

"With one particular member of the force, anyway. But I'm a free agent."

"How about the Los Angeles police?"

"I have had certain contacts with them, but I'm afraid they still believe a woman's place is in the home, or in the schoolroom."

Eileen seemed to make up her mind about something. She ran her thin well-manicured fingers through her Italian-cut locks. "I suppose, Miss Withers, you're wondering why I looked you up in the phone book and came out to see you?"

"Something like that has crossed my mind."

"I guess it was partly a desire to show off a little, and prove to you that a convicted murderess could come out of stir smelling like a rose. But now that we know each other a little better, I want to tell you something and ask your advice. I'm not just down here in Los Angeles to talk to the movie moguls. There's a very delicate errand that I promised to do for a friend of mine up at the Place who still has six months of time to do on a felony hit-and-run and is worried sick about her husband.

"He used to tend bar in Vegas and come up to Carson City every visiting day, but now he's moved down here and he doesn't come up to see her or even write anymore. Bunny has got it into her head that maybe he's taken up with another woman, and she's got to know the truth. You can't imagine how girls worry about things like that when they're locked up Inside."

"And sometimes when they're on the outside too, or so I've heard tell."

"Before I got out I promised Bunny that I'd check up on her man. But I've never met him, never seen him except for the picture over her bunk. I'm getting cold feet about just walking in on him." Eileen sipped her cold coffee. "Do you suppose it would be a good idea to hire a private eye?"

"The phone book is full of them, but I imagine the costs would run high."

"I'm not hurting for money—George divorced me while I was in stir, but my father and mother didn't disown me. And Bunny was such a good pal to me in stir! Miss Withers, you're supposed to be an investigator. Would you look into it for me?"

"My dear young lady, I'm not a licensed private eye."

"I'll gladly pay for your time."

Miss Withers hesitated—and was lost. "Sometimes the best way is the simplest. Why don't you and I go pay a call on the man? Perhaps your friend Bunny is only imagining things. If he's up to tricks, or living with another woman, it should be perfectly evident."

"Tonight? But—"

"There is no time like the present. I broke another engagement to see you, and I have the rest of the evening free. Do you have his name and address?"

"It's Bert Haas, 9877 Laurel Terrace Way."

The address, Miss Withers noted, would be somewhere in the hills above Laurel Canyon in Hollywood, no more than half an hour's drive from here. "Do you have your car?" she asked the visitor.

"Why, no, I came by taxi."

"Then we'll take mine."

It was no sooner said than done. Leaving the disconsolate Talleyrand behind, the retired school-ma'am and the rehabilitated murderess set forth on their errand of mercy—or whatever it was.

Had she but known . . . as dear Mary Roberts Rinehart used to write.

Eileen had little to say on the trip, either because she was apprehensive about the welcome she might receive on their arrival or because she was aghast at Miss Withers' individualistic way of handling a motorcar. The schoolteacher, as usual, talked enough for two.

The address proved to be a lonely, somewhat bedraggled-looking frame house, innocent of paint or pretense, perched above the roadway on stilts and clinging precariously to the edge of the cliff, and far off by itself on the edge of nowhere. But there was a light inside, flickering through drawn venetian blinds.

"I don't think I like the looks of the place," said Eileen, as the schoolteacher made a U-turn and came suddenly to a halt.

"Neither do I, but I'm not the type to turn now. Even if this Mr. Bert Haas is a very unpleasant character, he can hardly pull anything out of line, with the two of us there." But Miss Withers grabbed her heavy handbag and also her umbrella, both of which had proved excellent defensive weapons in the past.

"I guess you're right," admitted Eileen. "But better leave the engine running in case we have to make a fast getaway."

"Very well." Miss Withers hated to waste gas, but maybe Eileen had a point. They climbed a long flight of wooden steps, and the schoolteacher banged firmly on the door with her umbrella handle. There was a deep silence within. But all the same, Miss Withers had a sixth sense that somebody was in there—perhaps more than just one somebody. She hammered again, more loudly.

"Who is it?" came a guarded masculine voice from inside.

Miss Withers had to nudge Eileen into answering. The younger woman gulped and said, "We're friends of Bunny's. We want to see Mr. Bert Haas."

Another pause—but there were vague sounds of scurrying within. "I'm not dressed," came the same voice. "Wait a couple of minutes, okay?"

"He could be whisking feminine garments and lipstick-stained cigarettes out of sight," whispered the schoolteacher. "But he may be telling the truth. We should know in a minute."

But it was closer to five minutes before the front door opened to disclose a handsome but weakish-faced, actorish-looking man in his middle thirties, wearing a dressing gown but showing no other signs of having had to make himself suddenly presentable. His delight in receiving visitors was well concealed, but he let the ladies in and waved them toward overstuffed chairs facing a flickering television set.

Miss Withers noticed that the room was sparsely furnished, with no books and no magazines, no really intimate objects. However, the ashtrays were clean. The doors to what were presumably the kitchen and the bedroom were closed. But somehow, the place didn't really look lived-in.

Haas himself did not sit down, nor did he offer his visitors any refreshment. The situation was obviously strained. "Didn't Bunny ever mention my name?" asked Eileen. "Remember, I was her cellmate for a year."

"If she did, I don't remember," Bert Haas said bluntly, then turned to the retired schoolteacher. "Don't tell me you were a buddy of Bunny's too? You're too legit."

"Why—why, certainly!" The maiden schoolteacher had always fancied herself as an actress, and decided now that she might as well get into the act. "In certain select circles I am known as 'Light-Fingered Lil.' I did some time for shoplifting. Only the big stuff of course—like diamonds."

"Pleased to meetcha," said Haas. But the man seemed to be very much on edge, like an act left on stage in the lurch and forced to ad lib. "You girls got a message for me from Bunny, or what?" he demanded.

Miss Withers looked at Eileen, who suddenly spoke up and said, "Mr. Haas, you just don't know how that girl is worrying! She doesn't know if she's got anybody or anything to come out to, or not. You haven't been up to Carson City to see her since November, and the letters you used to write—what pitifully few there were—have just made her cry all the harder."

It occurred to Miss Withers that Eileen was being very dramatic about the whole thing, and the accompaniment of "Peyton Place" on the TV set was somehow completely in harmony. So she watched and listened.

"Bunny is still your wife!" cried Eileen. "You said your vows, and you can't let her down now, after all you've been to each other!"

Bert Haas was trying to shush her. "Take it easy! Yes, I know we were once married, but—"

Then he broke off, as the bedroom door was flung open. A small viva-cious, curvaceous brunette in silky pink nothings burst into the room, preceded by an Army .45 automatic held in both hands.

"*Wife?*" she shrieked. "Did I hear somebody say 'wife'?" There was a torrent of angry Spanish, of which Miss Withers caught only a few words.

Bert Haas moved forward. "Conchita, I was going to tell you! I'll divorce Bunny as soon as she gets out—"

"Tell it in hell!" cried Conchita. There was no time for anybody to do anything—Miss Withers could not even raise her umbrella or fling her handbag. The blast of the heavy gun seemed to make the entire house jump a foot in the air, with earthquake and thunder and lightning combined.

Bert Haas stood there in shocked surprise, as if he was unable to believe that this was actually happening to him. Then bright arterial blood spurted from his mouth. He grasped his dressing gown and crumpled forward to his knees, then collapsed into a sodden mass.

The girl called Conchita just stood there, frozen and wide-eyed. Perhaps somebody screamed—it might have been the schoolteacher. Come to think of it, it must have been—because dear Eileen was already out of the door.

Instant departure seemed the better part of valor, at the moment. Miss Withers tried valiantly to act on that precept, but by the time she had gathered her handbag and umbrella and had backed out of the corditesmelling room, it was a little too late. She heard the roar of a familiar motor in the street below, the howl of a tortured transmission. "Wait, wait!" she cried. But it seemed that Eileen had really panicked. She was now careening off down the canyon in the schoolteacher's beloved old Chevrolet, ricocheting first off one curb and then another. Just as she rounded the farther turn the tail-light came on.

"The things I get myself into!" said Miss Withers to herself, as she plodded off down the darkened street in search of a telephone.

Sometime later that evening Inspector Oscar Piper, roused from his bed and from the good book he had been reading, found himself down in the hotel's Tiki Room buying Miss Withers a much-needed glass of sherry. If she had expected any sympathy from him she was sadly disappointed. He seemed very amused at the whole story.

"And I'll take that dollar now," he grinned.

She paid it. "But anyway, Oscar, to make a long story short, I finally managed to wake up somebody in one of the big houses down the canyon and was permitted to use the phone and—"

"Just let me guess the rest of it," he cut in. "You yelled 'Bloody Murder' to the local law and you waited there until the cruise car arrived. And then you went back with them to the house on stilts where the killing took place and found the house dark and deserted. But at your frenzied insistence at being eyewitness to a murder the law broke in and found nobody and nothing. It's really a funny picture—"

"Go on. Mister Knowitall!"

"No dead body, no hysterical Conchita, no blood on the floor. Hildegarde, you were taken in by one of the oldest cons in the business— the one called the 'cackle bladder routine.' It's usually a blackmail gimmick. The supposed victim holds a chicken bladder filled with chicken blood in his mouth, and when he is supposed to be shot he bites the bladder and supposedly bleeds from the mouth and dies a horrible death right there in front of the 'mark.' Only in this case you were the mark.

"The rest is easy. The police naturally assumed that you are a little batty and they gave you a hard time and you probably had to talk fast to keep from being detained for psychiatric observation. You finally got home and found your ancient Chevy standing right in front of your front door, and so you called me to cry on my shoulder. Right?"

"Wrong, Oscar. I didn't know about the cackle bladder thing, but I did know the murder was phony. Because—"

"Wait a minute! You mean you *didn't* report the killing?"

"I did not. So all this beautiful scene you have been visualizing just didn't happen. Eileen and her friends were absolutely confident that I would be taken in; it wasn't blackmail but 'just a good try at making me look silly and ridiculous in the eyes of the local law.'"

"But that motive seems pretty mild for a girl like Eileen Travis. I'd have thought that she might want to take a pot shot at you, or something equally drastic."

"And risk going back to prison as a second offender? Not that clever wench! She just wanted to get even for that old business about the toe-prints."

"Okay. But I'd like to know why you didn't fall for it."

"Oscar, that was an Army-issue .45 that the girl fired at Haas—even I could see that. She fired point-blank at the man—and he fell *forward!* A real live bullet of that caliber would have knocked him backside-over-applecart backwards across the room, if you will pardon the vulgar but forceful expression. So I just called a taxi and went home, and when I found my car waiting there I knew I was right."

The Inspector ordered himself another highball. "But look," he said. "She still took you for a sucker, or tried to. She and her friends are probably out somewhere laughing themselves sick over how they conned you. But how do you go about getting even? You could never get a charge of auto theft to stick, not when you drove out there together and when she brought your car straight home. You might have her picked up for violation of parole, because it just occurred to me that parolees are not supposed to leave the state—"

"And get her sent back to prison? Oscar, I just thought of it. Do you happen to know what today is?"

"Sunday, I guess. Last day of March. Why?"

"If it were still March it would be the thirty-second. Oscar, it's Monday—April Fool's Day! You think I could get the girl sent back to prison for trying to play an April Fool's joke that didn't even work? Not a chance!"

"Then what?"

"I know where she's staying—at the Westwood-Hilton. And I just think I'll send her a bill for services rendered, perhaps a hundred dollars plus my taxi fare from Hollywood to Santa Monica. She did offer to retain me, you know. If I get the money I'll donate it to CALM, the anti-capital punishment group. And I'll bet you another dollar that she very meekly pays me, especially after she and her friends read the morning papers and find out there was no report of a murder and that their whole scheme was a fiasco."

"The bet is on," said Oscar Piper. But he had a deep feeling inside that this was one bet he was going to lose.

The Stripteaser and the Private Eye

The damsel in distress was already twenty minutes late. Howard Rook, his bulky body squeezed into a booth in Barney's Beanery, nursed a dark beer and thought of walking out on her—even if attorney Hal Agnew had promised over the phone that the potential client was the most gorgeous ecdysiast of recent times. But Rook the misogynist wouldn't have waited longer than half an hour for Miss Super-Universe in a topless.

Then the tall fur-bearing blonde came in—or rather, made an entrance. Every male in the place looked up and reacted, but she swept over to the booth and said breathlessly, "Mr. Rook? Sorry I'm late!"

"Miss Holly Wood, I presume?" He noted that she smelled good and looked younger than she probably was. Somewhat larger and more vividly colored than life, like a poster.

"No cracks about the moniker, it's legally mine." Her smile was disarming. "In my profession a girl has to have a tag people will remember. I'll just have a ginger ale, thanks." She studied him with startling amethyst eyes. "Mr. Agnew said you do private-eye work. Somehow I thought you'd be a much younger man."

"Confidentially, I am!" said Rook, unruffled. But the bulky, somewhat ursine, definitely middle-aged ex-newshawk wished that he had worn his other suit and stopped off on the way for a haircut. He admitted to meddling sometimes in crime, but he had no state ticket, and hence no standing with the police.

"I don't care much for the fuzz myself. They didn't believe me when I said I was eyewitness to a murder. But you see the spot I'm in. The killers must have seen me. And I'm a sort of public figure—I happen to drive a big pink convertible which is part of my image, like my mutation mink and my flowing locks and all the rest of it."

"Please take it again from the top. Who, what, where, when?"

"I'm the featured stripper at the Pink Peacock, down the street. Last night I was killing time in my dressing room after the last show, to make sure the stage Johns outside had given up and gone home. It must have been around three a.m. when I went out to the parking lot in the back and climbed in my car. I turned on the motor and the lights and then I saw something I won't ever forget, not if I live to be a hundred!"

"Just the facts, please."

"Three men were against the front of a beige sedan parked on the other side of the lot. One gangster-type in a sports jacket was arm-choking a smaller, older man in a black topcoat while another hoodlum in a sweater was sticking a knife in his belly. Caught in my bright lights, the two let the other one slump to the ground, jumped in their car, and roared away out the far exit."

She shuddered, and went on: "I got out and ran over to see if there was anything I could do. He was a little old guy with a big nose, and so forlorn-looking! I felt for his pulse, but he didn't have any. He was practically naked under the coat, just shorts and a pair of bedroom slippers. He had tousled gray hair and needed a shave."

"He didn't mumble any last words, then?"

"No, he was dead, real dead. But when I was trying for his pulse I saw he had something like a poker chip loosely held in his hand, and it had the initials G O on it. That's a clue, maybe?"

"Who knows what's a clue, at this stage? You kept the chip?"

She shook her head. "I started hell-bent for home, and then I decided to make like a good citizen and went over to the Hollywood police station and told my story. The cruise car they sent reported back that there wasn't any corpse, or even any blood, at the parking lot!"

"They thought you'd dreamed up a thing like that?"

"Well, they told me to go home and sleep it off, because they just couldn't open up a homicide investigation without a dead body. But I saw what I saw, and I didn't sleep much. This morning I called in and they said no body had been reported but that if I insisted I could go downtown and look through the photo files, which I did. The men I'd seen were typical gangster-hoodlum types but I looked at thousands of ugly faces and got nowhere. So I remembered meeting Hal Agnew at a party or somewhere, so I looked up his address and went over to his office on First Street and he referred me to you."

Holly put a jewel-encrusted hand on his arm. "I didn't get much of a look at the killers, and I don't know if I'd recognize them if they walked in here now. But they must have seen me, or at least my car. They could be thinking I saw more than I did. Isn't it the code of the underworld that eyewitnesses have to be knocked off because dead men tell no tales?"

"Probably they didn't see much of anything, blinded by your headlights. And Los Angeles hasn't had any gang activities in a long time."

"But how can I be sure I'm not on the spot? I wish I could take a full-page ad in the newspapers saying that Miss Holly Wood, now starring at the Pink Peacock, positively cannot identify the two men who—"

"Skip it, you'd only make matters worse," Rook interrupted. "What about the license plates on the beige car?"

"California. But I didn't get a good look at the letters or numerals."

"Probably intentionally spotted with mud or grease. Now from what I gather you were unlucky enough to witness an execution, old-time gangster style. The killers came back after you were gone and picked up the body to dispose of elsewhere. But that poker chip just possibly may be something else—" He caught a look at his watch. "Excuse me a minute, I have to make a phone call and break an appointment."

When he returned he found that Miss Holly Wood was standing up. "Let's get out of here," she half whispered. "Because just now a man in a dark suit and sunglasses came in and took a look around and then went into the bar—"

"It's the cocktail hour. Maybe he's just thirsty."

"But he didn't give me a second look. I'm just not used to that. He sort of made a *point* of not giving me a second look. Get it?"

Rook nodded and paid the check. As they went past the archway leading into the bar he saw the man in question sitting on a stool and nursing a glass; a *Racing Form* covered his face and he might or might not be looking their way in the mirror. "Looks like a harmless actor-type guy to me," Rook said as they came out the door. "Do you recognize him as one of the men you saw early this morning?"

"Could be slang for homosexual. Let's just keep "probably a man whose weakness". Only he walked different, and he's better dressed."

"Probably a man whose weakness is horses and booze. But I suppose we'd better play it safe. You driving the pink hearse?" She nodded, pointing. "Get in it and drive home. I'll follow."

But as he drove after her in his rackety but souped-up car he saw in the rearview mirror that the man in sunglasses was coming out of the Beanery, indicating that he had had a very quick drink—or else. . . .

Rook took all possible precautions against being followed as he tagged Miss Wood up Holloway onto the Sunset Strip, and then up the hill on Larrabee where she went to earth in the subterranean garage of a starkly modern apartment complex. "You'll come up?" she asked as they got out.

"Certainly." They got into an automatic elevator and rode to the top floor, Holly leading the way in rhythmic sway down the long hall. But for all his heft Rook moved to cut her off before she could use her key. "I think I'll go in first," he told her.

But just then a door across the hall was flung open and a barefoot young man in T-shirt and dungarees came out. He had a pageboy bob, a wisp of beard, and he seemed all a-dither. "Holly *darling*," he cried, "oh, have I been waiting for you! Because when I came back from the shoppe about an hour ago—I had to walk up the stairs because the elevator wasn't working—there was a man in some sort of uniform standing here at your door with a box of flowers."

"What's so unusual about that, Willi?" she asked.

"*Well*, there was another big ugly man holding the elevator door open while this one here was diddling with your lock. With a strip of celluloid!"

"Oh, no!" whispered Holly. "They—they know where I live!"

Rook took over. "Could you identify the men in the mug files?"

Willi hesitated, looking at Holly—who hastily introduced them. "Mr. Benson, meet Mr. Howard Rook. He's working on the case."

The other then confided, "No, I—I couldn't identify them—they just looked like underworld characters in a bad play. The one at the door had a uniform cap over his eyes and the other kept his face turned away and they both got away so fast! You going to call the fuzz or shall I?" He was looking at the girl.

"Not much use in that, Willi," Rook answered for her.

"Well, they were both characters I for one would hate to meet in a dark alley, so if there's anything I can do . . ." Willi's voice trailed away and he finally withdrew into his own lair.

Rook took the key and led the way into Holly's apartment, deciding immediately that it was enthusiastically and lavishly overfurnished in a sort of Contemporary Byzantine. The framed prints on the wall were feminine nudes by Modigliani, Picasso, and Schiele, plus one enormous color enlargement of Holly in the buff. "You live here alone?" he demanded.

"Yes, except for my feathered friends." She pointed to a large gilt cage in which two small parakeets huddled on a single trapeze.

"No husband, no boyfriend who could move in with you for protection?"

"Nope, I shed my last husband a year ago and I'm between boyfriends. Resting, as we say in the profession."

Rook was soberly surveying the layout from a security angle. The locks were nothing to brag about, and the big picture windows in the living room and bedroom looked out across the street at a tall motel for transients.

Anyone over there with a sporting rifle could take easy pot shots. As he hastily closed the venetian blinds, the girl came closer and flung both arms around him. "I'm really scared now! Mr. Rook—Howie—will *you* move in here with me?"

"Best offer I've had today," he told her with an embarrassed grin. At moments like this his ears always seemed to turn a bright red.

"If you're worried about your virtue you can sleep on the sofa."

He shook his head. "Thanks, but this place is too much like a goldfish bowl. Better pack everything you'll need for a week."

"But this is my home! And my parakeets—and my phone calls—"

"Bring the birds and forget the calls. You wouldn't be getting any calls if and when your address is Forest Lawn. Nobody will be out looking for you at my humble abode. And don't worry, I don't make passes at lady clients."

"Who said I'd worry? I always went for the Paul Douglas type of older man."

And in less than fifteen minutes Rook was carrying a queen-sized suitcase down to the garage, while Holly lugged the cage of disgruntled parakeets. They got out of there fast, in Howie's souped-up jalopy. After using every trick Rook knew or could imagine to make sure of eluding a possible tail, he finally drove up a narrow dead-end alley.

"Hope you don't mind it's over a garage. And you'll have to excuse the way the place looks," he told her as they climbed the creaky outside stair. "Some acquaintances call it The Hoorah's Nest."

"So this is how a bachelor private eye lives!" Holly gasped as they came in. "Anyway, you don't keep goats!"

The apartment was littered with empty beer cans, overflowing ashtrays, masculine garments, crumpled manuscript paper, a great many books, and faded newspaper clippings overflowing from shoe-box files on shelves covering one whole wall. Rook hastily whisked some of the debris off the couch so she could sit down, rolling aside two five-gallon cans of paint, explaining that one of these days he planned to do some redecorating. He showed her the kitchen, which was larger than the living room, and the bedroom, which was a sort of sleeping porch. "Care for a beer?"

"Liquor is the only vice I haven't got," Holly told him.

He poured himself one and lighted a pipe. "Now let's get down to cases. That poker chip could be a gambling chip. I seem to remember there's a casino in Las Vegas called the Gold Oasis—"

But Holly was interested in the sheet of paper in his old Underwood. "So you write, too? *The Black Dahlia Case*," she read aloud. "Wasn't that the murder right here in L.A. where a girl got slashed to ribbons?"

"And cut in two." Rook had worked on that one to no avail, and he knew that the killer of lovely Beth Short had got away scot-free and was now living happily not too far away. "Yes, I sometimes do a little truecrime stuff," he admitted. "When the rent's overdue."

"Then maybe some day you'll be writing my story!" Her face lighted up.

"Let's get you off the hook first. There's a newspaper clipping or two in those files that might give us a lead. You can help me look—"

"But I've got to be over at the Peacock by eight! There's a forfeit clause in my contract."

"The less you're seen in public the better," he pointed out. "But anyway, we've got to eat." He refused assistance, and set about preparing dinner out of cans. But over the coffee he decided, "Since you're determined to take the risk of going to work as usual, I'll drive you. But ditching the pink car isn't enough. You stand out. I suggest something quieter than that mink, and could you tuck your hair under a wig?"

"I guess so. But I don't have one. All the shops will be closed."

"There's one on Sunset that might be open and if it isn't, the owner lives overhead. I'll run up there now—bolt the door after me." He started out, then came back. "You happen to have thirty-five dollars on you? The lady won't be in a mood to give me any credit."

Holly pressed two fifties on him. "Money we got, lover!"

After what seemed a rather long time to Holly he returned bearing a box marked ESTELLE—COIFFEURS. Holly did things to her own blond tresses in front of the mirror and said this red job was a fright wig to end all fright wigs. "And what took you so long?" she wanted to know. "Did your girl friend give you a bad time?"

"Not at all," lied Rook. "She's just an occasional bowling companion." But Estelle, a cuddly though heavily upholstered welterweight, had been rather irritating in her insistence that he was making a fool of himself in this case. Sometimes he was almost afraid that she, like most of the others in his little black book, was getting strictly honorable intentions.

He drove Holly to the Pink Peacock and took her to the stage door. "You're among friends here," he said confidently. "I'll be back later."

"But I want you to catch my act—and I don't feel safe without you!" She was clinging to his lapels.

"Nobody is going to try anything in a crowded nightspot. Get in and work, and make like nothing's happened."

The amethyst eyes clouded. "Okay, I'll strip. But my heart won't be in it." And suddenly she put both arms around him and pressed a fervent kiss on his mouth. Then she turned and almost ran inside.

Rook walked dazedly out into the night. "At my age!" he told himself derisively. He shook his head and went out to survey the supposed scene of the murder, deciding that Holly couldn't have been more than forty or fifty feet from the spot as she described it—and that she must have seen more than she would now let herself remember.

Then he drove home and buried himself among his clippings. It was his detective credo that there was nothing really new in the crime field—everything had happened before and was almost certain to have found its way into print. Though his filing system wasn't much better than that of the late Mr. Sherlock Holmes—who was said to have filed his notes on the voyage of the *Gloria Scott* under V—he managed, in a couple of hours, to discover a whole sheaf of clippings of possible pertinance.

He also made a great many telephone calls, mostly to the downtown saloons where newspapermen were likely to be drowning their sorrows, one call to the detective bureau, and one to Hal Agnew at his top-secret home number. He went out and bought a bulldog edition of tomorrow's *Times* (which was disappointing), and had a dark beer (which was not).

It was with mixed emotions that Rook finally parked his car outside the Pink Peacock Club and came in to catch most of what was left of the owl show from a front-row table. He immediately decided that burlesque had changed since the old Main Street days; these girls—as well as their costumes, music, and lighting, were all *class*. No baggy-pants comics in the tradition of Bert Lahr or Joe Yule; humorous relief was offered by a master of ceremonies with a ribald repertoire.

Miss Holly Wood, evidently the *pièce de resistance*, came out finally to the strains of Rimsky-Korsakov's *Scheherazade*, wearing her own honey-colored hair again and—for a time at least—a beautifully designed evening gown of iridescent green. When their eyes met she gave him a special smile and ground him a special bump (so understated as to be almost ladylike), and he raised his hand in a mechanical salute. For now, in spite of himself, he was seeing the fair Holly in a new light.

She finally got undressed down to two pasties and a glittering G-string, taking five bows at the demand of an enthusiastic if semi-drunk audience, and then disappearing with an alluring if automatic smile.

Leaving some currency on the table to pay for his untouched highball, Rook headed backstage by the shortest route. He arrived at Holly's dressing room after a slight delay, finding her busily removing war paint. She did a double-take at his appearance. "Migawd, Howie! Wha-hoppen?"

Rook was making repairs before her mirror. "A man said I couldn't come backstage," he said, ruefully surveying the tear in his jacket.

"But that must have been Bud, one of the bouncers! You tried to come in through the front instead of the stage door. You could have been hurt—Bud carries a sap!"

"Not anymore, he doesn't." Rook laid the object down on the table. "Suppose you hurry and get dressed. I'll be out front in the car—I want to talk to you."

"Yes, Master! I love dominant males. Something come up?"

"You might say that, yes."

He had to wait in the car for not too long a time, and then she came hurrying out, in fright wig and quiet topcoat again. But he kept his eyes on the road as they drove.

"You're not afraid anymore that I'm being followed? Then can I buy us some steaks at Barney's or somewhere?"

"If you're hungry there's stuff at home." Holly cocked her head at this, and gave him a look, then subsided. They rode on in silence, and they climbed the creaking stairs in silence.

But once inside she flung off the coat and wig and faced him. "Just what's wrong, lover-boy?"

"Why should anything be wrong?"

"You've gone a million miles away. What's the matter, was my act indecent, immoral, and probably habit-forming?"

"The act? Oh, you were great, just great."

Holly gave up that approach. "You had no luck with the clippings?"

"Some. You may look if you like." He showed her, but she didn't see the connection.

"*Total recall through hypnosis, says psychologist . . . John (the gimp) Anselmo wiped out in Cicero Alley . . . roving reporter at Vegas Casinos . . . F.B.I. says unique $25,000 car can't be sold . . . new Police Chief for L.A. takes over next month . . .*"

She raised her eyebrows. "So?"

"The one from Chicago says that the murdered man had a dime for carfare put in his hand after he was dead, as a derisive gesture. Said to be common practice back in the Al Capone era, when this is dated. But the idea comes from the ancient Romans, who used to put an obul, a small coin, in the hand of the corpse—"

"To pay Charon to ferry the soul across the Styx!" she put in. "Don't look so startled, I read all sorts of things."

"No doubt. By the way, I found out the name of the doctor who gave a reporter that feature story on total recall through deep hypnosis. In that condition you might remember a useful description of the two men you say you saw commit murder. Theoretically it would be possible for you to remember everything that happened to you in your entire life."

"Perish forbid!" cried Holly.

"But it takes full cooperation. And you can't lie under deep hypnosis. Want me to make an appointment for you with the doctor?"

She flung herself down on the couch, nervously lighting a cigarette.

"Frankly, I'm not too hot about it. Hypnotism scares me."

"Okay. The clipping about the bulletproof limousine gave me a wild idea, the one on Vegas is only background, the one on the new police chief reminds me that I used to know the present interim chief. But Holly, there's one more clipping that I didn't find in my files—not the sort of thing I collect. But Hal Agnew read it to me over the phone—he keeps a scrapbook of his cases. The date was February something, 1965. The story got a big play, because of the cheesecake art that went with it. *Striptease Queen Loses Hundred Grand in Gem Theft* was the headline. Shall I quote some more?"

"Oh, *that!* The reporters exaggerated the value of my baubles."

"And you didn't meet Agnew 'at some party or other,' you retained him to get you off the hook for making a false report to the police and a phony insurance claim. Seems your jewels weren't stolen, just mislaid."

"It wasn't *quite* like that!" Holly said in a suddenly tight voice.

"But you got a lot of free front-page publicity, didn't you? And no doubt a new contract? Is it option time again, Miss Holly Wood? Sergeant Corey at the detective bureau says they didn't buy your report of the murder because they had a hunch you made it all up."

"And *you* believe that?"

"It occurred to me that nobody saw the murder but you, nobody saw the corpse or the killers but you, nobody backs up any part of your story except Willi with his account of the men trying to get into your apartment and he could have been rehearsed. The man in the bar at Barney's may or may not have acted strangely—I was away phoning. You chickened out on the hypnosis when I told you that it's a sort of lie detector, and you were too interested in how your story might be written up for some magazine."

He shook his head. "It all adds up. Holly, you're one hell of a good actress. But I don't like being conned by a pair of beautiful amethyst eyes—"

Her face was frozen, uncontrite. "Thanks at least for mentioning my eyes instead of my shape, like everybody else! Sorry to bother you. Now if you'll be kind enough to call me a taxi—"

"It's awfully late. You might as well bunk out there on the sleeping porch as we planned." But she shook her head, busily packing her things. "Well then, I'll drive you home," he conceded.

"*Mister* Rook, I wouldn't let you drive me to the hospital if I had two broken legs!" Then she turned to face him. "Just for the record, when did you get wise to my conning you, as you call it? You were all on my side until you went out and bought that fright wig. I bet it was your girl friend Estelle who flung the feathers in the electric fan! All I can say is, you two deserve each other!"

Nor, when the cab came, would she permit him to help her down the stairs with the suitcase and the cage of birds. "I've put you through quite enough trouble already," she said over her shoulder. "Don't forget to send me a bill."

And she was gone. Howie Rook, a sadder but wiser man, wearily sought his monastic couch; to tell the truth he was feeling somewhat relieved. Miss Holly Wood had swept into his life like a hot Santa Ana windstorm, and as suddenly swept out of it leaving only a tantalizing scent of perfume. Chalk it up to experience.

He slept like a log, without nightmares. The nightmare was to come when, around noon the next day, he picked up the early editions of the afternoon papers.

The body of a man, partially clad and dead of stab wounds, had been discovered at sunrise in one of the La Brea tar pits in Hancock Park.

An attendant had noticed a black topcoat floating in the shallow sump water which covered the pit—from the depths of which once had been recovered the bones of sabretooth tiger, hairy mastodon, and dire wolf. But in recent years the viscid tar had hardened almost to asphalt. Whoever had forced a way through the ornamental shrubbery and cut through a wire guard-fence hadn't known how obvious a hiding place they'd chosen.

"Hellfire and damnation!" was Rook's only comment. "She didn't lie!"

Then to further brighten his day, Sergeants Corey and Bickel of the downtown detective bureau came hammering on his door. "Okay, where's the dame?" demanded Corey, hard-nosed as always.

"If you mean Miss Wood—at her apartment, I imagine."

"We been there," Bickel put in. "A Mr. Willi Benson across the hall says she's shacked up with you."

Rook silently stood aside and waved his hand. They searched, without apology, and then Corey barked, "Well, where is she then? She's eyewitness to a gang murder, and she has to be locked up in protective custody."

"I haven't the slightest idea. Tell me, did you identify the stiff?"

"Sure, from prints," Bickel said obligingly. "Name is Joseph Twitchett, known as 'The Professor,' age fifty-eight, former vaudeville magician and card mechanic. Did time in County four years ago on a poker con. Last address was a rooming house, now torn down—"

Sergeant Corey gave his associate the eye. "Let him read the papers."

"And there'll be plenty to read, I imagine," observed Rook almost cheerfully. "*Gangdom Returns to Los Angeles* or something like that—just like the old days, eh, Sarge?"

"It looks like a typical mobster job, all right. You could cooperate with us, but I suppose this calls for another of your snide letters-to-the-editor in some yellow journal, panning the department. Rook, if that dame shows up or contacts you, it's your duty to tip us off. And you mess in what is now a homicide case and you'll get the book thrown at you!"

The door slammed behind them. Frowning, Howie Rook made a frugal breakfast of coffee, liverwurst, and crackers. What to do? Unless Holly had had the sense to grab a plane for parts unknown she was hiding out somewhere in the vast rabbit warren of Los Angeles. It shouldn't be too hard to trace a beautiful girl carrying an outsize suitcase and a cage of birds—the cab company would have trip records. But he had no intention of helping the law locate Holly and lock her up among the tarts, dipsos, addicts, and bulldykes who swarmed like maggots in Women's Detention.

There must be some better answer. He couldn't drop the whole thing as Corey had ordered, nor could he sit at home by the phone all day in case she did call up to say, "I told you so!" after she saw the papers. And later editions would soon be out with the whole story, including pictures of her. The killers-at-large would be spurred on to greater efforts to silence the one possible witness against them.

What did he know, or what could he deduce, about the killers? Probably gang backgrounds—which meant out of city or even out of state. Los Angeles had plenty of crime, but it had been free of classic gang rule for a generation. Possible link with Las Vegas, the gambling-and-sin center? Trying to use the La Brea tar pits might indicate they were old-timers—it had been common underworld practice in the Forties.

But why had they brought their victim to the parking lot? Hauling a prisoner around, at that late hour, would have been asking for trouble with prowl cars on the alert. And why had they relieved the man of almost all his clothes?

Yet the dead man had been mixed up with cards and gambling, and had held what was probably a gambling chip in his lifeless fingers. That *must* indicate Las Vegas. Rook got on long distance and finally managed to locate a former contemporary on the old *Express*, who now was a semiretired flack in the gambling city.

"Howie, the things I have to do because I left L.A. owing you a measly twenty bucks!" complained Bob Sullivan. But he promised to ask around town about a character who may have been known as Professor Twitchett, and to check out the Gold Oasis in particular.

"If you get anything, don't phone, wire. I may be out." Then Rook hung up and set out to ring doorbells, because it occurred to him that the victim might never have even been in the killer's car, or completely dressed that early morning. He could have been roused from bed in some lodging in the neighborhood of the Pink Peacock, and frog-marched down to the parking lot—and to his death.

It was a brilliant inspiration, but it proved faulty. Rook covered every apartment and every rooming house in the tawdry section, but there was nobody named Twitchett on any mailbox, and no information from any landlady or janitor. Dead end.

But wait! A former variety performer, an old vaudevillian, would undoubtedly put *Billboard*, that bible of the fringe world of show biz, ahead of any other contact with the profession. And the magazine would be cheaper by subscription than buying it on the newsstands.

It took one long-distance call, and the promise of a bottle of Scotch to a sub-editor who was a fellow Guild member, and Rook learned that one Joe Twitchett, Apartment 4, 7960 Morton, was on the subscription list. The address would be almost facing the rear of the Peacock parking lot!

Rook burned rubber to that address, knocked gently on the door of Number 4—which happened to be in the name of Mr. and Mrs. Jonathan Twist. Same initials—he should have spotted that earlier. At his second knock the door opened to the extent of a short chain. "Yes?" came a hoarse but definitely feminine voice, in a tone that said, "No!"

"Mrs. Twitchett—I mean Twist—do you know where Joe is?" That was a fairly safe opening, unless she'd heard some flash report on the radio.

"He's not home. Go away!"

"But I'm Bozo—Bozo Jones—Joe and I worked together a coupla times. I know of a club in Downey that's putting on old-time variety, and there's a spot for a good illusionist, if Joe is free. Or is he still tied up with that Vegas caper?"

That got him inside. The woman was fat, blowzy, and clad in a reddish housecoat that matched her eyes. She wore thick-lensed glasses, indicating that she might once have had an operation for double cataracts. There was a can of beer in her hand, and it was obvious she was feeling no pain.

And she hadn't heard the bad news. It went against his finer feelings, but under the circumstances he had to play along, using whatever he could remember of the patois of carny talk from his one memorable week with the circus in the Unhappy Hooligan case. She was a woman, though somewhat toadlike in appearance. And she was obviously lonely, itching for somebody to talk to. When he wished, Rook could exert a certain ingratiating, middle-aged charm. He consented to accept a beer.

"No, Joe ain't home now, but he got home from Vegas on Monday."

Rook had glanced at the small bookcase and seen a whole shelf devoted to the works of John Scarne, Dr. Thorp, Maurice Lemmel, and so forth, all various approaches on How To Beat the Dealer. "The blackjack bit worked okay, then?"

The fat woman nodded complacently. "He did right good. But that sorta thing is risky. I wish he'd stick to the old act. Used to be The Professor and Gertrude, you know, before I put on weight. Pantages, Orpheum, all the circuits. But those days are gone forever. Wisht Joe could get on TV."

"He isn't out on a job now, is he?"

"Honest, I got no idea where he went. He must of took off in the middle of the night—night before last it was. I was asleep in the bedroom in there and he was sacked out on this couch. Somebody knocked on the door and off he went. Maybe it was some all-night poker game, and it's still going on."

"He went without his—I mean, what was he wearing?"

"How should I know? I don't check his clothes. Say, Mr. Bozo Jones, you sure do ask a lot of questions. And come to think of it, I don't remember Joe ever mentioning your name."

"Since Joe and I did that time in County four years ago it looks like we both changed monikers," Rook put in quickly. "But I'd sure like to reach him. D'you suppose he went off with his Vegas friends?"

"You mean Hymie and Slim? Never did get their last names. They come here only oncet, and then Joe made me go in the bedroom while they talked. It was all sort of hush-hush, and I'm surprised Joe told you as much as he did, if you really wanta know."

She was getting wise, tipsy or not. Rook stood up. "When Joe comes home tell him to phone me—he knows the number. Thanks, Gertie."

Just then there came a heavy knocking at the door. Both of them froze. The knock came again, and then the unmistakable accents of Sergeant Hard-Nose Corey. "Open up, Mrs. Twitchett!"

The fat was really in the fire for Howie Rook. The Sergeant would be more than delighted to really throw the book at him. But the fat woman came suddenly alive. She cried, "Just a minute—I ain't decent!" and at the same time motioned Rook toward the kitchen, pantomiming out and *down.*

For a heavy man Howie could move swiftly and silently, and he did. In a flash he was through the kitchen and down the service stair, coming out in the alley behind the Pink Peacock.

His car was parked on Morton, but luckily not right in front of the entrance from which Corey would be bringing out the Twitchett woman for a trip to the Morgue. She didn't look and act like a type who would readily unbosom herself to the law, but that was a calculated risk. He'd give them ten minutes, no more.

It was enough. In fifteen minutes he was back home and on the phone again, for there'd been a Western Union slip on his door. It was from Bob, and he took it down word for word.

NOW YOU OWE ME. CHARACTER KNOWN ONLY AS THE PROFESSOR WAS A REGULAR AT GOLD OASIS BLACKJACK TABLES FOR COUPLE OF WEEKS, LEAVING ONLY TO EAT AND SLEEP. DEALERS SAY HE PLAYED VARIATION OF SCARNE'S MEMORY SYSTEM, WINNING SOME, LOSING MORE. WHEN BUSTED HE WOULD GO OUT AND COME BACK WITH FUNDS, SO MUST HAVE HAD BACKERS. LAST SATURDAY NIGHT FOR ELEVEN HOURS HE PLAYED ALL FIVE HANDS AT ONE TABLE. BIG KILLING, TOOK HOUSE FOR FIFTY GRAND ACCORDING TO PRESS RELEASE. GOT WINNINGS IN BIG BILLS AND CHECKED OUT OF HIS MOTEL. BOB.

Which for Rook filled in some more bits of the jigsaw puzzle. But the most important pieces were still missing; the men who called themselves "Hymie" and "Slim" were still anonymous menaces. Holly had got nowhere trying to find their faces in the mug files. Perhaps now, with nicknames, that angle could be checked out more thoroughly, but it would take weeks.

And Rook didn't have weeks, or even days. Hours, maybe. He wired back to Bob: RECHECK CASINO. ASK BLACKJACK DEALER DID PROFESSOR WEAR GLASSES AND DID ANYBODY CHECK THE USED CARDS. WERE TWO ROUGH TYPE

MEN REGISTERED AT MOTEL SAME TIME AS PROFESSOR. IF SO GET FULL NAMES AND DESCRIPTIONS. ANSWER SOONEST.

Then he made other calls, being most interested in a certain unique automobile, then in getting past red tape to the ear of an amiable, grizzled old man with whom he had once played penny ante in the press room at the Hall of Justice, and finally down the list to the detective bureau, where he found that Sergeant Corey was out.

Probably still grilling Gertie Twitchett, Rook guessed. "Have him call me back. It's regarding Holly Wood—the girl, not the place."

That brought almost immediate results. Rook had had barely time to open a can of beer when Corey called back, his voice hopeful. "Well, Howie! So the dame *did* call in. Where is she?"

"She didn't call, but I know where she's hiding," lied Rook. "But I can't tell you unless you make a promise—"

"No deals! You're harboring a fugitive and interfering with police officers in the performance of their duty!"

"Correction. She's committed no crime, so she's not a fugitive. And I'm only trying to help you do your job, if you'll just shut up and listen. Only you're not going to put that nice kid in Detention!"

"Nice kid, my behind! She's thirty if she's a day, and she's a—"

"Say that to me sometime when you're not wearing a badge and I'll take pleasure in breaking that hard nose of yours!"

"Any time at all!" bellowed Corey.

"But meanwhile we got a problem. The killers think she saw the murder and can recognize them. If you lock her up, what about Willi Benson, who saw two men trying to break into her apartment? What about the Twitchett woman, who saw two men planning a Vegas caper with her late husband? How about—?"

"Aha! So that was your heap parked on Morton, and you did get to Gertie!" The Sergeant was almost frothing at the mouth.

"Easy, now. I'm the only one who knows where Holly is." It just occurred to Rook that he did know—it had just popped into his mind.

Corey suddenly changed his tone. "Well, I hope you got more out of Mrs. Twitchett than we did. She was all cut up over seeing her husband's body. You and I ought to compare notes sometime. Now where's the dame?"

"I'll tell you when you promise to keep your hands off her. And remember, right now Holly is the bait that will lure the killers out into the open—if you play your cards right. I know where there's a bullet-proof limousine gathering cobwebs. . . ." He went on to explain.

"A theatrical grandstand play?" Corey almost laughed. "Rook, you're absolutely and completely nuts."

"Am I now? Acting Chief of Police Chad Green didn't think so."

"You went over my head to the top? You couldn't—"

"Chad was always friendly with the working press. If you haven't heard from him, you will."

"Rook, let me tell you something for your own—hold it, I got a call on the other line." Rook strained his ears, but could only hear indistinguishable mumblings. But finally Corey's voice came back. "Sorry to keep you waiting," he said, with abnormal politeness.

"So that call *was* from Chad Green, eh? Now maybe—"

"No, Howie." Corey spoke very gently, as to an idiot child. "The call was none of your damn business, but you might be interested so I don't mind telling you. It was a flash report that Mrs. Gertrude Twitchett got herself fatally shot about ten minutes ago. We'd sent her home from the Morgue in a taxi, which pulled up in front of her place only to get met by a lot of lead thrown by two men in a gray or green coupe. The taxi driver talked on the way to the hospital. Now will you make some sense and tell me where the Wood girl is?"

Holly was in her dressing room at the Pink Peacock, where else? At the moment she was stretched out on a cot borrowed from the night man, with the mink coat over her for warmth and not display. She had read herself to sleep with a paperback whodunit, but it was a troubled sleep—she tossed and whimpered in her dreams.

Beside her the parakeets complained in soft chitterings and at the other end of the building a fat chef and his assistants were busy with preparations for the Famous Sizzling Steak dinners included in the cover charge. At the service bar a dreamy busboy was polishing a mountain of highball glasses and humming "Guadalajara" off key.

It was the quiet hour for the nightspot, suddenly broken by alarums and excursions offstage. There were loud voices raised in anger, the sickening thud of blows, the crash of boards and the rip of canvas. The melee gathered around the stage door, then moved inward slowly like one of the hurricanes which now and then come upon Florida from the Gulf, no less frightening because they are given the names of girls.

Call this one Hurricane Holly. Only it took her a minute or so to come awake and sort out dreams from reality. She burst out of her dressing room clad in not much of anything and saw that a lone intruder was getting somewhat the worst of it from a chef, a doorman, a busboy, and several others. "Cut!" she screamed.

The busboy, with a switch-blade held low at his knees, seemed about to take the command literally. But Holly stiff-armed her way into the scrimmage, then clasped Howie Rook to her heavily insured bosom. The others reluctantly drew back, and she led him to her dressing room and slammed the door. The burly man let her swab his cuts and bruises, which luckily were superficial.

"Thanks," he managed to say through a split lip. "Am I to understand I'm forgiven for leaping to all the wrong conclusions this morning?"

"No," said Holly. "Not by a damn sight." But she kissed him again, so that he felt his ears flaming. "I know, I know," she said wearily, "The man said you couldn't come in, but you did."

"I've been accused of stubbornness," he admitted. "Will you please put something on, so I can keep my mind on business? Things have been happening."

"Too many things for this particular chick." She did a quick striptease in reverse, slipping into a housecoat. "Now tell me."

And he told her about the specially designed limousine, built at the order of a Central American dictator who had been liquidated before he could get delivery. "Right now it's in Dutch Damn's body shop being tuned up and given a lovely shade of Shocking Pink."

She jumped ahead of his story. "Wonderful, right out of a grade B movie! How bulletproof are those windows really? It's not just my fair white body, but the mink coat—it isn't completely paid for."

"You won't be in the car, you'll be with me," he told her.

"Now I'm beginning to like the whole idea," Holly said firmly, flicking her long eyelashes.

"It's not so bad, if I do say so myself." Rook was to remember that rash remark for many a year, with appropriate shudders. But he went on, "I must get back home, where there may be an important telegram for me. I'll be back before Zero Hour. You'll be safe enough in here. And you might fix it with the staff so I don't have to battle my way back in. I was an amateur wrestler when I was in journalism school at UCLA, but that was years ago and I'm afraid I'm a little rusty."

"You're not rusty in the think-tank, anyway!" she told him. "And before you go—if it makes any difference, I have forgiven you for not believing my tale of woe. It's so wild I hardly believe it myself. And I didn't tell you about the jewel thing because—well, it was my boyfriend who had walked out with the stuff, so you see—"

"Forget it," Rook told her.

"This is for luck," Holly said, and kissed him again.

"This could be habit-forming," Rook told himself as he made his exit. "Probably she has an Electra complex. But they say any pretty girl will flirt when the train is pulling out."

Back home there was another notice to call Western Union. It was from Bob.

ADD DATA. PIT BOSS AT OASIS ACTING ON TIP FOUND FIVE DECKS OF CARDS USED BY HOUSE ON NIGHT OF PROFESSOR'S BIG WIN. ALL HAVE FINGERMARKS DAUBED ON BACKS OF TENS AND FACE CARDS. IT WAS A MAGICIAN'S TRICK NOT A LEGIT SYSTEM. PROBABLY PROFESSOR HAD DAUB IN POCKET. THEY WOULD HAVE SUSPECTED SHENANIGANS HAD PROF WORN GLASSES.

"Contact lenses!" interrupted Rook jubilantly. "Special lenses to spot the markings. Read on, please."

CASINO MANAGEMENT NOW ADMIT HE ONLY WON $36,000. ANY BIG WIN GOOD PUBLICITY FOR HOUSE AND BRINGS IN SUCKERS. THEY PADDED FIGURE IN PRESS RELEASE JUST LIKE THEY DO SALARIES FOR STARS' PERSONAL APPEARANCES. NOTHING ON MOTEL WHERE PROF STAYED. REST OF UNITS TAKEN OVER BY CAST AND CREW OF TV COMPANY MAKING PILOT FILM QUOTE UNDERWORLD UNQUOTE NOW FINISHED AND GONE. YOU OWE ME MONEY REPEAT MONEY. BOB.

More bits of the jigsaw. And Rook began to see glimmerings of a possible answer to two things which had been puzzling him all along—the why of the killers reverting to old-time gangster tactics, and their determination to wipe out everyone who'd even caught a look at them.

Inelegant but unmistakable inner rumblings reminded him now, however, that he had only had breakfast today, and a skimpy one at that. He had promised to get back to the Pink Peacock—but he had his doubts about the Sizzling Steaks; so he took time out to heat up and consume a packaged and frozen TV dinner—which turned out to be as vapid and tasteless as the entertainment medium itself. Come to think of it, it would be funny if the answer to the last remaining question in this whole puzzle was linked with what he referred to as the "boob tube."

It was still early in the evening—or at least not too late to follow this new lead. Any port in a storm. But first he took time out to phone Willi Benson, Holly's helpful neighbor, and give him a warning about keeping out of sight while the heat was on. Rook already felt guilty about the

Twitchett woman, and didn't want any other deaths on his conscience. But Willi wasn't home—or he wasn't answering his phone.

But Estelle answered at the first ring. She was openly disappointed that the call did not concern an invitation for bowling, late supper, or a slumming trip down the Sunset Strip, but had only been made because he wanted to locate a book.

"I don't play the horses anymore," she told him.

"I mean a special book—with pictures in it," Rook explained impatiently. "Maybe you don't have it, but maybe you know somebody who knows somebody who does."

Finally she promised to see what she could do, if he'd come over for coffee and dessert. It was a relatively small sacrifice for him to make under the circumstances.

What with one thing and another it was almost zero hour when Rook got back to the Pink Peacock, leaving his car out on the street in a yellow zone and hoping that his new status of co-belligerence with the law would cover any parking ticket. Lugging the reference book, he walked around the side of the building to the stage door, noting that the substitute limousine, newly painted, had already been delivered and was waiting in the parking lot for its role in what he had begun to think of as "Operation Sitting Duck." A cold wind whistled about his knees, promising rain.

Inside he found that Holly was engaged onstage in doing her last strip of the evening. And Sergeant Hard-Nose Corey, having forgotten his original disparagement of the whole idea, was very much the generalissimo. Holly would finish her act and come off at 2:10. At about 2:30 her double, dressed in her coat and clothes and wearing a blonde wig matching her hair, would leave by the stage door, get in the pink limousine, and drive home over a prescribed route—up Santa Monica to the turn, straight ahead on Holloway, along Sunset Boulevard, and up to the apartment on Larrabee.

"Followed and preceded and guarded at most intersections by unmarked police cars," explained the Sergeant. "For extra protection there's a police marksman crouched down out of sight in the back seat of the limousine."

Rook at the moment couldn't find any flaws in it. "Of course we don't know that the hoods have their eyes on this place, or that even if they do that they'll strike tonight," he pointed out.

"If nothing happens tonight, the double spends the rest of the night and tomorrow in the dame's apartment and is covered the same way coming to work tomorrow night and going home tomorrow night. And so on.

As for you, Howie, I know you don't want to miss the excitement, but you and the Wood dame have to keep the hell out, understand? There may be lead flying all over the street, and we don't want any kibitzers."

"'They also serve who only stand and wait,'" quoted Rook sadly.

Just then there came the loud and indignant voice of Holly from behind them. "What's this hairy ape doing in my dressing room?"

It turned out that no policewoman had been found who cared much about volunteering to be the Target for Tonight, and that Officer Mike Something-or-other had been selected on the basis of being the minimum for height and weight of policemen. He had managed to get into Holly's dress and coat, but as for the rest of it—

"No cracks," hastily put in Sergeant Corey. "Mike captured the Griffith Park mugger who'd been attacking women, and going drag isn't his idea of fun, either." He glared at both Holly and Rook.

"Well, I don't care much for his idea of makeup! And that wig—" Holly pushed the young policeman down in a chair and set about putting on his face for him. She had quite forgotten that she was wearing only pasties and the sequin G-string, and no rouge was necessary because Officer Mike was turning redder than a beet.

"Oops!" cried Holly, putting on a robe. She did what she could, combed out the wig, and put a pink beret on top of it. "If you get any bullet holes in my mink I'll tear you apart with my own fair hands," she promised him. "Take small steps and swing your body when you walk. And I hope to heaven the hoodlums are near-sighted."

She gave him the pink handbag and shoved him maternally on his way. "If you don't get hit tonight, the key to my apartment is in the bag. There's food in the fridge and Scotch in the cabinet and don't use my toothbrush!"

And the sacrificial victim marched out the stage door. Sergeant Corey lingered a moment to give them a final warning about staying put and not getting into the act, then left hastily through the front to mingle with the departing customers and join his cohorts.

The Pink Peacock was quiet, too quiet. Miss Honey Barr and Miss Sandy Monica and the other girls had long since departed. Maxie the night man had borrowed back his cot and was obviously more than anxious to fold.

"So I guess we just sit here," Rook advised Holly. "You might pass the time by studying the book I brought you. Because it occurred to me that the men we're looking for might not be in the mug files of the police, but in the Central Casting Directory. Character types, actors, and bit players and extras. There was a company in Vegas making a pilot for a gangster TV show when the Professor was doing his stuff."

"What? You mean a couple of hams trying to live their hoodlum parts in real life?"

"Stranger things have happened. You and I both know a former movie star who's running a gambling joint in London, and a female star who tried shoplifting."

Holly obediently looked, but finally handed back the book. "No dice."

"Nobody pictured in there looks like the men you saw?"

"They all do—the male gang and Western players, I mean. The gangster players look more like hoods than the real wrong-gos did in the police mug files! It could be any of dozens—"

Just then the backstage phone rang—or rather flickered its light, because any bell would interrupt the show. "This could be it!" gasped Holly. She and Rook ran a dead heat to the phone. It was also a dry run, for it was only an exasperated Sergeant Corey reporting that Operation Sitting Duck had failed. Holly's double hadn't been hit.

"They saw through your disguised rookie," Rook told him.

"And you forgot that it's Saturday night and the Sunset Strip is a jamup of teen-agers and kooks so no car can hardly get through! Enough to scare anybody away! But we'll give it another try tomorrow. Nighty-night, lovebirds!"

"Damn!" said Howie Rook ineffectually, as he hung up.

"Doubled in spades," agreed Holly. "So a cop gets to sleep in my nice soft bed, and we're supposed to camp out here?"

"Where else? You're not safe on the street."

Holly, it developed, had foreseen this possibility. "When the Sergeant came rampaging around earlier tonight, I sneaked away and phoned Willi Benson to bring me down some of his clothes—we're about the same size except maybe in the chest. I'm going out of here in reverse drag. In a taxi to a hotel—unless you act sensible and let me come home with you. I can't sit up in a chair all night, not in this dump! I'm getting cabin fever!"

Rook had his doubts. But Holly shoved him out of the dressing room. "You go and make sure Santa Monica Boulevard is deserted, and I'll fix myself up so my own mother wouldn't know me! I'll be a lot safer with you than here with only Maxie as a guard and him asleep!"

In less than twenty minutes she rejoined him, looking like nothing human—and certainly nothing like herself. From a cape with a monk's hood which effectively covered her hair down to red slacks and open sandals, she was a beatnik teen-ager of a sort all too common in the Sunset Strip area. She had darkened her face with makeup until she looked Mexican, and a large cigar stuck out of her unrouged lips.

"Okay?" she demanded.

"No comment. But it's raining hard, which will help some. Hardly any traffic on the Boulevard, and my car is just outside."

They came out together, purposely unhurried, and climbed into the jalopy. There were no pedestrians about, and only a couple of trucks and one empty sports car parked a block or more to the east, in the direction of Hollywood.

The motor choked, then finally caught, and they drove off into the rain, with Rook's foot heavy on the accelerator. "It'll be duck soup," said Holly with supreme confidence. "We'll have a cozy little supper, and then I'll get a good night's sleep in your bed and you on the sofa."

"It just occurred to me," said Rook, "that somebody could have been watching the Peacock front from a window, maybe with binoculars. Or the parking lot—and seen the light go out in your dressing room."

"Worry wart," Holly told him.

Suddenly he opened the throttle full and went through a red light at the corner of La Cienega. "Wow!" said Holly. "For that I need an acceleration couch, like in the science-fiction stories."

"We're being followed," said Rook.

"I don't see any headlights."

"It's a black car—a little foreign number," Rook told her. "No lights. That figures. They first used a gray one and then a green one, both stolen probably. I'm afraid I've got you into a trap, Holly."

He turned suddenly on two wheels and swerved sharply off the boulevard, winding and twisting in the tangle of streets below the Strip. The little black car hung on.

"The hoods saw through the pink car," Holly whispered. "I was afraid they could tell a limousine from a convertible."

"More likely they saw through your double," Rook said, fighting to get every ounce of speed out of his souped-up rattletrap, risking their necks at every intersection. "If we come up to a police cruise car I'll crash it."

"The fuzz is never around when you want 'em, you know that."

"If I can get a little farther away from them I'll turn a corner and slow down and you can jump out—"

"And probably sprain an ankle and just lie there when they come past! No, dear Howie. I'll stick with you."

Rook's mind was running around in frantic circles, with wild and impossible alternatives flitting past. Drive off the Santa Monica pier and swim for it? Turn back to Griffith Park and head off across the golf course? These and even more fantastic impossibilities came to him, and were discarded.

The black car hung on, sometimes dark, sometimes with headlights, sometimes with parking lights—and steadily inching closer. Holly was taking it amazingly well. "Being actors, they're probably lousy shots," she observed. "The Twitchett woman and the taxi driver were both hit only by ricochets in the cab, the papers said."

Rook, desperate, thought of racing up to the Sheriff 's substation, or into the lot where cars were impounded—but the black car was too close.

They had reached a familiar neighborhood when Howie made a reckless decision. "I'm going to head for my own alley," he told Holly grimly. "It's narrow, and I'll skid this car so it stops crosswise. Brace yourself and get ready to jump—I'll follow out your door and we'll race for my apartment. Ready?"

"I'm ready," she said. "Ready for Freddy, like the old saying goes. Freddy's an undertaker."

The black car was only half a block behind them when they skidded on the slick asphalt into the alley below Rook's place, skidded again, and almost overturned as they came to a stop.

Holly and then Rook exploded out of the jalopy and ran madly through the puddled alley, then as madly started up the outside stairs. "They'll be afoot from now on, anyway," he said, as behind them there was a minor crash of metal as the black car slammed into the side of Howie's. Then Howie had the door unlocked and they were inside.

"No lights!" he whispered. "You find the phone and get down on the floor and call the police—fast!" Somewhere around the place there must be a weapon of some kind.

He could think of a walking stick that had been his grandfather's, an ornamental Japanese sword, a meat cleaver. . .

From the living-room window he could see two dark shapes moving closer along the alley, outlined against the dim street lights. No other dwelling had its entrance on the alley: by the process of simple elimination the killers must come here, even if they hadn't seen or heard the frantic climb up the outside stairs. It was only a matter of moments.

"I *can't* phone," Holly's whisper came in the darkness. "Somebody's on the line!"

"Party line," Rook came back. "Try to break in and tell them it's an emergency!" Then he gripped her arm. "Hold it," he whispered. "I know that creak of the steps. But the bolt and door are flimsy—"

"I'm not very good at screaming out the window—"

"The *window!*" he came back. "I've got a clipping—in ancient days people in a besieged fortress used to pour boiling oil down on their attackers."

"Who's got boiling oil handy?"

"If I can only find a screwdriver—"

Probably Holly thought he was completely addled at turning to a household tool as a weapon, but he was fumbling with the two cans of paint—the big five-gallon cans that had been intended for redecoration purposes. The lids finally were prized off.

And standing on a chair, Howie Rook flung open the living-room window above the outside stairs and dumped ten gallons of paint, just house paint, on two very surprised and chagrined actors-turned-gunmen, in a deluge of canary yellow. They got it in the face, they got it from head to toe, then got it on the guns in their hands and the knives in their pockets and in their mouths and under their fingernails.

They were gone when the police arrived, but even the worst of thumb-fingered cops can follow a trail of canary-colored paint.

Hours later, or so it seemed, Howie Rook and Holly Wood were breaking their fast over the biggest porterhouse steaks that Barney's could find in the locker. They had hashed and rehashed the events of the past fortyeight hours, with Rook explaining how the jigsaw pieces finally fit.

"Okay," Holly said. "I get it all—only why did Hymie and Slim or whatever their real names are have to knife the Professor? Did he welsh?"

"They leaped to the conclusion that he had. He gave them their cut of $36,000—but the Las Vegas papers reported that the casino lost $50,000. Same thing goes with bank robberies—the authorities always release a magnified figure, hoping the bandits will fall out among themselves. And once Twitchett had been killed, the murderers had to go to any lengths to wipe out anyone who could possibly identify them—because as actors they expected to have their faces splashed all over the nation's TV sets."

"You're simply out of this world," Holly breathed.

"I can't really take the credit," he admitted ruefully. "The cans of paint happening to be right there was just fool's luck."

"If they hadn't been there you'd have remembered some other clipping and thought of something else," Holly told him. Her amethyst eyes were tender. "You remember my telling you about my crush on Paul Douglas, the actor? You remind me of him. Howie, have you ever thought of getting married and settling down and giving up crime chasing?"

"Have you ever thought of settling down to housework and dishes and giving up your career?"

"Not recently," she said with candor.

"And that goes double. We're ships that pass in the night unquote."

"Things that might have been. Well, I have my work—"

"And I have my clippings, and taking somebody like Estelle out bowling on Friday nights. You and I are worlds apart."

But from his vantage point across the room the elderly waiter could see that while this couple was staging a renunciation scene right out of soap opera, they were still holding hands under the table. So maybe it wasn't quite

THE END

How Lost Was My Father?

The Curious Case of David Lang

"It wasn't too much trouble to get ol' Dave started, but he sure has been hard to stop."

Elmer Hinton, The Tennessean, 17 February 1963

Who was the first person to recount how, after picking up a hitchhiker, they were stunned to discover that their passenger had somehow vanished from the car while it was moving?

And who was the first person to have known someone who knew a strict vegetarian who only ate nuts and seeds and eventually had to undergo an operation to remove a fully grown watermelon from their stomach?

The answer to these and similar questions is of course always just out of reach. The story happened to a friend or to the friend of a friend. Or even to the friend of a friend of a friend. That is the essence of an urban legend. But there is one urban legend whose origins might just be known, and that is the curious case of David Lang.

In 'How Lost Was My Father?', first published in *Fate* magazine in September 1953, Stuart Palmer presented what he asserted was a true story. Allegedly written in 1931, the story is presented as the affidavit of a woman, Emma Lang, in 1931, regarding the disappearance of her father on September the 23rd 1880. David Lang had been a farmer in Gallatin, Tennessee, and "Miss Lang" described how he had suddenly and inexplicably vanished while crossing a field. No explanation was provided; indeed, no explanation was possible.

For all its sensational aspects, the story was not unfamiliar. In a coda, Palmer brazenly pre-empted accusations of plagiarism with admirable chutzpah, alleging that possibly the best-known fictional story of an inexplicable disappearance, Ambrose Bierce's 'The Difficulty of Crossing a Field' had been based on the case of David Lang. Bierce's story was first published in October 1888 and concerns the disappearance in July 1854 of an Alabaman farmer, Orion Williamson. The circumstances are almost identical with those in Palmer's story. Elsewhere, Palmer also claimed that he himself had *first* come across the case of David Lang in an issue of a magazine called *Ghost* in 1936 or 1937. Palmer might have meant *Ghost*

Stories, which published several pieces by him but *Ghost Stories* ceased publication in 1932. In any case, no story about David Lang has yet been located in that or any other magazine prior to the publication of Palmer's story in *Fate*.

Bierce's story has never been widely considered as factual and is of course somewhat overshadowed by the author's his own unexplained disappearance. However, Palmer's "account", written with his characteristic ability to bring his characters and places vividly to life, caught the public imagination. Not long after he first appeared in *Fate*, David Lang stepped out of the magazine and into a place somewhere between folklore and history.

Two years later, a British journalist Harold T Wilkins described the disappearance in *Strange Mysteries of Time and Space* (London: Frederick Muller, 1955, as by Hugh Percival Wilkins). The book was an enormous success and three years later was published in New York by Citadel Press, 1958). An American writer, Frank Edwards, then included the case in *Stranger than Science* {New York: Lyle Stuart, 1959), based on a syndicated radio program of the same name. In Edwards' words, the case showed that it was *"possible for a human being literally to walk off the earth in full view of witnesses"*.

Which of course it isn't. Not that stopped the speculation. One explanation was suggested by a *"Dr Hern of Venice, Italy"* in an article for *The American Mercury* in November 1957. Hern suggested that Lang had been swallowed up by something akin to a black hole – *"In the universal ether there are void spots. They last for very brief periods. But during their existence they are capable of annihilating any material object entering their realm"*; alternatively, he might have walked into a magnetic field *"which speeded up vibrations of his body, propelling him into a fourth dimension"*.

The mysterious disappearance of the Tennessee farmer was repeated in magazines and newspapers all across America. However, on February the 7th 1960, Elmer Hinton, writing in *The Tennessean*, stated confidently that it was *"nothing more than the brain child of a traveling salesman from Cincinatti who used to stop over in Gallatin on his regular rounds"*. Hinton even gave the salesman's name, Joe Mulhatten, a real salesman whose gift for storytelling had led to his surname being accepted as slang for any tall tale. Hinton's efforts to debunk the myth failed and he was pestered by readers who wanted to know more. Writing two weeks later, seemingly exasperated by the response, he again stated firmly that the story had been made up by a travelling salesman, only this time "*his name was Ambrose Bierce, or something like that. One weekend bad weather caught him in Gallatin and he had to stay over for two or three days. While he was there he dreamed up the story of David Lang and wrote it in his hotel or boarding house room*".

More than any other writer, Hinton kept the story of David Lang alive, frequently reminding his readers of the "*fool story*" and producing entertaining addenda, such as a call he had received "*right after breakfast from Mrs Scott Whittaker of Bethpage*", alleging that David Lang had been her grandfather's brother. Only his name had been Jim Pursley and while the story was true "*in some respects*", he hadn't actually vanished – "*he left his wife and ran off with another woman*".

And the story never lost its appeal. In 1975, it was featured in *The People's Almanac*, edited by David Wallechinsky and Irving Wallace (New York: Doubleday, 1975), which prompted a flurry of fresh newspaper reports across America. And in 1981, Bill Boshears a journalist writing for the *Cincinnatti Enquirer*, the newspaper where in 1960 Elmer Hinton had alleged the story had first appeared stated that "*researchers claim that Lang literally stepped through a time warp barrier into the next dimension where the magnetic fields overlap and produce this time warp system where a person can exist*".

Frustratingly, the "researchers" were unnamed. Perhaps they were simply amateurs and not seen as outstanding in their field.

Rather like David Lang, in fact . . . or fiction!

"On a warm September afternoon in 1883
Let me tell you what happened at Gallatin, Tennessee.
There was an old dirt farmer, his name was David Lang.
What happened to him is a mystery, and is mighty, mighty strange.
He went to his mules one day to groom them for the county fair;
As his family watched him walk through the field, he vanished in thin air.
Bloodhounds trailed old David's steps to where he should have been;
At the spot where he disappeared, the trail came to an end.
Winter passed and spring came on and the grass came out so green,
But not one sprig would grow on the spot where David was last seen.
David Lang was never found, he never more appeared,
But his folks often heard him call for help from the spot where he
disappeared."

The Ballad of David Lang by Olan Bassham

Though it may seem strange to you, for a large part of my life I prayed and hoped that my father, whom I dearly loved, was dead.

But I searched for him as fruitlessly through mediums and séance chambers as I used to search, when a child back in Tennessee, in the meadow where he . . . went. My life, until last spring, was darkened by what may be one of the strangest tragedies ever to strike a normal, moderately prosperous country family.

I am an old woman now (in 1931) but I was 11 years old when it occurred. What happened on that peaceful, sunny September day is as much a mystery to me now as it was then. One moment my father was walking across his field, in full view of three people besides my little brother and myself. The next moment he was nowhere!

I had been playing with my eight-year-old brother George on the lawn and Mother was standing above us on the porch. Father had just returned from a business trip to Nashville and after talking briefly to the family he had changed into his outdoor clothes and started across the field to see the horses. They were his special pride, those blue-grass thoroughbreds.

"Hurry back, Davey," Mother called after him. "You know I want you to drive me in to Gallatin before the stores close." Father waved and called back something. It was the last time—with one exception—that we ever heard his dear voice.

The sun was slanting low above the elms that lined the country road, the sky was clear and cloudless. It was September 23, 1880, and summer, in that sheltered Tennessee valley, had not yet given way to fall. Our house, a rambling, brick place covered with vines, faced south to the road. Between was the long sloping yard, its grass now brown from the late summer drought. Down the road, perhaps a quarter of a mile away, came a 'top' buggy drawn by an old white horse which my brother and I had already identified as that of "Judge" August Peck, a Gallatin lawyer and a friend of Father's.

George and I had begun to argue about the little wooden horses and wagon that Father had brought us from Nashville when a terrible scream rang out above our heads. It was Mother!

For a moment neither of us could move. Mother screamed again and we rushed up to her. She was staring off across the fields toward where Father was—but Father was gone. One moment he had walked in the middle of the forty-acre pasture, and the next moment he had vanished.

There was not a tree nor even a large stone in that entire field where he had been. Yet now it stretched empty under the hot sun.

Mother already was running toward the spot where she had last seen Father. Her first thought, and ours, was that there had been a cave-in and that Father must have fallen in. As we climbed the barbed-wire fence George pointed down the road. Judge Peck had jumped out of his buggy, followed by a fat man in a white coat, and was hurrying across the pasture to meet Mother. The judge, standing where Father had been, spoke first, in a voice that was reedy and thin:

"I was coming to see him. Had to get his signature on some papers. I was watching him cross the field, because I wanted to wave to him to come back. And I was just going to holler when—when—" He broke off, mopping his face.

Mother stood there, holding onto us children as if she feared that we too would be spirited away. It was easy to see that there had been no cave-in: the pasture grass was level and green.

"There must be an old well here," said Judge Peck after a moment. "There just must be."

We watched the grownups as they searched. Around and around the field they went, covering every inch of the ground. It was useless. Mother soon stopped and made us children walk with her toward the fence. Suddenly she sank down on the ground and began to laugh, her mouth all twisted and funny. George broke away and ran toward the house but I, being older, tugged at Mother's dress begging her not to laugh like that.

Judge Peck and the fat man, who was his brother-in-law from Akron, Ohio, came back and helped Mother through the fence and back up to the house. Mammy Sukie, our colored cook and friend, took us to the kitchen and kept us there. She wouldn't let us talk about what had happened, nor run back to Mother, and I couldn't help noticing, and being frightened, that her pleasant face was gray-green. I think Mammy Sukie knew that Father was gone and wouldn't come back ever.

We could hear Mother's voice upstairs; it sounded different, pitched like the high notes on the piano. I knew when Doctor Anthony came because I saw his little spotted mare being led back to the barn.

We children were put to bed early that night and for once Mammy Sukie sat and told us stories and sang "Sweet Chariot" and "Ebenezer, A Slave" and "Vandermeer's Stream" as long as we wanted her to—and after that she still sat, her rocker creaking back and forth, back and forth.

George woke me later. "Sary," he whispered, "Father isn't in his bed. And Mother is downstairs with a lot of company; everybody is just sitting there, not playing cards or anything." He got back into his own bed. "Sary," he went on, "I went to the window in the front room and there are a lot of people with lanterns out in the pasture. Are they—are they looking for Father?"

They were. The neighbors searched all that night and all the next day. But they never found a trace of David Lang. The pasture was combed from one end to the other. They found his heel prints where he had jumped over the fence into the pasture, but that was all.

Our pasture was full of people for weeks—at first well-meaning people who sincerely wanted to help and then later curiosity-seekers.

If it had not been for the word of Judge Peck and his brother-in-law, Mr. Wade, nobody would have believed Mother and us. But there had been three witnesses, five, if you count George and me, who had seen Father vanish in the middle of a field.

Some people said that there must have been a cave-in but there was no hole. Besides, the county surveyor came and said there was limestone bedrock only a few feet beneath the surface of our pasture, with no chance of the surface giving way. One or two newspapers hinted that Father had run away. But the grass in the field had been pastured down by the horses until it was inches short—no one could have crawled through the grass unseen as they suggested. There was no place he could have hidden himself in that open field even if he had been unwatched. Wherever Father went, he went in a split-second, from under six adult eyes.

Besides, Father liked his family, his farm and his blooded horses. And if he meant to leave us why had he returned from Nashville? Father was a sensible man, almost fifty years old at the time, and he never went away of his own will—he was *taken* in a way that we cannot understand.

People, trying to be kind to us children, said, "Your father will come back in a few days." But Mammy Sukie never said that; she prayed for us and for Father every night and she gave us little charm bags to wear around our necks. "Never, never," she said, "let me see either of you child'en go out into that field again; it's a bad, bad place."

We children knew about death. But Father hadn't died. When people die there is some outworn clay to be quietly put away in the ground, with a ceremony and later a monument. Funerals help a little for they make an ending. But we had no funeral for Father, not even of the sort held for fishermen who have been lost at sea, because while one can drown in the ocean nobody can drown in a meadow.

Mother was never well after that day. For a long time she insisted that Father would return, that he would walk back the way he had gone, in his old overalls. Her hair turned white that autumn. Everybody wanted her to take us and go back to her family in Virginia but she refused. "Davey is coming back," she said, "and we must be here when he comes." Eventually she let Judge Peck rent out the fertile farmland.

I think now that the event must have affected Mother's mind a little. She was always gentle and kind to us but she always seemed far away. Late at night she would walk down to the meadow, in spite of Mammy Sukie's warnings, and we could hear her calling, "Davey, Davey . . ." by the hour, until we fell asleep in our beds.

Autumn passed and winter. Spring came and the new tenant Judge Peck had found began planting. He wanted to plow up the big meadow but his men wouldn't work where Father had disappeared so he put his horses and cattle in there to graze, where ours had pastured before they were sold.

Mother was in bed most of the time that spring as her health got worse. Georgie and I were more and more together for companionship and comfort. One evening he came to me, his round face very serious. "Come with me, Sary. I want to show you something." I followed my little brother down the path—Mammy Sukie was in her quarters out back and Mother as usual was in her room. There was no one to stop us.

Georgie led me across the country road with its muddy ruts and we slipped through the barbed-wire fence that led into the pasture—the fatal meadow which had somehow swallowed up my father. It was just after sunset and a warm twilight glow lay everywhere. I could hear the whinnying of the horses which were running in circles at the far end of the field. I was afraid, though I tried not to show it in front of Georgie. Georgie bravely led the way. I went along, not ashamed to hold his hand. We walked straight to the spot where Father had *gone*. Suddenly Georgie pressed my hand and we both squatted down on the close-cropped grass of the pasture.

I noticed nothing until my brother pointed it out to me. Then I saw an irregular circle, perhaps 15 feet in diameter, where the meadow grass grew rank and tall and had an odd yellowish-green color. It was the exact spot where Father had disappeared. I was suddenly terribly frightened. I had read of fairy rings but this was nothing like that. This was only a spot in the pasture where the horses refused to graze. According to Georgie they wouldn't even walk through that circle. . . . He had been watching them.

We edged a little closer. In the twilight, we both noticed the same thing. There was no living thing in that circle of grass! Everywhere else night-moths were circling and grasshoppers and crickets moved cheerfully. Even ants were busy—everywhere else. Fireflies were beginning to glow. But in that circle, there was nothing but the sick grass.

Georgie hunted through the grass and pounced upon a cricket; a little black bug that chirped happily, even in Georgie's hand. My brother threw the insect into the circle of lush grass. Instantly it stopped chirping, and as we watched the cricket climbed quickly across the grass blades, hopping and skipping headlong out of the circle! As the insect completed its journey out it fell to chirping, again, as if nothing had happened at all.

"Let's try to call to Father," I suggested. "He must be here somewhere. He must be enchanted, like the White Princess in the fairy tale. Maybe if we call . . . both of us together . . . loud enough . . ."

Huddled in the deepening darkness, we raised our voices in a wail of "Father, Father . . ." Again and again we called, hoping against hope, believing a little in magic. Only the echo of our own voices came back to us. Once more and then we would have to go—before we were missed at the house.

Then the unbelievable happened. From far, far off, in a faint, hollow and very tired voice which neither of us could ever fail to recognize, there came the voice of Father. I will swear it here and before the Last Court of Judgment!

What were the words—what did he say? How I wish I could remember but we were two small, frightened children. We could not remember, we could not hear plainly. Father's voice was strange and far-off and troubled. But it was the voice of a man—a man lost but alive, and I shall swear to that as long as I live.

"Help!" it seemed to say, and "Help!" again. But Georgie and I could not wait, though it might have been infinitely better if we had stayed. We might have learned things long hidden from the world but we had already gone too far and with panic-stricken shrieks we both set off across the pasture for the lights of home, to pour our story into the ears of Mammy Sukie, who already was out looking for us with a lantern. We told her the story, while Father's dearly-remembered voice still rang in our ears. She shook her head and sent us up to our room. And the next day all the servants left except dear Sukie.

Of course we told it to Mother . . . in spite of her sickness. But she only shook her head. "I have heard his voice too," she told us. "I have called to him and he has answered me, but his voice grows fainter every day . . ." Mother's strength was about at an end and she was never to be up and around again. She just lay in her bed in the big front room and always seemed to be listening. . . .

I realize now that our story must have got around, reviving the mystery of Father's disappearance. Other people noticed the circle of untouched grass in the middle of the pasture. Then everything happened at once. Grandfather and Grandmother came from Virginia. They insisted that the farm be sold and that Mother bring us back to her old home. Mother did not care what happened any longer and amidst the confusion of moving she died, without a last word to us. Georgie and I did what we were told and went where we were told. We understood that Mother had busied herself with other things—perhaps with listening.

We lived with our grandparents in Virginia and went to school and grew up as children grow.

The man who bought our place, so I have heard, plowed up the pasture in hope of putting an end to the story that the place was haunted but he must have failed for I hear that until this day there is a fence around that circle of land and that nothing grows there but rank grass and weeds. I once, as a young woman, returned there. I even crept out onto the meadow to the fatal spot and cried out my father's name. But there was no answer. Perhaps Father then had drifted deeper into that strange dimension so that he could no longer answer or hear.

This story is a famous one now. Ambrose Bierce, the writer of stories, was one of the many visitors who came that month after Father went and he wrote several of his most famous works about our mystery, cloaking it under the guise of fiction. But Mr. Bierce, whom I remember as a frightening man with angry moustaches, went off to Mexico and they say he got shot by a firing squad. Anyway, he never lived to learn the end—if it is the end—of my father's story.

My brother George, being a boy, adjusted himself more easily to our new environment and finally went off into the Army, eventually married, and had a family. My brother, now (in 1931) Captain George Lang, has no explanation for the things we saw and heard as children. And I must admit that he has never had any sympathy with my attempts to find an answer, nor does he accept the answer which has finally satisfied me.

It was not strange that when I came out of the finishing school to which my grandparents had sent me—a pleasant place in Baltimore—I turned my attention toward spiritualism. I was desperately determined to contact the Hereafter, to find out what had happened to my father, to locate Mother if it were possible and to see if she, beyond the veil, had learned any of the secrets.

I wasted years of time and thousands of dollars cultivating the most famous mediums—including Margery of Boston. But I was perpetually disappointed. I met two types of mediums—plain fakes, who did parlor magic with trumpets and other gadgets, and honest, sincere, inept people who got no results at all, or got messages which were pointless, foolish and childish.

Then one night I was sitting in a small séance in Philadelphia, in a group where nobody could have known my name. The medium, an elderly woman, was in trance and was giving messages that were meaningless generalities. Suddenly she paused, choked, and in a new voice spoke, a man's voice, harsh and grating. I learned later that it was the voice of a control she called "Hugo," who sometimes came to her.

"Someone is calling for Sarah, Sarah Long; I think the name is Long. It is—"

"Is it a man, is it Father?" I cried out, hoping against hope.

"No, it is a woman," continued the voice. "It is a woman, very young, though all white." (I knew he meant Mother, for her hair had turned white before she died.)

"She says that she is seeking as you are seeking . . . and that she is waiting as you are waiting. And she says that you can come to her directly. . . ."

That was all—the contact broke. I left the place puzzled and confused. The message had said too much or not enough. Was this a summons for me? Mother wanted me to be with her. She was seeking as I was and waiting for me to come to her even as I waited. And I could come to her "directly."

But that wasn't what Mother would have said. She would never use the word "directly" to mean "at once." Nor would she, a former schoolteacher, have made the mistake of saying, "You *can* come to me" unless she meant to imply that coming to her was possible for me. I puzzled over it a long time, and then one night the whole thing cleared up as I awoke from a deep sleep. I had been wrong in my first guess. The message meant just what it said and no more. Mother was still seeking for Father and waiting for news of him just as I was. And she meant that I could come to her, that I was able to come to her, "directly," not "at once," but without using a third party, without using a medium!

I shall pass over the long weeks which I spent trying to develop my own powers as a medium. For a long time I wandered up and down a blind alley and then a friend gave me a planchette. I soon learned that the little piece of wood with its pencil was no toy. I received, over a period of years, numerous messages from Mother, loving tender messages—but they bore no news of Father. About three years ago worry about financial affairs put me in such a confused mental state that I could not concentrate on the planchette and I let it accumulate dust in my closet until spring-cleaning day last spring, April, 1930. Then something impelled me to stop my dusting at 10 o'clock in the morning and take up the little heart-shaped board again. Quickly I prepared the table and the paper and pointed the same little pencil which had served me in the past.

I tried to think of Mother, the lovely young mother I had lost so long ago. Then I placed my fingertips lightly on the wood. Instantly it dashed violently under my fingers, as it had never done before. There were meaningless scrawls and whirls but then the pencil steadied, and words spread themselves across the big white page. I was disappointed for this was not Mother's neat script. I thought I had come into contact with some meddling, malicious spirit. . .

But the message, strange and unfinished, seemed to have a meaning. "Together now," it began. "Together now and forever . . . after many years. . . God bless you." That was all and the planchette was quiet under my fingers. What on earth—or outside of earth—could it mean? I waited in vain for another hour and then put the little apparatus away.

A thought came to me. Feverishly I went into the closet and opened the lock of my little hair trunk, which had come all the way from Tennessee with me. In it were the souvenirs of my childhood, the school-prizes and dance-programs and pressed flowers and books which were all that remained of dear, bygone days. Finally I found it—a little volume of Charles Lamb's *Tales from Shakespeare*, faded and discolored by time. But there should be—and there was—an inscription on the flyleaf: "To Sarah, on her tenth birthday, from her Father." It *was* in the same handwriting as the scrawled message I had received from the planchette that morning! Later a handwriting expert said it is so.

To Sarah:—
On her tenth birthday,
From
her Father

I have been happy since in the certain knowledge that my father is now dead. I have laid the planchette away forever for I know what I need to know. Mother and Father are together now in the World Beyond, after the nightmare years of separation.

Where my father was, during the forty-nine years that elapsed between his strange passing and his "death," I dare not think. I shall know some day and that will be soon enough.

To Whom It May Concern:

 I, Sarah Emma Lang, hereby affirm and depose that I have read the accompanying hitherto unpublished account of my father, David Lang's, disappearance, and that in every detail this story is true.

       Signed *Sarah Emma Lang*

      Witnessed by *Stuart Palmer*

Subscribed and sworn to before me this 30th day of October, 1929 *William C. Wemlling*

     Notary Public in and for the County of New York, State of New York.

My Commission expires March 30, 1931

The Adventure of the Marked Man

It was on a blustery afternoon late in April of the year '95, and I had just returned to our Baker Street lodgings to find Sherlock Holmes as I had left him at noon, stretched out on the sofa with his eyes half-closed, the fumes of black shag tobacco rising to the ceiling.

Busy with my own thoughts, I removed the litter of chemical apparatus which had overflowed into the easy chair, and settled back with a perturbed sigh. Without realizing it, I must have fallen into a brown study. Suddenly Holmes's voice brought me back to myself with a start.

"So you have decided, Watson," said he, "that not even this difference should be a real barrier to your future happiness?"

"Exactly," I retorted. "After all, we cannot—" I stopped short. "My dear fellow!" I cried, "this is not at all like you!"

"Come, come, Watson. You know my methods."

"I had not known," said I stiffly, "that they embraced having your spies and eavesdroppers dog the footsteps of an old friend, simply because he chose a brisk spring afternoon for a walk with a certain lady."

"A thousand apologies! I had not realized that my little demonstration of a mental exercise might cause you pain," murmured Holmes in a deprecating voice. He sat up, smiling. "Of course, my dear fellow, I should have allowed for the temporary mental aberration known as falling in love."

"Really, Holmes!" I retorted sharply. "You should be the last person to speak of psycho-pathology—a man who is practically a walking case history of manic-depressive tendencies—"

He bowed. "A touch, a distinct touch! But Watson, in one respect you do me an injustice. I was aware of your plans to meet a lady only because of the excessive pains you took with your toilet before going out. The lovely Emilia, was it not? I shall always remember her courage in the affair of the Gorgiano murder in Mrs. Warren's otherwise respectable rooming house. And indeed, why not romance? There has been a very decent interval since the passing of your late wife, and the widow Lucca is a most captivating person."

"That is still beside the point. I do not see—"

"None so blind, Watson, none so blind," retorted Holmes, stuffing navy-cut into his cherry-wood pipe, a sure sign that he was in one of his most argumentative moods. "It is really most simple, my dear fellow. It was not difficult for me to deduce that your appointment, on an afternoon as pleasantly gusty as this, was in the park. The remnants of peanut shell upon your best waistcoat speak all too plainly of the fact that you have been amusing yourself by feeding the monkeys. And your return at such an early hour, obviously having failed to ask the lady to dine with you, indicates most clearly that you have had some sort of disagreement while observing the antics of the hairy primates."

"Granted, Holmes, for the moment. But pray continue."

"With pleasure. As a good medical man, you cannot fail to have certain deep convictions as to the truth contained in the recent controversial publications of Mr. Charles Darwin. What is more likely than that in the warmth of Indian Summer romance you were unwise enough to start a discussion of Darwin's theories with the Signora Lucca, who like most of her countrywomen is no doubt deeply religious? Of course she prefers the Garden of Eden account of humanity's beginning. Hence your first quarrel and your hasty return home, where you threw yourself into a chair and permitted your pipe to go out while you threshed through the entire situation in your mind."

"That is simple enough, now that you explain it," I admitted grudgingly. "But how could you possibly know the conclusion which I had just reached?"

"Elementary, Watson, most elementary. You returned with your normally placid face contorted into a pout, the lower lip protruding most angrily. Your glance turned to the mantelpiece, where lies a copy of *On the Origin of Species* and you looked even more belligerent than before. But then after a moment the flickering flames of the fireplace caught your eye, and I could not fail to see how that domestic symbol reminded you of the connubial felicity which you once enjoyed. You pictured yourself and the lovely Italian seated before such a fire, and your expression softened. A distinctly fatuous smile crossed your face, and I knew that you had decided that no theory should be permitted to come between you and the lady you plan to make the second Mrs. Watson." He tapped out the cherrywood pipe into the grate. "Can you deny that my deductions are substantially correct?"

"Of course not," I retorted, somewhat abashed. "But Holmes, in a less enlightened reign than this our Victoria's, you would be in grave danger of being burned as a witch."

"A wizard, pray," he corrected. "But enough of mental exercises. Unless I am mistaken, the persistent ringing of the doorbell presages a client. If so, it is a serious case and one which may absorb all my faculties.

Nothing trivial would bring out an Englishman during the hour sacred to afternoon tea."

There was barely time for Holmes to turn the reading lamp so that it fell upon the empty chair, and then there were quick steps on the stair and an impatient knocking at the door. "Come in!" cried Holmes.

The man who entered was still young, some eight and thirty at the outside, well-groomed and neatly if not fashionably attired, with something of professorial dignity in his bearing. He put his bowler and his sturdy malacca stick on the table, and then turned toward us, looking questioningly from one to the other. I could see that his normally ruddy complexion was of an unhealthy pallor. Obviously our caller was close to the breaking point.

"My name is Allen Pendarvis," he blurted forth, accepting the chair to which Holmes was pointing. "I must apologize for bursting in upon you like this."

"Not in the least," said Holmes. "Pray help yourself to tobacco, which is there in the Persian slipper. You have just come up from Cornwall, I see."

"Yes, from Mousehole, near Penzance. But how—?"

"Apart from your name—'By the prefix Tre-, Pol-, Penye shall know the Cornishmen'—you are wearing a raincoat, and angry storm clouds have filled the southwest sky most of the day. I see also that you are in great haste, as the *Royal Cornishman* pulled into Paddington but a few moments ago, and you have lost no time in coming here."

"*You*, then, are Mr. Holmes!" decided Pendarvis. "I appeal to you, sir. No other man can give me the help I require."

"Help is not easy to refuse, and not always easy to give," Holmes replied. "But pray continue. This is Dr. Watson. You may speak freely in his presence, as he has been my collaborator on some of my most difficult cases."

"No one of your cases," cried Pendarvis, "can be more difficult than mine! I am about to be murdered, Mr. Holmes. And yet—and yet I have not an enemy in the world! Not one person, living or dead, could have a reason to wish me in my coffin. All the same, my life has been thrice threatened, and once attempted, in the last fortnight!"

"Most interesting," said Holmes calmly. "And have you any idea of the identity of your enemy?"

"None whatever. I shall begin at the beginning, and hold nothing back. You see, gentlemen, my home is in a little fishing village which has not changed materially in hundreds of years. As a matter of fact, the harbor quay of Mousehole, which lies just beyond my windows, was laid down by the Phoenicians in the time of Uther Pendragon, the father of King Arthur, when they came trading for Cornish tin."

"I think in this matter we must look closer to home than the Phoenicians," said Holmes dryly.

"Of course. You see, Mr. Holmes, I live a very quiet life. A small income left to me by a deceased aunt makes it possible for me to devote my time to the avocation of bird photography." Pendarvis smiled with modest pride. "A few of my photographs of terns on the nest have been printed in ornithology magazines. Only the other day—"

"Nor do I suspect the terns," Holmes interrupted. "And yet someone seeks your life, or your death. By the way, Mr. Pendarvis, does your wife inherit your estate in the unhappy event of your demise?"

Pendarvis looked blank. "Sir? But I have never married. I live alone with my brother Donal. Bit of a gay dog, Donal. Romantic enough for us both. All of the scented missives in the morning mail are addressed to him."

"Ah," said Holmes. "We need not apply the old rule of *cherchez la femme*, then? That eliminates a great deal. You say that your brother is your heir?"

"I suppose so. There is not much to inherit, really. The income stops at my death, and who would want my ornithological specimens?"

"That puts a different light on it, most certainly. But let us set aside the problem of *cui bono*, at least for the moment. What was the first intimation that someone had designs upon your life?"

"The first threat was in the form of a note, roughly printed upon brown butcher's-paper and shoved beneath the door last Thursday week. It read: 'Mr. Allen Pendarvis, you have but a short while to live.'"

"You have that note?"

"Unfortunately, no. I destroyed it, thinking it to be but the work of a stupid practical joker." Pendarvis sighed. "Three days later came the second."

"Which you kept, and brought with you?"

Pendarvis smiled wryly. "That would be impossible. It was chalked upon the garden wall, repeating the first warning. And the third was marked in the mud of the harbor outside my bedroom window, visible on last Sunday morning at low tide, but speedily erased. It said, 'Ready to die yet, Mr. Allen Pendarvis?'"

"These warnings were of course reported to the police?"

"Of course. But they did not take them seriously."

Holmes gave me a look, and nodded. "We understand that official attitude, do we not, Watson?"

"Then you can also understand, Mr. Sherlock Holmes, why I have come to you. I am not used to being pooh-poohed by a local sub-inspector! And so, when it finally happened last night—" Pendarvis shuddered.

"Now," interrupted Holmes, as he applied the flame of a wax vesta to his clay pipe, "we progress. Just what did happen?"

"It was late," the ornithologist began. "Almost midnight, as a matter of fact, when I was awakened by the persistent ringing of the doorbell. My housekeeper, poor soul, is hard of hearing, and so I arose and answered the door myself. Imagine my surprise to find no one there. Without all was Stygian blackness, the intense gloomy stillness of a Cornish village at that late hour. I stood there for a moment, shivering, holding my candle and peering into the darkness. And then a bullet screamed past me, missing my heart by a narrow margin and extinguishing the candle in my hand!"

Holmes clasped his lean hands together, smiling. "Really! A pretty problem, eh, Watson? What do you make of it?"

"Mr. Pendarvis is lucky in that his assailant is such a poor shot," I replied. "He must have presented a very clear target, holding a light in the doorway."

"A clear target indeed," Holmes agreed. "And why, Mr. Pendarvis, did not your brother answer the door?"

"Donal was in Penzance," Pendarvis answered. "For years it has been his invariable custom to attend the Friday night boxing matches there. Afterwards he usually joins some of his cronies at the Capstan and Anchor."

"Returning in the wee sma' hours? Of course, of course. And now, Mr. Pendarvis, I believe I have all that I need. Return to your home. You shall hear from us shortly." Holmes waved a languid hand at the door. "A very good evening to you, sir."

Pendarvis caught up his hat and stick, and stood dubiously in the doorway. "I must confess, Mr. Holmes, that I had been led to expect more of you."

"More?" said Holmes. "Oh, yes. My little bill. It shall be mailed to you on the first of the month. Good night, sir."

The door closed upon our dissatisfied client, and Holmes, who had been leaning back on the sofa in what appeared to be the depths of dejection, abruptly rose and turned toward me. "Well, Watson, the solution seems disappointingly easy, does it not?"

"Perhaps so," said I stiffly. "But you are skating upon rather thin ice, are you not? You may have sent that poor man to his death."

"To his death? No, my dear Watson. I give you my word on that. Excuse me, I must write a note to our friend Gregson of the Yard. It is most important that an arrest be made at once."

"An arrest? But of whom?"

"Who else but Mr. Donal Pendarvis? A telegram to the authorities of Penzance should suffice."

"The brother?" I cried. "Then you believe that he was not actually attending the boxing matches at the time of the attempted murder of our client?"

"I am positive," said Sherlock Holmes, "that he was engaged in quite other activities." I waited, but evidently he preferred not to take me further into his confidence. Holmes took quill and paper, and did not look up again until he had finished his note and dispatched it by messenger. "That," he said, "should take care of the situation for the time being." Whereupon he rang for Mrs. Hudson, requesting a copious dinner.

My friend maintained his uncommunicative silence during the meal, and devoted the rest of the evening to his violin. It was not until we were at the breakfast table next morning that there was any reference whatever to the case of the Cornish ornithologist.

The doorbell rang sharply, and Holmes brightened. "Ah, at last!" he cried. "An answer from Gregson. No, it is the man himself, and in a hurry, too." The steps on the stairs came to our door, and in a moment Tobias Gregson, tall, pale, flaxen-haired as ever, entered.

Smartest and sharpest of the Scotland Yard Inspectors, Holmes had always called him. But Gregson was in a bad frame of mind at the moment. "You have had us for fair, Mr. Holmes," he began. "I felt in my bones that I should not have obeyed your unusual request, but remembering the assistance you have given us in the past, I followed out your suggestion. Bad business, Mr. Holmes, bad business!"

"Really?" said Holmes.

"Quite. It's this man Pendarvis, Donal Pendarvis, that you wanted arrested."

"No confession?"

"Certainly not. And moreover, the fellow is no doubt instituting a suit at law this very minute, for false arrest."

Homes almost dropped his cup. "You mean he is no longer in custody?"

"I mean exactly that. He was arrested last night and held in Penzance gaol, but he made such a fuss about it that Owens, the sub-inspector there, was forced to let him go free."

Sherlock Holmes drew himself up to his full height, throwing aside his napkin. "I agree, sir. Bad business it is." He stood in deep thought for a moment. "And the other request I made? Have they located a man of that description?"

"No, Mr. Holmes. Sub-inspector Owens has lived in Penzance all his life, and he swears that no such person exists."

"Impossible, quite impossible," said Holmes. "He must be mistaken!"

Gregson rose. "We all have our successes and our failures," he said comfortingly. "Good morning, Mr. Holmes. Good morning, Doctor."

As the door closed behind him, Holmes turned suddenly to me. "And why, Watson, are you not already packing? Do you not choose to accompany me to Cornwall?"

"To Cornwall? But I understood . . ."

"You have heard everything, and understood nothing. I shall have to demonstrate to you, and to the sub-inspector, on the scene. But enough of this. The game is afoot. You had best bring your service revolver and a stout ash, for there may be rough work before this little problem is solved." He consulted his watch. "Ah, we have just half an hour to catch the ten o'clock train from Paddington."

We boarded it with but a moment or two to spare, and when we were rolling southwest through the outskirts of London my friend began a dissertation upon hereditary tendencies in fingerprint groupings, a subject upon which he was planning a monograph. I kept my impatience to myself as long as I could, and finally interrupted him. "I have but one question, Holmes. Why are we going to Cornwall?"

"The spring flowers, Watson, are at the height of their season. The perfume will be pleasant after the fogs of London. Meanwhile, I intend to have a nap. You might occupy yourself with considering the unusual nature of the warning notes received by Mr. Allen Pendarvis,"

"Unusual? But they seemed clear enough to me. They were definitely intended to let Mr. Pendarvis know that he was a marked man."

"Brilliantly put, Watson!" said Sherlock Holmes, and placidly settled down to sleep.

He did not awaken until we were past Plymouth, and the expanse of Mount's Bay was outside our window. There were whitecaps rolling in from the sea, and a gusty wind. "I fancy there will be more rain by dusk," said Holmes pleasantly. "An excellent night for the type of hunting we expect to engage in."

We had hardly alighted at Penzance when a broad man in a heavy tweed ulster approached us. He must have stood fifteen stone of solid brawn and muscle, and his face was grave. An apple-cheeked young police constable followed him.

"Mr. Holmes?" said the elder man. "I am Sub-inspector Owens. We were advised that you might be coming down. And high time it is. A sorry muddle you have got us into."

"Indeed?" said Holmes coolly. "It has happened, then?"

"It has," replied Sub-inspector Owens seriously. "At two o'clock this afternoon." The constable nodded in affirmation, very grave.

"I trust," Holmes said, "that you have not moved the body?"

"The body?" The two local policemen looked at each other, and the constable guffawed. "I was referring," Owens went on, "to the suit for false arrest. A writ was served upon me in my office."

My companion hesitated only a moment. "I should not, if I were you, lose any sleep over the forthcoming trial of the case. And now before going any farther, Dr. Watson and I have just had a long train journey and are in need of sustenance. Can you direct us to the Capstan and Anchor, Inspector?"

Owens scowled, then turned to his assistant. "Tredennis, will you be good enough to show these gentlemen to the place?" He turned back to Holmes. "I shall expect you at the police station in an hour, sir. This affair is not yet settled to my satisfaction."

"Nor to mine, sir," said Holmes, and we set off after the constable. That strapping young man led us at a fast pace to the sign of the Capstan and Anchor. "Into the saloon bar with you, Watson," my companion said to me in a low voice. He lingered a moment at the door, and then turned and joined me. "Just as I thought. Constable Tredennis has taken up his post in a doorway across the street. We are not trusted by the local authorities."

He ordered a plate of kidneys and bacon, but left them to cool while he chatted with the barmaid, a singularly ordinary young woman from all that was apparent to me. But Holmes returned to the table smiling.

"She confesses to knowing Mr. Donal Pendarvis, at least to the point of giggling when his name is mentioned. But she says that he has not been frequenting the public house in recent weeks. By the way, Watson, suppose

I asked you for a description of our antagonist? What sort of game are we hunting, should you say?"

"Mr. Donal Pendarvis?"

Holmes frowned. "That gentleman resembles his extraordinarily dull brother, from best accounts. No, Watson, dig deeper than that. Look back upon the history of the case, the warning messages—"

"Very well," said I. "The intended murderer is a poor shot with a rifle. He is a person who holds a grudge a long time—even a fancied grudge, for Mr. Allen Pendarvis does not even have an idea of the identity of his assailant. He is a man of primitive mentality, or else he would not have stooped to the savagery of torturing his intended victim with warning messages. He is a newcomer to the town, a stranger."

"Hold, Watson!" interrupted Holmes, with an odd smile. "You have reasoned amazingly. Yet I hear the patter of rain against the panes, and we must not keep our constable waiting in the doorway."

A brisk walk uphill, with the rain in our faces, brought us at last to the steps of the police station, but there I found that the way was barred, at least to me. Sub-inspector Owens, it appeared, wished to speak to Mr. Holmes alone.

"And so it shall be," replied Holmes pleasantly, to the burly constable in the door. He turned to me. "Watson, I stand in need of your help. Would you be good enough to occupy the next hour or so in a call on one or two of your local colleagues? You might represent yourself as in search of a casual patient whose name has escaped you. But you have, of course, some important reason for locating him. A wrong prescription, I fancy."

"Really, Holmes!"

"Be as vague as you can about age and appearance, Watson, but specify that the man you seek is a crack shot, he is very conversant with the locality, of unimpeachable respectability and—most important of all—he has a young and beautiful wife."

"But Holmes! You imply that is the description of our murderer? It is the exact opposite of what I had imagined."

"The reverse of the coin, Watson. But you must excuse me. Be good enough to meet me here in—shall we say—two hours? Off with you now, I must not keep the sub-inspector cooling his heels."

He passed on inside and I turned away into the rain-swept street, shaking my head dubiously. How I wished, at that moment, for the warmth and comfort of my fireside, any fireside! But well I knew that Holmes had some method in his madness. With difficulty I managed to secure a hansom cab, and for a long time rattled about the steep streets of the ancient town of Penzance, in search of the ruby lamp outside the door which would signify the residence of a medical man.

My heart was not in the task, and it was no surprise to me that, in spite of the professional courtesy with which I was greeted by my medical colleagues, they were unable to help me by so much as one iota. Owens, for all his pomposity, had been correct when he reported that of all the citizenry of Penzance, no such person as Holmes sought had ever existed. Or if he had, he was not among their patients.

I returned to the police station to find Holmes waiting for me. "Aha, Watson!" he cried genially. "What luck? Very little, I suppose, else you should not wear the hangdog look of a retriever who has failed to locate the fallen bird. No matter. If we cannot go to our man, he shall come to us. I have to some extent regained the confidence of the sub-inspector, Watson. You see, I have given my word that before noon tomorrow Mr. Donal Pendarvis shall have withdrawn his suit for false arrest. In return we are to have the support of a stalwart P. C. for this night's work."

In a few moments there appeared down the street the figure of a uni-formed man astride a bicycle. It turned out to be our friend Tredennis, who apologized for his delay. This was to have been his evening off duty, and it had been necessary to hurry home and explain matters to his better half.

"Maudie, she worries if I'm not reporting in by nine o'clock," he said, his pink cheeks pinker than ever with the exertion of his ride. "But I told her that any man would be glad to volunteer for a tour of duty with Mister Holmes, the celebrated detective from England."

"From *England?*" I put in wonderingly. "And where are we now?"

"In Cornwall," said Holmes, nudging me gently with his elbow. "Ah, Watson, I see that your hansom has been kept waiting. Any moment now and we shall be setting our trap, somewhere near the home of Mr. Pendarvis."

"It's a good three miles, sir," said Constable Tredennis. "By the road, that is. Along the shore it's a good bit less, but it's coming high tide and no easy going at any season."

"We shall take the road," Holmes decided. Soon we were rattling along a cobbled street that wound up and down dale, past looming ranks of fisherman's houses, with the wind blowing ever wet and fresh against our cheeks. "A land to make a man cherish his hearth, eh, Watson?"

We rode on in silence for some time, and then the constable stopped the cab at the head of a steep sloping street that wound down toward the shore. There was a strong odor of herring about the place, mingled with that of tar and salt seaweed. I observed that as we went down the sloping street Holmes gave a most searching glance to right and left, and that at every subsequent street corner he took the utmost pains to see that we were not followed.

Frankly, I knew not what near-human game we were hoping to entrap in this rain-swept, forgotten corner of a forgotten seaside town, but I was well assured, from the manner in which Holmes held himself, that the adventure was a grave one, and nearing its climax. I felt the reassuring weight of the revolver in my coat pocket, and then suddenly the constable caught my arm.

"In here," he whispered. We turned into a narrow passage near the foot of the street, passed through what appeared to be in the dimness a network of mews and stables, and came at last to a narrow door in the wall, which Holmes unlocked with a key affixed to a block of wood. We entered it together, and closed it behind us.

The place was black as ink, but I felt that it was an empty house. The planking beneath my feet was old and bare, and my outstretched hand touched a stone wall wet with slime. Then we came to an empty window with a broken shutter, through which the dank night air came chilly.

"We are in what was once the Grey Mouse Inn," whispered the young constable. "Yonder, Mr. Holmes, is the house."

We peered across a narrow street and through the open, unshaded window panes of a library, brilliantly lighted by two oil lamps. I could see a line of bookcases, a table, and a mantelpiece in the background. For a long while there was nothing more to see except the dark street, the darker doorway of the house, and that one lighted window.

"There is no other entrance?" demanded Holmes in a whisper. "None," said the constable. "The other windows give out onto the harbor, and at this hour the tide is passing high."

"Good," said Holmes. "If our man comes, he must come this way. And we shall be ready for him."

"More than ready," said young Tredennis stoutly. He hesitated. "Mr. Holmes, I wonder if you would be willing to give a younger man a word of advice. What, do you think, are the opportunities for an ambitious policeman up London way? I have often thought of trying to better myself."

"Listen!" cried Holmes sharply. There had come a sharp screaming sound, like the shriek of a rusty gate. It came again, and I recognized it as the cry of a gull.

The silence crept back again. From far away came the barking of a dog, suddenly silenced. Then suddenly appeared in the room across the way, a man in a wine-colored dressing gown who entered the library, turned down the lamps, and blew them out. It could be none other than our client, Mr. Allen Pendarvis.

"As usual he keeps early hours," said Holmes dryly. We waited until one might have counted a hundred, and then another light showed in the room. The man returned, bearing a lamp—but mysteriously, in the few minutes that had passed, he had changed his apparel. Mr. Pendarvis now wore a dinner coat with the collar and tie askew. He crossed to the bookcase, removed a volume, and from the recess took out a small flask, which he placed in his pocket. Then he put back the book and left the room.

"A lightning-change artist!" I cried.

Holmes, gripping my arm, said, "Not quite, Watson. That is the brother. They are very alike, from this distance."

We waited in silence, for what seemed an interminable length of time. But no light reappeared. Finally Holmes turned to me. "Watson," he said, "we have drawn another blank. I should have sworn that the murderer would have struck tonight. I dislike to turn back."

"My orders, sir, are to remain here until sunrise," put in the constable. "If you wish to return to the town, rest assured that I shall keep my eyes open."

"I am sure of it," said Holmes. "Come, Watson. The game is too wary. We have no more to do here."

He led me back across the sagging floor, through the door into the mews, and finally brought me out into the street again. But once there, instead of heading up the slope toward where our hansom was waiting, he suddenly drew me into the shadows of an alleyway. I would have spoken, but I felt his bony fingers across my lips. "Shh, Watson. Wait here—and never take your eyes off that doorway."

We waited, for what seemed an eternity. I stared with all my might at the doorway of the Pendarvis house. But I saw nothing, not even when Holmes gripped my arm.

"Now! Watson," he whispered, and started out in that direction, I tardily at his heels.

As we came closer I saw that a man was standing with his finger pressed against the Pendarvis doorbell. Holmes and I flung ourselves upon him, but he was a wiry customer, and we for all our superior strength and numbers were flung back and forth like hounds attacking a bear. And then the door was opened suddenly from within, and we all tumbled into a hallway lighted only by a candle held aloft in the hand of the surprised householder.

Our captive suddenly ceased his struggles, and Holmes and I drew back to see that we had succeeded in overcoming none other than Constable Tredennis himself. He held in his right hand an extremely businesslike revolver, which fell to the carpet with a dull thump.

"Mr. Pendarvis," said Holmes, "Mr. Donal Pendarvis, permit me to introduce you to your intended murderer."

No one spoke. But the apple-cheeked constable now had a face the color of the under-side of a flounder. All thought of resistance was gone. "You are uncanny, Mr. Holmes," the young man muttered. "How could you know?"

"How could I fail to know?" said Holmes, arranging his disheveled clothing. "It was fairly evident that since there was no citizen in Penzance who possessed both an ability as a marksman, a knowledge of the tides, and an attractive young wife, our man must be a member of the profession where marksmanship is encouraged." He turned toward the man who still held the candle, though with trembling fingers. "It was also evident that your brother, who still sleeps soundly upstairs, was never intended as a victim at all. Else the murderer would hardly have bothered with warning messages. It was you, Mr. Donal Pendarvis, who was the bull's-eye of the target."

"I—I do not understand," said the man with the candle, backing away. I kept a close grip upon the unresisting form of the prisoner, and watched Holmes as he quietly produced his cherry-wood pipe and lighted it.

"There was an excellent motive for Constable Tredennis to murder you, sir," said Holmes to our unwilling host. "No man cares to have his garden plucked by a stranger. Your death would have begun an inquiry which would have led straight to the husband of the lady you see on Friday nights."

"That is a black lie!" shouted Tredennis, and then subsided.

"Unless," Holmes continued quietly, "it was obvious to all the world that Donal Pendarvis was killed by accident, that he met his death at the hands of a madman with an unexplained grudge against his brother Allen.

That is why the warning notes so unnecessarily stressed the name of *Allen* Pendarvis. That is why the murderer-to-be carefully missed his supposed victim and shot out the candle. I did my best, Mr. Pendarvis, to assure your safety by having you taken into custody. That subterfuge failed, and so I was forced to this extreme means."

Tredennis twisted out of my grasp. "Very well, make an end of it!" he cried. "I admit it all, Mr. Holmes, and shall gladly leave it to a jury of my peers—"

"You had best leave it to me, at the moment," advised Holmes. "Mr. Pendarvis, you do not know me, but I have saved your life. May I ask a favor in return?"

Donal Pendarvis hesitated. "I am listening," he said. "You understand, I admit nothing."

"Of course. I venture to suggest that, instead of remaining here in the household of your brother and amusing yourself with dangerous dalliance, you betake yourself to fields which offer a greater opportunity for the use of your time and energy. The wheat fields of Canada, perhaps, or the veldt of South Africa. "

"And if I refuse?"

"The alternative," said Holmes, "is an exceedingly unpleasant scandal, involving a lady's name. Your lawsuit for false arrest will present the yellow press with unusual opportunities, will it not, when they learn that it all arose from an honest attempt upon my part to save your neck from a just punishment?"

Mr. Donal Pendarvis lowered the candle, and a slow smile spread across his handsome face. "I give you my word, Mr. Holmes. I shall leave by the first packet."

He extended his hand, and Holmes grasped it. And then we turned back into the night, our prisoner between us. We went up the cobbled street in silence, the young constable striding forward as to the gallows.

We found the hansom still waiting, and set off at once for Penzance. But it was Holmes who called on the driver to stop as we pulled into the outskirts of the town.

"Can we drop you off at your dwelling, Constable?" he asked.

The young man looked up, his eyes haunted. "Do not make sport of me, Mr. Holmes. You copped me for fair and I am ready to—"

Holmes half-shoved him out of the hansom. "Be off with you, my young friend. You must leave it to me to satisfy your sub-inspector with a story which Doctor Watson and I shall contrive out of moonbeams. For your part, you must make up your own mind as to your tactics in dealing with your Maudie. After all, the immediate problem is removed, and if you wish to transfer to some other duty with less night work, here is my card. I shall be glad to say a word in your behalf to the powers at Scotland Yard."

The hansom, at Holmes's signal, rolled onward again, cutting short the incoherent thanks of the chastened young constable.

"I am quite aware of what is in your mind," said Holmes to me as we approached our destination. "But you are wrong. The ends of justice will be better served by sending our young culprit back to his Maudie instead of by publicly disgracing him."

"It is of no use, Holmes," said I firmly. "Nothing that you can say will change my decision. Upon our return to London I shall ask Emilia to become my wife."

Sherlock Holmes let his hand fall on my shoulder, in a comradely gesture. "So be it. Marry her and keep her. One of these days I shall return to the country and the keeping of bees. We shall see who suffers the sharpest stings."

The Adventure of the Remarkable Worm

Sherlock Holmes turned abruptly away from the bay window, against which all day a raw April wind had been driving rain. The spring of '93 will be remembered as unusually inclement, even for London, and as always the dreariness of the weather conspired with professional inactivity to force Holmes farther and farther into the depths of black depression.

I was therefore not surprised to see him cross to the mantelpiece in three quick strides, obviously in search of the needle I abhorred. "Holmes, I beg of you!" cried I, half rising from my easy chair. Ordinarily I should not have ventured to remonstrate with my friend, but all day the Jezail bullet in my shoulder had been sending excruciating pains down my right side as far as the knee, and I was not in the most tolerant of moods.

Holmes stopped short and turned toward me, the morocco case in his hand. "My dear Watson," he said, "can you suggest anything better than a seven percent solution of cocaine?"

I turned toward the table, decanted three fingers of good Irish whiskey into a tall glass and then filled it to the brim with sparkling water from the gasogene. "If you will not listen to me as a medical man, then give heed to an old comrade in arms. Try this, I beg of you. It is a far milder poison."

Languidly Holmes accepted the glass, raised it to his lips, and then put it aside with a wry smile and a shake of his head. "Revolting, Watson, most revolting."

More than a little nettled, I replied, "But my dear fellow! As a man who makes a point of keeping good Burley tobacco in a Persian slipper, and who toasts two-and-six Trichinopoly cigars in a coal scuttle before the fire, your sense of taste cannot be so terribly affronted by a whiskey-and-soda."

Holmes bowed mockingly. "*Touché*, Watson. I must confess that in the process of developing my faculties to their highest point it is possible my sense of taste has atrophied. Tobacco in its moist normal state repels me. So, by the way, does this atrocious mixture of fermented potato juice and carbon-dioxide gas. Granted for the moment that you are correct in arguing that the final results are less deleterious to the system than the habitual use of cocaine, still I have always found the latter drug a specific in exalting and stimulating the mental processes."

Here he stopped, cocking his head toward the door. "As exalting, shall we say, as the sudden appearance of a new problem?"

There was another quick step in the passage, and then a nervous hammering upon our door. Holmes paused only to adjust the shade of the reading lamp so that it fell upon the vacant chair in which our visitor must sit, and then crossed to the door and flung it open.

The man who staggered into our sitting room was perhaps of some eight-and-thirty years, though his cadaverous aspect made him appear superficially older. His apparel spoke of Savile Row, though it hung loosely upon his gaunt frame like the dress of a neat scarecrow. He looked about him anxiously, turning from Holmes to me and back again. I could not help noticing that there were deep gentian circles beneath his faintly bulging eyes, and that the man was obviously in the grip of a powerful emotion.

"Mr. Holmes?" he gasped.

"Please sit down," said Holmes, indicating the visitor's chair. "I am he. And this is Dr. Watson, my friend and colleague. If I may say so, it would appear that you are far more in need of his professional services than of my own."

"I must be the judge of that," retorted our caller sharply. He sank wearily into the chair, grasping the arms with bloodless trembling hands. "I will begin at the beginning," said he. "My name is Persano." He hesitated, took a deep breath, and went on. "Isadore Persano."

Holmes nodded. "Indeed? Can it be that you are the journalist over whose signature have recently appeared a number of controversial articles? In the *Sketch*, I believe."

Persano bowed, brightening a little. "I had no idea, Mr. Holmes, that my poor efforts had come to the attention of such a celebrated person as yourself. It is true that I have published a few diatribes dealing with widely held popular superstitions. . . ."

"Incidentally sinking home a few good thrusts at the medical profession, I believe?" Holmes nodded toward me, a flicker of amusement in his eye. "The good doctor here has not read them, so we may all still speak as friends. And now, Mr. Persano, having had a recent opportunity to study organized medicine at first hand in one of our London hospitals, you wish to consult me—"

"But this is black magic, sir!" interrupted the journalist.

"Not in the least. The faint but definite odor of iodoform and ether which clings to your person, plus an obviously recent loss of weight, plus the fact that you are wearing a hospital nightgown in place of a shirt, can only indicate the conclusion I mentioned."

A flickering smile crossed Persano's face. "Oh, I see. For a moment you gave me a start. But now that you explain I see how simple it all is."

Holmes nodded wearily. "As usual, I have made a mistake in disclosing the steps by which I arrive at my deductions. But let us get on, Mr. Persano. You wish to consult me about the object which bulges in your right-hand coat pocket?"

Isadora Persano fumbled nervously, and then thrust out at us a small glass flask, well stoppered. Even as he held it forth he kept his eyes averted, as if the very sight of the thing in the bottle were to be avoided as the glance of Medusa.

"Mr. Holmes, you must help me! I must find out the truth or lose my reason forever. Only a day or so ago—I have somehow lost track of time—I was the happiest man in the realm. Today"— and here he shuddered, a full perspiration breaking out on his pale brow—"today I am the most miserable. This—this *Thing* that I hold in my hand is the reason."

Holmes accepted the flask and held it to the light, so that we both saw clearly its contents. Floating in a clear viscous liquid was an object both strange and repellent, a slender, wormlike creature no more than six inches in length, with an eyeless, swollen head.

I must have given vent to an involuntary exclamation, for Holmes turned to me and nodded. "Exactly, Watson! You were about to say that we are looking upon a representative of the *phylla* group—possibly one of the *Platyhelminthes*; but most certainly of a venomous breed hitherto unknown to science." He turned back to our visitor. "Mr. Persano, how did you come by this thing?"

"In all my life," cried Persano wildly, "I have never intentionally caused harm to any living being. I have avoided Error and pursued Truth as my guiding star. Why, then, should anyone send me this object of horror incarnate?"

Holmes turned the flask, so that the motion induced in the supporting liquid caused a faint serpentine movement of the creature inside. "You have an enemy, no doubt?"

"Yes, and no, Mr. Holmes," the man replied. "All Harley Street has been my enemy since I published those articles. I was even challenged to a duel last week. But I cannot believe that any civilized human being could take so foul a revenge as this. Imagine it, Mr. Holmes! One moment I was walking along Oxford Street, my mind filled with happy, constructive thoughts, concentrating upon Health and Truth. Then—I can hardly believe it even now—a blackness descended upon me. I have vague formless memories of lying there on the pavement, with the avid faces of a curious crowd staring down at me. And then—nothing!"

"Nothing at all?" pressed Holmes.

The man shook his head. "Nothing until I awakened. In the charity ward of Charing Cross Hospital I found myself, weak and hungry and filled with the illusion of pain. Some poor soul at the other end of the room was passing on to his reward, his last struggles occupying the attention of the doctors and nurses. I seized the opportunity to recover my clothing from the locker at the foot of my bed, and made my escape, bringing with me that flask which had been placed on the night stand for my waking eyes to light upon."

"I begin to understand," said Holmes, grimly. I had expected to see him impatient at this hysterical, maudlin narrative, but on the contrary he had listened with the greatest concentration of attention.

"You have an enemy? This former dueling antagonist, perhaps?"

Persano shrugged. "Honor was satisfied when the secretary of the College of Surgeons fired over my head, and I over his. No, Mr. Holmes, I cannot believe that my persecution arises from such a source."

"Very well," said Holmes. "By the way, when did you separate from your wife?"

Persano started. "Mr. Holmes, this *is* unfair! You have had prior knowledge of me and my affairs."

"Not in the least. There is very clearly the mark of a wedding ring upon the proper finger of your left hand, and one of the buttons on your waistcoat has been replaced with thread of a different color, plainly indicating a change to a bachelor existence. Please answer the question."

"Marina and I separated last autumn," Persano said. "She returned to the practice of her profession, and is, I believe, at the moment telling fortunes at the Red Rose teashop in Lambeth. But we had no quarrel—it was just that she could not, would not, follow me into the new fields, the fresh world which opened to me when I finally got hold of the Key of the Scriptures."

I could not but detect a noticeable intensification in Holmes's manner. "Never fear, Mr. Persano. I shall do my very best to help you. Suppose you leave this unholy object with me for the time being? I think I shall have news for you within the fortnight. Your address?"

"Number 31 Tottenham Mews."

"Thank you. Will you be kind enough to note the address, Watson?" Holmes ushered our visitor to the door, then closed it after him and turned back toward the fire, his face grave and thoughtful. "Quite an unusual little problem," he said. "You will find parallel cases, if you care to consult the index, in Malvern in '84, and Hammersmith as late as year before last. The man himself was most interesting."

"No doubt you read a good deal in his appearance which was invisible to me," I remarked, rubbing my lame shoulder tenderly.

"Invisible? Ah, no, my good Watson. Just unnoticed. The man is obviously a recent convert to one of the new sects, such as that which recently came to us from Mrs. Eddy in the United States of North America. Christian Science, I believe they call it."

"Science!" I interposed sarcastically.

"Exactly. However, it was a conversion hardly likely to appeal to his wife, with her Romany background. What is more likely than that the gypsy girl probed among the deeper, darker secrets of her race to secure revenge upon the husband who had cast her aside? I seem to remember a similar case in Prague some years ago, when a jilted Romany woman secured a most horrible revenge upon a rival by feeding her the spores of a new species of mushroom, developed to thrive only upon human detritus. Myriads of tiny mushrooms burst from the victim's scalp, from beneath the fingernails— "

"Holmes!" I cried, shocked to the marrow. "This is too much!"

"All the same," said Sherlock Holmes quietly, "I believe that a visit to the Red Rose teashop is indicated."

"I refuse to believe that such things can exist in this civilized world!" I insisted.

Holmes shrugged. He took up the flask again, carefully removed the wax stopper, and poured out the liquid into a basin. The odor of raw spirits filled the room. He took a pair of forceps and lifted out the blind, lifeless worm, laying it on a bit of newspaper.

"No doubt we should burn this unholy object at once," he said thoughtfully. "But I intend first to take it with me when we journey to Lambeth. Will you be good enough to go down to the corner and summon a hansom?"

"In this deluge?" I shook my head, sinking back comfortably into the velvet lining of the easy chair.

"Come, come, Watson! The game is afoot. It is not every day that we are confronted with a worm unknown to science."

I hesitated, savoring my expected triumph. "Forgive me, Holmes. If you wish to visit the lady fortune teller, my best wishes go with you. But

I can see no reason for my accompanying you, nor for taking along that repulsive object on the table."

"Of course you do not see. You never do, until afterwards. But in this case . . ."

"In this case, Holmes, you are well off the target." I smiled, having waited for this moment ever since the day Holmes talked me into giving away Fusilier, my bull pup, on the grounds that the poor fellow snored. "As a matter of fact, it is perfectly clear that Mr. Persano was seized with a sudden intestinal attack while strolling down Oxford Street. Removed to Charing Cross Hospital, an emergency operation was found necessary, and the unhappy little man recovered consciousness alone and unattended, with the evidence of the operation exhibited beside his bed."

Holmes surveyed me coldly. "I fail to see what, if anything, you are driving at."

"Only this," I said. "The 'worm unknown to science' is unknown only to *Christian* Science. That unpleasant object before you is nothing more than an infected vermiform appendix."

Sherlock Holmes hesitated, swallowed, and then a reluctant smile broke across his face. He extended a lean brown hand toward mine. "Apologies, Watson! I forgot for a moment that medicine and surgery are your chosen field, in which I have but dabbled. This is your triumph. What disposition do you care to make of the case?"

"I should suggest returning his appendix to Mr. Isadora Persano, together with a note explaining the truth of the situation."

Holmes nodded. "It shall be done. This matchbox should serve as an excellent container. And now, by the way, I think that a good dinner at Simpsons would not be out of place. A good dinner for you, I should say. For myself I intend to order a double serving of humble pie."

The I-O-U of Hildegarde Withers

The detective story, for practical purposes, originated with the first public appearance of Mr. Sherlock Holmes. True enough, there were *The Moonstone* and "The Purloined Letter", but Sergeant Cuff and Dupin bear the same relation to Holmes as did Eric the Red and that other blond voyager remembered in Mexico as Quetzalcoatl to Christopher Columbus.

Collins and Poe made literary history, but their detectives were cut out of cardboard and animated with strings. Sherlock Holmes was the first living, breathing detective, the first immortal. Indeed, he has taken on an added vitality with the years, and not only in the Peter Pan clap-yourhands-if-you-believe-in-fairies school either. So truly and completely alive is the Brain of Baker Street that he has still a vitality to spare, a sort of spiritual sperm fathering sleuths wherever the Canon has travelled, in all of its eighty-odd translations.

Under these circumstances I cannot deny if I would that my own Hildegarde Withers owes a great debt to Dr. John Watson's erstwhile roommate. She could never have existed at all if it had not been for her illustrious predecessor, and neither could any other of the horde of fictional sleuths who fill our rental libraries, magazine pages, motion picture screens, and radio programs.

It was during my twelfth year that I was first introduced to Sherlock Holmes, and a strange sort of reverse-angle introduction it was. At the time I happened to be working my catholic way through the top shelf of an ancient pine bookcase in the attic of my father's farmhouse surrounded by apple orchards, in the cow-country of central Wisconsin—a hot stuffy attic, full of the scent of stored hickory nuts, dust, old clothes and black hornets' nests. Right between *Lorna Doone* and O. Meredith's *Lucile* a new comet swam into my ken, in the shape of a small yellow volume with an intriguing sketch on the cover. It was—no, class, guess again. It dealt with the Master, right enough, but the title was *The Return of the Houseboat*, by John Kendrick Bangs. This book of definitely pawky and dated humor was, although I did not immediately realize it, a sequel to *The Houseboat on the Styx*, which had had a fair though seemingly undeserved success some years previously.

But in spite of Mr. Bangs, Sherlock Holmes dominated his little parody. I wonder if any other disciple of the Master ever made his acquaintance in any such roundabout, double-roundabout fashion—through stumbling entranced upon the sequel to a parody? I also wonder, in passing, if there could be any connection between the Kendrick in Bangs' ancestry and my friend Baynard Kendrick, whose famous blind detective has his own obvious debt to the Sage of 221B?

Somehow, in that musty attic, I worked my way backwards through *The Houseboat*—which obligingly turned up on another shelf—and at last it struck me that I had been sipping a very diluted brew indeed, comparable only to the war-time beer served in the British pubs to us of the American Army some years ago.

The real stuff was to be found, one hundred proof, on the "D" shelf in the fiction wing of the Baraboo Carnegie Free Library, and heaven bless the acidulous spinster librarian who led me there, when my family returned to town for the winter, and with a disapproving sniff handed me *The Valley of Fear*.

The rest is history. My history at any rate. Within a year I had memorized, roughly speaking, most of the *Adventures* and the *Memoirs*, and had become official story-teller for the local troop of the Boy Scouts of America. Around the campfire, on our weekly hikes and yearly camping trips to nearby Devil's Lake, I burbled forth as much of the stories as I had been able to retain. My repertory was limited, it later proved, by the fact that our library's only copy of *His Last Bow* had been borrowed and never returned. The name on the card of the missing book was that of our little town's only author, an ex-convict. Nobody today remembers that name.

Not too long ago, when I was laboring in the Hollywood vineyard as a writer of B-picture melodramas, I found myself assigned by a producer at Columbia Pictures to do the script of a Boston Blackie whodunit. Nobody at the studio saw fit to mention, in the publicity advertising, or screen credits, that the character of Boston Blackie had originally been created, back in the little Wisconsin town of Baraboo, by one Jack Boyle—God rest his thirsty black-Irish soul. When Boyle and his lady moved out of town between two days, leaving a number of unpaid bills and a cellarful of empty bottles in their little yellow house on Oak Street, most of the town's parents spoke forcibly to their children about the evils of drink and the wickedness of story writers in general. It was then, I think, that I definitely chose what was to be my life's work.

At any rate, it was out of such mingled antecedents that Miss Hildegarde Withers finally came into being, in the summer of 1931. I fancy that she was—apart from the basic S.H. pattern from which so many of us have cut our cloth—a composite of my memories of the acidulous, sniffing librarian, of a horse-faced English teacher in the local high school, of my own Yankee father's sense of humor, and of an impression of Edna May Oliver whom I had seen one night, as a standee, in the last weeks of the first run of Jerome Kern's *Showboat.*

That was the same Edna May Oliver who stepped out of her brilliant portrayals in *Cimarron, David Copperfield,* and *Ladies of the Jury,* to make Miss Withers come alive upon the screen. In their infinite wisdom, the great brains of Hollywood decided, after three pictures, to substitute other actresses in the part, and I think I understand now how Kendrick felt when another studio decided that Eddie Arnold could no longer be wasted playing his blind Captain, and how Fred Dannay felt about losing Ralph Bellamy in the film role of Ellery Queen.

But all this is ancient history. Basil Rathbone still continues on the screen as Holmes himself, with as brilliant a portrayal as we have seen since Mr. Arthur Wontner in his series of British pictures. For that, and the tendency of Mr. Rathbone's producer to adhere somewhat more to the sacred traditions of 221B, let us be thankful.

In looking over the eleven volumes in which to date Miss Hildegarde Withers has had her fling, it surprises me to note how immediate, how deep a debt is owed to the Holmes saga. Indeed, in one of her several adventures south of the Border, the maiden schoolteacher is caught trying to stick a banderilla into the carcass of a pig, and is relieved and surprised to find that the Mexican detective who takes her into custody has also been indoctrinated with "The Adventure of Black Peter," and that he remembered what was done in Allardyce's back shop.

On still another occasion, according to the record, my maiden schoolma'am felt herself impelled to set up in her flat a dressmaker's dummy, topped off with one of her quieter hats and a spare switch, in order to settle once and for all the point as to whether a certain New York literary figure was a murderer or simply a man driven to justifiable homicide. The reference is fairly obvious, involving the view across the street from Camden House and what happened to a wax-colored model (what color is wax, anyway?) while Mrs. Hudson on her knees was moving it about.

One could go on at great length to point out such obvious borrowings of background and machinery. And yet the real indebtedness of Miss Hildegarde Withers (and most of our fictional sleuths) to Sherlock Holmes lies far deeper down.

Because of Sherlock Holmes, Miss Withers loves a knotty problem for its own sake and is possessed with a tireless curiosity and burning desire to get at the truth. Because of him she is a little too apt to withhold her deductions and her results in order to present them at the right time and before the right audience in a dramatic *dénouement*. As the saying goes in show-business, there is a touch of ham in the best of us, and by the word "ham" we mean the widespread human tendency to play up to an audience, particularly to an audience consisting of a reader who identifies himself with a muscular, thick-witted medico with a Jezail bullet near his clavicle, or a wiry little inspector assigned to Homicide.

It is true that Miss Withers has made her mistakes, and at times has even played Watson to Inspector Piper's Sherlock. I do not immediately recall that Sherlock Holmes was ever wrong but once, and that of course was in the affair of "The Yellow Face" (not one of the greater tales) at the culmination of which he requested Watson to whisper "Norbury" in his ear whenever he seemed to show overconfidence. True infallibility is a difficult cloak to wear, much too heavy for a maiden schoolteacher.

Did Watson ever take Sherlock Holmes at his word, and actually whisper "Norbury" to him? Perhaps when that collection of notes and records, now somewhere in the vaults of Cox and Co., at Charing Cross, is finally brought to the attention of the public, we shall find a mention of it.

I confess that some years ago when I was stranded at an Army post in the wilds of Oklahoma, as an instructor at the Field Artillery School, it occurred to me to attempt on paper certain pastiches, involving memoirs and adventures and bows patterned in the great tradition and yet conceived in all humbleness and respect. One or two of them later appeared in a magazine of detective stories, and yet the one story, the story of stories, in which Holmes was to triumph in defeat and resolve for once and forever the problem of the aluminium crutch, was never to see the light. In it Holmes not only heard Watson whisper "Norbury," he found it printed on a slip of paper and pinned to his hat.

Perhaps it was all for the best that the legal heirs of the late Sir Arthur Conan Doyle set up shrill wails of agony at the very idea of the continuance of the series. And yet it is hard to leave forever the intriguing problems of the stories that should have been written and now can never be—the lost, delightful stories more precious than the missing Songs of Sappho. I think that sometimes in the long watches of the night Vincent Starrett awakens with a new slant on the shocking affair of the Dutch steamer *Friesland*, that Tony Boucher dreams an answer to the singular tragedy of the Atkinson brothers at Trincomalee, that Augie Derleth or Fred Dannay devises the only perfect answer to what happened to the Grice Patersons in the Island of Uffa. Not to speak of the Amateur Mendicant Society, the arrest of Wilson the notorious canary trainer, of the repulsive story of the red leech. . . . Ah, Arcady!

Doubly sad it is that the lineal descendants of that utterly dull oculist, Artie Doyle, should rise up at this late date to prevent the continuance of the tradition with which he was so slightly associated.

Personally I have always held with that school of thought which maintains that for some reason, perhaps modesty, Dr. John Watson preferred to market his literary works under the *nom de plume* of Arthur Conan Doyle. There may have been a real person of that name, who immediately seized upon a good thing and started cashing royalty checks. Perhaps later on he attempted some authorship of his own, publishing some of the dullest volumes on spooks and mediums that ever saw the light of day. They too were on that "D" shelf in the public library, but I decided then, and am of the same opinion still, that there must be two separate and distinct Conan Doyles . . . one of them gloating over photographs of ghosts and pixies, or moaning over the understandable ingratitude of Oscar Slater, and the other the friend and intimate of the most loved, admired, and copied of all detectives, that disorderly reformed drug addict and Americanophile, Mr. Sherlock Holmes.

When I was thirteen I wrote him a letter at 221B Baker Street, and mailed it, too, with the proper weight of postage to take it to London. It was the only fan letter I ever wrote, and it must have been delivered somewhere, for it was never returned. I like to think that somewhere in the excellent postal service of Britannia there still is a clerk who could not bring himself to write the words "*No such person.*"

Sources for the
Hildegarde Withers Short Stories

Collections:

The Riddles of Hildegarde Withers, ed. Ellery Queen. New York: Lawrence E. Spivak (Jonathan Press), 1947.

The Monkey Murder and Other Hildegarde Withers Stories, ed. Ellery Queen. New York: Lawrence E. Spivak (Bestseller Mystery), 1950.

People vs. Withers and Malone, with Craig Rice. New York: Simon and Schuster, 1963

Hildegarde Withers: Uncollected Riddles. Norfolk: Crippen & Landru, 2002.

Hildegarde Withers: Final Riddles?. Cincinnati: Crippen & Landru, 2021

Individual Stories:

The Riddle of the Dangling Pearl, *Mystery,* November 1933 [Collected in *Hildegarde Withers: Uncollected Riddles,* 2002]

The Riddle of the Flea Circus, *Mystery,* December 1933 [Collected in *Hildegarde Withers: Uncollected Riddles,* 2002]

The Riddle of the Forty Costumes, *Mystery,* January 1934 [Collected in *Hildegarde Withers: Uncollected Riddles,* 2002]

The Riddle of the Brass Band, *Mystery,* March 1934 [Collected in *Hildegarde Withers: Uncollected Riddles,* 2002]

The Riddle of the Yellow Canary, *Mystery,* April 1934 [Collected in *The Riddles of Hildegarde Withers,* 1947]

The Riddle of the Blueblood Murders, *Mystery,* June 1934 [Collected in *Hildegarde Withers: Uncollected Riddles,* 2002]

The Riddle of Forty Naughty Girls, *Mystery,* July 1934 [Collected in *Hildegarde Withers: Uncollected Riddles,* 2002]

The Riddle of the Hanging Men, *Mystery,* September 1934 [Collected in *Hildegarde Withers: Uncollected Riddles,* 2002]

The Riddle of the Black Spade, *Mystery,* October 1934 [Collected in *Hildegarde Withers: Final Riddles?,* 2021]

The Riddle of the Marble Blade, *Mystery,* November 1934 [Collected in *Hildegarde Withers: Uncollected Riddles,* 2002]

The Riddle of the Whirling Lights, *Mystery,* January 1935 [Collected in *Hildegarde Withers: Uncollected Riddles,* 2002]

The Doctor's Double, 1st publication unknown, 1937; reprinted in *Ellery Queen's Mystery Magazine*, August 1946 [Collected as The Riddle of the Doctor's Double in *The Riddles of Hildegarde Withers*, 1947]

The Riddle of the Jack of Diamonds, 1st publication unknown; reprinted in *Fifty Famous Detectives of Fiction*, 1938 [Collected in *Hildegarde Withers: Uncollected Riddles*, 2002]

A Fingerprint in Cobalt, *New York Sunday News*, 1938; reprinted as The Blue Fingerprint, *Ellery Queen's Mystery Magazine*, May 1942 [Collected as The Riddle of the Blue Fingerprint in *The Riddles of Hildegarde Withers*, 1947]

The Purple Postcards, 1st publication unknown, 1939 [Collected in *The Monkey Murder*, 1950]

The Riddle of the Beggar on Horseback. *Winnipeg Tribune*, March 30, 1940 [Collected as Tomorrow's Murder, *The Monkey Murder*, 1950]

Miss Withers and the Unicorn, *Chicago Sunday Tribune*, August 3, 1941 [Collected in *The Monkey Murder*, 1950]

Miss Withers and the Green Ice, *Chicago Sunday Tribune*, April 13, 1941; reprinted as Green Ice in *Ellery Queen's Mystery Magazine*, Winter 1942 [Collected as The Riddle of the Green Ice in *The Riddles of Hildegarde Withers*, 1947]

The Puzzle of the Scorned Woman, *Chicago Sunday Tribune*, December 27, 1942; also *New York Sunday News*, 1942; reprinted as The Lady from Dubuque, *Ellery Queen's Mystery Magazine*, March 1944 [Collected as The Riddle of the Lady from Dubuque in *The Riddles of Hildegarde Withers*, 1947]

The Hungry Hippo, 1st publication unknown, 1943; *Australian Women's Weekly*, 19 February 1944 [Collected in *The Monkey Murder*, 1950]

To Die in the Dark, *Boston Post*, 9 March 1944 [Collected in *Hildegarde Withers: Final Riddles?*, 2021]

The Riddle of the Twelve Amethysts, *Ellery Queen's Mystery Magazine*, March 1945 [Collected in *The Riddles of Hildegarde Withers*, 1947]

Snafu Murder, *Ellery Queen's Mystery Magazine*, November 1945 [Collected as The Riddle of the Snafu Murder in *The Riddles of Hildegarde Withers*, 1947]

The Riddle of the Black Museum, *Ellery Queen's Mystery Magazine*, March 1946 [Collected in *The Riddles of Hildegarde Withers*, 1947]

The Monkey Murder, *Ellery Queen's Mystery Magazine*, January 1947 [Collected in *The Monkey Murder*, 1950]

The Riddle of the Double Negative, *Ellery Queen's Mystery Magazine*, March 1947 [Collected in *The Monkey Murder*, 1950]

The Long Worm, *Ellery Queen's Mystery Magazine*, October 1947 [Collected in *The Monkey Murder*, 1950]

Fingerprints Don't Lie, *Ellery Queen's Mystery Magazine*, November 1947 [Collected in *The Monkey Murder*, 1950]

The Riddle of the Tired Bullet, *Ellery Queen's Mystery Magazine*, March 1948 [Collected in *Hildegarde Withers: Uncollected Riddles*, 2002]

Once Upon a Train, with Craig Rice, *Ellery Queen's Mystery Magazine*, October 1950 [Collected in *People vs. Withers and Malone*, 1963]

Where Angels Fear to Tread, *Ellery Queen's Mystery Magazine*, February 1951 [Collected in *Hildegarde Withers: Final Riddles?*, 2021]

Cherchez la Frame, with Craig Rice, *Ellery Queen's Mystery Magazine*, June 1951 [Collected in *People vs. Withers and Malone*, 1963]

The Jinx Man. *Ellery Queen's Mystery Magazine,* December 1952 [Collected in *Hildegarde Withers: Final Riddles?*, 2021]

Autopsy and Eva, with Craig Rice, *Ellery Queen's Mystery Magazine*, August 1954 [Collected in *People vs. Withers and Malone*, 1963]

Rift in the Loot, with Craig Rice, *Ellery Queen's Mystery Magazine*, April 1955 [Collected in *People vs. Withers and Malone*, 1963]

Hildegarde and the Spanish Cavalier, *Ellery Queen's Mystery Magazine*, December 1955 [Collected in *Hildegarde Withers: Final Riddles?*, 2021]

You Bet Your Life, *Ellery Queen's Mystery Magazine*, May 1957 [Collected in *Hildegarde Withers: Final Riddles?*, 2021]

Withers and Malone, Brain-Stormers, with Craig Rice, *Ellery Queen's Mystery Magazine*, February 1959 [Collected in *People vs. Withers and Malone*, 1963]

Who is Sylvia? *Ellery Queen's Mystery Magazine*, July 1961 [Collected in *Hildegarde Withers: Final Riddles?*, 2021]

Withers and Malone, Crime-Busters, with Craig Rice, *Ellery Queen's Mystery Magazine*, November 1963 [Collected in *People vs. Withers and Malone*, 1963]

The Return of Hildegarde Withers, *Ellery Queen's Mystery Magazine*, July 1964 [Collected in *Hildegarde Withers: Final Riddles?*, 2021]

Hildegarde Withers Is Back, *Ellery Queen's Mystery Magazine*, April 1968 [Collected in *Hildegarde Withers: Final Riddles?*, 2021]

Hildegarde Plays It Calm, *Ellery Queen's Mystery Magazine*, April 1969 [Collected in *Hildegarde Withers: Final Riddles?*, 2021]

In 1952, Palmer wrote that there were about 50 Withers stories to that point; only about 30 are recorded through that year (33 including the collaborations with Craig Rice). Twenty or so remain unrecorded, perhaps from the period 1937-1942 when at least some were appearing in newspapers.

Sources for the Other Stories

The Stripteaser and the Private Eye. *Ellery Queen's Mystery Magazine*, November 1968 [Collected in *Hildegarde Withers: Final Riddles?*, 2021]

How Lost Was My Father? *Fate*, July 1953 [Collected in *Hildegarde Withers: Final Riddles?*, 2021]

The Adventure of the Marked Man. *Ellery Queen's Mystery Magazine*, July 1944. [Collected in *Hildegarde Withers: Final Riddles?*, 2021]

The Adventure of the Remarkable Worm. *The Misadventures of Sherlock Holmes*, ed. Ellery Queen, 1944. [Collected in *Hildegarde Withers: Final Riddles?*, 2021]

The I-O-U of Hildegarde Withers. *The Baler Street Journal*, Volume 3, Number 1, January 1948. [Collected in *Hildegarde Withers: Final Riddles?*, 2021]

Hildegarde Withers: Final Riddles?

Hildegarde Withers: Final Riddles? by Stuart Palmer is set in 12-point Garamond font, typeset by G.E. Satheesh, Pondicherry, India and printed on 60 pound natural acid-free paper. The cover painting is by Jacqueline Webber and the Lost Classics design is by Deborah Miller. *Hildegarde Withers: Final Riddles?* was published in November 2021 by Crippen & Landru, Publishers, Cincinnati, OH